```
1      8     28     56     70     56     28      8      1
   1      7     21     35     35     21      7      1
      1      6     15     20     15      6      1
         1      5     10     10      5      1
            1      4      6      4      1
               1      3      3      1
                  1      2      1
                     1      1
                        1
```

The Right Amount of Brilliance

by Nicole Wachell

```
                        1
                     1      1
                  1      2      1
               1      3      3      1
            1      4      6      4      1
         1      5     10     10      5      1
      1      6     15     20     15      6      1
   1      7     21     35     35     21      7      1
1      8     28     56     70     56     28      8      1
```

ISBN-13: 978-0-578-74061-4

Cover design by: Nicole Wachell
Library of Congress Control Number: 2020914751

Quick Note

Pascal's triangle is a pattern of numbers constructed through recursion (by adding up the two numbers above each number).

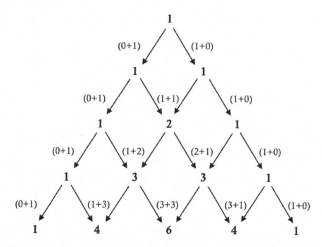

The triangle has many applications and properties. While the Western world generally refers to the triangle as "Pascal's" in honor of Blaise Pascal (a French mathematician and philosopher), other mathematicians used the triangle centuries earlier in India, China, Persia, and other areas.

The Zero Row

The Start of Everything (or Nothing at All)

1

Where n = the numbered rows in Pascal's triangle, our "1"
starts at n = 0. It may as well not exist.
Regardless, it is where we will begin.

"For after all, what is man in nature? A nothing in regard to
the infinite, a whole in regard to nothing, a mean between
nothing and the whole; infinitely removed from
understanding either extreme." – Blaise Pascal

1

This is how science works for me: it's a series of endless
pictures. Right now, the world forms, falls apart, and
reconstitutes itself. I'm pretty sure I'm the only person in the
lecture hall with my eyes closed. I don't keep them shut long.
Just long enough to flood my mind with images of a
beautiful, messy beginning. The lecturer discusses the
recently discovered Kepler-11 planetary system. I visualize a
molecular cloud core collapsing: a star is born.

"This is an unbelievably flat system," Dr. Bhattacharya
says. "Remarkably compact."

I wonder what it's like to be so tightly coiled, so
powerfully economical. There is a graphic representation of
the Kepler-11 planetary system projected at the front of the
lecture hall, but it's all lines and black space. I close my eyes
again and envision the planets: gaseous, rocky. It amazes me
that we keep finding these exoplanetary systems—other
planets orbiting stars outside the bounds of our Solar System.
When I leave the lecture, my mind is still full of impressions
of another world.

I'm craving espresso and ask a passing Stanford undergrad where the nearest café is. He seems surprised at my question but points me across the main quad.

"Have a good one, Professor Barnabas!" the kid says as we part.

I look around to see if anyone else is nearby, but I'm alone. Professor Barnabas?

When I finally get to the café, a college-aged barista greets me with frightening familiarity.

"Double ristretto?" she asks.

"Right," I say. "Pretty neat trick. How'd you peg me?"

"Is that a joke?" she asks. "You're so predictable."

An uncanny feeling worms through me. Am I that ordinary? A standard fortysomething professor with expectedly off-beat taste?

"But you don't even know me," I say.

"Of course I do," she responds. "Multivariable calculus?"

"Now I'm really lost," I tell her, hoping for an explanation.

"Dr. Barnabas, are you feeling all right?"

There was that name again.

"*What* did you call me?" I ask.

"Dr. Barnabas?"

"I'm Dr. Washington. Jake Washington," I tell her. "I have no idea who Dr. Barnabas is. I'm a planetary scientist at Berkeley. I'm just here for a lecture."

She clutches my arm and looks over my face as if she thinks I'm not real. It frightens me, watching this stranger staring at me the same way I look at wax figures in museums. I pull away from her and leave quickly. I try to write off the interaction as one of those bizarre encounters that might be explained by the right information. But after I leave the café, it happens three more times as I walk across the campus. My supposed acquaintances remark on my striking similarity to Dr. Sebastian Barnabas and use words I resent.

Dead ringer. Spitting image. Carbon copy. Twin.

As I drive home, I try to think about Kepler-11, but it doesn't stick. Instead, I keep thinking about one name: Sebastian Barnabas. Sebastian Barnabas, who's a professor. Sebastian Barnabas, who has a doctorate. Sebastian Barnabas, who works at a prestigious university across the bay. Sebastian Barnabas, who orders double ristrettos. For a moment, I half-believe that I'm the one who has it wrong. When I get home, I do what anyone would do: I search the internet. With a few keystrokes, there is Sebastian Barnabas, wearing my face as if it were his own. The same narrow eyes. The same prominent nose. The same dark brown hair. I don't know how to deal with the sight of him.

My first sensations are shock and curiosity, but those feelings yield to something more primal: anxiety, confusion, panic. I click on one image, then another, and then another, sticking my face right up to my monitor while everything inside me beats and pulses, like there is someone trapped in my body, banging on my skin in an attempt to get out. I run to the toilet and retch. Just bile. My hands shake.

To steady the tremors, I latch onto the differences. Sebastian's hair is longer than mine, styled upward and veering to one side. He is ten-or-so pounds lighter than I am, slimmer in the gut and face. I pinch the extra roundness under my chin, telling myself that sagging is natural in middle age. Unlike me, Sebastian has a light beard hiding any loose skin. But the differences in our appearance are so minor that they do little to overshadow the impression that someone is masquerading as me just across the bay.

I find Sebastian's email address on the Stanford website and write to him, attaching a picture of myself. I ask questions: *Where are you from? Who are your parents? Are you adopted? Do you know who I am?* After I send the email, I read a scientific article, then re-open Outlook. I work, refresh my email, work, refresh my email. I ask my wife if she knows where my birth certificate is. She says my mother has it. Of course she does. At eight o'clock, I check my email one last time. There's a response.

I read the first line: *I thought you were dead.*

I shiver. Sebastian's email spells out the unavoidable truth that he and I are twins. According to Sebastian, his mother had given me up as a toddler. He has memories of me.

I feel lost, so I do what I always do when I need to make sense of the world. I wait for nightfall, grab my telescope, jump in my car, and head north to avoid light pollution. Once I am outside the city, I park my car and pull out my equipment.

Anxious to drown my nerves in the beauty of the infinite, I attach the lowest power eyepiece to the telescope. I swing the telescope toward Aquarius, using the finder to ensure that the Helix Nebula is within range. After fixing my position, I peer through the eyepiece, eventually finding the smoky oval of the nebula set against a triangle of stars. With time and patience, I begin to see more details: the two interlocking coils and the darker center of the nebula. It's so ghost-like, this dying star. I look at the haze, knowing that the light is coming from the planetary nebula shedding its outer layers. I had seen more focused images of the Helix Nebula online—colorful pictures from infrared and ultraviolet NASA telescopes. The image I pick up is nothing that spectacular. But it is a vision nonetheless. I try my best to focus on the beauty, but all I can think about is how its interlocking coils are unraveling minute by minute, exposing the center to indifferent darkness.

The First Row
Reflection

1

1   1

The first row already shows us one property of odd rows in Pascal's triangle: symmetry. The numbers on the left half of the triangle mirror the numbers on the right half of the triangle.

---

1 :

For as long as he could remember, Jake Washington always had two bookshelves: one that he kept in his bedroom, another that he kept in the living room. The bookshelves were part of a matching set, handcrafted in sturdy oak with ornately carved embellishments along the sides. The bookshelf in the living room housed carefully chosen books. *A Brief History of Time* by Stephen Hawking. Postmodern tomes like *Gravity's Rainbow*. Classics like *Dr. Jekyll and Mr. Hyde*. The books in this bookcase were not alphabetized; they were clustered thematically. The combinations of texts had taken years to perfect. Now and then, he would still stumble upon a new work that would fit masterfully within a given collection. Whenever that happened, the impossibility of creating an "ultimate" bookshelf would become tragically apparent, and he would wonder whether there were parts of him that were just as incomplete, starved for missing components he didn't know were absent.

A couple of weeks ago, when his wife, Lilith, decided to redecorate the living room, Jake figured that the changes would be insignificant to him: fresh paint, an extra throw pillow on the couch, a reading nook built into the bay window. He encouraged her, thankful that she cared about enlivening their home. He had to give her credit. The powder blue color she picked for the walls brightened the room. The silk drapes she bought were elegant and homey. The redecoration was going well until she made a request on the morning of September 12, 2011, just days after Jake's world had changed forever.

"I'm going to bring in the second bookshelf. Restore some symmetry to the room," Lilith said, passing by Jake, who was staring at the ceiling in a fully reclined chair.

"I want it to stay in the bedroom," Jake insisted, yanking the seat upright.

"Those bookshelves deserve to be seen. They're beautiful," Lilith said, standing in the center of the living room, framing a segment of space with her hands. The gesture called attention to her manicured fingernails, the delicacy of her features. Even casually dressed in jeans, an open-collared shirt, and a camisole, she looked prim, the product of money. She accessorized with pearl studs and eye-catching red heels. Never too much.

"That's why I think that we should keep *one* in the living room. To be seen."

"They're a set, Jake," Lilith said, narrowing an eye.

"And that's supposed to mean something?"

"They work together. I can put one on either side of the china cabinet," she said, moving to the proposed location. "See," she motioned, raising her arms to the approximate height and width of the bookshelf. Tall but thin, Lilith wasn't the perfect stand-in for the furniture, but her angular features and understated prettiness did echo the wooden carvings. Her dirty blonde bun even mirrored the oak rosettes.

"They're just as beautiful when they stand alone," Jake said.

"Why are you so defensive about this? I thought you didn't care about interior decorating. I thought you said I could do whatever I wanted."

He had said this. At the time, it had seemed innocent enough. She was the one who cared about motifs and dominant hues and undertones. She was the one blessed with a sense of aesthetic compatibility, handed down through generations. Her job as senior vice president of marketing for her family's winery only cemented her claim to good taste. Jake had let her fulfill her ancestral role, never imagining that her love of interior decorating would infringe upon his sense of self. He never realized that his sense of self had unexpectedly built itself upon objects: not entirely, but enough to be unnerving.

"Aren't I allowed something beautiful too? Something for me to see, not something for everyone else to see?" Jake asked. He wondered if Lilith could read his desperation or understand it. They had been married for over a decade, but there were still times when Jake couldn't tell if Lilith misconstrued his intentions or simply ignored them.

"We can't have blank wall space," she said.

"Why not? Do we have to fill every square inch of this house with things? Can nothing just *exist* anymore?"

"Because a *wall* has so much significance," Lilith said, knitting her eyebrows the way she always did when she started to lose her patience.

"I just don't share your compulsion to occupy everything in sight," Jake replied with an edge that he couldn't control. He knew he was testing her, but she was testing him too.

"You make me sound like Napoleon."

"I've always kept that bookcase in the bedroom. You never complained before."

"Maybe I should've," she said, sitting on the couch, eyeing the space where the bookshelves would go. She closed one of her eyes and squinted the other like she was taking aim. She took mental pictures, loading the film, shooting. "I'm going to do it. I'm going to move the other bookcase out here."

"I asked you not to," Jake said, even though he knew that when Lilith set her mind to something, personal pleas wouldn't deter her. He appealed to her anyway, if only to justify his righteous indignation when she inevitably did what she planned.

"You also told me I could redecorate however I wanted."

"I changed my mind. Let me keep my bookshelf," Jake said, this time more earnestly. These were the moments when he liked her least, but he knew that her fierce independence was also cause for admiration when it wasn't coupled with unkindness.

"This is how it starts. One concession, and then another. I just want balance."

Seeing she was not giving up, Jake went into the kitchen, headed toward the knife block, and grabbed the biggest knife they owned. He stormed past Lilith with the knife in his hand, a man on a mission.

"What are you doing?" she called out from the couch, rising and following him.

Once he was in the bedroom, he took the knife and etched lines through the carvings on the side panel of the bookshelf, brutalizing the flourishes that he had kept pristine for years. Jake turned around to find Lilith staring at him. She didn't say anything. The damage was done. There was no way she would showcase a mutilated bookshelf in the living room, and he had known as much. He collapsed on the floor and fingered the spines of the books that were on his bedroom bookshelf. Unlike the living room bookshelf, this one was alphabetized, making it easier to find his favorite texts. Most of the books were science fiction or other genre works, formulaic books that lacked the literary merit which would have warranted placement on the living room bookshelf. He assessed the destruction, still gripping the knife, an instrument of violence that he needed to feel the weight of. It was lighter than he expected.

"What's gotten into you?" Lilith demanded, recovering from the situation.

"I told you I didn't want to move the bookshelf," Jake muttered.

"Those engravings were priceless," she said, admiring the baroque design.

"You're wrong. They had a price."

"Well, you got what you wanted. We'll keep the thing in here," she assured him. "Are you happy now?"

There was no response.

"This is about Sebastian," she deduced, sinking to the floor and putting her arms around her husband. She rubbed his back. Her warmth felt nice. Jake appreciated it when she made an effort. He usually craved this from her, the tenderness cultivated from years of shared living. But after a moment, he pushed her away.

"You're probably right," he said, diverting his gaze toward the ground.

Lilith recovered from the sting of his recoil and took the knife from his hand gingerly, uncurling his fingers as a mother might. "Tomorrow will be fine," she said.

"I don't need assurances. I just need the bookshelf to stay here."

"Well, thanks to your theatrics, that won't be a problem," she said, using the edge of her shirt to clean the wooden debris from the knife as she left the room.

The next day, everything did seem fine, at least for the most part. In preparation for his meeting with Sebastian, Jake laid out a pair of khakis and a white Oxford shirt. He picked up a copy of *Being and Nothingness*, the gargantuan work that, like many other books in the living room bookcase, he had only read a single chapter from. He scanned the table of contents and found Part Four, Chapter Two: "The Body." Jake leafed through the pages in his underwear before getting in the shower. He read about the murky tension between the body of oneself and the body of

11

others. The language was opaque: the language of philosophers, not scientists. He wasn't sure he understood what it meant, but the words held sway over him with the inexplicable force of a stranger who has something familiar buried beneath the layers of alien-ness. He stepped into the shower and soaped his body. When he emerged, steam had clouded the mirror, and he was reluctant to smear off the condensation. He didn't need to see the extra weight around his waist, the face that wasn't his alone.

"Hurry up. It's time," Lilith urged from the other side of the bathroom door.

"I still have to shave," Jake called back to her, peeved.

"You don't need to shave," she responded through the door.

Jake opened the door and looked her in the face. "Lilith, I *have* to shave."

"I don't know why you have to make this an issue. You look great," she said, casting the back of her hand across his stubbled cheek. He caught her wrist mid-stroke and lowered it. Even as he did it, he worried that his distance might stunt her affection for him.

"Don't treat today like it's any other day," he said. "Shaving is something I need to do. You might not understand it, but it's important to me."

"But you..."

"Lilith, this has nothing to do with you," he said.

"You're wrong, Jake. Your life *is* my life," she said. Jake looked into her green eyes. They were soft and inviting, but he couldn't fight the resentment he felt at her remark.

"Except that it's not. *My* life is my life," Jake shot back.

Lilith picked up the copy of *Being and Nothingness* that was lying on the bed. "A little light reading on the second most important day of your life?"

"Put that down...*Second* most important day?"

"You're kidding, right?" she said, wiggling her fingers in the air and flashing her wedding band. "Sartre? Please tell me you're not going to plummet into existential despair."

"Do I look like I'm in existential despair?"

"Your eyebrows are furrowed."

"There's another explanation for that," he quipped before shutting the bathroom door on his wife. He began shaving, not looking any closer at his face than he had to, and nicked himself on his cheek. He grabbed a piece of toilet paper to staunch the blood.

"Jake, I just want to tell you something," she said from behind the door.

"I'm *not* going to plummet into a pit of existential despair," he called out. "And if I do, I'll keep you out of it."

"That wasn't what I wanted to say. I just want you to remember that nothing changes because of today. You'll still be the same person you've always been."

"I know, Lilith. You're right," Jake lied, trying to believe her. He opened the door to her. "And I appreciate the support. But if it's all the same, I need to do this alone. I don't need you here while I'm getting ready, and I don't need you to drive me or wait up for me. I could use the time to myself."

"Fine," she said, turning her back to him and leaving without another glance.

After finishing his shave, Jake walked to the bed to pick up his freshly pressed shirt. He noticed something: the edge of the bedsheet was undone, peeking out from beneath the comforter. The sight was jarring. Had he forgotten to tuck in the corner when he'd made the bed earlier that morning? It was hard for him to believe. Jake was not one of those people who made his bed with the perfunctory laziness of a teenager. His mother had taught him how to crisply fold the edges using hospital corners, a skill she'd honed during her years as a nurse. His mother. Jake remembered how her career had seemed like a fantasy. The hospital corners. The nurturing bedside manner when he'd caught an illness. The improvised tourniquet she'd made when he'd sprained his elbow. These were the only vestiges of her work identity that he'd ever witnessed, and they became part of a deeper mythology about who she was when he wasn't with her. How fitting that of all days, this day, Jake had forgotten to fastidiously fold the fabric, forgotten to emulate the woman he didn't want to think about. And yet here he was, thinking about her. There was no escape. He remembered how gently she'd kissed his scrapes, how well she'd advised him during moments of confusion, how accepting she'd been of his life choices. But this was the same woman who'd concealed his adoptive roots from him. He couldn't shake that. He wanted to leave her behind, so he left the bed undone, put on his clothes, and went to confront his future.

: 1

Remnants of sleep were still fresh when Sebastian Barnabas stirred at three in the morning until suddenly, he was wide awake. Within minutes, he was in the kitchen, putting on coffee. Black, obviously. Strong, of course. His clothes were in disarray. There were ashtrays everywhere—both improvised and commercially produced. At 3:16, Sebastian went to his workspace and cleared papers from his desk. Beside his current cup of coffee, there was an abandoned mug from earlier that night. He would intermittently take a swig of the stale coffee by accident, but he was perfectly content with whatever his hand reached for. Coffee was coffee was coffee.

Sebastian's hands worked furiously. He was onto something: a new entry point to a mathematic theory, a potential break in his work. While he filled his composition notebook with symbols and arrows and Greek letters and equal signs, the pleasure of exploration was intense. It felt as if through his notations, he interrogated something at the very core of him, an intuitive sense of order that he translated

14

into the language of mathematics. He was convince
heart was constructed out of binary code; his lung,,
on a Cartesian plane; and his hands, mere vessels to
logarithms.

He took a drag of his cigarette. He reached the end of the composition book and shoved it into the shelving unit that was attached to his desk. It was brimming with notebooks full of ideas that had spun themselves from his brain in other monomaniacal fits. Most of the ideas in these composition books weren't destined for publication. These scribblings spoke to pure passion; they expressed the tangled mass of his internal circuitry. The compulsion to write, to think, to produce defined him. He continued to smoke his cigarette, feeling the addictive clutch of nicotine weaken its grip in the face of the more powerful force of his mind. He inhaled deeply to balance the adversaries, to unite them.

"Hey," a waifish girl said, groggy-eyed as she entered the living room where Sebastian was at work. Her long brown hair was down, wavy from the braids she'd worn during her night shift. She was wearing his T-shirt from the U.S.S. Hornet Museum over her underwear. She looked down at the shirt and toyed with the bottom seam.

"You a war buff?" she asked.

Sebastian glanced up long enough to recognize her reference to his T-shirt. "You could say that," he responded. He didn't want to discuss his preoccupation with the American military. If he did, he'd have to consider his father's service in Vietnam. Today was not the day to think about that. He shifted focus and returned to his work.

"It's six in the morning," she said.

"Is it?"

"What are you doing?"

"Nothing," he said, continuing his writing. She sidled up next to him and looked over his shoulder while he scrawled more numbers, more symbols on the page. She squinted her eyes, scrutinizing his handwriting as if she could translate the cipher.

"So...you're some kind of genius or something?" she asked.

"Or something."

"Why didn't you tell me last night?"

He didn't respond. He couldn't. The math was motoring his hand, overtaking his body like the Pentecostal spirit that takes residence in the tongues of the faithful.

"Sebastian?" she nudged him.

"I'm not a genius. I'm not that interesting," he assured her. Even though he knew that his nonchalance would make him more attractive to a girl like her, that wasn't why he'd said it. He wanted her to get the hint that the whole conversation was uninteresting to him. He kept working. She moved away and leaned against the wall opposite him. She dropped her chin and sighed loudly. Too loudly. He didn't look up.

"Say, do you have any tampons lying around?" she asked, tilting her head to get more squarely into his peripheral view. "I think I might be getting my period."

"No."

"You sure you never had an old girlfriend leave some in the bathroom?"

"No," he said, just as plainly as the first time.

"No, you're not sure, or no, that never happened?"

"What's the point of this?" he asked, looking up from his work with a flat affect.

"What do you mean?"

"I mean, are you asking me this so you can find out whether or not I've been in a serious relationship with some other woman who left her things at my place? Are you asking about tampons to make me uncomfortable because you're mad at me for being here at my desk instead of in bed with you? Or are you asking me about something that no man wants to hear about because you want to establish intimacy

16

and cross a personal boundary that might make it seem like we're more than we are?"

Throughout his rant, she took her medicine like a child, which she might as well have been. How old was she anyway? Twenty-one? Twenty-three? She wore a sour expression but tried to contain her frustration, cowering in the face of Sebastian's judgment as though he were her father.

"It was just a question," she said meekly. "It was just something I needed."

"Well, right now, *I* need to work," Sebastian said, barely even looking up.

"Right now, you sound like an asshole," she said, amplifying her voice.

"I don't care what I sound like."

"You're one slippery motherfucker," she said, removing Sebastian's T-shirt, throwing it on the ground, and grabbing her generic white blouse from the floor. "You know you're not as charming as you think," she continued, quickly buttoning up her shirt and getting into the black pants she'd grabbed from a nearby chair.

She pressed her body flat against the floor and sent a roving hand under the couch. "My nametag, you seen it?" she asked. "I have another shift this afternoon."

Sebastian turned to her and shrugged his shoulders. The missing nametag presented an opportunity. If he found it before she did, he could save some face and act as if he remembered something about her. But the place was a mess. It would take effort to track down the nametag. The risk of getting distracted didn't seem worth the potential upside of seeing her again. Besides, what was a name to a girl like this? Everything? Nothing? It was immaterial now.

"Fat lot of good you are," she said, searching on her own. "Christ, I've got to stop sleeping with fucking drunks. Hazard of the job, I guess. You're all so useless."

"I'm not a fucking drunk," Sebastian said. He had it on good authority that he was right. Last night had been a rare indulgence. There had been shots: ounces of tequila that the girl, whatever her name was, had matched with him covertly under the counter. But mostly there had been beer and relatively low-proof beer at that. Even in his leisure, he was a mathematician, considering the impact of each drink on his blood alcohol level using far simpler equations than he was used to. Real drunks didn't take such precautions. He knew this all too well. He knew about the precipitous collapse from tipsy to blacked out, knew about the vomiting (and with enough time and practice, the not vomiting), knew about the incontinence, the embarrassment, the lack of embarrassment, the utter failure to curb addiction, the delirium tremens, the apologies and apologies and apologies ad infinitum.

He was not a fucking drunk.

"That's what they all say," she replied just as she unearthed her nametag. She proceeded toward the door, and in one final insult, said, "and by the way, if you were a genius, you wouldn't need a calculator the size of a planet."

The old Hewlett-Packard calculator from the 1970s took up prime real estate on his desk. "It has sentimental value," he yelled out as she left. He grazed its edge where dried blood from decades past still tarnished it. He tried to get back to the numbers, but he hit a roadblock and put down the pencil.

Sebastian showered and got dressed. Even though he was about to meet his twin, Sebastian convinced himself there was nothing special about today. There would be the specter of the past hanging over him and Jake, that couldn't be helped, but Sebastian could tolerate the ghost since he'd learned to live with it long ago. He had an advantage since he'd already seen the silhouette and heard the voice of their shared history. Even though Sebastian hadn't looked it square in the eyes, he knew the vague shape and substance of this ghost in a way that Jake did not. Regardless, when

Jake reached out, Sebastian should have felt shocked. Instead, he felt the strange sense that he'd always known someone else was still co-opting his face, and that the entire course of his life could be explained by this subliminal knowledge.

After receiving Jake's email a couple of days ago, Sebastian had called his mother and confronted her about her massive lie: that Jake had died at age three.

"Not true," she'd insisted on the phone. "I never said, 'dead.' I just said he was gone. I said he was never coming back. I never said 'dead.'"

Sebastian hated the way she twisted the truth, but it was what he expected of her. The worst part of their conversation came after Sebastian mentioned he was meeting Jake. "Tell him I love him," she'd said.

Even now, as Sebastian got ready to meet the man, her request made him want to throw up. Determined to put this all behind him, Sebastian hopped into his car and drove on the 101. He made his way to the arranged meeting place, a small café in South San Francisco. When he opened the door, he scanned the tables and booths, unable to place his twin. But upon second inspection, Sebastian locked eyes with Jake Washington. He wondered how he could have missed him the first time around. Sebastian had looked in his direction. Approaching the booth, Sebastian neared the man whose face was nearly identical to his own, except for one key detail: the man had no beard.

The Second Row
The Double

1

1   1

1   2   **1**

When there is an even amount of numbers in a given row, each number will have a symmetrical counterpart. The reflection is seamless. But in a row with an odd amount of numbers, there will always be a number in the middle that stands alone, divided against itself. Pascal's triangle produces a doubling effect but an imperfect one.

---

1 : :

Everyone in the café was drinking coffee. The arm movements of the coffee drinkers transfixed Jake, hands moving up and down, up and down, out of sync as each person found their rhythm: a mutual act performed at different tempos. Jake was making a decision—coffee or no coffee—when he saw his twin walk through the door. Sebastian overlooked him once, then twice, as though Jake could have been anyone else in the café, any*thing* else. Jake thought about the double ristretto he'd ordered days before. He decided he didn't feel like coffee.

Sebastian approached the booth and shook hands with Jake. The handshake was equally firm on both sides. Jake tried not to read much into the gesture, but something about the perfectly matched pressure struck him.

"I'm starving," Jake lied, using hunger as an excuse to bury his head in the menu. Sebastian took the cue. They sat in silence until the waitress came around. They both ordered the same bacon-and-egg combo, only with a different cook on the eggs.

21

"Great minds think alike," the waitress said. "Look alike too," she smiled, pointing her pen in the direction of Jake then Sebastian. She was upbeat, the standard pretty-enough, twentysomething waitress whose smile alone warranted generous tips.

Sebastian smiled back flirtatiously, offering a gentle chuckle. It was harder for Jake to reciprocate the smile because he was uncomfortable with the comparison. He blindly handed his menu to the waitress.

"So...how do we do this?" Sebastian asked once she'd gone. "What do you want to get out of this?"

"I'm not sure even I know."

"You called me," Sebastian reminded him, as if there were rules to this sort of thing. The words sounded like a challenge and an unfair one at that. Even though Jake had emailed Sebastian, it was chance that Jake had been the one to stumble upon their situation. There was a long pause, and Jake knew that Sebastian wouldn't be the one to end it.

"So...you remembered me?" Jake eventually asked. "I mean, before I reached out to you...you had memories of having a twin?"

"Sure," Sebastian said, his baritone even and calm.

"What was it like? Having a brother?"

"It was so long ago, I hardly know. What I remember most is playing. Digging together in a sandbox. Not feeling alone. I remember being sad when you left. You *really* never remembered me?"

"No," Jake said, ripping his paper napkin. "I did some googling about repressed memories. Childhood trauma can distort the past. I've been trying to remember, and I do get flashes of images here and there, but I can't tell if they're real."

"What images?"

"The one that comes to me most is a trellis with wildflowers and berries on it. The vines are all tangled, and

I'm running my hands across the wood and the stems, getting splinters and cutting my hand."

"Mom lost control of the garden," Sebastian said. The casual "mom" threw Jake. Sebastian spoke the word as though she were a shared relative, which of course, she was. Jake tried to imagine a woman near the trellis, but the only mother he could picture was the one who had raised him. It was jarring to superimpose one life over another, so Jake shook his head to dispel the scene.

"So...the trellis...it was real?" Jake asked, feeling vindicated. Over the past few days, it had been hard to trust himself, his thoughts, his dreams.

"Still is. Well, sort of. The wood is broken and rotting, and the plants have overtaken it. She should have taken it down a long time ago, but that's not her way," Sebastian said with an edge of resentment. His face was serious—his lips pursed together, his eyes cast downward—and Jake couldn't help but wonder: was this what *he* looked like when he was frustrated? Did he seem as distant? As lost?

"You all right?" Jake asked.

"Fine. My mom's just a real piece of work."

"Does she look like me?" Jake asked. As soon as the words came out of his mouth, he wondered if he should have asked, "does she look like *us*?" but he was still getting used to the idea of the same-faced man across the table from him. Jake fidgeted.

"A lot, actually. Here. From the eighties. She must've been in her early thirties," Sebastian said, pulling out a picture of their mother on his phone. Her dark brown hair was parted down the middle, running in pin-straight tracks to her waist. Jake grabbed the phone and zoomed in. He felt awe at the sight of his creator. He saw his high forehead in hers. Beneath her too-bright blue eyeshadow, he saw his eyes. Her lipsticked mouth sparkled pastel pink, but the average fullness of her lips matched his. She and Jake shared a pronounced cleft in their top lip. Her image felt right, but that rightness felt like a betrayal of everything he grew up knowing and loving. There were striking similarities, but her nose was different than his...maybe an inherited trait from his biological father?

"Thanks," Jake said, sliding the phone across the table. "What about your dad?" Jake asked, aware of pronouns again. He couldn't keep the words straight: which people, objects, and traits were Jake's? Which were Sebastian's? Which belonged to both of them?

"Out of the picture," Sebastian said. "We weren't exactly a fairytale family."

"Yeah, well, my parents never even told me I was adopted."

"And you never figured it out?"

When Jake tensed up, Sebastian paused. "It's just that you're a scientist," Sebastian continued, softening his tone. "Scientists are observant by trade. Weren't there any clues that you were adopted? That you were a twin? What about your birth certificate?"

"I never needed it until I got married. And my mom came with my wife and me to process the marriage license. I didn't look at the documents too carefully," Jake said, realizing how unobservant and pathetic this must have made him sound.

"What about a passport? You need a birth certificate to get a passport."

"I've had one since I was young. I just renew it when it expires."

"And none of this seemed suspicious to you?" Sebastian asked.

Jake breathed in and out to escape the tension. He hated being interrogated. But Sebastian's questions did make Jake think about the extent of his parents' deception, the constant upkeep they must have done to ensure he never found out the truth.

"Listen, my mother was supportive. I never questioned her. And it's not like my parents look *entirely* different than I do. My dad has dark hair. My mom's eyes are almond-shaped. I also know a lot of people who look nothing like their parents," Jake said. "Besides, when I'm researching, I can be objective. In a situation like this, it's easy to get blinded by emotions. I'm sure you can relate. It's not as if your mathematical skills made you any better at figuring out that I was alive."

"I guess it just goes to show how far a Ph.D. will get you. None of us are gods."

"I have some colleagues who might fight you on that."

"Come to think of it, so do I," Sebastian responded. "The fools." They both laughed slightly. Almost as quickly, Jake averted his eyes, trying to figure out what to say next. When Jake had the strength to look up, he felt shaken by Sebastian, the man with his face. Jake rested his elbow on the table and took solace in the bare skin of his cheek against his hand, thankful he had shaved, unlike Sebastian. The only way Jake could escape the panic that beat inside him was to find details that separated them from one another. He stared at the unmarred, brown hairs along Sebastian's prominent brow and reflected on the scarred, hairless edge of his own left brow ridge. He looked at Sebastian's slightly crooked teeth, untouched by orthodontia, and he considered how they looked more natural than his own artificially crafted smile. Jake was there, and Sebastian was there, sitting opposite one another, but some small part of Jake worried that if he looked anywhere other than Sebastian's beard, his eyebrow, or his smile, he just might disappear.

"Not what you expected?" Sebastian asked.

"No."

"You aren't what I expected either," Sebastian noted. "Starched collar, nicked face," he pointed out, using his coffee spoon as a visual aid, labeling all the ways that the

Jake Washington of right here misaligned with the Jake Washington of his imagination.

"I'm not usually clumsy," Jake said, pulling the toilet paper scrap from his nick.

"You'll bleed."

"Are you afraid of blood?"

"No," Sebastian replied, neutral. "Are you?"

At first, Jake didn't respond. The mention of blood activated the scientist in him, summoning biological terms: plasma, leukocytes, platelets, hemoglobin. But blood was also a reminder of genetics, of heritability, of what bound Jake and Sebastian to one another.

"No, I'm not afraid of blood," Jake eventually replied. "I just don't want to look ridiculous with this scrap of paper stuck to my face."

"And you won't look ridiculous with blood running down your face?"

When Sebastian's question was met with silence, he apologized.

"Listen, this isn't easy for me," Jake said.

"You think it's easy for me?"

"No, I...it's probably hard for you too. I just meant...well, I don't know what I meant. But the day I found out about you, it was like a switch went off in my head. I can't even stand the sight of my reflection. The other day, I did the strangest thing. I was working at my laptop, writing notes for a lecture, and I got the impulse to open the camera on my computer. I looked at myself on the screen and tried to imagine my face was yours."

"And?"

"And, I thought I would try to script a conversation...you know, try to anticipate what you and I might say to one another. But I couldn't find the words," Jake said.

"You can try to find them now."

"I'm not sure they exist."

"We're talking, aren't we?"

"I guess I was hoping for a revelation. I mean, I'm looking over at you, and you look like me, but obviously, you're not me."

"And you expected something different?"

"No," Jake continued, "but when I was looking at myself on my laptop, the thing was, I didn't recognize myself. Not entirely."

"That sounds like it has nothing to do with me and everything to do with you."

"Forget it," Jake said, feeling exposed.

"I say we start simple," Sebastian said. "This doesn't have to be some life-changing conversation. We can just get to know one another. Do you like working at Berkeley?"

"It isn't Stanford," Jake countered, as though sibling rivalry were something innate.

"I didn't mean it that way. I just want to know what your experience is like over there. Honestly," Sebastian said, but Jake couldn't tell how genuine he was. Before meeting up, Jake imagined he'd be an expert at decoding Sebastian's tone. After all, they had the same midrange, California-accented voice, even similar inflections. But listening to Sebastian was strangely dissociative, like hearing a recording of himself.

"Great. My research is going well right now," Jake said, hating himself for the need to boast. "I got my hands on a newly discovered Martian meteorite. It could make me."

"Provided you find something interesting," Sebastian said, off-handed.

"Yes, provided that."

"Easier said than done," Sebastian responded, eyebrows arched as he took gulps from his water. Jake tensed at Sebastian's bluntness.

"Sorry," Sebastian said, leaning onto his forearms and moving closer to Jake. "I know I can be direct. It's not always charming. Maybe it never is. Let's start simpler."

"Simpler?"

"Music?" Sebastian asked with an inviting shrug.

"What about it?"

"If you had to pick a defining album, what would it be?"

"That's hardly simple," Jake said. He loathed this sort of question. It felt like a test, a measure of coolness. Jake was one of those middle-aged men who had stopped listening to new music not long after he graduated from college. Now, when he wasn't listening to public radio, he was listening to songs from the past.

"Come on," Sebastian said. "No judgment. Just curiosity. You tell me, I tell you."

"All right. *War*," Jake caved. The title tripped off his tongue more easily than he'd anticipated.

"U2...Me too," Sebastian smiled.

"*War* was your defining album?" Jake asked, skeptical.

"*The Joshua Tree.*"

Their similar responses shouldn't have been a big deal. They were the same age, and they grew up listening to the same radio stations. But there were plenty of other bands they could have chosen from their formative years: New Order or the Smiths or Depeche Mode or R.E.M. or the Violent Femmes or the Cure. For some reason, this surface connection felt meaningful. It went beyond physical likeness, beyond the shared gestures and identical lips. They talked about eighties' and nineties' alt-rock for a substantial time, discussing jangly guitar riffs and divisive lead singers and flawed critical responses to underappreciated albums. It cooled the tensions Jake felt.

But then the food came. Jake stared at the sunny-side-up eggs on his plate. One yolk sat in the center of the egg while the other yolk teetered on the edge of the egg. In an act of mercy, Jake sliced down the middle of the wayward yolk first, watching the life drip out from it and saturate his potatoes. He took a bite, then eyed Sebastian's eggs, regretful that he hadn't opted for the scramble too.

"My mother should be here," Sebastian said as he ate his breakfast. The abrupt shift from the fluff of musical preferences to the substance of familial bonds reminded Jake of how fraught their interaction was.

"I can meet her another time," Jake said, realizing it would have been too much to meet both of them anyway. Seeing her picture triggered a desire to meet her, but that could come later. Jake had barely been ready to meet Sebastian. One new person at a time.

"She had her reasons," Sebastian offered in what passed for kindness. "But you should count yourself lucky she's not here. And lucky she gave you up."

"Lucky?" Jake scoffed.

"Yeah, lucky. To hear her tell the story, she was young. She…"

"I don't need to know," Jake interrupted, overwhelmed by the circumstances of his adoption. The question Jake wanted to ask was the one he knew he couldn't broach: why not you? Although unuttered, it was there, occupying all the space inside him. The fact that *he* was the one left behind stoked his deepest insecurities. Jake knew his life with his adoptive family might have been far better than his life would have been with Sebastian's, but that didn't lessen the sting of rejection.

"My mother, or rather, the woman who raised me, she's wonderful. She's compassionate and smart. My father's like that too. Great man," Jake said. He didn't know why he was defending his parents, especially given the way they had betrayed him. But it made him feel better to idealize them the same way he would have a week ago.

"Like I said," Sebastian managed between bites, "count yourself lucky."

There was that word again: lucky. It was intolerable when Jake felt so profoundly unlucky at that moment. Jake watched as Sebastian shoveled scrambled eggs into his mouth, chewing with his mouth open like a slob.

29

"I need to get out of here," Jake said, knowing that another second spent watching Sebastian cram eggs into his mouth would prove unbearable. "Sorry about the rush." He took cash from his wallet and put it on the table before leaving.

After he got to his car, Jake wanted to steady himself, so he hurried to his office. Once he arrived, he retrieved his Martian meteorite from the vacuum desiccator he kept hidden in a locked cabinet. Tens of thousands of meteorites had been discovered on Earth, but only a little over a hundred were from Mars. Such rarity provided opportunities for discovery, and by extension, possible recognition. He needed to keep the specimen safe.

He brought out the meteorite, or what was left of it, and smiled. Not long ago, the rock had been sawed in half so that Jake's friend and fellow investor, Chris, could keep the other half. There were also thin sections that Jake had cut from the rock in preparation for spectral analysis and radiometric dating. To an ordinary onlooker, the meteorite would look like any other rock. There were only a couple of distinguishing features: a black fusion crust on the surface of the meteorite and a vitreous luster from the maskelynite. But to Jake, the rock was a sight to behold. He kept the meteorite on his desk in its glass desiccator while he sat at his computer. He opened up the preliminary data from his spectral analysis of the rock and tried to work. The only problem was that the more he tried to accomplish, the more futile his efforts became. Jake tried to reclaim the energy surge he'd felt when he received the rock. He remembered how captivated he'd been when he first observed it under the high-powered university microscopes.

But no matter how much he tried to focus on work, Jake couldn't stop thinking about his recent encounter with Sebastian. He recalled the image of his birth mother, her eyes like his. Jake tried to summon her face, not from the picture on Sebastian's phone, but from the fragments of his memories. Foolishly, he assumed that with a few keywords, he might be able to pull up complete accounts of who he had been, who his mother had been, who his family had been. But there were only the jagged shards of the past. Ignorance. At least Jake had the wildflowers and blackberries on the trellis: an artifact his three-year-old brain had tucked away. He wished he had retained something more significant, maybe a memory of an outing or an everyday experience with his twin. But he'd take the yellow flowers, the thorns, the fruit, the whitewashed wood. He just wanted more.

There must have been a million questions Jake could have asked Sebastian in the diner, a million details they could have discussed. But what had Jake done? Bolted. He had always been on a perpetual quest for knowledge. But now, he wondered what good would come of learning more about something as enigmatic as his past.

: 2 :

There was a war going on. Tensions had built after recent attacks on the home front, and now warfare threatened a suburban location: Glendale, California. The army was quick to respond to the threats of a mastermind, Communist scientist from across the Pacific Ocean who had done the unthinkable: birthed a race of warrior dinosaurs in their quest for world domination. Excited by the prospect of seeing the carnage, Little Jakey Washington prepared to serve his country at the ripe age of seven years old. At 12:10, on January 2nd, 1977, Little Jakey was right in the thick of it. Loud engine noises emanated from above. The fringe of Jakey's bowl cut swooshed to the right when he tilted his head skyward. He watched the aerial attack and followed the trajectory of the enemy combatant with his eyes. The descent happened fast. The B-17 Flying Fortress replica zoomed closer toward the ground, and Jakey's bangs swooshed downward.

"Watch out!" Jakey called out to the officers on the ground, but it was too late. The enemy had already dropped a bomb, and a number of the men perished.

"You're dead! You're dead!" Sebastian shouted at the downed warriors. Little Jakey looked over at Sebastian in anger. Sebastian lowered the plane and brought out the big guns: a Tyrannosaurus that had a rifle attached to its head with scotch tape.

"Rawwrrr...I'm gonna eat your face off and have your liver for dessert," Sebastian growled huskily, T-rex in hand. "Bang!" he shouted, firing at one of Jakey's army men. Sebastian knocked the figure over by pushing on the man's forehead right where the bullet would have gone through. The Tyrannosaurus pounced on the corpse of the lame army commander and started gnawing on the plastic helmet.

"You'll never get away with this," Jakey proclaimed. "Besides, you're no match for my fleet of bombers." Jakey whirred an engine using the back of his throat and rolled one of his model airplanes across the carpet and into the air. The plane dropped a bomb directly over the Tyrannosaurus.

"You'll regret that," Sebastian said, looking into the deep brown eyes that mirrored his own. Almost every feature on Sebastian's face reflected the features on Little Jakey's face—their noses, still young and unformed, were equally button-like in the center of their faces; their freckles, nearly invisible, were patterned with the same blueprint. Their faces had the appeal of American austerity, adorable but dulled around the edges. Jakey and Sebastian would be perfect facsimiles of one another if not for something in Sebastian's eyes.

"Mutant dinosaur takeover!" Sebastian called out. "All the humans are dead! I win, Jakey loses!"

"No, Sebastian, *I* win!" Little Jakey yelled, throwing a Triceratops across the room. Jakey picked up another dinosaur, a brown Brontosaurus, and swung it around his head like a lasso, gripping the tail while its body picked up velocity. "Check this out, Sebastian," Jakey called out, prepared to launch the dinosaur. Suddenly, he noticed his mother standing in the doorframe. Jake lost his grip on the toy, and it flew across the room.

Rachel Washington had several mom-faces that Jakey had grown accustomed to over the years. The proud mom-face. The happy mom-face. The don't-embarrass-me-right-now mom-face. The I'm-not-mad-I'm-just-disappointed mom-face. But little Jakey didn't know how to react to the new mom-face that emerged. Her almond-shaped eyes seemed larger than usual as she stared at him, forehead wrinkled in concern. Little Jakey might have attributed her stare to his dinosaur-twirling performance, but he could tell something else disturbed her. There was no rage or frustration in her eyes, nor had she chanced to look around at the mess Jakey had made. Instead, she fixated on him in a stupor. It was almost as if she were looking through him. She took breathed deeply and averted her eyes. When she looked back up at Jakey again, she salvaged herself with a warm, motherly smile.

"Jakey pie, come here," she said, bending her knees and descending onto the balls of her feet to meet his eye line. He approached her cautiously.

"What is it, Mom?"

"Sweetie," she said, lightly gripping one of his arms and whisking his bangs over his forehead in gentle strokes. "Who were you talking to when I came in here?"

"Sebastian," Jakey said plainly with a shoulder shrug.

"Who's Sebastian?"

"He's my friend."

His mother scanned the room. "Jakey, I don't see anyone else in here," she said.

"That's because he's hiding. He's scared of adults."

"Jakey, I want you to be a big boy. I want you to see what I see," Rachel said, gripping both of Jakey's arms and turning them clockwise, like a mechanism on a wind-up doll. She adjusted his stance so that she and he were both facing the center of the bedroom. Rachel went onto her knees and wrapped her arms around her son's waist. She lowered her chin toward his shoulder and spoke into his ear: "Now, just look around the room. I'm looking around, and I can't see anything. There's no one here."

After Jakey looked around the empty room and cast his head down, Rachel spun her son toward her once more. "What I mean to say is, Sebastian's not real."

"He is *too* real. He's just hiding, I told you. He's scared," Jakey responded, his face shriveling into a caricature of frustration.

"Now what kind of sense does that make? I'm not scary, am I?"

"You're not scary to *me*, but Sebastian thinks you're a stranger."

Rachel paused. Her warmth evaporated. She retreated to the same blank stare from before. She breathed shallowly and looked up at Jakey.

"But *you* know I'm not a stranger," she said, clutching him desperately.

"*I* know that, Mom."

"All right, all right. Now, I want you to repeat what I say: Sebastian isn't real."

"He is too!" Jakey protested, stomping and raising his chin in revolt.

"Then show me where he is sweetie, show me where Sebastian is."

"I don't know where he is now. You scared him away! He knew you'd be mad at him. He *told* me so. He *knew* you wouldn't like him, so he left. Sebastian! Sebastian! Come back!" Jakey shouted, walking through his room and stepping on the clutter of dinosaurs and army men that lay in the wake of his battle.

"Stop saying his name, for God's sake," Rachel said, losing her patience.

"Sebastian!"

"Stop saying his name!" she yelled.

"I will not. Sebastian, Sebastian, Sebastian, Sebastian..." Jakey repeated in defiance, turning the name into a chant that flitted along on nursery-rhyme melodies.

"Jakey, don't you see you're making Mommy upset?" Rachel pleaded with her son, her eyes on the verge of tears. "You said Sebastian left because he was scared. Well, right now, you're scaring *me*. You don't want to do that, do you?" she asked, regaining her calm.

"No, Mom," Jakey muttered.

"Good. Now come give me a hug," Rachel said, pulling Jakey toward her. She drew away from the hug and braced his shoulders. "And promise me, no more talking about Sebastian."

"Okay, Mom," he conceded with a weak smile.

After his mother left, Jakey looked around the room. "Sebastian?" he whispered, lifting the comforter on his bed. "Sebastian?" he whispered once more, opening his closet and rifling through his clothes. He looked everywhere: under the bed, out the window, and down the street, but there was no sign of him. Jakey sighed. He picked up his Brontosaurus and sat on the floor, his back against his bed. He thought about the way his mother had looked at him. Had he done something wrong? Jakey loved playing with Sebastian, but some burgeoning empathetic part of him didn't want his fun with Sebastian to come at the cost of his mother's happiness.

Jakey wished away Sebastian for the better part of the afternoon, but before dinnertime, Sebastian resurfaced. Jakey was playing with his Lincoln Logs when he noticed Sebastian sitting next to him, on hand to construct a home. Jakey had already organized the pieces. He was attuned to the importance of order when laying a foundation. He grabbed one of the longer logs. Carefully, he lined up its notches with another piece that Sebastian pointed to. Jake followed the direction of his imaginary guide while he erected an artifact of the real world, shrunken down to his size. Together, Jakey and Sebastian assembled the base, one interlocked piece at a time. Jakey loved the way the grooves fit into place, the carved-out joints preventing everything from falling apart.

Jakey's mom announced that dinner was ready. Sebastian was hungry. The two of them made their way to the dinner table.

"Jake, why haven't you touched your asparagus?" Daniel Washington asked his son, looking at the parallel spears on the edge of the plate.

"I'm saving them for Sebastian. He loves asparagus," Jake replied. Daniel looked over at Rachel, who pursed her lips. Jake folded an extra napkin he'd taken from the kitchen and placed it onto the empty chair at the end of the table.

"Jakey, you promised me you were going to cut that out," Rachel said, irritated.

"But Mom, Dad asked me about the asparagus. I didn't want to lie."

"It seems Jakey has an invisible friend. Apparently, he made him up today," Rachel informed her husband, giving him a serious look.

"I didn't make him up. He's real, Dad. He's just invisible to adults."

"Jakey, cut it out," Rachel intervened. "It's not healthy for you to have an invisible friend. You're old enough to know the difference between reality and make-believe. Now, if you want to play with your action figures, that's fine, but you have to keep in mind that it's not real. Somewhere inside, you need to *know* when you're pretending."

"Where'd you come up with a name like Sebastian, anyway?" Daniel asked, glancing at Rachel using his peripheral vision as he tilted his head toward Jakey.

"That's just his name, Dad. He *told* me his name was Sebastian. And I'm not pretending," Jakey protested.

"I've had enough of this," Rachel said. "You've had enough to eat. Now go up to your room. I told you to quit it with the Sebastian business, but you just had to bring it up at the dinner table, so go upstairs."

"But Mom..."

"Jake..." Daniel said sternly.

With a sour expression on his face, Little Jakey made his way up the stairs, pausing intermittently to grunt. Jakey watched as his mother continued to eat her dinner, ignoring him. Once Jakey reached the top of the stairs, Daniel looked to ensure he was gone. But Jakey, accustomed to the ways that adults waited for children to leave before unleashing the truth, was not gone. Jakey emerged from the darkness, crouched down, and peered between the slats of the railing. He watched as his father undid his tie and slung it over his chair. Jakey turned to look for Sebastian, only to find that he was gone.

"Does he know?" Daniel asked his wife.

Know what? Jakey wondered. There was weight to his father's question, but nothing gave form to that weight.

"I don't think so," Rachel said.

"This just started today?"

"As far as I know. I don't know what to do," Rachel said, tearing up. Jakey nearly cried himself, feeling powerless at the sight of a withering parent.

"Maybe he knows," Daniel said.

There it was again: the space between Jakey's ignorance and his parents' knowledge. Jakey was a mess of loose ends. All he was *sure* he felt was an intense desire to know.

"I don't think so," Rachel said.

"Maybe we should tell him the truth," Daniel said.

"He wouldn't understand," she responded, speaking as emphatically as she could while maintaining a hushed tone. "And what if we told him and he started remembering more? What if he remembered too much? I don't want his past to haunt him. I don't want him to get hurt. I just can't." Rachel burst into tears, collapsing. Daniel comforted her.

Jakey didn't understand his parents' embrace and retreated to his room to avoid it. When he opened the door, Jakey saw the half-assembled Lincoln Log cabin that he and Sebastian had started building before dinner. Jakey thought about finishing the structure, giving it a roof to provide insulation from the outside world. But he couldn't. Instead, Jakey grabbed one of the longer logs, twisting the wood between his fingers and his thumb. He grazed the notches on both ends. He used to appreciate those divots, but now he hated them. The grooves made everything seem so easy when the pieces fit together. But when the parts were disassembled, the logs just looked broken. Mutilated. Jakey threw one log against the wall. He cried, unsure why. When his mother came to get him ready for bed, Jakey wiped his tears away and lied about their origin. A stubbed toe, he claimed. He tore down the partially constructed cabin and put the Lincoln Logs back in the box. He slept in his room alone; Sebastian was gone for good.

For decades, the imaginary Sebastian went unremembered until forty-two-year-old Jake scavenged the wreckage of his past and resurrected the memory of his phantom twin.

: : 1

The real Sebastian Barnabas, the flesh-and-blood Sebastian, was alive and well. While Jake grew up with Sebastian's image lurking in his depths, *Jake* lurked in the depths of Sebastian. Only instead of overtly thinking about Jake, Sebastian just felt divided against himself: incomplete, amputated. He found his consolation in the poetry of mathematics. He made up for the loss of Jake by solving trigonometric proofs, analyzing the unchanging relationships between sines, cosines, tangents, cotangents, secants, and cosecants, whose bonds were fixed and absolute. Sebastian loved that expressions were set equal in a proof. This balance restored equity to a world that felt off-kilter, skewed against him. The goal of proofs was also his own: to use relationships to legitimize an identity, to prove that the self equals the self. After learning that Jake was alive, Sebastian wondered if there might be an inherent bond between them, a fixed and absolute relationship encoded into their DNA. But their first encounter hadn't gone as anticipated.

"I met Jake," Sebastian told his mother, speaking on his cell phone while driving home from the diner. "I thought you'd want to know."

"And?"

"You should've been there, not me. I didn't ask for this. I didn't make the decisions that led to this mess. I felt bad for him. I nearly apologized to him when I shook hands with him, but I couldn't. It would have been weird. I had nothing to be sorry for. You, on the other hand…"

There was silence on the other end of the phone.

"Did you explain everything to him? Why I had to do it?" Jacqueline asked.

"He barely even gave me a chance to explain."

"Did you at least tell him I love him?"

Sebastian was about to respond when he realized he was headed the wrong way, driving toward work instead of home. He made a swift U-turn at the nearest light with such force that he dropped his cell phone on the floor. He sent his right hand toward the floor while driving, grasping for the device. He glanced down. He managed to locate the phone and grab it, but when he pulled himself back up, he noticed that a jaywalker was in his path.

Sebastian braked hard, swerved, and narrowly avoided hitting the guy.

"What just happened?" his mother asked, reacting to the sound of the brakes.

Sebastian looked in his rear-view mirror. The person whom he had almost hit—a twentysomething white kid with dreadlocks, a hippie wardrobe, and a guitar slung around his back—was in the middle of the road, both arms raised, giving Sebastian two middle fingers. Sebastian heard honks behind him. He knew he should press on without a thought for damage that wasn't even done, but his eye returned to his rear-view mirror. The guitar-slinging free spirit hadn't crossed the street but had continued walking in the middle of the lane in protest, impeding traffic. Sebastian couldn't believe the kid's audacity. Sure, the guy had nearly been killed, but his unwillingness to get out of the road was reckless.

"Sebastian?" his mother repeated, tearing his concentration from his mirror.

"Nothing happened. I just dropped my phone for a second."

"Are you driving? You could kill someone."

"I know," he muttered.

Enough distance passed to make the drifter invisible to Sebastian, but Sebastian kept checking his mirror regardless, searching for the phantom of his antagonist.

"You never answered my question," Jacqueline reminded Sebastian.

"What question?"

"Did you tell Jake I love him?"

"Jesus, Mom, this is not a time for love!" Sebastian yelled, frustrated that he had nearly killed someone, yes, almost *killed* another human being, and here his mother spoke of love. Not even real love or deep love but imagined love, dead love, lost love. There were more pressing matters to consider.

"So…you didn't tell him?" his mother asked.

"Did you expect me to? I just met the guy. You haven't even laid eyes on him since he was three years old. Can you even claim to love him at this point? Is that a valid message to send to someone who didn't even know you existed until a week ago? You're a stranger to him," Sebastian reminded her, feeling no guilt about extinguishing the life of her fantasy child, the long-lost son revived.

"I'm his mother," she said, her voice dropping an octave and cracking with weight.

"His *birth* mother."

"His *mother*," she protested, raising her volume.

"You're nobody's mother."

His mother didn't respond but managed to stay on the line. Sebastian considered: the boy in the road has a mother, somewhere. "Listen," Sebastian explained, "this person may have been your son once, but he's not your son anymore. I could tell he was uncomfortable even thinking about us."

While at the diner, Jake had exhibited nervous habits: tearing his napkin, tapping his fingers, averting his eyes, and withdrawing his hands from the table as if Sebastian were dangerous or contagious. Had Jacqueline been there, she might have understood.

"But he was the one who reached out to you. He must want to know about us," she reasoned.

"He must've changed his mind. You should've seen how fast he left."

"Do you think it was something you said?"

It took Sebastian too long to respond, but in moments like this, he couldn't couch his frustration. "Not at all," he managed. "I was cordial. It was just a bad idea from the start."

"So...that's it? You're not going to see him again?"

Sebastian nearly responded with a resounding no. But the more he thought about it, the more Sebastian felt an intense desire to open Jake's eyes to where he came from.

"I don't know. I don't know anymore," Sebastian confessed. "I'm sick of talking about this." He looked in his rear-view mirror, and even though he was miles away from the site of his near-accident, he was still half-expecting to see the kid in the road behind him, fingers upturned. Instead, he saw a row of cars—lifeless, weaponized metal that concealed

41

the capacity for destruction beneath the more visible promise of utility.

"Listen, I just got home," Sebastian said, as he pulled into his parking space. "If you're so interested in finding out more about him, I can give you his number."

"But I..."

"That's what I thought," Sebastian said and hung up.

When Sebastian walked through his front door, he noticed he had a message on his machine. It was from his lawyer's office, or rather, Stanford's lawyer's office. The office assistant said Sebastian needed to meet with the lawyers to prepare for his deposition. Sebastian sighed. He couldn't believe that the frivolous lawsuit levied against the university by his former colleague, Mallory Specter, was proceeding. Sebastian had hoped Mallory would come to her senses and drop the whole enterprise.

Sebastian didn't want to think about the lawsuit. Instead, he thought about the hippie kid in the road. He'd looked like the type of boy who'd gone to a wealthy private school and converted to his crunchy, Birkenstock-wearing style to get under the collar of his blue-blooded parents. He'd looked like Sebastian's father. Sebastian had probably given the kid everything he wanted that day: another excuse to justify his righteous indignation against the Establishment, adults, rules, and industrialized society.

That night, Sebastian dreamed that his own hair was longer, itching, twirled together. In the dream, he scratched his head with his left hand, trying to get rid of the feeling that he was someone else. In his right hand, he could feel the weight of an encased acoustic guitar. Sebastian noticed that the guitar case was the one his father had carried around after he'd returned from Vietnam. It was hand-painted with bleeding hearts and flowers shooting from guns—everything half-beautiful and half-violent, the detail work half-original and half-clichéd. He dropped it to the ground, and the case opened when it hit the pavement. The guitar flew onto the road, and a car ran it over, strewing splintered wood across lanes of traffic. Sebastian bent down to pick up some of the pieces. He salvaged the strings rather than the wood, the tension rather than the form. Hearing the sound of a motor, Sebastian looked up to see a car headed toward him. Sebastian dropped the guitar strings so he could lift his middle fingers. He stared down the vehicle, unblinking as the headlights approached, until finally, with the force of his conscious mind, he woke up and opened his eyes.

The Third Row
Binomial Coefficients: Shortcuts

```
            1
        1       1
    1       2       1
1       3       3       1
```

One application of Pascal's triangle concerns the binomial theorem. When determining the polynomial expansion of a binomial power, you can use a mathematical shortcut by consulting Pascal's Triangle for the coefficients you need.

For example, when you have a binomial power like $(x+y)^3$, and you want to multiply $(x+y)(x+y)(x+y)$ to create a polynomial version of the expression, you come up with:
$$(1)x^3+3x^2y+3xy^2+(1)y^3.$$

Notice, the coefficients of this polynomial expression are: 1, 3, 3, 1, which appear in the third row of Pascal's triangle.

So instead of doing the multiplication, you can get the coefficients from Pascal's triangle.
For better or worse, it helps you cut corners.

---

1 : : :

Jake Washington had a history of avoiding shortcuts where he could help it. Although he convinced himself that he did this out of a moral imperative, in truth, he was not good at recognizing safe shortcuts where they did exist. On the occasions when Jake did devise a quick route, he found the path plagued by obstacles. There was the time when he was eager to get home one night after playing ball with friends at the local park. Instead of walking around the well-lit periphery, Jake ran the quicker route through the center of the park, sprinting in the darkness because he was afraid a child abductor might be lurking. In his haste, Jake tripped over the roots of a tree, twisted his ankle, and hobbled the rest of the way home. As he grew older, Jake fared no better where shortcuts were concerned. In high school, he cut through the locker hall only to find football players who threw elbows into his side. Rather than brave that again, Jake took the long way around the building.

Because there had never been a time in Jake's life when he had benefited from cutting corners, he learned to value his walks along the edge of the world. But Jake was not oblivious to the workings of modern society. He knew the world didn't prize longer routes or riskless ventures. He watched as others profited from the fast tracks that he was disinclined to take. Whenever he jealously watched people succeed this way, he comforted himself with the notion that at least he was safe, looking on from a distance. He never entertained the possibility that someone else's shortcut might run through his winding path and shatter the very security he esteemed so highly.

When Jake first met William Radenport during a shared graduate class in 1991, he could already tell that Radenport was someone who moved fast. Radenport, in his late thirties at the time, was already a model of the aging intellectual he'd eventually become. He wore professorial clothes, right down to the tweed jacket with leather elbow patches. His hair had streaks of gray, a precursor to the silver mane that would define him later in life. His face was weathered even then, carved with deep creases that made him seem serious. Originally from London, Radenport's upper-crust accent only amplified his air of superiority. The clothes, the pensive demeanor, the attitude, all of it was irritating but innocuous. It wasn't until later, when they worked on a group project together a few months into their studies, that Jake grew wary of Radenport.

"The lab's booked for this week," Jake told Radenport when they were scheduling time for data collection. "We can take the earliest opening next Tuesday. Work overtime."

"That won't do," Radenport said. "Let me look at the schedule," he continued, glancing at the calendar. With a rub of his eraser, Radenport wiped out a name. "This Wednesday at nine a.m. There we are."

"We can't just take someone else's lab time."

"No need to worry."

"What do you think is going to happen when the other scientist shows up and thinks the lab is reserved for him?"

"I'm quite certain he won't show up," Radenport said, his face crumpling into condescension. His expression suggested that Jake was being ridiculous and unimaginative.

"What makes you so sure?"

"Just trust me," Radenport said, walking away as though the issue didn't warrant another thought.

"Why should I?" Jake called out.

Radenport turned around and spoke in a low tone. "Because I'm your partner for this work. Our fate is tied. This other scientist is not going to be a problem. I'll handle it."

Jake buckled. When he and William went to the lab on Wednesday, the other scientist didn't show up. At the time, Jake assumed Radenport had made an arrangement with the other scientist. Years later, Jake considered other possibilities: bribery, deception, impersonation. The moment when Radenport smudged out the name of a fellow scientist should have been an omen. But Jake had been naïve. Perhaps if Jake had known the other scientist whose name William had erased, he might have seen the action as a more grievous offense. Maybe he might have been able to prepare himself for the day when William Radenport would come after his name with a greater weapon than an eraser.

Radenport moved in on Jake slowly. When they first met, Jake and William focused on different specializations, but it didn't take long for William to change his concentration to meteorites, just like Jake. When William told Jake about this change, Jake bit his tongue, but he was frustrated. As if that weren't bad enough, the department gave them a shared office to "facilitate collaboration." For a while, Jake worked in the same space as Radenport without incident. But then it happened.

Jake went out for lunch at midday, leaving his work behind. When he returned, he found Radenport rifling through his desk drawers.

"What are you doing?"

"Just looking for a pencil," Radenport replied, finding one and retreating to his desk.

Jake distrusted Radenport but returned to his research. He thumbed to a Post-it in one of his books. He noticed something. The corner of the page had a faint impression left behind from a dog-ear. As someone who loved the smell and feel of books almost as much as the words in them, Jake never dog-eared anything. Instead, he used bookmarks and sticky notes to mark his place. Jake searched through one article after another in the book, jumping to each Post-it Note. At every turn, he saw that damned mark, mocking his trustworthiness. William had scoured his research sources. But what should Jake have done? Locked up his resources? Wouldn't that have been paranoid and unsupportive? And was it so bad that they would be relying on the same research materials?

Jake left the office at the end of the day but returned when he could be sure William was gone. Once there, he rifled through William's area but found nothing. Jake believed that any sensitive materials were in the small locked drawers under William's desk. For the next week, Jake carefully monitored William, keeping track of where he kept his wallet, his keys, anything of importance. Pockets. That's where his keys usually went. At an opportune moment, Jake "accidentally" took William's lab coat instead of his own. Only instead of going to the lab, Jake left campus, went to the nearest locksmith, and had the keys from William's coat pocket duplicated. When he returned to the office, Jake put William's lab coat back on the rack. Returning the next night, Jake unlocked Radenport's drawer set. When he did, he was overwhelmed. There were copies of everything: relevant passages from articles Jake had found, notes from his readings, personal data from his lab work, early drafts from his dissertation proposal, and the worst: a copy of William's dissertation draft that plagiarized Jake's research. Jake had to confront him.

"Did you think I wouldn't find out you were stealing my research?" Jake asked heatedly when William came into the office the next morning.

"I don't know what you're talking about," William said, impressively straight-faced.

"My research, my data, my writing, all of it. You know plagiarism is grounds for expulsion. I can have you kicked out of the program."

"Are you sure you want to expose yourself to that sort of risk? Could *you* handle getting dismissed on plagiarism charges? Because I'm not sure your career would recover," William countered, not flinching for a beat. His stony confidence was terrifying, and Jake worried he had underestimated his adversary.

"What do you mean?"

"Well, the way I see it, if the university starts looking into a plagiarism case, you'll be on shakier ground. Not only do I have your research and data, but I've also added data. I've also shared drafts with my advisor. Have you gotten to that point yet, mate?"

Jake saw that William had bested him. Jake stormed out of the office, contemplating his next move. He could talk to his adviser, try to build a case against William, and launch an investigation, but Jake worried Radenport was right. Maybe all of his efforts would backfire, especially since Radenport was more unscrupulous than Jake had imagined.

William also had a pristine reputation at the school because he had ingratiated himself with the faculty. No, Jake couldn't rat out Radenport; it was too risky.

Jake drowned his frustrations at the local bar, dousing his cowardice with beer. He hated himself for giving up, but he didn't have the stomach for conflict. He drank alone and decided he would have to move on. He could still use some of the articles from his research, but he would need to focus on a new radiochronometer and gather data to differentiate his work from William's. As he considered all of this, Jake watched the carbonation of his beer dead-end into a pillow of white foam. He mused on the lab work he and William had once done together for a class. Jake remembered how appreciative he'd been when William allowed him to spend most of the time at the microscope, investigating the samples. Jake loved getting lost in the intricacies of the specimens, finding compelling patterns, and escaping the largeness of the world. Even now, charting the golden bubbles in his beer calmed him, pulling focus from the despair gnawing inside. But the moment also forced Jake to realize that his attention to detail sometimes made him myopic and that Radenport saw a bigger picture from outside the microscope's lens: a picture of himself—a man who wanted to increase the size of his world, not diminish it.

:   3   :   :

Rachel Washington, Jake's adoptive mother, once loved anything red. Out of fondness for the color, she planted red roses in the front yard when she and her husband, Daniel, bought their first home in Glendale back in 1969. She knew it was beyond traditional, the flowers crisply vibrant against the white picket fence in the suburbs, but she didn't care. It flew in the face of the feminist ideals she clung to in this age of revolution, but she still felt attached to older customs, and she didn't want to apologize for it. She was a modern woman

50

who distrusted others who weren't equally so. Still, this prejudice only applied to values of equality and empowerment, not to the superficial signs of liberation or convention that too many women used to showcase their political views. Besides, she loved roses.

When she went to the nursery, she learned the basics of what roses needed to thrive. She worried she might not be fit to care for them, too untested to cultivate flowers that required so much attention. But a man at the nursery assured her that it didn't take a seasoned gardener to care for them. Besides, she wasn't going to grow the roses from seeds. She would transplant potted roses into her lawn. Anyone could do it, he claimed.

Rachel got her hands dirty, burying the roots deep in the ground. In the heat of the sun, she patted down the soil that cradled the infant flowers in their new home. The plants grew more beautiful every day, releasing an intoxicating scent that she'd drink in when she'd walk to her doorstep. They were a source of comfort for her. But that was before she started hating the color red. It was only three years after planting the roses that they began to mock her rather than console her. Their petals were the exact wrong shade of crimson: deep and dark and saturated like blood.

It was 1972, and Rachel was beginning to feel defective. It wasn't anyone's fault, her fellow nurses told her. She needed to be patient—plenty of obstetricians in the hospital offered that kernel of wisdom. At first, she believed them, but with each passing month, she grew increasingly convinced that she was one of nature's rejects. She didn't understand how her body could rebel against the preeminent impulse it was programmed to obey. She felt the most acute agony she'd encountered in her twenty-six years of life, and while in the throes of her emotions, she believed that no purer form of torture existed. She was still young, but young was no longer a consolation because it had been years of trying, years of waiting for the thirtieth, the thirty-first of the month hoping nothing would show up, only to be destroyed by the color red.

She grew resentful of the brilliant hues of the roses, so she stopped watering them. She told herself that if she could rid her house of every shade of red, maybe it wouldn't haunt her with its monthly appearances. The roses shriveled quickly, and Rachel wondered if they might have been more resilient had she cultivated the plants from the beginning. As much as she'd wanted the red gone, it still hurt to watch the flowers fall apart. Once the last petal fell from the bushes, Rachel uprooted the bones of the plants, and with them, her grief, and threw away the remains, determined to change her fate if nature would not change it for her. She inquired about adoption. The agency workers told her to prepare for a long process. She was willing to wait. If it took a year or two, it took a year or two.

Days after she filled out the initial adoption paperwork, Rachel experienced the most maddening day in her career as a nurse. Working in an emergency room always brought carnage—severed fingers, projectile vomiting, compound fractures—but most of the damage was minor, caused by cooking accidents, food poisoning, or childhood hijinks. On this day, however, there was a riot after a Dodger game. The downtown Los Angeles hospitals were overwhelmed, so ambulances brought patients to Glendale and Pasadena. Suddenly, the emergency room was overrun with drunken sports fans shouting at one another as the nurses tried to contain them. Rachel witnessed her first gun-shot victim ushered past her. One man gesticulated so wildly during a profanity-fueled rant that he accidentally knocked Rachel in the mouth, jostling a tooth and sending blood down her chin.

Rachel ran toward a nearby bathroom to appraise her injury when she came across a six-year-old girl crying in the middle of the chaos. Rachel used her wrist to wipe away her blood before approaching the child. Once Rachel got close, she noticed bruises on the girl's right forearm and a burn across her left arm in the shape of an iron. As Rachel neared the girl, a messy-haired pregnant woman barreled over and grabbed the girl's hand.

"There you are," the mother said to her child, bending down and exposing her bra. Rachel swore she could smell alcohol on the woman's breath, but Rachel also knew that the stench of stale beer had followed the rioters into the emergency room. She couldn't be sure. Rachel stared at the woman's pregnant belly and cursed the world for its injustice.

"I was just about to take her to a bed," Rachel said to the mother, then squatted to meet the girl's eye line. "Can you tell me what happened to you?" Rachel asked the child, who evaded her eye contact. The girl hunched her shoulders and shrank into herself. She had an overbite that pushed out her upper lip and drew her lower jaw inward. Rachel couldn't tell if the girl was preparing to speak or just resting her teeth against her lip.

"She was playing around..." the mother interjected, but Rachel silenced her.

"I was asking your daughter," Rachel said. "Go ahead, sweetie."

The girl looked at her mother, whose eyes were bloodshot. The mother's glare was expectant. The girl looked back at Rachel and stammered out what seemed like a rehearsed answer: "I...I was just playing and didn't know the iron was on."

"I told you," the mom said. "She was playing around and pretending. Didn't even realize the damn thing was hot till it burned her."

Rachel didn't believe their story, not when the iron mark's position was too awkward to be self-inflicted, and the bruises' locations matched the placement of fingers. This injury was a clear case of abuse, and Rachel would have to report it.

"All right. Let's set you up, and I'll call one of the docs," Rachel said, guiding the girl to a bed on the edge of the madness. After taking the girl's vitals and providing initial primary care, Rachel filled in one of the attending doctors and left him to his business.

Rachel finally made it to the bathroom, headed toward the sink, and started crying. Her tears merged with the blood from her mouth, forming pink rivulets that ran toward the drain. When the worst of her emotions was through with her, she washed her face, spat out blood, and retrieved pressed powder and lipstick from her purse. She painted her face back on, nearly as perfect as it had been that morning. She traded in the nude shade of lipstick she'd worn earlier for a bold red that had been sitting at the bottom of her purse for years. She wanted something to mask the blood or recreate it or both. She gave herself five minutes to recover and then went back to work.

Once the rush ended and Rachel was ready to clock out, she spotted her friend and fellow nurse, Carol Wickering. Carol was twenty-four years older than Rachel, so she served as a mother figure. The nurses who were Rachel's age were all single and didn't understand why Rachel kept working after she got married. Carol was unmarried but had a daughter. She understood not just the need to work but the desire to work.

That evening, Carol looked almost as worn down as Rachel probably did. Carol's curls had lost their bounce, and her feet hobbled with each step. Fortunately, her signature, crooked smile remained intact when Rachel greeted her. They headed for the exit together, commiserating about the stressors of the day, exhausted by the toll it had taken on them.

"Is my tooth still attached?" Rachel asked, projecting her lower canine toward Carol for inspection.

"Yeah. Barely," Carol said, scrunching up her broad face as she neared Rachel's mouth. "Tell me you weren't holding out hope of seeing the tooth fairy tonight."

"I stopped believing in fantasies a long time ago."

"Well, maybe you should start believing again."

"What do you mean?" Rachel asked as they passed through the hospital doors. Carol paused when they got outside, and Rachel turned to her.

"Bobbie's friend wants to give away one of her kids. *Needs* to. Is set on it. Bobbie told her friend you might be interested in adopting him. Sweet boy. Three years old," Carol said, softening into a smile. "Miracles do happen."

"I've already submitted my paperwork for adoption. I'm in line for a baby. It might take a while, but it's the right way to do this," Rachel said.

"Everyone wants a baby, Rachel," Carol said. "Not many people will take in a three-year-old kid. His mom's unfit. She's giving him up whether you take him or not. He's gonna end up in the system. And you and I both know the system's no good. He needs someone like you. You've got the heart for it. Others don't."

Rachel thought about the little girl with the burn across her arm. The girl had been mousy and skinny like Rachel had been when she was young. Rachel believed that if she'd had a natural-born daughter, her child might have looked like the abused girl, green-eyed and button-nosed with buck teeth. In a kinder world, the girl would have been hers.

Rachel dwelled on Carol's phrase, "the system," and imagined the future that the three-year-old boy might have in foster care: cigarette burns and resentful foster fathers and loveless homes. It wasn't a guarantee, but it was a possibility. Rachel had already done some good today; she'd reported the abusive mother to the authorities. But Rachel regretted that she couldn't save the girl. Maybe she could save someone else instead. That night, she talked to Daniel, and they agreed to look into the boy. The day that Rachel learned little Jake would be hers, she planted a new set of roses, white ones this time, transforming the grave of her dashed hopes into a wellspring of promise.

With Jakey by her side, Rachel was full of optimism until the neighborhood women started tearing her down. It all began with their horror and shock that Rachel would continue working as a nurse while raising Jake. Never mind that Rachel had hired a competent nanny and was only working part-time. Katherine Worthington had the gall to knock on Rachel's door in the middle of the day and deliver a Phyllis-Schlafly-esque speech about how a woman's place was in the home. Sandra Jones, the mother of a three-month-old baby, offered to nurse Jake so he could get the proper nutrition only a *real* mother could provide (at which point Rachel reminded Sandra that Jake was *three*). Rebecca Smith discussed her upcoming Tupperware party in Rachel's company without extending an invitation to her. Abigail Knightley sarcastically asked Rachel if she was going to burn her bras with Gloria Steinem over the weekend.

Frustrated, Rachel took to her imagination for vindication against these women, creating nightmarish fantasies. She imagined that Sandra—the neatly kempt wife of an older man—would take lipstick late at night and smear it clownishly around her mouth with a kindergartner's imprecision. Rachel imagined that Katherine—Catholic mother of six—would superimpose Christ's face onto that of her husband whenever they had sex, fabricating the sensation of long, shaggy brown tendrils against her exposed breasts. Rachel imagined that Rebecca—the oldest of the group—would pull off her skin by its edges every night, place it in a sauna to prevent wrinkling, and sleep cautiously with her nerves and muscles exposed, only to reconstruct herself in the morning. Rachel imagined that Abigail—the only one of them who had worked at all before the birth of her first-born—would play dress-up when her husband wasn't looking, stealing his suits and briefcases, and walking around in high heels that were too big for her.

These musings helped Rachel shoulder her neighbors' pettiness and judgment, but the jabs still stung. After months of passive-aggressive gestures, Rachel started doubting her maternal impulses, questioning the depth of Jakey's love for her, and wondering whether or not he might have been better off with his birth mother despite all indications to the contrary. She reminded herself that she and Daniel had tried to get pregnant, and there was nothing fundamentally wrong with her as a person just because she'd failed to conceive, even though her biological, social, and psychological impulses squarely blamed herself.

:　:　3　:

Sometimes shortcuts are not taken flippantly or out of a need to get ahead. In 1972, Jacqueline Barnabas, mother to Jake and Sebastian, took her shortcuts out of necessity. When Jacqueline decided it was her turn to cut corners, she knew she had no other viable options. It had been three weeks since she'd heard the news about her parents' fatal car accident, and not much had changed since she'd dropped the phone in the middle of the police officers' condolences. She sat around numbly in the living room of her parents' house, the house that no longer carried the scent of her mother's perfume or her father's pipe tobacco. She had SpaghettiOs crusted on a dress that she couldn't motivate herself to change. Her hair was in disarray. Just as she did every morning, she finished off the remaining wine that had been left on the kitchen counter the night before. She chugged the soured sludge to feel normal again or at least to make everything more manageable.

The last drop of wine was fresh on her lips when she felt the crush of responsibility. One of her little boys bumped his head on the glass table. He started to cry. It seemed like he was always crying about one thing or another. She thought he was supposed to be out of that phase by now. She ran to him, but the second she started wiping back his hair and kissing his forehead, there was a cry coming from another room. "Mommy," she heard, "Mommy, come here!" Another bumped head? A lost toy? A scuffed knee?

Instead of responding to this new demand, she sat in the middle of the rug, paralyzed, looking at the frayed edge of her sleeve that had once been pristine, embellished with handmade lace. She let the world fall around her, ignoring the little hands and the little voices (they would go away eventually) while she pulled at the unraveling threads. Slowly, the intricate circles in the lace pattern started disappearing until the largest ring in the center was nothing but a crescent moon, waning and waning while the world ebbed.

Suddenly, the doorbell rang. How long had Jacqueline been sitting in the middle of the room, pulling the edges of the lace? She thought about going into the nearby powder room and fixing her hair, wiping away the excess smudges of mascara from under her eyes, or even appraising the state of herself without doing anything, because what could she do in a minute or two? How much could she accomplish if the visitor became impatient and rang again? And how long had she already been sitting here, thinking about going into the powder room? A couple of seconds? A minute? Longer? There was no point, so she approached the entryway without even pulling down the bunched-up fabric of her dress that exposed too much of her legs.

She opened the door to Bobbie, her oldest friend. Bobbie looked every bit the twenty-year-old girl Jacqueline wished she could be: pretty, thin, blonde, and effortless. Jacqueline had a charm all her own, but she was more of a dark-haired Midge than a Barbie, and who wanted to be Midge?

"Jackie," said Bobbie, hugging Jacqueline briefly before coming into the house. "I've been calling you. Your phone broken or something?" she asked.

"No, I..."

"Holy hell, Jackie," Bobbie said, snapping her gum. "You're still in that dress?" she asked, pulling down the fabric so that it covered more of Jacqueline's thighs and edged toward her kneecaps. "Have you even showered since Sunday?"

Instead of answering, Jacqueline teared up. "What am I supposed to do?" Jacqueline asked.

"You're supposed to live is what," Bobbie said, putting an arm around her.

One of the boys started crying.

"Is he okay?" Bobbie asked.

"I should check on him," Jacqueline said tiredly, walking toward the boys' room while Bobbie followed.

"Man," Bobbie said, barely entering the room before recoiling her neck from the smell. "Did he shit his pants or something? I thought he was potty trained."

"He is," Jacqueline said. She picked up her son and asked, "Are you sick?"

He nodded and said, "I couldn't make it."

"It's okay. It's okay," Jacqueline assured him. She looked over at Bobbie and said, "Give me a minute. I'll take care of this." Jacqueline took off her son's soiled clothes and threw them in the trash because she couldn't bear to do anything else with them. She wiped off her son with a nearby bath towel, tossed the shit-stained towel on the floor, and sent him back to the playroom with new clothes on. Bobbie looked at Jacqueline, serious.

"Something's not right here," Bobbie said.

"It's temporary."

"Not temporary enough for your boys."

"I don't know what else to do. Bobbie, I'm trying."

"Bullshit. You haven't taken off that dress in a week. You're not trying enough."

"I made this dress," Jacqueline said, gliding a finger up the side seam and gazing off blankly as she recalled the memory of her mother. "I used fabric from an old dress of hers."

"I know you made the dress, and you know, it's a beautiful dress. Or at least it *was* a beautiful dress. But you've spilled tomato sauce down the front. The sleeve looks like it got caught in the garbage disposal. It's riding up so high you look like you belong on Hollywood Boulevard. You're a mess."

"She loved lace," Jacqueline noted, fingering the threads of the sleeve that were undone and dangling, the edges of a crescent moon slivering further toward oblivion.

"Who cares about the lace? There are bigger issues you need to deal with."

"You think I don't know that?" Jacqueline asked angrily, frustrated that Bobbie acted like someone with all the answers. What did she know about getting pregnant with twins at seventeen? What did she know about losing your parents at twenty?

"You're freaking out on me, Jack," Bobbie said, approaching Jacqueline with her hands raised as if she were dealing with a dangerous person.

"I can handle this. It'll just take time," Jacqueline said, standing up and making her best impression of someone composed.

"Let me stay over for a night or two and help you out. We'll figure out what to do."

"Don't you have finals to study for?" Jacqueline asked, trying not to act too jealous about the fact that Bobbie was attending UCLA, that she had a future.

"My books are in the car. If I need to do some studying, I can do it here. Besides, this is more important."

Jacqueline fought a smile, but it came anyway. It was impossible to resent Bobbie when she was as steadfast and kind as ever. Grudgingly, Jacqueline accepted Bobbie's offer to stay the weekend. But there were complications. With Bobbie around, Jacqueline couldn't open another bottle of wine, at least not until dinnertime, which would be too late. Even then, more than two glasses might trigger concern. So Jacqueline snuck off to the liquor cabinet whenever Bobbie was preoccupied and poured vodka into a water glass. Beyond the sneaking around, Jacqueline also dreaded the looks that Bobbie routinely gave her, alcohol in hand or not. It wasn't so much that Bobbie was harsh or critical, but her stares *were* heightening Jacqueline's internal judgment.

Eventually, Jacqueline let her fear of criticism slip away. At dinner, she poured wine until both she and Bobbie got obliterated, reminiscing and crying and laughing and stumbling, if only because that's what would be expected of them at their age anyway, had life been kinder. After a while, Bobbie confessed that she had resented Jacqueline when the kids were born. There'd been no time for the two of them anymore. It'd happened when Bobbie had needed her best friend the most—at the end of adolescence, the beginning of heartbreak, and the middle of everything. Bobbie had gone through her losses without the companionship that seven years of playing invented games with her buddy Jack had led her to expect out of life.

Jacqueline apologized. She never imagined that she'd robbed Bobbie of her youth while stripping away her own. Bobbie had always seemed like she'd everything together, and Jacqueline had been too preoccupied to notice otherwise. She'd been dealing with the demands of raising children when it wasn't supposed to be her time yet. Until a week ago, she'd had help from her parents—too much help because now she felt incapable of dealing with her children.

"I get it, you had your hands full," Bobbie said, "and if I'd said anything to you about how I felt cheated by your new life, I would've seemed like a selfish bitch."

"No, you wouldn't have. You should've said something."

"Well, I guess it's out there now. I don't mad...I mean, I'm *not* mad anymore. Man, I'm drunk," Bobbie said, her words falling out lazily, her eyes starting to fold.

"I've got a joint in my car. You interested?"

"Nah, I think I might be sick as it is," Bobbie said, rubbing her stomach. "Besides, we should somber up in case something happens with the boys."

"*Somber* up, that's a good one," Jacqueline laughed. "You are drunk. I think that's the last thing we need. Listen, don't worry. The boys are *fine*. They're just sleeping."

As if on cue, one of the boys began crying. Jacqueline and Bobbie laughed at the timing. They both took in a big breath as if to prepare them for the task of dealing with the kids, sitting up straighter as if that made them fitter for the job.

"Bobbie," Jacqueline said seriously, "it's time to make a decision."

"Now?" Bobbie asked, laughing a bit. Her face collapsed into her arm, which was resting on the bar in the kitchen.

"Isn't this why you're here? Didn't you say you were going to help me?"

"Aren't you going to deal with the crying kid first?"

"Come with me," Jacqueline said, grabbing Bobbie by the wrist and forcibly pulling her dead weight toward the boys' room.

"What's wrong, buddy?" Jacqueline asked her son, kneeling by his toddler bed. Bobbie looked on from the doorway, using the frame of the door as a crutch.

"I wet the bed," he said timidly.

"Yuck," said his now-awake brother, looking on.

"Quiet," Jacqueline hissed reproachfully. She lifted her son, stripped the sheets from the bed, and walked toward the door, saying, "Mommy'll be back in a second."

"Where are you going?" Bobbie asked.

"I'll be back," Jacqueline said. She returned a minute later with a stack of newspapers. She unfolded them and put them over the mattress.

"He's not a dog, Jackie," Bobbie said.

"Yeah, I'm not a dog," her boy said in imitation.

"This'll be fine. There's nothing else," Jacqueline said, picking up her son and placing him on the newspaper.

"You're a mess, Jack."

"That's why you need to help me."

"I have a family friend who wants to A-D-O-P-T," Bobbie said slowly, stammering out the letters with drunken deliberateness. "They're good people. The K-I-D-S would be comfortable."

"I can't give them up," Jacqueline said.

"Give who up?" Jake asked.

"No one," Jacqueline told him. "Just go to sleep," she said, grazing his hair.

"You can't keep them," Bobbie said. "Not like this."

"Maybe I could just keep one. I think I could handle one," Jackie assured Bobbie.

"One what?" little Sebastian asked.

"Nothing, Sebastian," Jacqueline said. She kissed both of her sons on the forehead, and at their request, she sang until they'd dozed off. After singing her last note, Jacqueline turned to Bobbie, who had fallen asleep in a chair in the corner of the room.

"Bobbie," Jacqueline said, stirring her awake, "how do I decide?"

"Can't we talk about this in the morning?" Bobbie asked, yawning and dozing off.

"Eeny-meeny-miny-moe," Jacqueline began reciting, pointing her finger in one direction, and then the other. "My mother said to pick the very best one and you are it," Jacqueline continued in a whisper, ultimately pointing her unsteady finger toward Sebastian, who slept peacefully in his toddler bed. Clumsily and nearly disastrously, Jacqueline climbed into the toddler bed as best as she could, cradling her son in her cramped arms while her legs hung off the edges of the bed. It should have been obvious that she couldn't fit, not just in the bed, but in that role. She should have known that even one child was more than she could handle. But in her broken world, there was nothing wrong with staying attached to something you were supposed to outgrow. Even if this habit deformed you, even if your legs dangled or your neck cramped, you were still allowed to live in that stifling world, and so you would; there were no other options that sounded decent anyway. And so she slept, breathing softly onto the nape of the neck of her elected son while little Jake, a stranger now, slept restlessly, jerking around as if that might make the crumpled newspaper beneath him feel more tolerable.

:   :   :   1

If Jake Washington suffered from other people's shortcuts, Sebastian Barnabas profited from his own shortcuts to an equivalent degree. Brilliant and unafraid to showcase his academic prowess, Sebastian skipped seventh and eighth grade after demonstrating mathematical skills that far surpassed the humble abilities of his middle school teachers. Growth-wise, Sebastian was a late bloomer, which proved to be a blessing when he went to high school. Any other grade-jumping weakling might have been routinely beaten up by insecure muscle-heads, but Sebastian garnered sympathy from their girlfriends. Far from knowing that Sebastian was simply two years younger and slow to mature, his classmates thought that Sebastian was, well, there were different names for it. If you asked someone from the already politically correct crowd, he was a "little person"; if you asked a run-of-the-mill student, a "midget"; and if you had the privilege of asking the insecure muscle-heads, he was a "stumpbucket."

The primary hypothesis was that Sebastian had a rare growth-stunting disease that was going to be named after him. He was content to let everyone think what they wanted if it would spare him physical harm. If he'd wanted to, Sebastian could have set the record straight. But what was the point? What he wanted came from textbooks, not other students.

Besides, there were perks to letting other people think you were a mutant. He was crowned Homecoming King during his senior year. Had he won the title as part of a collective joke? Or had he won because other kids pitied him, and those same students wanted a self-congratulatory recognition of their empathy? Sebastian knew his win was *somehow* linked to the presumed seriousness of "Barnabas disease," but he didn't care. He was glad he won but not because of the title. His real prize had been an experience: the touch of his hand against the exposed back of Mary DePaul, the flowery smell of her mother's Coco Chanel fragrance on her neck, her smiling willingness to let his "diseased" fingers inch toward the boundaries of acceptable terrain. That dance allowed him to conceive of something he wanted, something elusive that he could feel but not describe.

After graduating from Palos Verdes High School at the tender age of 16, Sebastian had a tremendous growth spurt, just in time for college. Suddenly six-foot-two, Sebastian was gangly, but at least his height made him look more age-appropriate. Moreover, he could finally shake the name "stumpbucket," which some of his close friends had re-appropriated from the meatheads as a term of endearment. As he grew out of his awkward phase, Sebastian gained confidence. This confidence came from a concerted effort to learn how to lure women into bed.

Ever the methodical mathematician, Sebastian began his education in seduction with a notebook, a pencil, and a fake ID. Sebastian brought these materials with him to the local drinking circuit. For a long time, Sebastian was just an observer, watching young men approach young women. Rejection. Rejection. Success. Rejection. Sebastian would take careful notes on the interactions he witnessed. He rated the physical attractiveness of both the men and the women in terms of facial appeal, physique, and *je ne sais quoi*. He recorded lines of dialogue. He noted facial expressions. He estimated people's drunkenness. He described the outcome: silence, genital fondling underneath the table, an eye roll, a phone number, a slap across the face. As time went on, he added new metrics. Race. Political leaning. Dialect. Indications of wealth or poverty. Breadth of vocabulary. He pressed on. He knew the importance of a large data set if he wanted to extrapolate his findings to womankind, or even to the more modest set of female students at Yale.

In his quest for answers, he created graphs and charts, using statistical analysis to unearth a mathematically defensible strategy for approaching women. Sebastian—a guy who was a solid 7.5, maybe an 8.5 to a particular brand of lady—knew it wouldn't help him to chart the obvious ways that physical attractiveness correlated with stronger performance with women. Sebastian was more interested in the deviations from the expected line of regression: those 5.0 men who outperformed more attractive competitors. Sebastian found that one of the greatest determinants of a man's success was his willingness to move on to other women, even after facing the sting of rejection. Persistence was essential, and persistence was a trait that Sebastian knew he could exercise without much difficulty.

Sebastian also found that some attributes helped men, no matter their attractiveness: confidence, wit, and a knack for finding common ground with women. More than anything, like was attracted to like. Sebastian conducted regression analysis using several indices. He examined the specificity or generality of men's dialogue. When he did, he found that men fared better in finding like-minded women when they provided vague statements (like "I love music") rather than more focused statements (like "I love new wave"). The women mattered too. Physical attractiveness played a role, sure, but a strong determinant of whether or not a woman would be receptive to a single guy was the number of men who had already approached her. Whether she was a 6 or a 10, if the girl had fewer contenders, she was more likely to engage with someone who approached her.

After sifting through his research, Sebastian knew that any path forward would have to be personalized to him. There was no generic formula that worked for every person on every occasion. Still, Sebastian trusted in the math well enough to establish a foolproof plan. Or so he thought. When Sebastian first left the shadowy world of covert spying and started approaching girls himself, he was hopeless. He was ignored. He was laughed at. He was humored and then discarded. He felt the acute sting that so many statisticians experience when their theoretical findings don't bear out entirely foreseeable results. Bound in the world of humans, this sort of math was a fallible prognosticator. Nonetheless, the statistics gave him the confidence to keep trying.

The first time his approach worked was when Sebastian tried a location that would make it most likely for him to find girls who were similar to him: the Mathematics Library. Sebastian had intelligence on his side, and he knew that intelligence won over the most when the woman was intelligent herself. Before doing his statistical analysis, Sebastian never would have imagined that the Mathematics Library would be a fruitful environment for finding girls. Most people in the library were young men. But there were *some* girls there. And Sebastian noticed that other males never approached any of the girls in the library. He remembered: *a scarcity of choice*, one of the determinants of potential success.

"Newcomb's paradox," Sebastian said, eyeing an article that a mousy girl was reading at a nearby desk. She was makeup-less, dressed in a gray pullover. She kept back her long, brown hair with a headband. Sebastian thought she was cute in her modesty. He'd noticed her a half an hour ago and knew that not a single guy had approached her. He sidled up to her and said, "Interesting. I like thought experiments."

"Me too," she said, keeping her eyes averted. "Obviously."

"I wish I knew what you were thinking right now."

"I'll let you try to crack that thought experiment on your own," she said, returning to her article. Sebastian gave her space, knowing that overly aggressive behavior often backfired. He cracked open a book and began reading an article on Fermat's last theorem, which at that time hadn't been proven. Sebastian could feel her eyes peering over his shoulder, glancing at the material he was reading.

"Actually, I would like to know what your take on Newcomb's paradox is," she turned to him and said. "Since you find it so interesting."

Sebastian started to worry. His seduction research had told him to keep the discussion general. If he chose the wrong viewpoint, she might stop relating to him. Newcomb's paradox was a divisive topic. It was a thought experiment that included two possible choices that were equally defensible, and yet, it was hard for people to understand how anyone could make a choice that ran counter to their own. Sebastian wanted to showcase his intelligence and prove his familiarity with the paradox. Still, he didn't want to scare her off if she viewed its central problem differently than he did.

"Can we start by discussing the being that oversees everything?" Sebastian asked, diverting the conversation to a critical element of the experiment: the premise that there is a hyper-intelligent being capable of predicting the future. "Because beyond the debate about the paradox itself, I find myself wondering how different my life would be if I could predict what was going to happen ahead of time."

The gamble paid off. Sebastian successfully segued his musings into a probe of her life and interests. She opened up. He brought her to the book stacks and kissed her in the quiet, narrow walkway, where the proximity of genius served as an aphrodisiac.

But all of this was just the beginning. Sebastian developed a talent for luring timid, intelligent if naïve girls into his bed. Throughout his time at Yale, he pushed his track record from zero sexual encounters into the sought-after double-digit range, quite a feat for a former stumpbucket brainiac like Sebastian. Not everyone was impressed.

"Have you ever told these girls that they're *breaking the law* by sleeping with you?" Sebastian's pimple-faced roommate, Travis, asked once Sebastian hit girl number three.

"What do you think?"

"It just seems like pertinent information," Travis remarked from the couch, shoving his hand into a nearly empty bag of Cheetos. There was orange dust all over his dingy T-shirt and cargo pants, but he didn't seem to care. "They should know what they're getting into when they jump into your bed."

"It's not like I'm going to press charges against them."

"I'm just putting myself in their shoes. I would like to know if a girl I was sleeping with was *sixteen*."

"I'm seventeen now," Sebastian said in vexation, his slack face showing his irritation.

"Listen, all I'm saying is, maybe you should slow down until you, you know, *come of age*," Travis said with mocking formality, casting a dandyish flip of his wrist in the air.

"Travis, it's not my fault that you're not getting laid."

"You arrogant prick. You think I'm jealous of you?" Travis asked from the couch, throwing a few Cheetos at Sebastian.

"Nice arsenal," Sebastian said, picking up one of the Cheetos and eating it. "Let's just drop this, okay?"

"No, let me get this straight. You think I'm jealous of you because I don't know, you're freakishly smart, and you've managed to con a few girls into bed using rudimentary statistical techniques. Well, guess what? You're at Yale. Everyone here is freakishly smart. And I am perfectly satisfied with my love life, or lack thereof."

"*Rudimentary* techniques?" Sebastian asked.

"What?" Travis shrugged. "You think I haven't seen the data points you've charted on napkins? Or the standard deviations you've recorded in your notebooks, that Jesus, could you clean up once in a while? I just think you could have better controlled for confounding variables here and there."

"There's a lot of analysis you haven't seen."

Travis continued eating his Cheetos on the couch, rubbing orange crust on his white undershirt after every few bites. "I guess I just don't understand why you do it," he said.

"Do what?"

"Sleep with these girls once and never bring them around again."

At that moment, Sebastian tried to psychoanalyze himself. Perhaps he was overcompensating for the physical inadequacies he'd felt in high school. Perhaps his intelligence set him apart from his peers and prevented true intimacy. Perhaps growing up without a reliable father figure had perverted his sense of healthy romantic relationships. He wasn't sure what was most to blame, so he remained silent.

Sebastian's womanizing continued after he graduated from Yale. The problem was that the shortcuts Sebastian had used with such success as an undergraduate began backfiring once he started his graduate studies. While at Yale, he'd never had to deal with any backlash from the girls he'd slept with. They were all so unassuming that they would never dare confront him for his behavior. The girls had been duped by his flattery, yes, but they'd been consenting adults, so they'd blamed themselves. But once Sebastian began pursuing his doctoral degree at the University of Chicago and wooing local women, he found the women to be much more vocal about their needs and their distaste for his.

The third-wave feminist movement was also gaining traction just as he began his graduate work in the early 1990s. No matter where he went, he couldn't escape one rally or protest held in the name of women's rights. Banners and posters reclaiming the names "bitch" and "slut" waved across campus. There were rumblings that a Women's Studies major might appear on campus. Feminist puns like "herstory" were used in hip cafés. Madeleine Albright was a prominent political figure, and the world was watching women assert their collective voice. Not that Sebastian took any issue with the advancement of women. It was simply not the ideal setting for seducing meek women since that contingent was growing smaller by the day. He would have to take the long route with women, getting to know them better and staying more connected with them, even if all he could think about was how to devise another shortcut.

The Fourth Row
The Beginning Stages of Getting Even

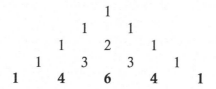

```
            1
         1     1
      1     2     1
   1     3     3     1
1     4     6     4     1
```

Even numbers don't yield odd results. At least certain
principles suggest this. An even number (like 4) multiplied
by another even number (like 6) is always going to be even
(like 24). An even number (like 4) plus another even
number (like 6) is also going to be even (like 10). Despite
these mathematical properties, in real life, getting even can
be truly odd indeed.

---

1 : : : :

For years after William Radenport stole Jake Washington's
research in graduate school, Jake cursed his parents for his
upbringing. Jake's frustration arose whenever he was
dreaming up elegant revenge fantasies. There were plots,
born of too many late nights watching spy dramas, where
Jake imagined himself extracting a confession out of
Radenport, covertly recording it, and getting Radenport's
degree taken away. Later, when Radenport returned to
Berkeley as a professor, Jake fantasized about posting
vitriolic rants about Radenport under the guise of "students"
on websites devoted to anonymously rating professors.
Once, Jake dreamed of murdering Radenport—a dream, yes,
nothing really, the unwieldy sputtering of the unconscious
mind, and yet...

Jake could never act on any of his plots. Instead, he
considered ideals that his father had ingrained in him:

character, integrity, accountability. And so, revenge was only a passing reverie. It was devoured by the larger nightmare called conscience, which sucked up desire with the invisible force of civilized history. Daniel Washington had molded Jake's conscience from boyhood, laying out a solid defense of the American legal system whenever the occasion warranted it. Daniel was so rigid in his morality that Jake wondered if even his father could live up to the expectations he set. His father's dogmatic adherence to principles felt desperate, as though he worried Jake would tumble into hell if his father made any concessions. Even the slightest moral failing was a major moral failing in the Washington household, so Jake feared being less than perfect. It crippled him. Sometimes he worried he might blow up his life just to shatter those expectations, but the more pragmatic, moralistic side of him usually prevented that.

As a result, there was only one avenue for getting even with Radenport: fair and professional gamesmanship. Jake needed to focus on his career. He needed to do what he could to surpass his rival using intellect and diligence. But Jake never expected that his one-up-man-ship would lead him to such unexpected places. Jake's ultimate prize was his Martian meteorite, but the road to his rock was a long one.

The journey started five years ago in 2006 at the Mars Desert Research Station in Utah, where Jake went to conduct experiments in a simulated Martian environment. The vastness of the desert expanse stirred something in him, and Jake and Chris—a colleague from the Utah expedition—decided to set their sights on an even more foreign enterprise: traveling to Northern Africa as meteorite hunters in 2010.

On their meteorite expedition, Jake and Chris ended up in the barren reaches of Algeria. They spent days wandering the desert and didn't find any rocks worth taking home, but that was fine. They knew any success would likely come down the road. When they arrived in a merchant-filled desert town, they met with local Berber traders in hopes of establishing a network of meteorite hunters on the ground. Jake and Chris spent the next couple of months training local dealers to look and test for meteorites. They described fusion crusts and ablation and regmaglypts. They showed dealers and native nomads pictures of different Martian meteorites that highlighted the particularities of the rocks. The dealers offered no guarantees of discovery, but as long as they got paid, they agreed to send Chris and Jake shipments of rocks that looked promising.

More than a year passed, and without finding anything meaningful in the boxes Jake and Chris received from Africa, Jake began to get discouraged. Everything sank back into the mundane routine of university life. There were lectures to prepare, mounds of academic journals to read through, and laboratory research to do.

The day that the meteorite finally arrived, Jake was meeting with Jessica Fleming, a young graduate student whose dissertation he was advising. She wore little makeup, like so many female Ph.D. candidates who wanted to be taken seriously, and she wore her hair as she always did, pulled back in a ponytail. She dressed plainly in jeans and a black top, keeping the focus on her intellectual curiosity rather than her subtle natural beauty. They were starting to talk about the latest articles she'd been researching when his phone rang.

"Don't worry about that," he said, pressing a button. "It can go to voicemail."

The phone rang again, but Jake let it ring through.

"You're popular today," Jessica replied.

Less than a minute later, the phone rang again. "Do you mind if I take this?" Jake asked Jessica. "It seems whoever is calling isn't going to give up."

"Sure," Jessica said. "I'll step outside."

When Jake picked up the phone, he heard Chris on the other end of the line, exclaiming that they had a "gen-u-ine"

Martian meteorite on their hands, and he would be sending half of the rock to Jake. After a brief, excited interchange, Jake hung up the phone and called Jessica back into the room.

"I heard you scream," she said, her face goading him into disclosing details about the phone call.

"Would you call that a scream?"

"Would you prefer I called it a loud giggle?" she asked, verging on flirtation. Jake scoffed, trying to bat away any intimation of familiarity. He pushed himself further away from his desk and settled deeper into his rolling chair to establish distance.

"All right, I..." Jake started, trying to redirect the conversation.

"I also saw you dance," Jessica interrupted. She scrunched her face in faux judgment, then raised an eyebrow to elicit a reaction from him.

"Now you're just making stuff up," Jake said, laughing, drawn in by the charms of her banter. Almost as soon, he squirmed in discomfort, wishing they could get back to her research. But he knew she would keep prodding, so he told her about the meteorite. It felt good to tell someone, even if the meteorite held more potential than realized success.

"Congratulations," Jessica said electrically. "I feel lucky to have snagged you as a dissertation advisor."

It didn't take long before the news of the meteorite spread. Even before the carefully sealed box came for Jacob Washington c/o Berkeley University, there were rumblings that the Earth and Planetary Science Department would be conducting significant research. The rumblings had grown so loud that they'd reached William Radenport, who intercepted the package in the mailroom and hand-delivered it to Jake.

"So...this is the Martian meteorite people have been talking about?" he asked, bringing the box into Jake's office.

"It's personal, William."

"That's not what I heard. I heard this is a new endeavor the department is undertaking. New research."

"Just let me do my job," Jake said, taking the box out of Radenport's hands.

"Only if you let me do mine."

"What does that mean?"

"I'm the department chair. You know I'm responsible for supervising research. Let's work together. Bring glory to the Berkeley program," William said, wearing a smug grimace. The half-smile was transparently artificial, telegraphing his strained collegiality.

Jake was about to respond when his eyes fixated on the leather patches on William's tweed jacket. They felt so falsely pretentious, evoking images of stodgy old professors pontificating on arcane subjects. Was the additional elbow support *really* necessary for academics who rarely sat like the Thinker in contemplation?

"What are those elbow patches for anyway?" Jake asked.

"They extend the lifetime of your clothes," Radenport said. "Elbows are the first areas to wear out. The patches are about honoring the integrity of your jacket. Looks like you could use some yourself," he said, fingering the elbow on Jake's jacket. Jake hated that William defended his clothing choice based on practicality; it seemed insincere.

"Listen, you might be able to convince yourself that you're looking out for my interests by offering your help on this project, but the bottom line is, I can handle this research myself. The meteorite isn't on loan from NASA. It's something I own. So just give me space and let me work. You can rest assured that any findings I publish will reflect excellently on the department and the university," Jake said, ushering Radenport out by the leather-patched elbows.

Jake smiled as he closed the door and locked it. Jake figured his father would be proud of him for finding a principled way to handle Radenport. After all, when Jake first got the meteorite, he still craved his father's approval, still considered him a pillar of virtue.

But weeks later, Jake had to reckon with the existence of Sebastian, and by extension, the descent of his parents from paragons of morality to whatever they actually were. What were they? Flawed, assuredly. But that word minimized the extent of their actions. Monsters? No, loath as Jake was to admit it, they weren't. But it was hard for Jake to categorize his parents because his father had provided him with such a black-and-white framework for understanding the world. The truth was, they had lied to him his entire life. He began to wonder: had he learned to be virtuous from his parents, or had he learned how to *seem* virtuous? Part of him wanted to dismiss the question. He was a middle-aged man. He didn't need his parents to determine his morality for him. Another part of him knew that his foundation was cracked, and reasonable adult or no, it would be foolish to dismiss the fissure as inconsequential. It wasn't as if his moral foundation had never been shaken. Jake was far from perfect. But now, he felt corruption deep inside himself, corruption with a family legacy, and he wondered just how far from perfect he might stray.

: 4 : : :

Lilith Washington was well versed in her husband's failings. For a long time, these failings seemed minor, and in the beginning, they were born from noble intentions. Back when they first began sleeping together, Jake was keenly focused on her sexual satisfaction. An honorable pursuit, to be sure. After spending her collegiate years dealing with oblivious sexual partners who were easily convinced by unconvincing orgasms, Lilith didn't want to complain when Jake made a concerted effort to please her. But there was something about the way he went about his pleasure crusade that did not fully satisfy her. The bedroom became a laboratory, a sterile environment of experimentation where hypotheses needed testing, areas of her body needed deliberate exploration, and questions needed to be answered: how is that? What about there? Is this doing anything for you? Do you want me to talk more? Less? Was that good for you? He wouldn't let her do any of the pleasing, and Lilith realized Jake was indulging in a perverse martyrdom that had nothing to do with her and everything to do with him. She put up with it because now and then, he would make a discovery that warranted praise—an erotic kiss behind her knee or a new position that left her screaming in bliss—but at some point, she'd halt his investigation and plead, "Just fuck me already."

As the years wore on, he engaged in less experimentation, seemingly convinced that he was a man with answers. By the later stages of their marriage, Jake could make her come with the rehearsed ease and expedience that only comes from so much practice with the same partner. His compulsive need to please her in inventive ways faded. Although his preoccupation with her pleasure had been one of his early failings, the gradual decline of this impulse was yet another failing in Lilith's eyes. She knew it was unfair. He couldn't win. But there were other minor failings she felt justified in holding against him. He wouldn't clear his browser history after he'd watch porn on the desktop computer in the office. He would meticulously order everything in the house and wouldn't tolerate an item out of place. He would smile too widely whenever other men eyed Lilith's body. He would shut her out when dealing with everyday disappointments.

She still loved him, of course. It would be easier if she didn't. But she knew that all people were imperfect, all love was imperfect, and all marriages were imperfect. She had acquiesced to the inevitability of imperfection long ago.

The minor failings were not what ultimately undid Lilith: Jake's egregious transgression, his affair—that was the failing that mattered. Lilith did not find out about Jake's indiscretion in the traditional manner. Since he hadn't been at home when the infidelity happened, Lilith had never had any clues to give her cause for suspicion. The affair had occurred five years ago, back in 2006, when Jake had been working at the Mars Desert Research Station in Utah, conducting a month-long scientific study. Jake had only called Lilith once throughout his time there. She had been expecting as much. Before leaving, Jake had explained that the intensiveness of their work would make it difficult for him to communicate with her. The crew needed to work in isolation. Once the month-long study ended, Lilith went to pick up Jake from the airport without any thought that he might have been unfaithful. There had been no reason for her to question him. But when she saw him waiting at the airport terminal, he was serious. Too serious.

"Lily, there's something I need to talk to you about," he said once he settled into the car on the way home.

"Whatever it is, can we talk about it once we get back to the house? There's construction on McDonnell, and I have no idea where this detour is going to take me. The freeway entrance is blocked off where I usually get on," she said, ignoring the urgency in Jake's voice. She had more significant concerns to focus on, like not getting lost in the convolutions of the detours. More than fearing death, she feared getting lost.

"This construction's been going on all year. I figured you'd have adjusted to it by now," Jake said.

"Well, I haven't," Lilith responded. Orange construction cones and cautionary signs were everywhere, warning drivers to maintain slow speeds and merge when necessary. Lilith did not heed the reminders that speeding fines were doubled in construction zones. She believed it was best to rush through disaster areas.

"Why do they have to do so much construction anyway?" Lilith asked, tapping her manicured nails against the steering wheel.

"Rebuilding is important."

"If you say so," she noted, unconvinced. She eventually found her way out of the construction zone, breathing a sigh of relief, glad that the worst was over, convinced that no matter what happened now, she could find her way back from here.

"Lily, I slept with someone," Jake finally said.

"I hate when you call me Lily. I'm not some delicate flower."

"Christ, would you listen? I said I slept with someone," he said more forcefully.

There it was, repeated, impossible to ignore. Lilith didn't want to face her husband's betrayal while operating a moving vehicle. She thought about stopping the car in the middle of the road. She considered rear-ending the vehicle in front of her just to get out of this. But she couldn't bring herself to do it.

"How many times?" she asked.

"Just once," Jake said.

Lilith thought about everything for a moment. "Why are you telling me this anyway?" she asked.

"It's going to come out."

"What do you mean it's going to come out?"

"It'll be part of the report."

"Part of the report?" she asked. The road was clear, and she kept moving straight ahead, emboldened by an empty horizon. "You've got to be kidding me, Jake. In what way could the fact that you *fucked* some woman be relevant to a scientific report? So, what, will there be sections on…I don't know, metamorphic rocks and fossils and *fucking sexual positions*? Explain it to me, Jake, because it sure as hell doesn't make any sense why you would publish something personal about our *marriage* in a fucking scientific article," she said, feeling the heat of rage flush throughout her body.

"There was a socio-psychological component to the mission," he said.

"A socio-psychological component?"

81

"Yeah, there was a psychologist on the crew evaluating the dynamics of the crewmembers. Noting anything that could affect efficiency and group cohesion."

Lilith got quiet for a moment, processing everything. All she could think about was damage control. At the next red light, she turned to Jake and said, "Deny it. Lie to the psychologist."

"I can't," Jake said.

"Why not?"

"Well, I already told him everything. Besides, I want the report to reflect what happened. Other scientists need to get a realistic sense of social conditions that might impact future studies."

"So…your answer is, 'because of science'? You could have denied this whole affair, but you're disclosing it, not just to me, but also to the world…because of science?"

"You make it seem like science is unimportant. This is my career. These are my values you're talking about. And listen, my name won't be mentioned in the description of the…event. The paper will describe what happened in broad strokes. It'll mostly be about how everything impacted the team," Jake explained.

"Well, thank God for small favors," Lilith said. But Jake's clarifying remark about his name being left out of the report offered more than just a "small favor." Lilith was relieved that people wouldn't know about his infidelity. The public shame: that would have been the worst part of all of this. She wondered if she should feel guilty for thinking so deeply about the optics of the situation, but she let go of the thought. She reminded herself that she was the one who'd been wronged. At least she and Jake didn't have kids. She never thought she'd be happy about that fact, but here she was, glad for it.

"Are you okay?" Jake asked timidly.

"Jake, I just can't deal with this right now," Lilith responded. She didn't say another word for the rest of the car ride home. The punch of betrayal was coupled with shock. Jake was a good man, after all. Or she'd always thought he was. His earlier sins had barely registered as sins: they were the type of nitpicking imperfections that only emerged when deeper flaws were absent. But now, who was this man? Did he get points for honesty? He probably saw it that way. He could have lied. She would never have known. The paper wasn't even going to use his name. How likely was she to read the report anyway? It felt like Jake's disclosure, honest though it might have been, was a way of cleansing himself of guilt and shifting the burden onto her. While she appreciated the truth, she also knew the comfort of ignorance. Jake's confession felt like unnecessary antagonism. He hadn't said he loved this other woman. He hadn't said he wanted a divorce. He'd only said he'd slept with someone. Lilith thought about asking him what this woman meant to him, but she couldn't bring herself to it. He had shoved her into the discomfort of knowledge, but she could choose to constrain that knowledge rather than expand it. So she let him sigh in the passenger's seat without so much as a sigh in return. If she had to breathe in the discomfort of knowledge, he could manage the discomfort of ignorance.

At home, she dropped her keys in the bowl of marbles near the entryway, shed her coat, and went to the master bedroom. She returned to the living room with her husband's pillow and threw it onto the couch before retreating to the back of the house.

"You don't have to go," Jake told her the following morning as she packed her things into a suitcase. His plea might have meant more if he'd been more visibly distressed. But he was too even-toned, casually leaning against a wall.

"You fucking cheated on me," she said, stuffing her clothes into the suitcase.

"But it's done," he said, this time a bit wounded. "I told you about this because I want to move past it."

She wondered whether his plea was rooted in her or rooted in his fear of loneliness. Like so many other couples, Jake and Lilith had built a life together from mundane experiences. But they were shared mundane experiences, *their* mundane experiences. She wondered if he would miss her off-key singing in the shower, wondered if she would miss the way he folded his underwear into squares. As she prepared to leave, there was some part of her that wanted to stay. But she remembered her rage, felt it worming upward toward her throat, and she felt entitled to a fight.

"You told me about it because you want to feel better about it," Lilith responded. "So please, don't pretend that anything you've done has been for my sake."

"Is there anything I can say to make you stay?"

"I don't know. Why don't you try to figure something out?" Lilith said. He sat there, mute, maybe trying to come up with something, maybe reckoning with the inevitability of her departure. It was hard to tell since his eyes weren't meeting hers. With one arm crossed and the other propped up, he began biting the cuticles of his thumb. Lilith could only take so much of his consternation.

"Christ, you are a disappointment," she said before she left.

Unlike most spurned wives, Lilith Washington's revenge was not in leaving but in returning. After a month of living at her parents' place, Lilith came back to Palo Alto, knowing she was more potent with Jake under her control than she could have been living on her own. Their time apart had helped. Lilith had fielded Jake's many phone calls, dismissing him whenever she pleased, knowing that if he wanted to prove himself, he'd have to pursue her, succumbing to her command. When she returned, Lilith knew that on some level, she would never be able to forget what Jake had done, but at least she could retake charge of her life, moving spice jars from their alphabetized slots in the pantry without fear of reprisal. How could he criticize her for such minor offenses when he had committed the ultimate act of disloyalty? Small retaliatory actions like these consoled Lilith. But now and then, the memories of Jake's infidelity would torment her so powerfully that her frivolous acts of rebellion couldn't compensate for the pain. She would picture him in bed with someone else, someone brunette or redheaded, not dirty blonde like her. She would imagine Jake and the other woman laughing and talking in whispers. She would look in the mirror and think, "he chose someone else," and it would take everything inside her to correct the record and think, "he ultimately chose me."

The worst moment in recent memory came when Jake agreed to serve as an advisor overseeing the dissertation of Jessica Fleming, a young graduate student.

"I thought you weren't going to advise any dissertations this year," Lilith said when she learned the name of his advisee, a woman's name.

"No, I told you about this. Listen, I should..." Jake started.

"How old is she anyway?" Lilith interrupted.

"Mid-twenties, I guess."

"So she's beautiful," Lilith said. She knew her naked jealousy was ugly, but she couldn't get rid of it. It was stuck there. It was better not to hide it anyway. Jake needed to feel the consequences of his transgression.

"I never said that," he protested.

"You didn't have to."

"Don't be ridiculous," Jake said. Lilith couldn't believe that he used that word: ridiculous. "She's just a graduate student who needs a dissertation advisor. This *is* part of my job."

She could have pleaded with him and made an honest confession of her doubts. But she didn't want to feel weak. She didn't deserve that. Instead, she asked, "Did you follow the new policies about assigning advisers and advisees? Did you fill out the paperwork?"

"You and I both know that's just bureaucratic bullshit."

"That bureaucratic bullshit provides safeguards for students and teachers. If you try to work around the process, you might find it harder to secure grant money from the Foundation. We spent a lot of money on the educational consultants who came up with those procedures and helped put them in place."

"Are you trying to bully me or something?" Jake asked.

"Jake, I'm just trying to help," she said.

Lilith's position on the Board of Trustees at the UC Berkeley Foundation had been a way for her to get even with Jake. She didn't take on the post as part of a revenge plot, not really. She'd always been adept at fundraising. Even before she became senior vice president for her family's vineyard, she was organizing galas and charitable campaigns. She was a Berkeley alum, just like Jake, and when the Foundation tapped her as a member of the board, she eagerly accepted the position. The offer had been years in the making. She knew the right people and worked the right angles.

"So now I can't even set my own metrics for evaluating my students?" Jake asked his wife a week after the Jessica dispute. A new idea had just come down the university pipeline: standardizing grade weighting across the department.

"Don't get so worked up. You still have complete freedom over the content of the curriculum and all the issues that matter," Lilith said, pouring herself a glass of Duckhorn Vineyards Merlot and sitting down in the living room.

"But regulating the weight of the midterms and final exams? What purpose does that serve?"

"It's about setting uniform expectations within the department," she said, smelling her wine before her first sip. She closed her eyes. She took a drink and tasted the smokiness of the oak, the cloves. She opened her eyes to see the annoyed look Jake gave her whenever she opened a bottle during a serious conversation. He took her wine glass from her hand and put it on the counter.

"Uniformity? Since when has uniformity been an admirable trait in anything, much less in academia? We should be encouraging students to go against the grain."

"And going against the grain is always so admirable?" Lilith asked, sending an arm across Jake's chest to pick up her wine glass.

"I'm just saying autonomy is important. We all have Ph.D.s. We're smart enough to be trusted when it comes to setting expectations for our students."

"Intelligence and trust aren't necessarily related. Not every Ph.D. deserves our trust," she said. Another barb. She lingered on that thought before speaking again, letting the implication of mistrust reach him until he pursed his lips in reproach. Just when she thought Jake might respond or act out, she qualified her response: "Did you hear about Matthews? Last semester in his freshman seminar, a hundred percent of the students' grades was based on their performance on his final exam. It incorporated information from one of his graduate courses. Half the class failed."

"So talk to the administration about disciplining Matthews. Don't impose restrictions on the entire department."

"Matthews isn't an isolated case. Listen, these restrictions are just for your undergraduate classes. Throw whatever you want at your graduate students, but those undergrads are still kids. Establishing uniform expectations across the department is important to ensuring their success."

"They have to grow up sometime."

"Listen, the Foundation didn't even make this decision. We just funded committees to oversee changes across departments that would improve student success. If you have a problem, talk to Radenport about it," she said. She was right. This decision was not within the purview of the Foundation. The board controlled the purse strings of

87

various grants, while administrators and departments controlled academic policy decisions.

"Are you even listening to yourself?" Jake asked.

"He *is* your department chair."

"I'm not going to talk to Radenport."

"Suit yourself," she said, continuing to drink her wine. She liked the spice in the bottle. The full body. She relished it.

"Can't you talk him out of it? I know you've gotten closer with him now that you've been working with him on your committee."

She took a bigger sip of her wine, only this time, a dribble that looked like blood trickled down her chin before she wiped it away with her hand. By this point, her teeth were stained.

"And why would I do that?" she asked casually. She watched her husband slink off toward the master bedroom while the sunset peered through the sliding glass doors. The pink glow highlighted the wine stain on her chin. Lilith Washington luxuriated, stretching out her legs and pointing her toes before conceding to a languorous collapse of loose limbs.

:   :   6   :   :

Rachel Washington knew as well as anyone that the past seeks vengeance. When Rachel first decided to conceal the adoption of her three-year-old son from him, her husband had tried to dissuade her. There was no way it could work, he'd told her. The boy was old enough to form memories. He was old enough to ask questions about his estranged brother. But Rachel was convinced it was the right thing to do. From the moment little Jakey came into their home, he had violent night terrors, screaming and kicking. Whenever Rachel would rock his sweating, shaking little body in the recliner to soothe him back to sleep, she'd worried that his experiences with his unfit birth mother had warped him. Once before taking a nap, Jakey had asked Rachel why she never played the "stay still, lock-up game," which she learned meant physically restraining him before naptime using her arms and legs to pin him to the ground. That was when Rachel decided that full concealment of the past was the only way to eradicate his trauma.

Daniel understood her desire to help Jake, but he worried about the logistical difficulties of blocking out the past. Daniel had asked her, what are you going to do when he needs to process paperwork and sees his birth certificate? She had already thought about that. She would handle all the paperwork herself. "Even his marriage certificate?" Daniel had asked. "When he's an adult?" Yes, even his marriage certificate. Even when he's an adult. "And what if he wants to see baby pictures?" Daniel had asked. There had been an answer for that too: a fire had destroyed the pictures.

Rachel had figured out a way to handle everything. She never had any doubts about building a fortress of lies if it meant that Jake could be safe and whole. Erasing the past also quieted the dull ache of infertility that had throbbed from her uterus to her heart. By the end of their conversation about how to manage Jake, she had appealed to Daniel with the full grief of her womanhood, assuring him that his anatomy prevented him from understanding the reaches of her evolutionary maternal urges. So Daniel had acquiesced, admitting that maybe Rachel was right, perhaps the trauma needed to be wiped clean.

Rachel's deception worked for far longer than they ever expected, but it could not survive a lifetime. Rachel and Jake had always been close, and even into his middle age, they'd spoken on the phone weekly, sometimes more. But after Jake learned about Sebastian, he got his retribution against his mother by shutting her out. Suddenly, for weeks, Jake wouldn't answer her calls or respond to her emails. Ever the optimist, Rachel initially assumed he was too engrossed in his job to respond. It was out of the ordinary, but he'd just acquired his meteorite. He had work, lots of it. But the more her calls went unreturned, the more her anxious she became. When she finally heard the phone ring and recognized Jake's number on caller ID, she answered with dread.

"How could you keep something like this from me?" Jake started in, cutting off her introductory hello.

"Calm down," Rachel urged him. "Something like what?"

"Guess," he said.

Rachel didn't need to guess. Jake spoke with such force that she knew he was referring to the only secret she'd ever kept from him, *the* secret she'd kept from him. She tried to summon the right words but didn't know what the right words were.

"Come on, guess," he repeated.

"I don't like games," she deflected, trying to buy herself time. She could feel her anxiety ratcheting up, knowing she would have to confront her past decisions.

"This isn't a game."

"Then why don't you say what's bothering you? We've always been able to talk to one another."

"You're not my mother," he paused. "You wanted me to say it, so I said it."

Rachel was speechless. Over the years, she had anticipated the possibility that Jake might eventually figure everything out, but it had been at least a decade since she'd last considered what she might tell her son. Once she'd gotten past the tough years, she'd thought it was over. Rachel had made it through the childhood years, past the imaginary friends and the vestiges of his memories. She'd made it through the teenage years, when he had started looking less and less like their child, growing into a nose that neither she nor Daniel could lay claim to. Once all of that had seemed buried, she'd started letting down her guard. By the time Jake hit middle age, she'd assumed the best: that the legitimacy of their bond, genetically or environmentally determined, was beyond question.

At Jake's repudiation of her role as a mother, Rachel cried. Jake stayed on the line for one minute, two minutes, until she finally pulled herself together enough to carry on.

"What do you think a mother is?" she asked, steadying herself on the firm ground of years of home-cooked meals, consolatory hugs, care packages, and financial support. She understood his frustration, but she couldn't bear his dismissal of her sacrifices and devotion.

"What kind of question is that?" he asked, anger still seething from his voice.

"It's exactly the kind of question you should be asking yourself."

"I'm not sure there's space in my head for another question."

"A mother isn't a vessel for childbirth," Rachel yelled, stunning herself with her volume and self-possession. Her son had struck her in the soft center of her insecurity, and she'd pounced back defensively.

"Maybe not entirely."

"Jake, I'm your mother, whether you like it or not."

"Whatever you are, no title makes you any less guilty for what you've done," Jake said. "I don't know who I am now. Do you understand that? I don't even know who I am!" he yelled, causing Rachel to pull her ear away from the phone.

Rachel hurt as he hurt. She cried for his pain and her share in it. She tried to imagine what he must be experiencing, but every attempt ricocheted backward in a double-pronged assault of sympathy and guilt.

"*I* know who you are. You're my son," she said, trying to assure herself of this truth.

"Did you know there are two of me?"

"There's one of you. Even if someone else looks like you."

"So, you knew."

"I knew," she admitted, figuring that nothing short of full disclosure would do her any good at this point.

"And you kept that from me too?"

"Would you have wanted to know?"

"Is that a serious question?" he asked, louder and frustrated.

"Don't shout," she pleaded, her voice earnest and raw. She couldn't remember the last time he'd raised his voice at her...maybe when he was in high school...that time he'd fried his bedroom carpet with chemicals, and they'd argued about his at-home lab.

"I didn't keep your brother hidden from you to hurt you," she said. "When you were younger, I thought it would trigger your trauma. When you were older, it just felt too late."

"Too late?"

"I didn't want to do any damage. Destroy the foundations your father and I laid for you. No time seemed like a good time," she responded, trying to be as honest as she could. "I didn't do any of this to be mean."

"I didn't say you did."

"Well, doesn't that count for something?" she asked, the question rising from her mind to her mouth without any advanced deliberation.

"Sure, it just doesn't count for everything."

"Jake, I'm so sorry," she said, genuine, pained. "I love you so much."

There was no immediate response. Jake's failure to reciprocate her love stung. After years of parenting, she felt owed a response. She'd scaled back her career to raise him. She'd endured the Sisyphean boredom of constant housework between her shifts in the hospital and still made time to read him stories about space to nurture his curiosity. She'd sacrificed for the love of this child, her child, and even now, as she saw how thankless his love could be, it didn't make her love him any less. He was in pain; she had to remember that. She'd caused that pain; she had to remember that too.

"Why didn't you just tell me?" he cried. His voice was still angry. Rachel was mad at herself too. She might have left their love unscathed if only she'd acknowledged the breach between them decades ago, early enough that they wouldn't have needed such a large bridge to span the divide.

"I couldn't. I thought I'd lose you," Rachel confessed. "We tried to conceive for so long, and I wanted a child so badly. I wanted *you*. I could have waited for a baby. I was on a list to adopt an infant. But my good friend's daughter knew you. Knew about your situation. Your birth mother, she couldn't manage you. She was practically a kid. Unfit. Negligent. She was going to give you up, and another family might have been worse. You don't know the kind of abuse I saw in my job. I didn't want you to be one of the kids in the emergency room. I knew I could give you a good life. I *did* give you a good life. But you were traumatized when your dad and I got you. You don't remember, but you would scream in the night. I wanted to help you. Move you past your trauma."

"And you don't think this is trauma? Years of deception? An identity crisis?"

"I don't know what else to say. I'm sorry. Maybe it was the wrong decision. But I can't change it. I can't turn back time. I did it because I love you."

"Forgive me if I have my doubts."

"You don't have to be cruel," Rachel said, struggling to reconcile Jake's malice with the kind person she knew him to be at his core.

"I'm not trying to be. It's just hard to process all of this. I need some time to figure everything out," Jake said, cold and distant.

"What's there to figure out?"

"More than you think," he said.

Even though Rachel wanted to keep engaging with him, she needed to let him be. The last thing she wanted was to push too hard.

"Fine," Rachel said. "I'll give you your space. But I'm here if you have any questions. If you want to talk. If you need time to process this, fine. Process it. Then come back to me."

After Rachel got off the phone with Jake, she sat on the couch, crying. When she finally pulled herself together, she made her way to the garage where she kept storage boxes filled with relics of Jake's childhood. She unearthed old birthday cards, science fair entries, prize ribbons, his collection of polished rocks, and other keepsakes that reminded Rachel he had once been young; he had once been hers; he had once been content with their life. These artifacts lifted Rachel's spirits.

She decided to organize the mementos into scrapbooks for Jake. She spent hours cutting flourishes and arranging colorful backdrops. She glued down old drawings and awards and notes. Daniel poked his head into the garage several times and tried to convince her to come inside.

"We did what we thought was best," he told her. "We gave Jake everything we could. He'll come around eventually. You don't need to stay up all night crafting. There'll be time for that later."

But Rachel was determined. Once it got late, he gave up trying to dissuade her and went to bed. She kept cutting and pasting, cutting and pasting, as if she might be able to rearrange the pieces of their family and reorder the edges that misaligned, gluing them down so the new configuration might stick.

It was verging on daybreak when she finished her sixth scrapbook. Once it was complete, there was only one object left in the storage bin: a small, white, cushioned box. She opened the box and found something she'd forgotten she'd saved: Jake's baby teeth. They were yellowed and brittle from years spent outside of his body. Most of them were broken, but there was one that was still whole. It looked like a kernel of sweet corn, uncooked and waiting for the stove to give it purpose. Rachel held it in her hand. It was so small. She remembered when Jake's mouth had been small. She remembered the gaps the teeth had left on his kindergarten smile. She couldn't bear to think of any of it for a second longer—not his childhood, not the spaces, blanks, and absences calling attention to themselves, whether on his face or in his genetic makeup. Rachel curled up on the concrete floor of the garage and fell asleep without dreaming.

*　　*　　*

Jacqueline Barnabas, on the other hand, was haunted by recurrent nightmares ever since Sebastian had called her and accused her of lying about Jake's death. The nightmares would open in the middle of a shift at one of the low-wage jobs she'd worked in her lifetime. Everything would go sideways, slowly at first, then rapidly. Customers would come into the grocery store, ask her complex academic questions, then mock her ignorance when she couldn't summon an answer. Diners at the French café in Lunada Bay, where she bussed tables, would speak in gibberish, then demand to talk to a manager when she couldn't process their requests. Cinephiles would barge into the video rental store, arguing about the lack of cult classics or Italian Neorealist films.

But it'd get worse. People would ask her where her child was, and she wouldn't know the answer. They'd summon police officers to arrest her for heinous crimes she never committed. They'd threaten her life at knifepoint, steal the top-shelf liquor from behind the counter, pour the alcohol over her head, and laugh maniacally. They'd show her pictures from the scene of her parents' fatal car accident. They'd tell her she'd always be alone.

Jacqueline believed her nightmares were her comeuppance for neglecting Sebastian. She could trace her role in his damage.

When he was three, she'd taught him how to pull the step stool over to the fridge, get to the milk, and dump it over a bowl of cereal so she could spend the morning sleeping in bed or puking in the bathroom. When he was four, she'd drunkenly blamed him for his father's reluctance to stick around, even though her own foolish, teenage decisions and inability to pick the right men had been responsible. When he was five, she'd taught him how to clean up urine from the carpet. When he was six, she'd woken up to him crying and poking her topless, limp body in the middle of the dining room floor after she'd spent a night partying. When he was seven, she'd poured herself a shot of vodka, only to find he'd switched out the liquor for water, and she'd angrily confronted him before shame washed over her. When he was eight, she'd found him sleeping outside the front door at four in the morning because she had absent-mindedly taken the spare key with her when she'd left the house the previous afternoon. When he was nine, he'd been too embarrassed to invite any friends over, and she'd yelled at him. She'd defending the beautiful home they'd inherited from her parents (the only thing of value that was hers), never considering that the source of embarrassment might have been her rather than the home. When he was ten, she'd watched from the swerving vantage of her car as he walked home from a restaurant they'd gone to together.

These moments also surfaced in her nightmares, forcing her to relive the times when she'd been the worst version of herself.

But there had been good times, too, and after the nightmares came, she tried to cling onto those. She remembered the way his toddler body had fit perfectly inside hers when she'd cuddle up with him during her darkest moments. She remembered their trip to Disneyland when

Barrie had briefly been around, the three of them pretending to be a family. She remembered creating a scavenger hunt for Sebastian after Barrie had left, leading Sebastian to a package of silly putty. She remembered sneaking him a macaron from the stack of cookies in the French bakery after wiping down the tables at the end of the day.

But her favorite memories were from her time as the manager of a local video store. She loved that job because she got to relax, smoke a joint in the back if Sebastian wasn't there, and put on all types of movies: comedies, period pieces, noir films, Doris Day classics. Plenty of times, she'd bring eleven-or-twelve-year-old Sebastian with her for a shift, and he would pick the movie for the main television display, *Star Wars* or *Superman*.

The two of them had a ritual. Whenever Jacqueline and Sebastian finished watching a movie, they would rewind the VHS using the slowest speed possible, keep the visuals playing, and anticipate what was coming. They tried to outdo one another with their knowledge of what came next, or rather, what came first. Famous lines. Explosions. Scene changes. The placement of a prop. The exit of a character. The head nod of an extra. The more they watched a film, the more nuance they would pick up. Jacqueline always lost to Sebastian, but she didn't mind. She liked that her son was more perceptive than she was; it made her feel like she'd done something right. Soon, they started watching films in reverse before ever watching them from the beginning. She remembered Sebastian saying stories should be as compelling from finish-to-start as from start-to-finish; he'd mentioned something about symmetry or inversion or linearity.

After waking from another dream, Jacqueline had a superstitious thought: maybe reminding Sebastian about the good memories would ease her nightmares. She called him.

"Sebastian," she greeted him on the phone. "Do you remember when we would rewind movies at the video store and blurt out what was about to happen?"

"Mom, it's six in the morning," Sebastian said gruffly.

"I know, I know. But do you remember?"

"Yeah, sure," he muttered. "Is that all?"

"What movie would you say you watched most back then? *Empire Strikes Back*?" she asked, trying to resurrect details as if doing so would vanquish the past.

"*The Deer Hunter*," he said without hesitation.

"No. I never would've let you watch that. Not at your age."

"*Let* me watch it?" Sebastian asked. "Do you remember how often you shoved me in the back room and told me to use the small TV and put on whatever I wanted while you were out front? Maybe you wouldn't have put *The Deer Hunter* up on the main TV. But the answer is *Deer Hunter*, mom. Now seriously. Can I go back to sleep?"

Jacqueline didn't know how to reconcile Sebastian's experiences with her own. She couldn't believe that, without her knowledge, her young son had been watching and re-watching a film with so much violence and personal anguish. Trying to put it past her, she let her adult son return to his bed. But when evening fell, and it was time for her to sleep, her nightmares glowed with the fires of Vietnam, blazing with a vengeance.

: : : 4 :

Although many women wanted to get even with Sebastian Barnabas, Mallory Specter, a former colleague from Stanford, went further than anyone else in her quest for vengeance. Mallory, the daughter of an elite lawyer, had an arsenal of litigators at her disposal. Lawyers had come through for Mallory before. If anyone doubted her capacity for revenge, she would turn their attention to exhibit A: her

98

multi-million-dollar, four-bedroom home in Palo Alto, outfitted with top-of-the-line appliances, remodeled bathrooms, and a sizeable swimming pool. A sprawling estate of glass, wood, and metal, the mid-century modern architecture still looked contemporary. Mallory had secured the home as part of her divorce settlement with her ex-husband, a man she'd loved who hadn't loved her enough. A man who'd cheated on her. There was no better endorsement of her ability to undo a man than that house.

But the truth was the house undid Mallory. When her divorce was fresh, and she would sit in the living room by herself, drinking a glass of whiskey, the spacious layout amplified her loneliness. On her way to the master bedroom, she had to pass the other three bedrooms in the house—the guest room, the fitness room, and the office—and in her grief over the collapse of her marriage, she would superimpose her lost dreams onto the rooms as she passed them. Dreams of having a nursery, a playroom. Dreams of working with her husband on a joint business venture in the tech industry. Living in that house meant living with the ghost of her once-imagined future. Sometimes, she could even hear children laughing in her mind, the soundtrack of the horror movie she was living.

The first time Sebastian came to Mallory's house, the memory of her ex-husband still haunted the place, so she didn't lead Sebastian to the master bedroom. Instead, she slept with Sebastian in the guest room in a bed made up for outsiders. Sliding her naked limbs across the brand-new sheets, Mallory pretended she was an exile in a foreign city rather than an abandoned wife alienated in her own home. When Mallory and Sebastian lay in the queen-sized bed after they had sex, she tried to savor the moment, recapturing the once familiar feeling of living with another person nearby. That was what she missed most about her marriage: not the intimacy or the conversation or the love, just the physical presence of someone else. The moment didn't last long.

Sebastian only spent a minute or so catching his breath before he reached for his clothes. He was fucking her; she was fucking him. There was nothing more to it. She was divorced and broken anyway, but the casual sex was more uncomplicated in impersonal spaces.

So the next time she slept with him in her house, it wasn't in a bed but on the treadmill in the fitness room. The time after that, it wasn't in a bed but on the desk in the office. And the time after that, it wasn't in a bed but on the kitchen island. Every one of those bed-less interactions was cold and uncomfortable and procedural. Still, she convinced herself that if she and Sebastian could conquer every room in her house with their intimacy-free sex, then the house wouldn't be a home anymore but a den of iniquity, and her previous hopes for a prototypical family life would disappear. But her plan didn't work. The more Sebastian came over, the more she turned him into an object designed to be there—a piece of furniture or a carved-out niche, something she could sink into.

"Are there any more rooms for us to christen?" Sebastian asked before they had sex in her house for the last time.

"Just one," Mallory said, leading him toward the master bedroom.

"I thought this place was off-limits."

"It was. But not anymore."

"I don't know," Sebastian said once they entered the room.

"Come on," she prodded. "It's not a big deal."

But Mallory was lying. When she and Sebastian slept together in her marital bed, his presence filled the absence left by her former husband too artfully. It was hard for her to look at Sebastian after she rolled over, flushed and satisfied, without admitting to herself that she wanted him to stay there with her. Lying in that bed, she came to terms with the fact that her divorce had nearly killed her. She remembered the moment she had found unfamiliar underwear, lacy and purple, wedged at the base of the bed against the footboard. She could still feel the shock of betrayal. She'd been debasing the rooms in her house because she'd hoped Sebastian could fuck her through the devastation. But some part of her knew he was only fucking her toward more of it.

"Could I come with you to the San Diego conference in June?" she asked, knowing he was scheduled to give a talk. She hoped this would be a getaway where they could grow roots outside the graveyard of her house. It took him too long to respond.

"I guess."

His tepid response was disheartening, but she convinced herself he might just need some time to come around. She knew he wasn't good at intimacy. At that point in her life, she wasn't either. If anything, that made them suited for each other—both of them could stumble toward vulnerability slowly. She thought they might make a real go of things, and this conference would be a start. But then Sebastian slept with Diana Hyland, the mathematics department chair, and so began Mallory's revenge campaign.

The first steps Mallory took weren't litigious in the strictest sense of the word. She filed a formal complaint with the university about Sebastian and Diana but not a lawsuit. But Diana had already processed paperwork disclosing her sexual encounter with Sebastian and had recused herself from any administrative decisions that would directly impact him. There were no censures or job losses. Mallory was frustrated her complaint hadn't brought about any real results.

The following year wore on Mallory. It would have been easier for her to avoid Sebastian and Diana if Mallory had other colleagues whom she trusted. But Mallory was one of only four women in a math department that boasted fifty or sixty professors. There were times when she lurked near her male colleagues and overheard conversations: conversations about which of their female colleagues was most fuckable, conversations about the biological basis for men's superior mathematical prowess, conversations about how a woman had conned her way into winning the Blumenthal Award, conversations about which of the female faculty members were probably lesbians, conversations about how oversexed she and Diana were without so describing Sebastian Barnabas, conversations about who should replace Diana as department chair.

Mallory should have been comforted that a woman ran the department. She might have been if that woman hadn't been Diana. When Mallory didn't get the teaching assignments she'd wanted, she blamed Diana's bias against her. But Mallory's complaints to the Provost did nothing. The only thing the university did was shift administrative decisions that pertained to Mallory to another department chair. Unfortunately, the other chair was one of the men who had deemed her "supremely fuckable" in private conversation, citing her "tight ass but maybe not her face" as sufficient evidence for her desirability.

Everything about the work environment felt toxic, and it started to degrade the quality of Mallory's work. She found it harder to think, suffocating on the emotional exhaust. She was alone in her anguish, infantilized by the men and traitorously abandoned by the women. Stanford failed to renew her teaching contract, and she found herself wishing she was back in her office, embattled but employed.

Alone in her house, after she learned she wouldn't be returning as a faculty member the following school year, Mallory stripped off all of her clothes. As dusk turned to night, she walked toward the long swimming pool that ran the length of her house in the backyard. She dove into the cold, poorly lit shallows. She didn't drown. Mallory emerged from the water and shivered in the night air. Her too-long, wet hair covered her breasts. It was as if nature instinctively recoiled from exposure, even in the face of nothing dangerous. She floated on her back, offering up her sex more conveniently, granting easier access to her womanhood. That was the trick of life: relinquishing any claim to your own gendered body, but only if you could get something out of it, only if you could float. She walked out of the pool, thinking of a phrase that her literary ex-boyfriend had repeated to her: unsex me here. She'd always loved that phrase.

Mallory wrapped a towel around herself and went inside. She grabbed a bottle of Hudson Baby Bourbon and poured some into a tumbler, neat. She drank to blunt the pain of her dismissal, of her divorce, of her isolation. But when she sat on the couch, she remembered lying there with Sebastian on top of her. Bourbon in hand, she got up and went through the house, looking for a place where she and Sebastian hadn't had sex. But she had led him on a deliberate conquest of her home; now, there was no place left for her. In trying to kill the ghost of her husband, Mallory had created the ghost of his replacement, and she couldn't enter any room without seeing her once-hoped-for children or her once-wedded partner or her once-desired lover. She worried she might have to burn down her own house just to make it livable again. At the very least, she needed to exorcise the residue left behind by Sebastian, so the next day, she called her father, assembled a team of litigators, and started the process of expelling Sebastian from her life with tools more potent than sage.

: : : : 1

Although Sebastian was inclined to let his adversaries fall prey to their self-destructive instincts, there was one notable time when Sebastian was the one who got revenge. He was ten years old. The day had started well. It was a show-and-tell day, and he had a prize to brag about: a 1973 HP-46 printing calculator from Hewlett-Packard that he lugged to school in its plastic case. From the outside, the case looked like a briefcase. It had a black, plastic handle and the brand name emblazoned on the exterior. Small and weak as he was, Sebastian liked carrying the massive case. It allowed him to pretend he was a businessman, or at least a man of some sort, which was so crushingly far from his reality that the whole scene looked ridiculous.

Sebastian's appreciation of the calculator was a new development. For years, he'd hated it. The hatred made sense. The calculator reminded him of the night his father had left for good, an abandonment that came after the longest stint his father had spent with Sebastian and his mother: six months. His father had been in Vietnam at the time of Sebastian's birth, and his re-entrances into Sebastian's life had always been brief. Their last moments together occurred on New Year's Eve when Sebastian was six.

That night, his father, Barrie, went out for a drink with a couple of his buddies but promised to be back before midnight. Left alone, Sebastian and his mother watched the CBS broadcast. When Sebastian's mother roused Sebastian near midnight with drunken finger jabs, Sebastian realized his father wasn't home. Jacqueline polished off another glass of champagne and passed out on the couch, so Sebastian went looking for his father. He started in the master bedroom, where he noticed that his father's belongings were missing from the shelves. He went into the master bathroom to find the deodorant, the razor, the after-shave, and the cologne all gone, squirreled away somewhere more masculine than this house. Sebastian kept searching, opening all the drawers and medicine cabinets, rooting through his father's closet, looking under the bed, and trying to find one forgotten item—a tie or a dress sock or a business card. He wanted to find anything that might offer hope that not all male presence had been stripped from his life.

The only thing Sebastian found was something he, already gifted in mathematics, had no use for: a calculator.

It was one of those accounting calculators that whirred like a typewriter and printed out the entries on a roll of paper. Sebastian would never need a printed record of his work because he never forgot anything, never made mistakes, and never lost his place in the middle of a calculation. His father, on the other hand, had relied on the calculator whenever he did the bills. He'd refused to make even minor calculations in his head because he didn't trust his addition and subtraction skills.

Barrie, Sebastian's father, had used the calculator for one primary purpose: examining the finances, and relatedly, tracking the spending habits of Sebastian's mom. As a result, the clacking of the calculator had always preceded fights between his parents. So when Sebastian found the accounting calculator in the office, he thought his father had played a cruel joke on him. His father could have left behind a pair of cuff links that Sebastian could have worn in commemoration at his wedding one day. Or a small bottle of cologne that Sebastian could have spritzed on himself before an important high school formal. Or the signed baseball that Sebastian had openly coveted. Instead, Sebastian was left with the worst of the worst: something both useless to him and reminiscent of painful memories. Maybe if the calculator had been a birthday present or a reward for his good grades, he might have relished it from the start. He might have been able to forgive its easiness. But as it was, Sebastian could not love the calculator, could not even like it, at least not at the beginning when the memories were too fresh.

Fourth-grade show-and-tell was a sign that Sebastian was healing. When asked to pick an object, the only item he could think to bring was that goddamn calculator. So at ten years old, Sebastian decided to stop hating the thing and instead grew attached to it, transforming his disappointment and his scars into an item of value.

"This is a Hewlett-Packard calculator," Sebastian told the class proudly on show-and-tell day, lifting the contraption with considerable effort.

"It does addition and subtraction and multiplication and division. You can put in the numbers like this," Sebastian explained, pressing on buttons while the printer tapped out the information, "then you press this button up here, and it tells you the answer."

"Can we keep it in the classroom?" one of Sebastian's ferret-faced classmates asked. "We'll never have to do math on our own again!" The class rang out in cheers.

"You're not going to stop learning math just because some machine can do it for you," the teacher replied, channeling the authority of her sixty years and gray hair.

"Says you!" one of the kids called out. More cheers erupted. The teacher took the troublemaker out of his seat and led him by the elbow to a corner.

"Mrs. Williams is right," Sebastian said. His classmates just stared at him. "But this calculator is still neat. I read the whole manual ten times, and I know everything about it."

"Yeah, right," a bigger kid with angry red hair and freckles interjected while the teacher was still dealing with the exiled student in the corner.

"Try me," Sebastian challenged him.

"What's that STO button do?"

"It's a storage function that can be combined with other operations to keep numbers in the system throughout your calculations."

That quieted the class. Sebastian thought he might get another comment from the redheaded miscreant in the front, maybe a "nerd!" or a "loser!" but everyone was too in awe of what Sebastian had just said to tolerate an act of betrayal against him. All in all, the show-and-tell session was a success, far more so than any previous presentation that Sebastian had made. On the heels of the school day, Sebastian walked home, satisfied with himself until a fourteen-year-old kid from the middle school confronted him. The boy was almost twice Sebastian's size and was ragged enough around the edges that he didn't look like he belonged in Palos Verdes. He had the feel of a kid from somewhere harder, grittier. His blond mullet ran scraggly down his back. His squinty eyes were bloodshot, probably because he'd been smoking pot like so many of the gutter-dredged, South Bay urchins that had access to too much filth too early.

"What's in there?" the kid asked, eyeing the case for Sebastian's calculator.

"Nothing."

"It doesn't look like nothing. Open it," the bully commanded. Sebastian unlatched the case and displayed the calculator for the bully's examination.

"What is it?" the bully asked, sweeping his mullet over his shoulder as he got closer.

"You haven't seen a calculator before?"

"Not all of us get fancy gifts for Christmas," the kid said before looking over the contraption once more with a wrinkled brow, struggling to decide whether or not this might be worth the investment of his time and effort. "I'll take it," he concluded. "Say, why don't you give me your money too."

"I don't have any," Sebastian said plainly. He should have been more intimidated by the kid than he was, but something about Sebastian's newfound love for the calculator emboldened him against fear.

"No lunch money?"

"I spent it."

"Rich kid like you with a machine must have some green hidden somewhere."

"I don't, I swear," Sebastian said. "I'm not even a rich kid." The bully approached him and began patting down his body, checking anywhere that Sebastian might have hidden some money. The kid got down on his knees and started feeling Sebastian's socks for a spare buck or two. This was Sebastian's opportunity. Even though the bully was older, taller, and stockier than he was, Sebastian recognized the power of his position. Sebastian would have to move quickly and decisively. Charged with a rage he didn't know he had in his heart, Sebastian reached for the heavy calculator, pulled it above his head like a sledgehammer, and as the bully struggled to get up, Sebastian smashed the calculator over the bully's head.

The kid fell to the ground, and a stream of blood flowed from a gash on his head. The boy was barely conscious, lying uselessly on the concrete, but Sebastian couldn't simply walk away. Delicately, Sebastian picked up his calculator, wiped some of the blood from its base, and put the machine back in the briefcase. Holding the case like a man, Sebastian took his weak, little, ten-year-old feet and kicked the bully repeatedly in the stomach, hitting the kid so dully that his large body barely moved in response. Sebastian kept kicking and kicking until he lost the energy to continue, collapsing on top of the boy's body in tears and dropping the case by his side. Sebastian looked at the bully's face, which was slack and bruised. He felt no pity for him. Instead, Sebastian felt disappointed by the boy, disappointed by himself, and simultaneously empowered by both forms of disappointment, thriving in the face of everything that hurt. He clumsily wiped away his tears, using the back of his hand like a child, and left the scene behind him, dragging the calculator case that was now a nearly impossible burden to bear.

The Fifth Row
The Power of Two

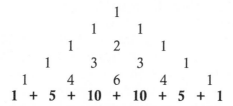

$$
\begin{array}{ccccccccccc}
 & & & & & 1 & & & & & \\
 & & & & 1 & & 1 & & & & \\
 & & & 1 & & 2 & & 1 & & & \\
 & & 1 & & 3 & & 3 & & 1 & & \\
 & 1 & & 4 & & 6 & & 4 & & 1 & \\
1 & + & 5 & + & 10 & + & 10 & + & 5 & + & 1
\end{array}
$$

Every row of Pascal's triangle is tied to the number two. When you add the numbers of any row together, their sum is equal to the number two raised to the power of the number of the row, such that: 2^n = the row's sum, where n = the number of the row.

For example, for the fifth row, the sum of the numbers 1+5+10+10+5+1 = 32.
Two raised to the fifth power is also 32.

This characteristic is present in every row, proving that the power of two is pervasive and significant.

$$1 \quad : \quad : \quad : \quad : \quad :$$

None of the people around Jake at the Golden Gate Bridge Pavilion were anything like him. They were foreigners, aliens, outsiders. Although Jake had agreed to meet Sebastian there, he now wished he'd put up more of a fight when Sebastian had suggested the location. Jake did everything he could to seem like the local he was. He waited as far away as he could from the gift shop area where people who were less Californian than he oohed and ahhhhh'ed over replicas of the bridge, flipping over paperweights in search of price tags for objects worth nothing. He hated the rows of mass-produced statuettes, which reduced an impressive worldwide attraction to a mere mold for clones. When a beautiful young woman picked up one of the small bridges, Jake resisted the urge to swat it out of her hand and onto the ground where it belonged.

Sebastian was running late. Jake looked at his Blackberry. He reread emails that he'd already responded to days ago. He did what he could to kill time, but eventually, he reached a breaking point. He strolled through the merchandise area, falling prey to boredom. He browsed coffee-table books, flipping through pictures of the bridge. He sifted through T-shirts. He found a large rack of personalized keychains, and despite the childishness of it, he scanned the alphabetized names until he reached Jake. Jacob. There were multiple rows dedicated to both iterations, and yet, there weren't any keychains left bearing his name. There were only cardboard cut-outs with his name at the base of the racks, serving as placeholders for the real thing.

"We're fresh out," a rugged, fiftysomething employee informed him.

"Oh, I wasn't..."

"You're a Jacob?"

"No," Jake said, "I mean, yes. But I don't need a keychain."

"No one *needs* a keychain," the employee said, gliding a hand across the merchandise. "No one *needs* any of this stuff. But that's not the point, is it?"

"I'm not a tourist," Jake said defensively.

"Neither am I," the employee said, pulling his keys out of his pocket and jangling a personalized keychain of his own: Luke.

"Why'd you assume I was a Jacob? What if I'd been shopping for a son or a nephew or a friend?"

"That's not how it usually works. People come over to this rack, and they find their names first. Sons, daughters, friends, all those people come second to numero uno. Who

110

doesn't want to find their name? It's nice knowing someone was expecting you to exist. Although in your case, we weren't expecting so many of you."

"I guess not," Jake said with a shrug.

"I keep telling our manager to order more Jacobs. More Jakes. I looked it up when we kept running out. It's the most common boy's name in America. Has been for over a decade."

"I hadn't realized," Jake said. "It wasn't always that way."

Jake rotated the rack and scanned further down the alphabet, using his finger to trace through the names: Samuel, Sandy, Sarah, Scott, Sean, but no…it wasn't there. He looked through the S names a second time, a third. Each time he restarted the process, he hoped he would catch an oversight and learn that there was something common about the name Sebastian after all, something universal and generic.

"I don't want a keychain anyway," Sebastian said, creeping up behind Jake, whose finger moved past the space where Sebastian should exist. "Certainly not from this place."

"Why'd you want to meet here, anyway?"

"Let's walk," Sebastian said, approaching the door. They left the Pavilion and headed toward the pedestrian walkway of the Golden Gate Bridge. The clouds dulled the orange of the bridge to a blunter shade. The loss of vibrancy reminded Jake that despite its grand aspirations, the bridge was ultimately the work of men. It was an engineering marvel, assuredly; a sight to see, without question; but it was not a divine icon. It was malleable, subject to the whims of the dead load, the live load, and the dynamic load, all competing to add the most burden to the charge of the suspension cables. The stability of the structure came with stressors that were invisible to most people. But not to engineers, physicists, or scientists, people like Jake, who looked at the structure and considered the catenary versus the parabola, the weight of gravity.

"You want to cross the bridge?" Jake asked, walking alongside Sebastian.

"You don't?"

"I've never done it."

"And you've lived in the Bay Area for how long?" Sebastian asked with a smirk.

"It's not exactly on my bucket list. I drive across the thing often enough. That takes away some of the allure of doing it the old-fashioned way."

"To be honest, I've only walked across it once," Sebastian said. "I never thought I'd go through with it a second time, but it's important now. I think it might restore balance."

"And yet, by including me, who's never walked across the bridge, it's not truly balanced," Jake pointed out. "It almost seems unfair."

"You're right," Sebastian said, looking up at the bridge with an emotion that Jake couldn't place. "It's entirely unfair."

"I'm still not sure how all this works," Jake admitted, feeling conflicted about this new relationship. "Our first meeting didn't inspire a lot of confidence."

"And yet you're here, and so am I."

"What made you decide to call me?" Jake asked.

"I guess I wasn't satisfied with how it all ended."

"What do you hope to get this time around?"

"I want to show you something," Sebastian said, "but we need to keep walking." As they proceeded, Jake looked to his left, eyeing drivers who were paying tolls at the booths. There was a price for safe passage across any obstacle. Jake remembered hearing on the news that in time, these tollbooths would be transformed. The hands that now exchanged money would no longer reach across the car window toward the booth: no more fingers touching fingers in the barely intimate way strangers connected. The transaction would still happen, but the cost would be deducted from bank accounts automatically. Jake walked with Sebastian, and unlike the people in cars, the two of them paid no toll.

"Here," Sebastian said, stopping at a point along the bridge that seemed arbitrary to Jake. "I'm sure it was here."

Jake looked at the view and saw nothing that he hadn't seen many times over. The bay. The clouds. The wind rippling across the water. What was he missing? Jake tried to find something remarkable about the spot.

"What was here?" he finally asked.

"When I was doing my graduate work, my mom, *our mom*, came to visit me over the holidays. She wanted to walk across the bridge. The day hadn't gone well. She'd been drinking. A lot. She was already drunk, so I told her we could come back another time, but she kept insisting. Fighting her sounded less appealing than indulging her. Anyway, we came, and once we got right here, she started making threats, telling me her life wasn't worth anything and had never been worth anything. Telling me she was going to jump."

"You stopped her?"

"Only by telling her to do it. I didn't hold her back or try to talk her out of it. I told her to swan dive," Sebastian said, his face stoic at the seriousness of his story.

"Why are you telling me this?"

"So you understand," Sebastian explained. "She was the worst type of parent: absentee, self-indulgent, threatening, childish. An addict. She would never jump, and I knew it. She loved herself too much. Those threats weren't about hurting herself. They were about hurting me. When you and I were at the diner, it seemed like you resented me. I'm telling you, there's no reason for that. You escaped. You got a stable two-parent home. You got the love I never got. And I'm not blaming you. I just want to give you perspective. The day my mom gave you up, you didn't lose anything. You gained everything."

113

"You might be right," Jake agreed, "but it doesn't change the way I feel. And right now, I feel robbed of something. I'm just not sure what that something is."

"That's how I've felt my whole life."

A breeze came through the slats of the gate along the pedestrian walkway. "It's cold. Why don't we get some coffee?" Jake asked.

"I know a place."

Jake followed Sebastian's lead and headed toward the warmth.

:   5   :   :   :   :

It was blisteringly hot in July of 2006 when Jake arrived at the Mars Desert Research Station as the leader of a month-long study designed to simulate missions on Mars. Jake gazed out at the striped hills and mesas. Some of the red and brown colors of the soil were vibrant; others were desaturated. To most people, such sights might seem beautiful or unique or alien, but few people would call it romantic...few people aside from Jake Washington and the rest of the crew. Jake had dreamed of being an astronaut when he was a child, and the thrill of recapturing those youthful fantasies painted a magical sheen over the expanse before him.

On his first day of exploration of the San Rafael Swell in the Utah desert, Jake put on a simulation spacesuit for the first time. The trickiest part was the backpack since it required looping his arms through the straps while getting his head through a large, circular collar that secured the helmet to the pack. Seeking help, Jake approached a colleague, Selene Thessalonia. She flashed him a smile when she reached for his oxygen tubes and secured them to his helmet. In an instant, he felt like he was about to collapse, destroyed by the perfect force of the moment. She was close enough that he could inspect the peculiarities of her face. Her eyes were large and brown. Her nose was Grecian with an aquiline shape that unexpectedly had freckles along its ridge. He already liked those freckles. They had no business being on her brownish skin, and yet there they were, small enough that they were undetectable to the uninterested eye. Looking at her through his helmet heightened his attraction to her. She was tied to his boyhood fantasy, part of the make-believe.

"Are you getting air?" she asked after flipping on the oxygen, checking that she'd properly attached the hoses. Jake was unresponsive, lost in her freckles.

"Jake," she asked more insistently, "are you getting oxygen?" He could tell that the oxygen was flowing in through the tubes, but he felt short of breath regardless. Recovering, he nodded and gave her a thumbs up. Not that the oxygen mattered. This was all part of a simulation. They wouldn't be on Mars. Still, the crewmembers were committed to preserving the integrity of the Mars exploration replication without "breaking sim." It was their job to imagine that the conditions on Mars applied to them and to work around any issues that would plague them if they'd been on the actual planet. This was their world, unreal as it might be, and they were determined to protect their fiction.

Another part of the fiction Jake imagined was that his earthly life no longer existed. He hadn't consciously arrived at this conclusion, but he did repel the residual memories of university life and husbandly duties that would pop into his mind. As a result, when Selene transfixed him, his imagination cherished the lie that his other life was paused. He slowly got to know her in the middle of the night. They both had insomnia and would go into the main living area of the hab—the stumpy cylindrical structure that they called home—while they tried to slow their restless brains.

"You too?" she asked the first night they met in the darkness. Jake gave her a brief nod as she entered the living area.

"Do you usually have trouble sleeping?" he asked her from his seat at the table in the center of the room.

"Are you kidding me? Always," she said, grabbing a glass of water. The moonlight erased her freckles but cast a glowing sheen across her face. Through her ribbed white tank top, Jake could see the braless outline of her nipples and the curves of her modest breasts.

"Me too," Jake said, sitting at the table, struggling to look away from her body.

"What do you think it means?" she asked, pulling up a chair at the table.

"Anxiety?"

"Only I don't feel anxious," she said, gently smiling at him with her full eyes wide.

"Me neither," he replied, breathing a subtle laugh through his nose and reciprocating her smile. He found it nearly impossible to feel anxious around Selene, especially when he was close enough to inspect the richness of her brown irises, the warmth of her expressions.

"So. Who are you when you're not here?" Selene asked, forcing him to break away from the illusion that nothing else existed beyond this station.

"A planetary geologist. A professor," Jake noted, trying to be as spare as he could in his description of life at home. He hoped this might make it seems less real.

"A husband?" Selene asked, eyeing his wedding band.

"A husband," he responded. "A wife?" he asked her in return, more playfully than he knew he was capable of sounding.

"Never," Selene said, shaking her head with a sideways wrench of her lips.

"Never? Are you one of those people who doesn't believe in marriage?"

"I guess I would just rather believe in love."

"Some people would tell you the two aren't mutually exclusive."

"Are you one of those people?"

Jake wasn't sure how to answer. Part of him was screaming, say no, say no, say no, please, for the love of god. This is your chance. It may be your only chance to let her know that you're interested in her, that your marriage feels...what? Old? Tired? Forgettable? Yes, *forgettable* when compared to the bond between the two of you. And yet, there was the weight—the weight of responsibilities, of character, of integrity. As much as Jake wanted to buy into the false narrative that he wasn't a husband here, he knew it was bullshit, and he would fault himself for giving in to the bullshit. But he felt off-kilter, thrown by his infatuation.

"It's not *impossible* to have both" was what he settled on, non-committal. "And who are *you* when you're not here?"

"In a metaphysical sense?"

"In any sense."

"Who am I when I'm not here?" she paused, lips pursed, gaze floating toward the ceiling in contemplation. "That's a tough question to answer."

"You're the one who posed the question to me in the first place," Jake reminded her, laughing. "Think about how I felt."

"I'm dangerous," she said, her eyes alight with moonglow.

"Excuse me?" he asked, even though he knew what she meant. She *was* dangerous, particularly to someone like him.

"Dangerous. Defective..." Selene went on, her tone, sober and contemplative.

"Deceptive?" he interjected, completing the series but unsure if he'd gotten it right.

"Not deceptive. Never deceptive."

"You must be deceptive if you're as dangerous as you say you are," Jake reasoned.

"Maybe I'm dangerous because no one expects it," she told him, as if in a warning. "But I never *intend* to be deceptive. I never *try* to deceive anyone."

Jake and Selene continued in much the same way every night, meeting in the half-light of the moon, slowly divulging secrets. There was no denying their chemistry, and neither of them took pains to do so, not at first. Their late-night interactions were innocent, at least in terms of discernible boundaries. Their conversations were personal, but there were no admissions of romantic feelings, no comments about the allure of her eyes, no mention of the palpitations haunting him in her presence. Every utterance was charged, highly charged. But because neither of them articulated the reasons why, Jake could convince himself that there was nothing wrong with their intimate conversations.

Yet part of him knew that without kissing her, without even touching her, he was already crossing a line, flirting with the flimsy boundary that separated platonic friendship from romantic interest. He was too interested in her history, too rapt at her every word, too conscious of his behavior around her to dismiss their interactions as inconsequential. If their conversations were as innocent as he wanted to pretend they were, he wouldn't feel guilty when he spent time with her. But there were reasons to feel guilty. He often imagined her naked. He regularly fantasized about sleeping with her. He actively considered what circumstances might lead to something physical. Ever since their first conversation, he could see the destruction of his marital fidelity on the horizon.

During the day, Jake and Selene were still friendly, but their conversations were collegial. Work was work, and their days were filled with routine. Jake was the commander, so he led her like he led the rest of the crew. He tried not to show favoritism toward her, but his affection for her made the task difficult. There was the time when one of the male crewmembers tried to explain what a volcano was to Selene.

Jake saw her rage and frustration rising, but she swallowed it. He stepped in, saying, "For god's sake, she's doing graduate work in the natural sciences. I think she knows what a volcano is."

She smiled at him slyly but appreciatively. Many other moments spoke to a subtle confederacy between them, but most only surfaced in a knowing look.

There were also moments of leisure among the crew. At the end of the first week at the Mars Analog Research Station, Jake and four of his crewmembers—Chris, Selene, John, and David—decided they wanted to take a break from their typical workday. They trekked to Olympus Mons, a ridge that was just over a half-mile away from the hab.

"Onward and upward," Chris said, taking the lead. They walked single file for much of the hike, and Jake hung toward the back. Selene was just in front of him, clad in her spacesuit like the rest of them. Her backpack bore the number five, serving as a reminder that her identity as Selene was subservient to her more anonymous numbered role as an experimenter. There was nothing personal or sexy about their circumstances. If anything, Jake and Selene were working together in just about the most unsexy way they could be. They were clothed head-to-toe in spacesuits. They proceeded along the ridge in a single-file line, whose rigidity evoked military drills. But Jake couldn't help but stare at her as she walked in front of him, swinging her hips.

When Jake and Selene went back to the hab, removed their suits in the airlocked prep room, and retreated to the upper floor of the structure, there was still nothing sexy about their work environment. All the furniture and equipment was built for function, and nothing seemed as clean as you might expect from scientists. The sleeping quarters consisted of nothing but a tight walkway and a raised narrow bed close to the ceiling. Their work schedules only made the prospect of a romantic relationship even more remote.

But Jake grew attached to Selene. Their midnight discussions got increasingly personal. He learned about her broken engagement, her struggles with depression, and her history with men who'd never transformed her from an ideal subject to a human being. And she knew about him too. She knew about the long stretches of sexless and companionless years that made him question his manhood during a formative time of his life; she knew about the rivalry with Radenport and the lingering trust issues that their competition had born. His intense connection to her was becoming dangerous to his marriage, so during the third week, he distanced himself from Selene. But not long after his distance campaign began in earnest, she knocked on the door of his sleeping quarters one night.

"Come in," he called out. Selene opened the door. "What's on your mind?" he asked as casually as he could manage, struggling to keep his cool while shirtless in his bed.

"Did I do something wrong? Do you have a problem with me or something?" she asked, standing in the doorway in an oversized sleep shirt and boxer shorts. "Because I thought we were getting along well, but lately, it seems like you've been avoiding me."

"I haven't been avoiding you," Jake said weakly.

"You don't have to lie. We're a close crew living in close quarters. If something is wrong, I need to know about it so we can fix this," Selene said, entering the room and closing the door behind her. Jake liked strong women and admired her assertiveness, even though it reminded him of Lilith.

"Maybe you're right. I have been avoiding you. I'm sorry. You haven't done anything wrong."

"So why have you been avoiding me?"

He took some time, looking away from her as he tried to find the words. "I'm married," he eventually said. "I've been avoiding you because I'm married."

"I get it. But the thing is, we still have a job to do here. We need to find a way to work together even if we're attracted to one another. You're the leader here, and no one is going to respect me if you keep avoiding me. They're going to think I'm not capable of doing the work," she said, back against the wall, posture easing once she made her case. The weak overhead light dulled her features, but her large, dark eyes penetrated him.

"No one is going to think that," Jake said. "You're too smart for them to think that." But even as he consoled Selene, all he could think about was one phrase she'd used: attracted to one another. Jake couldn't believe she'd felt something for him in return. Yes, there was an energy between them, one that felt shared, but she was so beautiful and intriguing that Jake had often wondered if their chemistry had been imagined, nothing more than the reflected glow of his intense feelings.

"I'm not so sure," Selene said. "Listen, you don't have to be overly nice to me or start spending all your time with me, just don't avoid me."

Jake got out of his bed, joining her in the narrow space beside it. He kissed her. She reciprocated with an urgency that surpassed his expectations about what their romance might feel like. Bodies clinging to one another, the two of them tumbled back onto the bed. The small dimensions of the space barely accommodated both of them, but neither of them minded. They still moved around passionately and occasionally bumped their elbows or heads or legs against the wall. They didn't care. After being isolated in their sim suits every day, they craved the close physical presence of one another and savored every second spent together in bed. At no time when he was with Selene in that bed did Jake think about Lilith. He didn't think about Lilith when he was running a finger down the smooth skin that covered Selene's spine. He didn't think about Lilith when he and Selene talked in nerdy amazement about the experience thus far, feeling united in an atmosphere designed to make them feel alone. He didn't think about Lilith when he told Selene about the ambitions he'd been too scared to reveal to anyone. He didn't think about Lilith when he laughed with Selene, poking her as if he were a flirtatious teenager.

It wasn't until the next morning that he thought about Lilith. Waking to Selene in his bed, Jake remembered the woman who was usually beside him, the one who first showed him deep but imperfect love. It had been so long since he'd first romanced his wife that it was hard to recall the passion of their initial attraction, the days when he'd thirsted for a mere glance from her. As powerful as his infatuation for Selene felt, Jake reminded himself that he'd once felt a similar, if less potent, lust for his wife's more measured beauty. His experience with Selene had renewed something he'd been missing from his life: novelty and excitement. But climbing out of bed, he worried about the cost of living his beautiful, indulgent fantasy, feeling the guilt of having carved a deep canyon inside his marriage.

:   :   10   :   :   :

Daniel Washington always hoped that his relationship with Rachel would provide Jake with a model for marriage. In the face of the routine difficulties that disbanded weaker unions, Daniel and Rachel stood side by side. Daniel knew that the stability of his marriage wouldn't ensure the security of his son's, but he hoped it would help. Daniel made a point of demonstrating his affection for his wife throughout Jake's childhood and adolescence. He'd kiss her on the stairwell or wrap an arm around her in the company of friends. He'd hug her before he headed for work and hug her when he returned home. They made important decisions together, modeling strong communication for their son.

Daniel wanted to ensure that his son knew what marriage could be at its best: intimate, grounding, and loving. When Jake struggled to find serious girlfriends in high school and college, Daniel pitied his son. But it wasn't until Jake, twenty-eight at the time, was home for the holidays and spoke with his dad that Daniel realized the high expectations set by his marriage might be partly to blame for Jake's problems.

"There's this girl I'm going to meet up with after the break. Lilith. Apparently, she's pretty. Nice. She just finished her last semester at Berkeley. Supposedly, the daughter of a winemaker or something. That's what Ken says, anyway," Jake said.

"Ken?" Daniel asked.

"Yeah, a post-doc in the department. He's the one who set it up. It's a blind date. Not exactly the love story of how you and Mom met."

Daniel thought back on all the times he'd recounted the early stages of his romance with Rachel. How many times had he told Jake the story? A few times? Ten times? More?

"Not all love stories look like ours," Daniel said.

"Yeah, so I've gathered. I guess I just want what you have."

"Listen, if you're open to finding someone, you will. Just know that when you find that other person, well, that feeling...? Love? It might not hit you over the head. Sometimes love takes time," Daniel said. Jake nodded in acceptance.

The trouble was that Jake was well aware Daniel had been struck over the head and thrust into love's path. It happened on June 23, 1967, when ten thousand people marched toward the Century Plaza Hotel. Daniel was one of them. When Daniel decided to protest the Vietnam War, he did so without the slightest hope of seeking romantic love. Love for his fellow man? Certainly. Love for the nation whose laws were the bedrock of his secular morality? Yes, that sort of love. Love for his best friend from high school who'd recently died fighting overseas? More than anything, that love was the love that drove Daniel to pick up a sign and join the legion of objectors.

123

He hoped to give voice not only to his righteous indignation, but also to his profound grief, which had no other outlet but tears that couldn't decontaminate, cleanse, and absolve the hurt. Since his identity was so intertwined with his sense of justice, Daniel knew he needed to be an advocate for the drafted men if he ever wanted to see himself as whole again—repaired, if shoddily, by his emerging legal voice. No, there had not been a passing consideration for romantic love when he descended onto the streets that day.

Perhaps if he'd been an English teacher or a dreamer, Daniel might have looked at a map, noticed that the Century Plaza was wedged between Avenue of the Stars and Constellation Boulevard, and deduced that an act of fate was bound to occur. But Daniel was literal-minded. Convinced he was the one in charge of his life and his future, Daniel prepared for the march in the early evening with little more than the hope of honoring Timothy Reinhardt.

"It looks good. Personal," Daniel's roommate Frank said, eyeing the poster Daniel made for the march. A photograph of Daniel's departed friend was in the center of the sign. In large letters, Daniel had written, "His name was Tim" over the picture.

"That's what I was going for," Daniel replied.

"No last name?"

"No last name."

"So your Tim is every Tim?"

"Right."

"There'll be others like yours," Frank said.

"As there should be," Daniel remarked. It didn't bother Daniel that Tim would be one name, one photo, in a sea of others. That was the point, wasn't it? Everything going on at the highest levels of government was tremendously personal, not just to a single citizen, but to far too many citizens.

"If Tim hadn't died, do you think you'd be marching in the streets?" Frank eventually asked, settling into the living room couch as Tim gathered his belongings.

124

"What kind of question is that?" Daniel asked, worried about where this was headed.

"It's just...I mean, how many brown children had to die before anyone here cared?"

The lawyer inside Daniel wanted to argue with his roommate, decrying the implications of his question, but this was no time for litigation. This was about Tim. Swallowing his frustration and gritting his teeth, Daniel grabbed his poster, put on his shoes, and headed to the march. When Daniel arrived, the protest had already begun in earnest. There were thousands of people walking toward the Century Plaza Hotel, signs in hand. Marchers began singing the national anthem, then "America the Beautiful." Daniel lent his voice to the chorus of his fellow patriots. The mention of "brotherhood" stung as it came out of his mouth, but he delivered a full-throated endorsement of the word regardless.

As the protestors neared the hotel, the shouts and whispers and conversation around him grew, buzzing with a chaotic fury that melded into harmony. Daniel surrendered himself to the chorus of the masses. He rubbed elbows with men and women whose names were unknown to him. There were no Toms or Marthas or Ryans here. There was no Daniel, either. There was only the collective will of the people. When the protesters rammed into one another as the police funneled the crowd through narrow pathways, Daniel didn't perceive the thuds as instruments of violence. Instead, the blows were shared war wounds that connected him to mothers, fathers, sisters, and brothers with the most potent adhesive: mutual pain that feels like a balm even as it stings. But the unity dissipated as the unrest mounted. Police helicopters circled in the sky, projecting threats and discord.

"I command you in the name of the people of the state of California to disperse. If you fail to disperse and leave the area, you will be arrested," a police officer said to the crowd over a loudspeaker.

Here was the hand of the law. Daniel's instinct to obey the law compelled him to leave. But when he neared the edges of the crowd, lined with police officers in white-helmeted riot gear, Daniel watched a cop raise a baton and pummel a middle-aged woman who had shouted, "Gestapo!" at the police. Daniel ran toward her.

"Is so much force really justified?" Daniel asked the police officer, whose face was still taut with rage at the woman he'd hit.

"You think I'm part of the Gestapo too? You don't look like a Jew," the officer said. Daniel gritted his teeth. "You heard the announcement to disperse. This protest is unlawful. You want to be arrested?" the officer asked.

"No, sir," Daniel said. "But I do want you to explain yourself."

"I don't need to explain anything," the officer said, grabbing Daniel by the arm. Daniel pulled away, trying to wrest his arm from the officer's clutches. That was when the baton struck Daniel's head, and he collapsed onto the ground.

Daniel felt people lifting him by his arms and his legs, removing him from the turbulent center of the protest. Once they put him down, it took a while for him to recover. He fell in and out of consciousness. When he came to, he saw the face of a woman leaning over him in the darkness. She attended to the gash on his head, using the first aid kit from her nurse's bag. Her white nursing gown stood out in the night. It reassured him, even as he noticed the blood, *his* blood, that was splashed across her chest.

Occasionally, she would lift her head to survey the scene, and Daniel would get a glimpse of her features in the half-light of the streetlamps. Camera flashbulbs went off as the media covered the tumult, and when the light shone too brightly on her, she flinched. Daniel only got to see her whole face illuminated for an instant at a time, but that was all he needed. In those seconds, the flash of the camera

126

generated a spark inside him: not just attraction but a strange feeling of belonging to this woman, this signifier of the unknown. In the absence of his connection with Tim, he welcomed the touch of the anonymous nurse whose fingers grazed his face.

"Stay calm," she told him. "You're all right."

"Are you real?" he asked her, stunned by her angelic features.

"Are *you*?" she responded, smiling.

"*Am* I?" he suddenly considered, dazed by his head trauma.

"That was cruel of me. I shouldn't have said that. You and I are both real. We're real, and we're alive. There is no truer statement than that. You just hurt your head."

"What's your name?" he asked, even though he worried that learning her name would box her into a set of expectations, as names often did.

"Rachel," she said. "But that's not important right now."

The name suited her, but Daniel was glad she dismissed its significance too. Right now, he was just a young man, and she, a young woman, and they both seemed to understand that all that mattered was her touch against his skin—compassionate and intimate, the sort of handshake their relationship already warranted. In the darkness and his wooziness, Daniel imagined her at other points in time, thrust into his infant past and his more-adult future, seeing the mother and wife she would eventually become already painted onto his psyche. Freed from the hesitation that would have gripped him if not for the effects of blunt force trauma, Daniel cast a hand across her face.

"Who are *you*?" she asked, laughing.

This was not the sort of love that grew out of friendship or collegiality or enough time. This was a love born from the Earth and the Underworld. This was the primordial love from The Beginning of Time that only strikes the exceptionally lucky, creating fodder for fairy tales that most people write off as unrealistic. Daniel should have known not to tell his son this story years later. Maybe if Daniel had kept this love story from Jake, Daniel might have spared his son the disappointment that comes from settling into a good enough marriage, knowing full well other people had it better.

:   :   :   10   :   :

When Barrie Stevenson met Jacqueline Barnabas on the day of his high school graduation in 1968, marriage and family were the furthest things from his mind. The graduation ceremony had just ended, and Barrie received the requisite shoulder pats from his old man and his grandfather, both of whom were former army sergeants wearing full military attire in honor of the procession. The sight of the pins and freshly pressed seams pushed Barrie over the edge. He was ready to bust out. Once he was out of his family's view, he wasted no time liberating his long, wavy hair from the constraints of the mortarboard. He kept on his graduation robe because it concealed the joint that was protruding from the pocket of his jeans. His priority was finding a place to smoke his joint, but as he was pushing through the crowd, Jacqueline approached him. Her eyes were wide and suggestive, ripe with innocence and intrigue. Even though she wore her mother's pearls around her neck and a ribbon tied across her flipped-up hair, her dress was short enough that Barrie could imagine some devil inside her.

"Barrie, right?" she asked him. He thought she might extend her arm out for a formal handshake. She seemed like the type to do that. Instead, she introduced herself with her arms anchored behind her back, shoulders moving sprightly at the sound of her name. "You know, I've been meaning to talk to you for a long time now, but I couldn't get up the nerve to say anything until today," she said.

"Oh yeah?" Barrie asked casually. Her intentions were obvious enough, but he knew he had to keep his cool if he wanted anything to progress.

"Yeah. I love listening to you play. So groovy. I've heard you at lunch. I thought you should know how great you are," Jacqueline smiled and blushed.

"Thanks," he said, considering his next move. Jacqueline looked at him like he was a god, and all he could think to do was to provide an offering to the faithful. "Listen, you wanna go somewhere and get high?"

"Only if you bring your guitar," she said. It was a bargain that Barrie was happy to strike. They hopped into his car and headed toward his place.

"So. What now?" Jacqueline asked him as they drove.

"I figured after I grab my guitar, we could walk to the cliffs."

"No, I mean, what are you going to do now that you've graduated?"

"Oh," Barrie said. He had a decision to make about how much of himself to expose. When she looked up at him with those doe eyes, he wanted to confess everything to her: his aimlessness, his father's insistence that he join the family business or serve his goddamn country, his reluctance to do either. But he knew such confessions wouldn't get him laid.

"I don't wanna think about that right now," Barrie said. "I just need to do some living for a while. If it turns you on, do it, you know?"

"I dig you," she said, nodding her head.

Jacqueline stretched out her arm and touched the wooden beads slung around his rear-view mirror. "I love this," she said, as she took the tasseled end and rolled the strings between her fingers. "What is it?"

"It's called a mala. It's a string of prayer beads that Hindus and Buddhists use."

"Makes sense. You look like a monk right now," she teased, tugging the edge of the red graduation robe he was still wearing. Her joke calmed him. Barrie preferred thinking of his robe as a symbol of monastic order rather than acknowledging its real purpose anyway.

"Why do you have this?" she asked, turning her attention back to the mala in her right hand. "You a Buddhist or a Hindu or something?"

"Nah, nothing like that. You know Salinger?"

"Who doesn't? We just read *Catcher in the Rye* in English class."

"That was one of the only books I read in school. I loved it, so I read the rest of Salinger's stuff. He's my god. And Buddhism, Hinduism, all that Eastern religion talk, that's Salinger's thing. Keeping this mala around, that's how I stay close to him."

"So you're one of those types who thinks he's Holden Caulfield?"

"I never realized that was a 'type.' I figured everyone felt like Holden Caulfield."

They pulled up to his house. He ran inside and grabbed his guitar. He and Jacqueline walked toward the cliffs. Mere feet away from the bluffs, the ocean air reached them. Barrie couldn't think of anywhere he'd rather be than here, staring at the roughly hewn edges of the world, breathing in the beauty without a thought for tomorrow. Barrie threw down a blanket, sat down, and lit up his joint. Jacqueline took a hit and had a coughing fit. She shrugged off any suggestion that she was inexperienced at this sort of thing. Barrie was flattered by the lie, drinking in the power that came from watching someone bend to his will before he even tried to exert it. It was nice, her innocence. Part of him wanted to protect her as he exploited her.

After whittling away the joint, Barrie held up his end of the bargain and played "Sunshine of Your Love" on the guitar, channeling Jack Bruce with an aptitude that only surfaced when he had just the right amount of pot coursing through him. At times, Barrie kept his eyes closed while

130

singing, capitulating to the pulse of the music. Other times, Barrie opened his eyes, looking at Jacqueline, who gazed at him with adoration. He knew the power of a guitar and a decent set of pipes because he'd melted girls before. Jacqueline was like the rest of them, a puddle of submission. After the song, he and Jacqueline made out on the blanket, slowly working their way through one another at a pace set by their lazy high, hands and lips seeking out pleasure without ambition. He couldn't tell how long this lasted because his high broke down the continuity of space and time, but he snapped back to reality when she told him, "I better go."

That was the beginning of the two of them, Jacqueline and Barrie. They continued meeting up to get high and fool around for months after that. It wasn't long before he took her virginity, and in doing so, bound her to him with an implicit promise he wasn't sure he could honor. It wasn't so bad, though, having a devotee. She was pretty. Sweet. Then on the night of November 10th, she asked if she could stop by his place. When she arrived, she told him she was pregnant. Maybe the condom had broken, maybe it'd just failed, she wasn't sure. Barrie didn't know what to say. All he knew was he couldn't be a father. And then it came out—the mother of all lies.

"Jackie, I...I should have told you earlier, but...I enlisted in the army," he said.

"What are you talking about? Is this some kind of sick joke? You hate the war."

"My dad served in World War II," Barrie explained, not just to Jacqueline, but also to himself, since he'd been almost as surprised by his words as she'd been.

"So did mine, but that wasn't 'Nam. And why enlist now? I didn't think we even needed any more troops after Tet. I thought we were going to get the hell out of there."

"The war's still on."

"And you're going to fight?" she cried. "Even with the baby coming?"

Especially with the baby coming, he thought. But he said nothing, only shushed her and held her tightly. Was he going to do this? Enlist? Yes, it was the only way to get away and preserve his dignity. His father would get off his back. His grandfather too.

The next day he signed up, and soon after that, he started his training. He deployed just as Jacqueline began to show. He thought about her carrying the baby over the coming months. He could picture her graduating in a robe like the one he'd been wearing on the day they'd met, only she'd be hiding a baby underneath the sacramental garb, not a joint. It was too much to bear. He decided not to tell her his deployment date because he didn't want to deal with the dramatics of a final farewell, the tears and the accusations and the frustration. Without so much as a goodbye, he was gone.

Other soldiers in Vietnam had girls back home: sweethearts whose faces got passed around any time anyone felt homesick, any time anyone needed a reminder that there was another world out there, an honest-to-goodness American world unsullied by blood and napalm, one where pretty teenaged fiancées went grocery shopping and had a gas with their girlfriends at the record store and wrote letters about it. There was so much hope in the men's eyes when they'd talk about Judy or Rebecca or Betty. Barrie wanted what those men had: the hope. Even though Jacqueline's beauty could best those girls on a bad day, Barrie didn't have a picture of her. He didn't need one. Didn't want one.

Whenever a guy would ask, "You got someone back home?" Barrie would lie and say, "No, man, I got no one," until he realized it wasn't a lie. Jacqueline, by virtue of that growing belly, was not his, would not be his, could not be his. Wasn't that the reason he was in this godforsaken jungle, evading gunfire, constantly looking for Charlie in the trees, wrecking his nerves?

At first, it hadn't seemed so bad, this plan of his—serve his country as his family had long expected him to, hang out at the base, and play football with the boys. But his time at the base was limited. Extended stays in the cushy base camps were for the rear-echelon motherfuckers: the commandos and the skilled labor with a specific task to do. Barrie was no REMF, just a boot, a combat heel, and he was going to have to tough it out in the hellacious heat, sweating himself apart while keeping an ever-vigilant eye out for the enemy. Much of the time in the jungle was horrifically boring. Nothing happened for days. The chronic monotony was all the worse because the men knew that it wouldn't last.

Barrie saw action like everyone else. After his first firefight, Barrie questioned his sanity, wondering why the fuck he ever thought this was a good idea. He went back to those moments on the cliffs of Palos Verdes, thinking about the scent of Jacqueline's perfume: the rose hips and jasmine and citrus. He remembered how it would combine with the plumes of pot smoke, suddenly earthy. Barrie could still taste the saltiness of the ocean that clung to her. The sea air turned the sweetness of her perfume savory. Every lick, every kiss of her skin, delivered both a meal and a dessert. Those times had been easy, and from the vantage of the Asian jungle after a firefight, perfect. But then he'd consider Jacqueline's abdomen and the way that it'd started to swell when he'd left, like the end of low tide sending mild yet building waves before an imminent storm. Whenever his mind would wander to the reaches of her uterus, he thanked the jungle for its distractions: its heat, weapons, camaraderie, marijuana, and terror.

There were times when Barrie and the men would come across villages that were seemingly abandoned by the enemy. Without the VC, children ran around as if there wasn't a war on. The villages were ramshackle—the dirt-floor huts were

133

dilapidated, there were piss and shit on the ground from the diaperless babies and toddlers, trash was preserved like keepsakes. But the poverty of the Vietnamese was no excuse in the eyes of many soldiers.

"Sympathizers, every last one of 'em," one of the soldiers said.

"Time to do a sweep, make sure Charlie doesn't have any weapons hidden," a lieutenant ordered when they arrived into one of the villages.

"I'll check over here," Barrie said, motioning to a makeshift "temple" that the villagers had created. There was a red paper tablecloth spread out over a stack of bricks, and on display were incenses shoved into empty Budweiser cans. Barrie could see his fellow soldiers toppling over people's meager possessions indelicately, and he was glad he would be the one to inspect the shrine. Carefully, he lifted the Budweiser cans, pulling out the incense sticks and looking down the pop-top holes to make sure nothing was stashed in the holy vessels. Barrie noticed an older man sitting near the temple in prayer. Unlike the other villagers whose totems and rituals served the gods, goddesses, and spirits of the local folk religion, this man had a mala in his hands.

"Buddhist?" Barrie asked the man after searching the temple. The man didn't speak English. He simply smiled and bowed his head, focusing on the prayer beads. The wrinkles around his eyes, eyes that had doubtless seen unspeakable violence in the previous months, betrayed nothing. This was no Salinger. This was someone wholly un-American. Barrie went to the man, got down on his knees, grasped the spare end of the mala, pressed a bead to his forehead, and wept. The Vietnamese man placed a hand on his shoulder and cried too. When Barrie looked up and saw the man's tears, Barrie dropped the bead and walked away, convinced that both he and the man knew nothing and would always know nothing.

Days later, still thinking of the older man, Barrie trekked through the jungle. The image of the prayer beads brought a blankness to his mind until the firefight started. It was far and away the most intense firefight Barrie had witnessed during his time in the bush. Barrie watched men around him, his brothers in arms, go down: one killed with a bullet to the head, one injured with a shot to the leg, and one blown apart yards away by a grenade. Barrie knew he wasn't equipped for any of this; he was the weakest kind of coward, and there wouldn't be any salvation for him, not now, not ever. The shot rang out. When the bullet pierced his skin, Barrie screamed out for help. A buddy turned around, saw Barrie, and pulled him to safety. By the time Barrie made it to a medic, he was fading from the blood loss. Even so, he had enough life in him to wonder whether or not the injury was severe enough to get him back to America.

He thought of Jacqueline. She would be there, stateside, and as the medic put pressure on his wound, Barrie countered the hard strain on his body by considering the softness of her body. In his moment of weakness, he ached for her and imagined waking to the sight of her face. But then Barrie remembered the child—the reason he ran, the reason he might still run. The blood sped through him, and even though Barrie had no idea that he would have *two* sons waiting for him at home, his pulse surged at a double pace. I can't do this forever, he thought. I can't keep running, can't fake my way through life, not forever, maybe a bit longer, a lot longer, there's still time…and just like that, he slipped out of consciousness.

:　:　:　:　5　:

Sebastian's father taught him how to disappear. His mother did too. It wasn't hard. Not when you were used to doing it. It didn't require the sleight of hand of a veteran magician, just a trained dissociation from other people. It turned out that when you were used to being abandoned, it became all too easy to abandon other people. But there were side effects. A lifetime of abandonment left Sebastian wondering whether or not he was capable of truly loving anyone. The thought colored every casual sexual interaction. But suddenly, in the middle of his life, Sebastian thought he finally felt it. Maybe. Love. It happened about a year ago. Sebastian was sitting in a conference room, waiting for Diana Hyland—his colleague and department chair—to arrive for her talk. Five minutes before the scheduled start of her lecture, she entered the room. Her brown curls were untamed but lovely; her angular features made her look distinguished. Her thick triceps bulged from her sleeveless dress as she wheeled in a couple of blackboards, one in each hand.

"You need help with those?" Sebastian asked, approaching her.

"Oh, hey, Sebastian," she said, cocking her head in greeting. "I've got them."

"Where'd you get these? I thought there weren't any blackboards on site."

"I bought them at an office supply store nearby."

"You didn't want to use digital slides like everyone else?"

"You and I both know that's not the same as giving a chalk talk," she said, arranging the blackboards so that they were front and center.

"Sure," Sebastian admitted. "But you committed. When the organizers told me there wouldn't be blackboards here, I didn't think twice about using PowerPoint."

"I'm sure you didn't," she said, flashing a quick, satisfied smile. "Anyway, listen, I should get set up. The moderator's going to introduce me any minute."

"Good luck up there," Sebastian offered. After she thanked him, Sebastian headed toward his seat in the audience.

Sebastian watched as Diana readied herself for the presentation. She put a jacket on over her dress, secured a nametag to the lapel, and drank bottled water. She removed colored chalk from a box and placed the sticks along the bottom of the blackboard. Sebastian still couldn't believe she'd brought chalkboards here. What would she do with them after the conference? Was she going to drive them up to Palo Alto from San Diego? Would she donate them somewhere before she left? How had she gotten them here in the first place? Had she strapped them to the top of her car like a Christmas tree? Had she walked them from an office supply store? It was compulsive, her decision to bring those blackboards into a conference that had explicitly told speakers their only resources would be digital. Still, Sebastian admired her for it, in part because he saw himself in her stubborn adherence to her preferences.

"I want to spend most of my time focusing on the combinatorics of non-crossing partitions," she began, "but I'll veer off here and there into some related topics if only to keep things interesting."

Sebastian watched as she constructed Cayley graphs on the blackboard—color-coded charts that mapped combinations of numbers. Her graphs looked like art: the lines, the colors, the curves, and the composition felt balanced and essential. The tangle of lines wove its way across the board in perfect synchrony with her words. Like any good lecturer, Diana did math with her entire body, channeling her mind onto the blackboard with a gesticular force that enthralled Sebastian. Not all professors knew how to animate their lectures with a narrative thrust, but Diana did. Sebastian was spellbound.

Eventually, she ran out of blackboard space, but she didn't skip a beat. Diana erased her previous work, a task most lecturing professors were unwilling to do. She started fresh. The blackboard was cheap, and her early work was never entirely erased, but Sebastian liked looking into the portal of her past thoughts as he listened to her lecture. It was all connected in a way that made sense to him: the way the past was always there, the way you could overwrite it with new thoughts that only partially obscured their origins. The pink wrote over the green, wrote over the blue. She was weaving her tapestry on the board when a much older mathematician interrupted her.

"In my early work, I relied on a unimodality conjecture related to Young's lattice. I think that's the best way to understand the problem you've laid out," he said.

"Dr. Krezlov, of course, I know your work well," she responded. "I'm thrilled to have you in the audience today. I have a different approach that I want to work through right now, but I'll reference some of your ideas as I continue. I can briefly touch on the conjecture you're referring to after I take this in the direction I'd envisioned."

Damn impressive, Sebastian thought. He knew he couldn't have handled that moment as Diana had. Whenever mathematicians tried to co-opt his talks and push their approaches, Sebastian became adversarial. He dreaded those interjections because he didn't have the patience to defuse the situation artfully. But Diana was able to cage the narcissistic beast. She continued, and whenever she noticed Krezlov preparing to raise his hand or open his mouth, she sidestepped the interruptions by casually addressing methods he'd used in his papers. It was masterful. Soon Sebastian would give his own lecture. He knew he wouldn't be able to manage interruptions as well as she could. He fidgeted at the thought but dove back into thinking about the math she was discussing. As promised, she ventured into unexpected territory after covering the basics of her most recent paper. She drew binary trees on the blackboard, speaking in mathematical terms that were evocative to Sebastian on multiple levels: words like "family" and "children" and "parents."

Later, when it was Sebastian's turn to give a lecture, he felt raw, like something had split open inside him. He was fortunate not to have a Krezlov type in his audience, but he did have to contend with Diana. She was sitting in the second row, smack in the middle. Every click of the PowerPoint felt inelegant when he looked over at her and recalled the way her hand had glided across the blackboard, keeping pace with her words. Her lecture had been so fluid and organic that his digital presentation felt rigid and rehearsed by comparison. He wished he had a blackboard, but at least the PowerPoint kept him focused, which eased the stress of looking at Diana. She was engaged, taking notes. Now and then, she'd smile. Whenever that happened, he would stumble, thinking about her thinking about him. He'd lose himself and then…click. Next slide. He'd be back in the thick of it.

Sebastian finished his lecture and was glad his presentation was the last of the day. Right after his talk ended, Sebastian made his way to the hotel bar with a flock of mathematicians. He spotted Diana and sidled up next to her.

"You were the most brilliant mind at the conference today," Sebastian said to Diana.

"Thanks," she said, taking a sip from her wine. "But I thought your talk was better."

"No way. It was incredible the way you dealt with Krezlov. I would have lost it."

"The benefits of being a woman. Knowing how to stroke men's egos to make them less threatening. Knowing how to smile when you'd rather tell them to go to hell."

"It's a gift."

"It's also a curse."

"Yeah. It can't be easy being a woman in math."

"It's not. But you know, life's not easy. Not for anyone," she said, drinking her highball. *Not for anyone*, he thought. A gracious gesture. She let him into the circle of pain and commiseration when she didn't have to. There was something easy about her. In her presence, Sebastian felt like he could just exist. He wasn't doing the mental calculus he

139

usually did with women, trying to say just the right thing. Sebastian and Diana continued talking for a while about her experiences at Stanford. She described a working environment that felt foreign to Sebastian, even though he worked in the same department at the same university. Diana showed him how much his maleness informed his experience. There were times when Sebastian thought he would say the wrong thing, and there were times when he *did* say the wrong thing, but he let himself be imperfect and authentic, and she seemed to recognize that.

Sebastian looked her over. He loved the casual way she leaned her arm against the bar. Her loose, unruly curls spilled onto her shoulders and framed her makeup-less face beautifully. The floral-print dress she wore under her blazer sensually stuck to her hips. He was taking it all in when his eye caught a smudge of green chalk on her jacket.

"Do you mind?" Sebastian asked, gesturing toward the chalk on her blazer with a wetted napkin in hand.

"Not at all, wipe away," Diana said. He cleaned the mess. "I can't believe I didn't notice that earlier. The perils of working with chalk. Look at this," she directed him, fanning out her fingers so he could see the residue underneath her nails. "I swear, I'm going to have color stuck under there forever. I've been working away at it all afternoon."

"Mathematician's nail polish," he replied, taking hold of her hand and examining her fingers more closely. "It suits you."

"I can't tell if that's a compliment or not."

"It is," he smiled.

"It doesn't make me seem like a slob?"

"No. You're no slob. Just a thinker. A colorful one," he said, realizing he was still holding her fingers. He let go but not before sending her a longing gaze. Once their stare became drawn out, she averted her eyes and took another sip of her highball.

"So...I have to ask," Sebastian started. "What are you going to do with those blackboards now that your lecture is over?"

"Why? You want 'em?"

"Are you crazy?" Sebastian responded, laughing at the thought.

"What's so crazy about it?"

"We're in San Diego. How would I get them to Palo Alto?"

"Who says you need to take them back to Palo Alto? Just use them while you're here. Leave them for someone else to use. Say, what room are you in?"

"Five-ten."

"All right. I'm going to settle my tab. Then I'm bringing the blackboards up to you," Diana said, her face mischievous.

"You're incorrigible."

"It's my best quality," she said, smiling.

When Sebastian got to his room after paying his tab, Diana was waiting outside with the blackboards, as promised. He opened the door, and she wheeled in the goods. He kept the overhead lights off but turned on a bedside lamp. Meanwhile, she positioned one of the blackboards in the center of the room. She handed Sebastian a piece of chalk.

"Chalk something for me," Diana said.

"You first," Sebastian replied, picking up a piece of chalk and placing it in her hand. She pushed him onto the edge of the bed, fashioning him into an audience member. She discussed partitions, speaking with a seductive authority that demanded his attention. But then she softened and began drawing Ferrers diagrams for fun, filling the board with dots. She extended her hand and pulled Sebastian up. He joined her, contributing dots of his own that completed her partition patterns. They made an organized mess of the board, scrawling a code that would appear random to an untrained passerby. They would ask each other questions that required numerical answers and use dots to respond to one another graphically. He asked her how many times she'd been in love. She paused before she drew a partition of the number five, her hand slowly forming the dots, her face contemplative.

"Your turn to answer," she said. Instead of responding, Sebastian dropped the chalk. Their lips found one another's. Everything moved fast from that point on. Diana and Sebastian spent the night together in his hotel room, exploring one another with an insatiable thirst that regenerated him, restoring life where he hadn't realized it was lacking. Sebastian had experienced wild sexual encounters in the past. But his night with Diana was unforgettable, not because she exposed him to a new sexual position or gave him a multi-orgasmic endorsement of approval, but because she harnessed raw sexuality and imbued it with an intimacy that didn't scare him. Perhaps this union felt so intoxicating because Diana was so much like him. She was as intelligent as he was, and her lecture at the conference had proved it. When he'd told her earlier that she'd been the most brilliant participant there, he hadn't just been flattering her. He genuinely believed she'd outperformed him that day. Like Sebastian, she was self-assured. But unlike Sebastian, she was soft. He held her, clutching the body of a woman who was older and larger than most of the women he'd been with. He liked it. Her substance. The way she took up space.

Was this love? He couldn't be sure. It was the closest he'd ever come to the emotion, but there were lingering questions. Was it possible to fall in love with someone so quickly? Could he love Diana without knowing about her elementary Girl Scout excursions or her middle school heartbreaks or her early role models or her broken bones? How much information did you need to know about another person before you could convincingly argue a case of love? He had a nagging feeling most people would write off his emotions as mere lust. Infatuation. A few years of casual acquaintanceship plus a day's lecture plus a night of drinking plus a night of sex could not possibly constitute love. Could it? But if it couldn't be enough, then why had it felt like enough? Whatever it was, this may-be, might-be love, it was over almost as soon as it had begun, ruined the way Sebastian ruined every relationship he'd ever had, torn apart by the wreckage of his womanizing. Diana went back to being his department chair, no longer his lover, and Sebastian waited for the day when he might know for sure what this thing called love was.

: : : : : 1

Sebastian didn't understand filial or fraternal love much better than he understood romantic love. But there was some amount of love that couldn't be trained out of him. No matter how much his mother and his father had hardened his heart, there was still a kernel buried inside him, even if it lay fallow. It must have been that kernel that compelled him to invite Jake to the Golden Gate Bridge. He needed Jake to understand how small the kernel inside him was, how untilled. That was why he'd taken Jake to the place where his mother had threatened suicide. Once Sebastian and Jake reached Crissy Field, the watershed moment when Sebastian had disclosed his mother's suicide attempt was already in the past. Wordlessly, Sebastian set his sights on their destination, the Warming Hut Café and Bookstore on the Presidio. The Warming Hut was an old Army building that had been converted into a café, a shelter from the San Francisco cold.

"This place has a history," Sebastian said as he and Jake waited in line to order coffee at the café. "This used to be a storeroom for an underwater mine operation that began at the turn of the century. The mines lasted through both World Wars."

One of the employees at the café had given Sebastian background about the place the last time he'd come, but he'd done a deeper dive into the history on his own afterward. Ever since he was old enough to understand the severity of war, and by extension, the likely shape of his father's service, he cared about war history.

"You know our father was a veteran. Vietnam," Sebastian said. "He was over there when we were born."

"Is that why he wasn't in the picture? I remember you saying he wasn't around."

"I don't know if it was just the war. Now and then, he and my mom would reunite when I was young. He'd talk to me about the war in vague ways. Mention the sacrifice. The buddies he'd had who never made it out. One year, he got me a model kit for building a replica of a Bell AH-1G Assault Copter," Sebastian said, remembering how much he'd cherished that plastic vehicle of war.

"I had replicas too. No helicopters, though. Mostly World-War-II-era planes. Anything too close to Vietnam made my parents uncomfortable."

"Did your dad serve?" Sebastian asked, but based on Jake's response, he could already intuit the answer. Sebastian watched Jake's face crumple in apprehension, brow knitted as he searched for the words to frame his family's narrative.

"No," Jake said, hedging at a slow pace. "He was finishing up law school when the draft began. He and my mom actually met at an anti-war protest. But in his early years as a lawyer, he represented a lot of veterans pro bono. Still does sometimes. He lost a good friend to the war and wanted to do his part. You know, in his own way."

Sebastian nodded, feeling on the other side of an invisible divide from Jake. It felt appropriate that Sebastian's father had taken a bullet...that Jake's father had dodged one. But

144

Sebastian knew this wasn't a war of nobility; neither side was free from blood.

"I wonder what my father might have been like if he hadn't gone to fight. Maybe he wouldn't have been so damaged. Maybe he would have stuck around. Who knows, you and I might have grown up together if he'd stayed put instead of leaving my mom on her own," Sebastian said, doubting the productivity of these musings even as he voiced them. He'd often thought about the legacy of his father's fighting. Usually, he found the war a convenient excuse to exonerate his father from too much blame. But now, envisioning this alternate reality made Sebastian more resentful of his father's decision to enlist. The talk of Jake's anti-war parents reminded Sebastian of the peace sign on his father's guitar case. Sebastian had traced it with his finger as a kid like a maze, but it struck adult Sebastian as hypocritical given his father's reluctance to fully support or fully denounce the war when he returned. Sebastian wondered whether it was a sign of cowardice or complexity.

"I've been torturing myself with 'what ifs' lately," Jake said.

"As in, what if your parents had told you about your adoption sooner?"

"Right. Your story adds another dimension. But I'm glad you asked to meet up again," Jake said, his almond-shaped eyes meeting Sebastian's with candor. "I needed to hear all this. About your father. Your mother. I would never have guessed you had it so hard. I mean, I know you mentioned it at the diner, but I had trouble focusing that day. I was still getting used to the idea that you existed. But I can't wish you away, and I'm getting the feeling your childhood was worse than I could have imagined."

"That's probably because you had a functional childhood."

"What good is a functional childhood if you can't have a functional adulthood?"

"You seem to be doing all right," Sebastian said, reluctant to admit that Jake's struggles were anywhere near as profound as his own.

"I guess," Jake responded, averting his eyes. Sebastian could see apprehension building in Jake's absent gaze, but he couldn't fully understand its source.

"Listen, no one *really* has a functional adulthood," Sebastian offered, losing his grip on any resentment he'd held against Jake. Jake was too fearful. He didn't warrant jealousy. "What about your family? Have you talked to them about this? About me?" Sebastian asked, curious how more reliable parents might have navigated these circumstances.

"To some extent," Jake sidestepped.

"To what extent?"

"Barely," Jake confessed. "It isn't exactly easy."

"It seems like 'barely' is a problem," Sebastian said. Despite his inability to get through to his mother, Sebastian knew that other families lived in a world where talking could bring resolution, closure, and growth.

Jake paused and sipped his coffee.

"Can I ask you a question?" Jake managed, sullen and introspective.

"Sure."

"Doesn't it ever make you shrink inside yourself to know I'm out in the world with your face and with your voice? I mean, doesn't it make you feel cheated? Like nothing is your own anymore, and at any second, someone could just take your life away from you? Because that's how I've been feeling," Jake said, tearing away at his napkin as he had done during their first encounter. "And I'm not trying to blame you. I'm just wondering if you've been feeling what I've been feeling."

"Listen. We may look alike. We may sound alike. But we are not the same person. So to answer your question: no. I don't feel what you feel because I'm not you. If anything, knowing I'm one half of a twin makes me feel less alone.

Like I'm part of something bigger," Sebastian said, processing his feelings.

"I'm just used to people taking what's mine," Jake said, hunched over the café table, looking up at Sebastian with pained intensity.

"You can't let anyone do that."

"It's not like I *let* them do it. Sometimes they use force."

"Then use force against them," Sebastian suggested. There was a flicker in Jake's eye, like the dawning of an idea. "Just don't use force against me," Sebastian continued. "I don't want to take anything from you. I'm not the enemy here."

"I know you're not," Jake said, reflexively moving his body closer to Sebastian in a show of solidarity. "I blame my parents. They could have told me everything years ago. Aren't you mad at your mom?"

"Sure. But that's not exactly a new emotion for me. My mom's got a whole lot of black marks against her, so what's one more added to the tally?"

"But don't you feel betrayed?" Jake asked.

"You can only feel betrayed by someone who had your trust to begin with. It sounds like your parents had your trust. Maybe it's time you let them earn it back," Sebastian said. He knew it was futile to get his mother to see past her damage and defensiveness, but perhaps he could steer Jake in a better direction.

"I don't know," Jake responded.

"Listen, maybe it's not my place to say anything. I don't know much about your family. What were your parents like when you were younger? Reasonable? Supportive?"

"Yeah. They were great. Until now, I couldn't complain."

"Well, all I know is, if I had loving parents who provided me with a stable life, I might be more forgiving of them. Just remember, you could have had a truly shit parent. You could have had my mother."

147

"Was it that bad?"

How could Sebastian consolidate a lifetime of neglect into a few sentences? He struggled to find the words. Just as he thought he might venture a response, his cell phone rang. He looked down at the number.

"You need to take that?" Jake asked Sebastian.

"No," Sebastian replied. "They can leave a message. It's the lawyer's office calling again. I'm involved in a lawsuit. I'm sure it's about the deposition I have to do."

"Are you the plaintiff or the defendant?" Jake asked.

"Neither exactly. A key witness, I suppose. My former colleague, Mallory, is suing Stanford for wrongful termination and gender discrimination. She blames me because I had a relationship with both her and the department chair, a woman named Diana. Mallory thinks Stanford let her go because of that whole mess."

"Sounds like a headache."

"You have no idea. This woman, Mallory, she's a nightmare."

"I think I have a colleague who could rival yours," Jake said before explaining the backstory of his fraught relationship with William Radenport. Jake and Sebastian spent the rest of the time talking about their lives as they were living them in the present: their jobs, their relationships, and their conflicts. Sebastian was glad to see that for all of their differences, there were too many similarities to discount. He left feeling better about Jake.

As Sebastian made his way to his car, he listened to his voicemail. "Sebastian," the message began, "This is Patricia from Westin and Carruthers. I wanted to confirm your appointment at our offices this Friday at 5:00. Please make it this time. We can't keep drawing this out. Believe it or not, we're on your team."

Sebastian deleted the message and went home. When he arrived at his condo, he pulled out a cigarette and lit it, contemplating his next move. Work. He wanted to pursue something new. He took a drag of his cigarette and thought about Jake. That's when Sebastian figured out his next passion project: the Twin Prime Conjecture. Prime numbers appealed to Sebastian—their strangeness, their unconventional properties. The Twin Prime Conjecture, which concerned the gaps between prime numbers, would be perfect. At a time when Sebastian was evaluating his relationship with Jake, an investigation into the relative spaces between strange entities seemed enticing. Sebastian hoped to prove that there were infinitely many "twin prime numbers," primes whose distance from one another is only two. Sebastian took one last drag of his cigarette. He went to his desk and began pouring over proofs that might help him access the conjecture. He settled in, confident he would show that he was not so rare, that he and Jake were not so rare.

The First Diagonals
Natural Numbers: Chronology

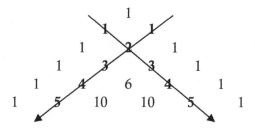

In Pascal's triangle, the numbers featured in the first set of diagonals (1, 2, 3, 4, 5, etc.) are the natural numbers in sequential order.

An incomplete record of the life of Jake Washington:

→ **Age 1 – 1970:** The first word Jake ever says is "nana": the baby-talk his family uses to label his grandmother. Her happy tears roll onto his scalp, barely catching in his hair since the follicles are too delicate to hold the weight.

→ **Age 2 – 1971:** Jake learns the contours of his face by perusing the form of his Other. Consulting an imperfect replica, Jake experiences toddlerhood under the misapprehension that his eyes are one-fifth of an inch further apart than they are.

→ **Age 3 – 1972:** This year is a hard one, so Jake blocks it out of his mind.

→ **Age 4 – 1973:** Jake calls Rachel "Mommy" now. Ever since he's started sleeping in his parents' bed, it's felt natural. Every time he wakes, he embraces his mom and tells her he loves her because it's the most visceral feeling in his body.

→ **Age 5 – 1974:** Jake hates the "I Can Do It!" chart in his kindergarten classroom. Other kids have stickers next to

151

their names. But Jake can't tie his shoes: no sticker. He can't snap his fingers: no sticker. Frustrated, Jake tries to rip off a sticker from David R.'s row, but the sticker resists. He leaves it alone in defeat.

→ **Age 6 – 1975:** Jake's mom tells him that in the year he was born, the whole world watched the first man walk on the moon. Drawing on a napkin, she crudely fashions an astronaut on top of a circle, and Jake decides who he might be one day.

→ **Age 7 – 1976:** Summer Sundays are Jake's favorite days because they mean family beach days. His mother and father seek refuge from the sun underneath an umbrella, smiling beside each other while Jake lets the waves lap at his feet.

→ **Age 8 – 1977:** Jake becomes obsessed with his Erector Set. Trying to make sense of the second grade, Jake builds towers and bulldozers in equal numbers.

→ **Age 9 – 1978:** There's a rerun of *The Twilight Zone* on television, and Jake watches Roddy McDowall's character, a brilliant young scientist, land on Mars.

→ **Age 10 – 1979:** The first telescope that Jake receives is not a real telescope at all but a prop that comes with a Halloween pirate costume. The lens doesn't magnify anything, but he aims the telescope at the sky and pretends.

→ **Age 11 – 1980:** There's a girl, Laura Stevens. She's new. She's not from Glendale, not even close. When he sees her, the feeling in his pants is tethered to his heart with faulty pre-teen wiring—the type that conceals itself so expertly he thinks this is love, deep love. He suddenly feels weak.

→ **Age 12 – 1981:** This year is so painfully awkward that Jake prefers to forget it.

→ **Age 13 – 1982:** Jake sits in his room listening to the Clash, trying to cultivate the cool he needs to arouse the interest of some girl, any girl, but even if none give him any attention, at least he has the electric downbeats, the dull words of resistance.

→ **Age 14 – 1983:** Some of Jake's friends talk about transferring to a private high school: all-boys, Catholic, academically rigorous. Jake wants to prove himself in an elite institution. He's not Catholic, but his parents support the change anyway.

→ **Age 15 – 1984:** Jake's school is having a mixer with the girls from his sister school. The regulations for the girls' attire are strict, so Jake learns the subtleties of female sexuality: the depression behind the knee, the wisp of hair that clings to the neck.

→ **Age 16 – 1985:** In theology class, as Jake questions literalist interpretations of the Bible, a fundamentalist student cries. At that moment, Jake feels grateful for his own unmessy belief in nothing and vows to stop taking communion solely because it's easy to play along. But the next thing he knows, he's saying, "Lord, I am not worthy to receive you, but only say the word, and I shall be healed."

→ **Age 17 – 1986:** For his birthday, Jake's parents get him a top-of-the-line telescope that lets him look at the sky through close magnification and see endless possibility.

→ **Age 18 – 1987:** Jake and Charles Thomasson both have the highest GPAs in the school, but Charles—more self-assured and charismatic—delivers the valedictory address, even though Jake knows he could have written a better one.

→ **Age 19 – 1988:** Jake's first kiss comes from during a chemistry study session with a classmate at Brown. Weeks later, he loses his virginity to her. He wishes he could tell the old boys from high school, but they've fallen out of touch already.

→ **Age 20 – 1989:** Jake buries his head in his books.

→ **Age 21 – 1990:** Jake takes an upper-division class on asteroids and meteorites. Through the analysis of these rocks, Jake feels as though he has finally found an instrument with which to understand not only the universe but himself.

→ **Age 22 – 1991:** During his last year at Brown, Jake goes to a bar and wears a retro band T-shirt that some Rhode Island School of Design students appreciate. He joins their clique for two months before they realize the depths of his uncool-ness.

→ **Age 23 – 1992:** Riddled with stress, Jake's father suffers a minor heart attack. Jake visits him in the hospital and realizes how hard it would be to lose a parent.

→ **Age 24 – 1993:** Jake passes his qualifying examinations.

→ **Age 25 – 1994:** Jake works overtime to make up for Radenport's plagiarism.

→ **Age 26 – 1995:** After complaining about the strains of non-stop research, Jake receives care packages from his mother: home-baked cookies, scratch-made pretzels, top-notch wine. He feels like a child for loving it as much as he does.

→ **Age 27 – 1996:** His dissertation is complete; he's defended it successfully, but he worries that the postdoctoral job he's landed isn't prestigious enough.

→ **Age 28 – 1997:** Jake takes Lilith out on a blind date. Perhaps their initial interaction warrants an account of the sweet details that comprise the beginnings of any love story, but it's better to forget they were ever so young.

→ **Age 29 – 1998:** By the time Jake's anniversary with Lilith comes around, she's become a second skin, a change of clothes. Sometimes she is a neatly pressed suit: impressive to colleagues and friends. Sometimes she is a pair of sweats: a source of comfort. When he proposes, his hand shakes, but he reminds himself that he wants this: insulation from the elements at the expense of his individuality.

→ **Age 30 – 1999:** Jake takes on a teaching position at Berkeley.

→ **Age 31 – 2000:** Jake feels weightless and breathless, tightly bound to Lilith, who'd convinced him to bungee-jump with her in the first place. She's transferred some of her fearlessness to him, just as he hoped she would.

→ **Age 32 – 2001:** Jake watches Lilith cry on the couch and in the bedroom and the bathroom, grieving over a third miscarriage. This goes on for days. He tells her to let it out, and she does, but she lets too much of herself get away in the process.

→ **Age 33 – 2002:** After a seven-year stint working abroad at Leiden University in the Netherlands, William Radenport returns to Berkeley and takes on a faculty position in the department. Jake nearly has a panic attack at the news.

→ **Age 34 – 2003:** Jake and Lilith buy their first home—a quaint two-bedroom house. A "starter home" they think, but they never move to a bigger property. Instead, they grow inward, thornily tangling until there is barely any room left for the self.

→ **Age 35 – 2004:** While Jake and Lilith are out at dinner, Jake notices a man at the bar staring at Lilith with naked lust. When Jake and Lilith get home, he rips her clothes off with ferocity, and for the rest of the night, she is transformed into the person she used to be, subtly beautiful and fresh.

→ **Age 36 – 2005:** Jake can't avoid hearing about Kramer Leighton, his classmate from Brown, who wrote a popular book on cosmology for the layman. Kramer appears on a talk show. Jake shuts off the television but cannot shut off his mind.

→ **Age 37 – 2006:** Selene is a fixation, but Jake worries his obsession is destructive.

→ **Age 38 – 2007:** The therapist is taking her side, Jake thinks. As he and Lilith work through issues of trust and betrayal, he feels like she no longer understands him.

→ **Age 39 – 2008:** Jake drinks too much when Radenport is named department chair.

→ **Age 40 – 2009:** Jake buys Lilith a bouquet of Stargazer lilies, thinking it would be a nice homage to her name and his favorite hobby, "the perfect union of the two of them." She hugs him sweetly before her allergies kick in. She sneezes so much that she has to throw them out, and Jake worries he can do no right.

→ **Age 41 – 2010:** Jake hates aging, and he worries about the state of his soul. He questions—not in a passing way but in an all-consuming way—what his purpose is and whether or not he's been valuing the wrong things from the start.

→ **Age 42 – 2011:** This is a crossroads, and Jake knows it.

An incomplete record of the life of Sebastian Barnabas:

→ **Age 42 – 2011:** This is a crossroads, but Sebastian doesn't know it.

→ **Age 41 – 2010:** Diana is a decade older than he is. Her chest is wrinkled, puckering her freckles toward the convergence of her breasts. She knows how to handle him, which makes her all the more dangerous, and he worries about how this will end.

→ **Age 40 – 2009:** Sebastian celebrates his birthday by parking his car in a lot by the Presidio and drinking beer on the rooftop. Gazing at the skeleton of the Golden Gate Bridge, he thinks it's a good time to be alone but only because he has to.

→ **Age 39 – 2008:** Sebastian earns the Frank Nelson Cole Prize in Number Theory.

→ **Age 38 – 2007:** After years as an associate professor, Sebastian earns tenure.

→ **Age 37 – 2006:** Even though he once swore off anything that would peg him as a South Bay native, Sebastian surfs for the first time. He falls often but likes the taste of saltwater. Eventually, he notices the riptide pulling him to the periphery.

→ **Age 36 – 2005:** Thirty-six feels indistinct.

→ **Age 35 – 2004:** Sebastian could have died in the car accident he just had. He realizes dying is not the worst thing that could happen to him.

→ **Age 34 – 2003:** Sebastian writes out numbers then uses the sieve of Eratosthenes to find the primes. As he crosses out numbers, he feels like a weaver, his fingers pulling a pencil across the page like a thread through fabric. But this isn't creation. He's just tearing away digits in search of rarities, but he enjoys the destruction.

→ **Age 33 – 2002:** Sebastian becomes an editor of a scholarly mathematics journal. He's excited to be on the front lines of mathematic thought, reading through groundbreaking papers that inspire him.

→ **Age 32 – 2001:** Sebastian wakes up naked in a foreign bed. For the first time in a long time, he has blacked out from drinking. Bleary-eyed, Sebastian recognizes that sometimes he is more like his mother than he would like to admit.

→ **Age 31 – 2000:** Sebastian buys a two-bedroom condo on Bayshore Road, deciding it's not his fate to be a family man, and there is no reason to pretend otherwise.

→ **Age 30 – 1999:** Even though Sebastian is living in California again, he refuses to go to Palos Verdes for Thanksgiving. His mother calls him, and he humors her for five minutes, even though he can't understand a word she is saying. It is a holiday.

→ **Age 29 – 1998:** Post-doc complete, he returns to the States from London and puts an end to his itinerant academic life. After jumping between universities, it feels right to settle down. He's home, even if he wouldn't use that word.

→ **Age 28 – 1997:** For the first time, Sebastian calls a woman his girlfriend, knowing he'll be Stateside soon enough. He doesn't love her. She breathes in expressively whenever he touches her. She roots her world in him while he breathes out.

→ **Age 27 – 1996:** Life in England deepens Sebastian's love of fish and chips.

→ **Age 26 – 1995:** It's so damn elegant, Sebastian thinks when he opens the *Annals of Mathematics* and reads Andrew Wiles' proof of Fermat's Last Theorem. Returning to the publication in the middle of the night, Sebastian thinks there is nothing more beautiful than that proof, even as a woman lies in his bed, calling for his return.

→ **Age 25 – 1994:** When Sebastian moves to Cambridge to do his postdoctoral work, it is the first time he lives outside of the United States. His identity is not defined by the boundaries of any nation but by the limits of his mind.

→ **Age 24 – 1993:** In Hutchinson Commons at the University of Chicago, Sebastian sees his face in the center of neon flyers on the bulletin board. Below his image are taglines: *I am the face of phallocentrism. Would you be able to spot a woman-hater like this one? Patriarchy could use a shave and some lipstick.* He grabs his coffee and goes.

→ **Age 23 – 1992:** The world is a world of promise.

→ **Age 22 – 1991:** Sebastian stumbles into a lecture on the Jacobean era of English and Scottish history, thinking it was going to be about the Jacobian conjecture. He stays anyway. With echoes of monarchs buzzing, he scribbles through an idea.

→ **Age 21 – 1990:** During his first year of graduate work at the University of Chicago, Sebastian admires the old-world buildings of Hyde Park, but he also enjoys going downtown to look at the skyscrapers where he appreciates the smallness of himself.

→ **Age 20 – 1989:** Sebastian Barnabas, summa cum laude, crosses the stage to shake hands with renowned scholars at Yale, but the only person he can think about is the one missing from the audience. Another disappointment.

→ **Age 19 – 1988:** While in town to visit his mother in the hospital, Sebastian goes through microfiche at the local library, trying to track down an old article about his grandparents' death. He finds something, but the records are too damaged to read.

→ **Age 18 – 1987:** In his leisure, Sebastian reads biographies of Euler, Gödel, Cantor.

→ **Age 17 – 1986:** Sebastian buries himself in proofs.

→ **Age 16 – 1985:** After a conversation with a painfully shy girl at a party, Sebastian has his first sexual encounter. It lasts fifty-eight seconds, and it only takes two minutes before Sebastian leaves the room without another word to the unsatisfied wallflower who buttons her cardigan, watching him turn his back on her.

→ **Age 15 – 1984:** Center stage, Sebastian dances with the most beautiful girl in school. The cheap crown on his head is uncomfortable, but wearing it means his hands can stay on Mary DePaul's hips. The spotlight blinds him. He refuses to shut his eyes but does squint, trying to let in the right amount of brilliance.

→ **Age 14 – 1983:** Sebastian stops by the Lunada Bay Market. A local drunk staggers through the aisles and calls out, "Where'd the other one of you go?" Sebastian turns and responds, "He died, asshole." Fucking drunk, Sebastian thinks.

→ **Age 13 – 1982:** Sebastian buys a Rubik's cube and solves it in nearly record time.

→ **Age 12 – 1981:** Sebastian watches a rerun of *Star Trek* where an evil Captain Kirk from a parallel universe boards the *U.S.S. Enterprise.* He parrots Kirk's expression.

→ **Age 11 – 1980:** Sebastian sits at home and reads about Goldberg's conjecture.

→ **Age 10 – 1979:** Sebastian wants to play dodgeball. He wants to approximate the ball's trajectory and calculate angles of attack. He wants to roast his skin under the sun, grabbing rubber that might burn his hands. He wants to know what it is to exist in the world instead of thinking about it, but no one lets him play.

→ **Age 9 – 1978:** Sebastian doesn't know where they come from, but there are books, math books that keep coming to his house. His mother is no mathematician, but Sebastian doesn't think about it. He loves them too much to ask questions.

→ **Age 8 – 1977:** Sebastian trips on the concrete and the wristwatch his father had bought for him at Disneyland shatters. Mickey's hands get stuck. Sebastian sees the words written on the hands: "hours" and "minutes." They remind him that someone had wanted to make his life easier and position him in the march of time. But now the watch is broken, and his father is gone, unable to replace it.

→ **Age 7 – 1976:** On Christmas morning, Sebastian calls 9-1-1. Once the emergency crew stabilizes his mother, Sebastian heads to his stocking and finds a magnifying glass inside. Sebastian takes his new gift out to the front yard. The world blows up under the magnification of the lens, and Sebastian harnesses the December sun, using it to burn the receipt from the liquor store that was stuck on the vodka bottle.

→ **Age 6 – 1975:** The yelling gets louder and louder. It's the end of the month, so Sebastian should have expected this. Sebastian pulls a pillow over his head, trying to muffle the sound. His efforts are futile. He pulls a lucky penny from his pocket, but all he can notice is that it's too dull to shine.

→ **Age 5 – 1974:** Sebastian's father takes him and his mother to Disneyland, and they hold hands down Main Street, stuck in a tableau that will come unstuck too soon.

→ **Age 4 – 1973:** Sebastian stumbles into his mother's bedroom on an early Sunday morning and watches her back heave up and down. She brushes tears away, and with red eyes, goes to make instant pancakes. It's one of the few times she makes him breakfast, and for the rest of his life, pancakes taste like love to him.

→ **Age 3 – 1972:** Sebastian wears his first suit: a small black one for his grandparents' funeral. He is too young to remember everything, but some details stick—the brilliance of the grass, the lowering of the coffins, the sobs of his mother.

→ **Age 2 – 1971:** Asleep in his crib for the last time before switching to a toddler bed, Sebastian can hear the pulsation of a second heartbeat nearby. The drowsy rhythm casts a soundtrack against his dreamscape, beating and beating and beating.

→ **Age 1 – 1970:** The carpet feels unstable, but that doesn't stop Sebastian from taking his first steps across the living room. He stumbles, but his grandmother holds his hands until he begins moving more steadily toward his future.

The Second Diagonals
Triangular Numbers: Life Gets Complicated

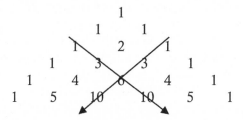

In Pascal's triangle, the numbers featured in the second set of diagonals (1, 3, 6, 10...) are also known as triangular numbers. These units represent the number of dots that fill an equilateral triangle. The equation for determining triangular numbers (where n = the place in the sequence and T_n = the total number of dots in the triangle) is:

$$T_n = \frac{n(n+1)}{2}$$

$T_1 = 1$

$T_2 = 3$

$T_3 = 6$

$T_4 = 10$

In short, aside from being a triangle itself, Pascal's triangle also gives us insight into the construction of other triangles that cut through the heart of things.

Part I. The Emotional Triangles Cutting Through Jake Washington's World:

$$1 \quad \rightarrow \quad \rightarrow \quad \rightarrow$$

Jake Washington wore his wedding ring everywhere. Lilith wouldn't have it any other way. But last week, there was a story going around the department about a grad student who had accidentally thrown away her engagement ring when it had gotten stuck to the nitrile gloves she'd trashed after her lab work. Even though Jake had always worn his wedding band underneath his gloves without incident, the story about the grad student made him worry. He knew he couldn't risk losing his ring, which Lilith monitored closely in the wake of his infidelity five years ago. Trying to do the right thing, Jake took off his wedding band before his lab work and placed it in the locked drawer next to his meteorite so the ring wouldn't find its way into the garbage. Unfortunately, the precautions he took to preserve his marriage undermined it later that night.

At around 10:00 p.m., Jake and Lilith were watching television in bed. Inspired by the sex scene on the screen, Jake sent a hand across her body. She accepted the gesture, letting his fingers inch past the waistband of her pajamas, past the elastic of her underwear. He spent the last fifteen minutes of the show grazing her skin in titillation, making his designs known. Once the credits came on, he turned off the television and the lights. He kissed her. He was used to this routine. Sometimes he longed for the freshness of another person, someone new and less predictable, but his wife was still attractive, make-up-less with her blondish hair tied in a messy bun. She kissed him back, receptive and eager, and grabbed his hand, interlocking her fingers with his. She retreated.

"Where's your wedding ring?" she asked, sitting up and flipping on the lights.

"Shit. I left it in my office."

"Why'd you take it off?" she asked, her face craggy with accusation.

"I was doing lab work and…"

"Did you see Jessica today?" she interrupted, her eyes fixed on his.

"My advisee?" Jake asked, struck by Lilith's unwarranted jealousy. How many times did he need to profess his devotion to her before she'd accept his penance?

"Who else?"

"No, I..." Jake said, hoping to explain the whole story— the grad student, the trashed ring, his desire to make good on his promise to protect this trivial symbol of their marriage— but Lilith was not in the mood for explanations.

"I want you to get it," she said, her thin eyebrows arched in expectation, her back stiff against the headboard. Her arms were resting in her lap, crossed in seriousness.

"Now?" Jake asked. "It's nighttime. The building's locked up."

"You have a key, don't you?"

"Sure, but the ring's safe. It's locked in my office. It's not going anywhere."

"I thought you understood how important that ring is to me," she said, her tough veneer cracking and her vulnerability pooling in her green eyes.

"I do," Jake tried to assure her, straddling the line between understanding and tired. "It's just not worth it right now. I can get it in the morning."

"Not worth it?"

He could have fought her. Maybe he should have. But he didn't want to fight. She was upset and would only grow more so. He was also partly responsible for her insecurities, so he conceded defeat. Besides, he wanted to escape. He got up and drove to his office.

He parked his car near the southernmost entrance to McCone Hall. Approaching the building in the darkness, he noticed the saber-toothed cat sculpture that guarded the door with its jaws craned open, its teeth bared, and its eyes narrowed. Jake hadn't come here in search of an adversary.

He'd come to appease one. He insulted it. You're extinct, he said. You're made of bronze, he said. I'm alive, he said.

Jake unlocked the door to the building and made his way to the third floor. To his surprise, he wasn't the only one there. The lights were on in the hallway. Jake figured there must be a janitor working a night shift. He was about to head to his office when the door to Radenport's office cracked open. Jake slunk back into the cover of the stairwell.

"Can we meet somewhere else next time?" Jake heard a female voice ask. It was a familiar voice, high-registered but gravelly...someone he knew, he tried to place it...then Jake caught a glimpse. Jessica entered the hallway with William.

"Nowhere in Berkeley," Radenport said, shutting off his office light.

"We could get a hotel room in San Francisco. Maybe in Nob Hill?" Jessica asked with a suggestive lilt, tugging on William's arm.

"Maybe," he said, locking his office door. He rubbed Jessica's arms in consolation and kissed her on the forehead. "It's going to take me a while to figure out something that won't make Sarah suspicious."

"I wish you wouldn't say her name," Jessica said with a quiet sternness, wounded.

"I'm sorry. But you can't wish her away. You need to understand what we're doing here," Radenport coolly explained, speaking as though she were a child.

Radenport walked down the hallway to shut off the hallway lights while Jessica stayed near the elevator and pressed the button to go down.

"It's so dark," she said, gripping onto his side once he returned to her.

"The elevator should come soon," Radenport said.

In the dark, Jake could hear the sounds of their kisses, brief and punctuated.

"I don't like this," Jessica whispered once the kissing stopped. Jake wondered what she meant: the kissing, the dark, the sneaking. Radenport ignored her, kissed her again.

The elevator doors opened, and Jessica and Radenport got in. Jake waited for the doors to close, then exited the stairwell. He used the light of his cell phone to guide him to his office. Once there, Jake unlocked his drawer where he found his wedding ring, right next to the meteorite in its vacuum desiccator. He thought about William Radenport, who wore a wedding band every day. Jake wanted to believe he was better than Radenport. Different. After all, Jake had only cheated on his wife once. He'd come clean about his infidelity. But he knew better than to rationalize his mistake. He felt sick at the comparison.

Jake picked up the gold band and placed it on his finger. It wasn't anything special. Precious metal but unadorned, no inscriptions or designs. He hadn't needed a ring at all, but it publicized his marital status, which meant something to Lilith, so it meant something to him. Difficult as she could be, there was much to love: her independence, her charm, her assuredness, her intelligence. He barely knew who he was without her.

Jake looked at the meteorite one last time, glad it was protected in its glass case, immune to outside influence. He locked up, turned off the lights, and surrendered to the darkness while he made his way out the building.

Jake stopped in front of the saber-toothed cat statue on the way to his car. Instead of hurling insults at it, Jake petted its cold, bronze back. Tamed, it was not a beast but a pet. Jake looked up at the stars, his other compatriots, and mourned the light pollution that kept him from connecting to the heavens. He craned his head back to the earth and left.

On the drive home, Jake considered exposing Radenport and reporting his relationship with Jessica to the university. The prospect was tempting, but Jake didn't want to make any decisions impulsively. He needed to think through the implications. Jake recalled the day when he'd first heard about the meteorite. How long had it taken for the news to get to Radenport? And whom had Jake told other than Jessica and Lilith? Jake began to wonder if William had seduced Jessica to get information about Jake's work. His paranoia hovered over the idea, but he knew there were other reasons why Radenport would want to sleep with Jessica. Perhaps getting information on Jake was just a bonus.

When Jake got home, Lilith was already asleep, but Jake's mind raced. He decided to test the waters before he said or did anything significant. Fortunately, Jake had an appointment to meet with Jessica the next day. At first, they discussed articles she'd researched. The whole time, Jake was distracted. He kept getting lost in the cupid-bow cleft of her top lip that smelled sweetly of watermelon lip balm, even from a distance. He watched her low-tied ponytail sweep over her shoulder when she flicked it away, the errant strawberry blonde hairs catching the light. He noticed how the conservative neckline of her shirt exposed only a sliver of her collarbone as if she knew that sexiness came from playfully hiding. He saw a glimmer of sweat clinging to her brow. That was what got to him the most. It didn't feel warm in the office, and this made the sweat more evocative, suggestive even of an encounter she might've had with Radenport before coming to the meeting. There were empty holes in the upper cartilage of her ear from the second and third piercings she must have had at some point. Her blue eyes were the type you could fall into, and now he saw it, she was beautiful, not obviously so, but in her own way, and...

"Jake?" she asked, recognizing his distractedness. "What do you think?"

"I think it's a good start," he said, snapping out of his reverie. "You know, I'm pretty sure William Radenport published an article that would be worth reading. I don't know how I overlooked it. Let me look up the title," Jake said, consulting his computer. "Have you ever met Dr.

Radenport?" he asked casually while the search results loaded.

"I'm taking one of his classes right now," she said.

"How do you like it?" Jake asked, appraising her reaction.

"It's great," she said with impressive normalcy. "I'm learning a lot."

"That's great," Jake said, turning to his screen. "Here it is: 'Redox models of SNC meteorites: Using ferric-ferrous chemistry to probe the crustal heterogeneity on Mars.'"

"I'll be sure to read it before our next meeting," she said after noting down the title, putting away her pen and notepad. "One more thing," she said as she packed up.

"Yes?"

"I was curious...how's your research going? It's a hot topic of conversation among the grad students," she said. Grad students...or Radenport? Jake wondered.

"It's going well," he said confidently. "It's an incredible specimen."

"Any observations you'd like to share with an inquiring mind?"

Her question offered Jake an opportunity. At that moment, he decided to fabricate details about the meteorite. Afterward, he would closely monitor Radenport, trying to figure out if Jessica had passed along the information. Looking into Jessica's bright eyes, Jake regretted that she was getting stuck in the middle of this rivalry. She had a genuine intellectual curiosity. But he reminded himself that she had placed herself in this situation. Thinking of information to plant, Jake went with a bold choice. He implied that the meteorite had biomorphs, fossilized bacteria that might serve as evidence of past life on Mars. Even though Jake knew he was inventing fiction, constructing nothing more than a trap for Jessica and Radenport, he rejoiced in his own words. He loved the idea of the meteorite yielding something remarkable, even in fantasy.

The other night, Lilith Washington had a fantasy of her own about Jessica Fleming. Even though Lilith had no idea what Jessica looked like, Lilith created her own version of Jessica in a dream. The Jessica of Lilith's unconscious had platinum blonde hair that fell to her waist. When this imagined Jessica flicked her hair over one of her shoulders, she denuded just the sort of breast that Lilith wished she could have: a large but buoyant dome with the gravity-defying vertical thrust of a cartoon character's chest. Lilith swiped away the hair on Jessica's other side, exposing the rest of her naked form. Jessica was thin but womanly. She had ample hips, but they didn't lead to the meatier thighs that Lilith possessed. There were no excess fat deposits anywhere on Jessica's body. Her skin was as flawless as the musculature it concealed. Lilith looked at Jessica's face, admiring the flush of young cheeks, the brightness of young eyes, the fullness of young lips.

Lilith kissed Jessica in a fit of ecstasy. Lilith was the first to open their lips with a tongue, the aggressor claiming territory. As Lilith's mouth opened, her hand roamed southward. She clutched onto Jessica's breasts, then pulled her to the ground. Lilith saw Jake looking on from a distance, vexed. With her eyes locked on her spectator, Lilith grabbed the flesh underneath her more firmly, kissing it more violently.

When Lilith woke up, she wanted to kill Jake for infecting her with this nightmare. For the next half hour, she felt the traitorous sensations of arousal pulsing through her body. Lilith was self-aware enough that she understood the subtext of these desires. For the past month, Lilith had worried about the possibility that Jake might cheat on her with Jessica. This vivid dream was the last straw. It was time to take action.

But before she could do anything, Lilith needed to make an appointment with her dermatologist. There was an opening the next Wednesday at 3:00 p.m., and Lilith booked the slot. When Lilith lay back on the reclining chair in her doctor's office, she tried to relax. She felt the first prick of the syringe. She breathed in and out to calm herself before the next one. She closed her eyes. She didn't want any warning about when the next sting would come. But without any visual stimuli to distract her, Lilith's mind summoned the details of her invented Jessica: the unrealistically blemishless skin and the eager lips. Lilith opened her eyes. Better to watch the needle.

When the procedure was over, Lilith's impulse was to consult a mirror, but the doctor explained the effects wouldn't be immediate. It would take days. So Lilith avoided reflective surfaces for a week, hoping the next glimpse of herself would offer a revelation. When she finally surveyed the work, the results were agreeable. The Botox hadn't been entirely restorative. Her past had stacked too many years on the promise of her face. But many of her wrinkles were smoothed over as if she had never known happiness.

"What do you think?" she asked Jake when she came to bed that night.

"I think it's toxic," he responded, not bothering to look up from his reading.

"Only in insanely large doses," Lilith argued, using her hand to lower his book.

"That's not what I meant," Jake told her, meeting her eyes with an exasperated expression before raising his book once more.

"Don't I look better?"

He glanced up and spent a few seconds surveying her face. "Maybe," he eventually said in appraisal, "but *are* you?"

"Is there a difference?"

"Part of you is literally paralyzed now," Jake said. Lilith couldn't tell if he was speaking so hostilely about her procedure out of concern or spite. Either way, Lilith knew

Jake didn't get it. He didn't understand how hard it was for a woman to age, how crippling.

"Don't be so quick to judge," Lilith cautioned him. "You're not any different than I am. You're stuck right here with me."

"Those wrinkles are going to come back," he said, putting down his book.

"You think I don't know that?" Lilith said, peeved that her husband felt entitled to state facts as if she were ignorant. "But I bought myself time. That's all you can do."

"You didn't get this work done for me, did you? Because I appreciate you just as you are," he said, resting a hand on hers.

"No," Lilith said, softening at his touch. "Of course I didn't."

Lilith had done it for herself. The treatment boosted her confidence. But she wasn't sure how long that surge would last. The real test came on Friday. Lilith knew that Jake had a meeting with Jessica at noon, so Lilith headed to Jake's office just in time to catch Jessica on her way out.

"Excuse me," Lilith said when she saw a strawberry blonde young woman leaving Jake's office. "Are you Jessica?"

"Yes, and you are...?"

"Lilith. Jake's wife. I understand my husband will be overseeing your research," she said, lingering on the word "husband."

"Yes. I can't tell you how happy I am to meet you," Jessica said with an enthusiasm that seemed genuine. "He's been so helpful in guiding my work."

Lilith examined Jessica, all the while maintaining her practiced political smile. This was not the Jessica Fleming of Lilith's dreams, not the paragon of perfection. Jessica did not have the stunning good looks of a celebrity, much less those of a sexual goddess of fantasy, but she did have a charm all her own. She was pretty, that much was unimpeachable, even if it was a measured prettiness that didn't call attention to itself. Jake had always told Lilith that Jessica wasn't attractive in his eyes. She's just a kid, he would say. But clearly, Jake had downplayed the girl's beauty. Unlike Lilith, Jessica could smile without agenda in the way only young people seemed capable of. Her teeth were tightly bound together, fresh from orthodontia that hadn't lost its straightening power. Like a teenager, Jessica had her hair tucked into a high ponytail that swayed as she spoke with animation. Lilith had worn her hair in much the same way during her adolescence in Napa when she would run through the vineyard and let her hair brush against the leaves. Those days were long gone. Reexamining Jessica's hair, Lilith noticed an imperfection that was all too common among young people who couldn't afford endless trips to the salon: the color of Jessica's ponytail was lighter than the darker section of hair near her crown.

"I know a great stylist who could even out your hair color if you'd like," Lilith said, picking up a strand from the ponytail and inspecting it as she spoke. "I'm sure she'd give you a fair price since you're a student."

"Oh," Jessica said, timidly. "Thanks, but it's ombré."

"Ombré?"

"Yeah, it's a new trend. The whole dark to light thing, it's intentional," Jessica explained buoyantly, her hands gesturing with youthful energy.

"And to think in my day, we just called that showing your roots," Lilith said, the edge in her voice barely concealed.

"It's supposed to add dimension."

"It takes more than color to do that. But it looks lovely," Lilith responded with a false smile.

"Thanks," Jessica said unsurely. "Are you here to see Jake?"

"Yeah, I was just dropping off some lunch for him," Lilith explained, holding up the takeout in her hands. "Anyway, it was nice meeting you."

Lilith retreated into Jake's office and handed him the food.

"To what do I owe this pleasure?" he asked, looking up from his work with a smile.

"I just thought you might be hungry," Lilith said, kissing him on the cheek.

"Did you have business on campus today?"

"Something like that," she evaded, brushing a hair from his forehead.

"This is nice," he said, looking at her appreciatively. "Stay. Have some with me," he commanded as he unpacked the salad, the fruit, the curried chicken.

"I can't. I've got another meeting," she lied. If she hadn't just met Jessica, Lilith might have been tempted to stay, but as it was, she was too emotional. "I just wanted to drop this off," she said as she turned toward the door.

"Lilith," Jake called out.

"Yeah?"

"The other night, I should've told you something," he said. "You do look beautiful."

Until Jake said that, Lilith hadn't realized how badly she'd needed to hear it. She was thankful to Jake for paying her a compliment, but it didn't ease her worries about Jessica. When Lilith got home, she rifled through Jake's possessions, thinking she might find evidence of another affair. Nothing. Email, she thought. After he fell asleep that night, she crept out of bed and opened his laptop. Lilith knew she was crossing a boundary in her marriage, but she was sure if she didn't, the whole enterprise would collapse anyway. She fell into a habit, checking his email routinely. A couple of weeks later, Lilith found an unread message from Selene. She had to read it ten times to digest it.

Subject: In San Fran!

Hi, Jake,

I hope this email finds you well. I know we haven't spoken in a while, but I have some news. Stanford offered me a position, and I've accepted the job. I'll be working with some great biologists, and I think they'll help me grow. Since we'll both be in the Bay Area, I was wondering if you wanted to grab some coffee and catch up? You know the area better than I do, so I'm open to recommendations (if you're interested in meeting).

I heard through the grapevine that you and Chris found a meteorite? And it might be Martian?! You two seem to be living the dream! I guess all that time looking at rocks in Utah wasn't good enough for you guys – you needed to track down the genuine article. Good for you. Once I found out about your research, I started searching for updates online, but there isn't a lot of information yet about your work. I'd love to hear about your findings if you've got the time to spare.

I know that the last time we spoke, you mentioned that we couldn't stay in touch. I'm sorry if I breached your trust by reaching out to you. It's just that I don't know anyone else in the Bay Area, and I couldn't stand the thought of running into you on the street without letting you know I live here now. I understand if you can't meet up with me because of your wife, but I swear, I won't cross any boundaries. If you want to know the truth, I do still love you (did I ever tell you in the first place? I don't know if I did, but you must have assumed as much), but I'll put my feelings aside. I just want to see you again, even if it's for one last time.

Let me know what you think,

Selene

Lilith thought she might cry, but she held off the tears. She typed a reply.

Subject: Re: In San Fran!

Selene,

Congratulations on your position at Stanford. I hope it works out for you. But you know I'm married. My wife and I moved past the affair, and our marriage is stronger than ever. It was wrong to betray her, and I don't want to be reminded of the past.

I never thought you were in love with me. Hopefully, you realize how silly that sounds. What we had was physical. To think that you might fall in love with me because we had sex when I was lonely and missing my wife shows how deluded you are. I never loved you, and I think you should move on.

Jake

After sending the email, Lilith deleted the original email and the response she'd written. She emptied the digital trashcan in Jake's mail. She checked his phone and made sure the emails had been deleted from that device too. Lilith climbed back into bed, devoid of the facial expressions that would have given away the tangled emotions inside her.

→　　→　　6　　→

Jake knew there was something wrong with Lilith when he looked on the kitchen counter and saw a bottle of 1996 Château Haut-Brion, opened and breathing. He poured himself a glass and set out to find her. She wasn't in either of the bedrooms. He checked the front and back yards, thinking she might have wanted to enjoy the night. While Jake was outside, he took a moment to look up at the sky and find the star Arcturus, as he compulsively did whenever the visibility was good enough, tracing the constellation Boötes in his mind. He allowed himself the consolation of the stars and the wine for a solid ten minutes, determined to keep some part of his Friday night unmarred before looking for his wife again. Lilith's car was still out front, which meant she could only be in one place.

He went inside, opened the door to the wine cellar, and climbed down the stairs. Lilith was sitting on the tile floor wearing all black, a crushed velvet top and a flared skirt. Her legs were splayed, wine glass in hand. She looked like a woman who'd escaped her own party.

"Is everything all right?" Jake asked her.

"Fine," she said unconvincingly. "Why?"

"It's just...well, the Haut-Brion. When I wanted to open it last month, you said it would be a travesty to open it so soon."

"I felt like drinking it tonight. That's all," Lilith responded, looking blankly at the wall before glancing up at her husband.

"I know you well enough to know you never open a bottle too young."

"You're right," she said, getting up and pacing the racks, looking through her collection with morose laziness. "I suppose I do care about that."

"So, what's wrong?" Jake asked, placing a hand on her shoulder. She put her hand warmly over his for a few seconds, then removed his hand.

"I told you. I just felt like drinking the bottle tonight. I don't mind that it's young. Daddy gave me a case of it anyway. I'll save the rest of the bottles for later. Let them age. I just wanted a taste of what's to come."

"It's still good," Jake said, nudging her and trying to weasel a smile from her.

"Yeah," she replied with a smirk. She drank the last sip in her glass. "Makes you wonder how good it's going to get."

"Sure. Just don't wait too long."

Lilith looked at him cuttingly. She continued appraising the bottles, picking up one here and there before replacing it. "I was thinking about picking out some older vintages from our collection and auctioning them off at the gala. What do you think?"

"I can part with them if you can," Jake said. "This is your collection, after all."

"I want to do it. I'm just not sure people at the gala will understand the value of these older bottles."

"What are you talking about? We're in the Bay Area. There are plenty of wine snobs around here."

"Wine snobs, huh?" she asked. Jake found it hard to gauge how light-hearted her comment was. He should have been more careful with his words. She was in a mood.

"I say that with affection. So…are you worried about the fundraiser? Is that what's bugging you?"

"Sure," Lilith said, grabbing a couple of bottles and sticking them under her arms.

"Care to elaborate?"

"I don't know, Jake. I'm sick of talking. I just want another glass of wine."

"But we hardly talked," he said, frustrated. "Did I do something wrong?"

"Not lately," she said, then walked up the stairs and left him alone in the cellar.

The next week, Lilith and Jake went to the Berkeley City Club Hotel for the UC Berkeley Foundation gala that Lilith had organized. Upon their entrance to the ballroom, Lilith grabbed a glass of champagne from one of the circulating waiters, and Jake did the same. She looked beautiful. She was wearing a sleeveless, gray satin dress with a conservative, boat-neck front. The dress slipped along the edges of her figure and pooled at the floor. The back of the dress dipped low, making up for the lack of exposure in the front. Lilith thrived in these environments. People gravitated toward her. She was at ease in the center of a crowd, unlike Jake, who preferred being on the periphery. Still, he served his purpose. Now and then, he cast his hand against the small of her back. He knew she appreciated that. He let her "work the room" and re-joined her when summoned.

Standing by her side in the middle of the evening, she prompted him to speak to some donors. "Go ahead, honey, tell them about your research," she insisted.

"I'm investigating a newfound meteorite."

"The meteorite that was found in Algeria last month?" asked a fiftysomething man in the crowd. "I read an article about it in the *Daily Cal*. There wasn't a lot of information, but Dr. Radenport said there were suspicions it might be Martian."

"William Radenport said that in *The Daily Cal?*" Jake asked, frustrated.

"Yes," the man responded, clearly unsure why Jake was upset.

"Excuse me," Jake said, leaving. Lilith shot him a death stare. Jake went to the bar and purchased a glass of Merlot, only to find William Radenport nearby.

"Can I buy you a drink?" Jake asked William.

"I'm six years sober."

"Sorry. I forgot," Jake lied. He drank his wine with ferocious gulps.

"I've been meaning to talk to you. I can put together a team to help with your research. No one ever works on these projects alone," Radenport said.

"I'm working with Chris Thurman from U of A."

"That hardly seems practical."

"I trust Chris. That's important to me. And speaking of trust, I would appreciate it if you didn't discuss my research with the press without consulting me first."

"*The Daily Californian*? I'd hardly call them the press."

"Still," Jake said, "if it's all the same, send any inquiries about my research to me so I can answer any questions."

"I don't know why you keep rejecting my help. You may need to bring in a biologist, and I know excellent scientists across all disciplines," Radenport said. Now that Radenport mentioned commissioning a biologist, Jake was sure that Jessica was passing information to Radenport. Why would William have said anything about biologists if Jessica hadn't told him about the invented biomorphs Jake had planted in his conversation with her?

"Thanks for your offer, but I'm capable of managing my research," Jake said.

The whole interchange exhausted him. Jake wanted to leave, but Lilith insisted they stay. An hour later, they took off. When they finally got home, Lilith went to her vanity and removed her jewelry, getting closer to the person she really was with the removal of each sparkle from her body. She undid her hair, taking out bobby pin after bobby pin until the weight of her long tresses unfurled down her back. She ran her hands through her hair, scouring the terrain for leftover bobby pins. Jake approached her as she struggled.

"Here," Jake said, finding one bobby pin and pulling it out.

"It's a mess," she admitted, grappling with the tangled terrain.

"No," he assured her. "It's fine. Just a little complicated to manage." As he picked through the maze of her hair, he tried to be as gentle as he could, but the hairspray made the bobby pins stick to her hair. He pulled out another bobby pin, but he accidentally took a few strands of hair with him.

"Stop," she finally said, pained. "You're hurting me."

"I'm doing my best, but the hairspray is making everything sticky. And without me, you'd be doing this blind."

"I'm used to it," she said, continuing to scavenge for bobby pins with both of her hands. "I prefer it. It hurts less that way."

Jake backed off, untying his bow tie and unbuttoning his shirt while sitting on the edge of the bed. She pulled her hair into a low ponytail and wiped off her makeup. This was not the version of her that Jake was used to seeing day in and day out. It was the version of her that he was used to seeing late-night in and late-night out. It was reserved only for him, ostensibly something special, even though it felt like a burden to be privy to her secret self.

"Unzip me?" she asked, walking toward him and turning her back. He complied and watched her take off her dress. She wasn't wearing any lacy lingerie, but instead, a girdle-like contraption. The spandex had given her so much sex appeal when she'd been in her dress. Now, it stripped away that same sex appeal. She took off the bodysuit in the way that the stricture of the fabric necessitated: inelegantly and forcefully. Once it was off, she put on flannel pajamas, brushed her teeth, and climbed into bed.

"I wish you'd dropped the Radenport thing. The mention of his name doesn't entitle you to be rude to a donor," Lilith said when Jake joined her in bed. "Right now, we need to butter up as many people as we can. The Foundation has been getting less money this year in grants. We're going to have to make some tough decisions."

"Nothing I'm working on is being defunded, is it?"

"No. I'll make sure of that. But the same can't be said of your dissertation advisee."

"Jessica?"

"There was a conference she'd hoped to go to, and the Foundation had provisionally approved the funds to cover

181

the expenses, but I have a feeling we're going to have to pull the money for it."

Jake felt conflicted. If anything, he should be glad that Jessica would suffer instead of him. Hadn't she been sharing secrets with Radenport? But Jake still felt some allegiance to her. She was his advisee, and Jake couldn't write her off entirely. She was probably just a naïve young woman in love with the wrong type of man. He felt sorry for her. Then his thoughts shifted from Jessica to his wife.

"You still don't trust me," Jake said, getting to the root of the issue.

"I don't know what you mean."

"You do. You're telling me the only reason my advisee is losing grant money is because of budgetary constraints? What about the other graduate students?"

"They'll be affected too. I'm not targeting your precious pupil because I'm trying to get back at you. I'm not that cold-blooded. Although now I know you think I am," she said, getting out of bed in offense and standing in indignation.

"It's just…this feels personal. I'm sure you didn't put up a fight when you found out about the cuts," Jake reasoned, trying to mellow his tone.

"We have to prioritize when we look at our budget."

"So, you didn't even try to help her?"

"What do you want me to say?" Lilith yelled. "No, I didn't try to help your advisee. And you're right. I don't feel bad about it. I told you from the start. I didn't feel comfortable with you taking on a young, female advisee, and you took her on anyway."

"Yes, in a purely professional capacity!" Jake exclaimed, hands raised in frustration.

"You were also working with Selene in a 'purely professional capacity.'"

"And now we get to it."

"Fine, I'll admit it," Lilith said, pacing beside the bed. "I don't trust you. I haven't trusted you for a long time. I can't even remember what it's like to trust you."

"What does this mean? Do you want a divorce?"

"I didn't say anything about a divorce."

"Well, how do you expect our marriage to work if you don't trust me?"

"The way it always has," she said, returning to the bed and turning away from him. She curled up against her pillow and shut off the light by her side of the bed. Jake didn't fight her. He did just as she did, hitting his light and retreating to his side. Maybe she was right. Maybe they could keep living this way, ignoring all the signs that there was something wrong with their marriage. It seemed as though many of the married couples Jake knew did the same. He wanted something more from Lilith, something she was reluctant to give him, but divorce sounded like hell. When they weren't fighting, Lilith offered him comfort, and Jake didn't want to lose that. Instead of consternating about it, Jake acquiesced to the darkness and fell asleep. It was the easiest thing to do.

$$\rightarrow \quad \rightarrow \quad \rightarrow \quad 10$$

Jake's world would soon get more complicated because of a past he'd been shielded from: the past of his father. For all of Jake's life, his parents' marriage had seemed perfect. But Daniel kept a mistress: his job at the law firm. In the early years, when Rachel would find an errant legal memo in his bedside drawers, she would lift it up and jokingly chastise Daniel for keeping "incriminating lingerie" in their marital space. When he would spend late nights in the office, she would ask him if his tart knew he was married. Rachel even gave his job a name: Charmaine.

"Say hello to Charmaine for me!" she'd cry as he walked out the door. "Don't let Charmaine spin one of her long stories for you tonight," she'd caution him. These lighthearted games were a way to ease the tension. Rachel loved her husband. She had married him for a reason, she explained, and that reason had not been so he could provide financial support to the detriment of emotional support. Daniel understood her frustration. If he could have, he would've spent more time with the family. But there were deeper issues that neither Jake nor Rachel knew about.

Daniel knew how to hide his workplace problems. Part of the charade was the suit. Every Monday, he wore the same suit, one he had inherited from his father. It was important for Daniel to start every week with a reminder of who he was and where he came from, even though the suit didn't fit him perfectly. The arms were too long, so he had to push the excess material into the crooks of his elbows whenever he got to work. Despite the inconvenience, the bunched fabric served a purpose: it steadied him. His joints stiffened into one position, and that made the surrounding muscles firmer. Daniel's father had told him that being strong meant coping with discomfort if it could better you; being weak meant fleeing from it. The strain Daniel felt in his forearm was part of the message he reserved for himself. He couldn't bring himself to tailor the suit. He liked to think his father's arms had been so long because he'd reached toward the best version of himself. Daniel wanted to imagine that one day, after stretching further toward his future, the sleeves would catch up to his achievements and end properly at his wrists.

"Must be Monday," Rachel said on one such weekday in 1973, looking at her husband and craning her neck toward his face for a kiss on the cheek. "When are you going to be home tonight?" she asked.

"Hopefully not too late," he said, adjusting his tie.

"Hopefully?" she asked, her eye narrowed, forehead wrinkled in expectation.

"Hopefully," he said with a smile and quick squeeze of her hand.

"You've got to stop working these crazy hours," she said, earnest. Her face widened to a smirk as she said, "I'm beginning to miss you."

"Beginning to?"

"Don't push it. After last week, you're in the doghouse. Charmaine's been greedy lately."

"You know I still have to prove myself."

"But to whom?" she asked, pursing her lips and widening her eyes. Daniel kissed her forehead. It was a question he'd already asked himself many times, and there was never just one answer. As Daniel headed toward the front door, his son jumped in his path.

"It's your daddy suit," young Jake said, pointing at his father. It made sense that this was how Daniel's son defined him. Hadn't Daniel done the same when he'd been Jake's age? Wasn't Daniel still doing it now, wearing his father's clothes because it was the only way he knew how to resemble the old man? If only Daniel could wear the suit as his father had worn it, new and pristine. After so many uses, the suit was not only ill-fitting but also damaged, showcasing the abuse of time with a frayed edge here or a loose thread there. Daniel worried these were the details Jake would forever see.

"Be a good lawyer, Daddy," Jake commanded before hugging his waist.

"I will. What about you? Do you want to be a lawyer someday?"

"No, Daddy, I'm gonna be an astronaut."

To say that Jake's response was disappointing would be an understatement. Daniel's father had been a lawyer, his grandfather had been a lawyer, and the legacy created by these two men alone was so strong it could surpass a legacy five generations in the making. Growing up with heroes like Clarence Darrow and Daniel Webster had shaped Daniel's moral constitution, and he was sad that his only son might not become a man through the same means as the other Washingtons.

185

"It's okay, Daddy," Jake assured him, "I still love you."

Daniel was glad Jake was still young enough for unvarnished admissions of love. He knew these days wouldn't last forever. Nevertheless, Daniel had to leave. With a quick dismissal, he went to the office. Once Daniel settled in, he returned some phone calls, dealt with paperwork, and then started to research information for a case. He probed the filing cabinets in search of old documents from a previous case, thinking the findings could have some bearing on his current one. As he bent to reach a file in the back, Daniel heard his jacket tear. Frantically, he searched the exterior, trying to find the rupture. Without success, he took the jacket off and looked inside. There was the tear: in the armpit of the lining.

"Is there a sewing kit around here?" he asked a receptionist, files underarm.

"Something I can stitch up for you?"

"No. But if you come across a kit, would you let me know?"

"Of course, Mr. Washington," she responded in her secretarial tone.

Daniel went back to his desk and began sorting through the files that had come at such a grave cost. In the process, he stumbled across some documents that he should never have been able to locate so easily. An accounting ledger from the case showed large sums of money coming into the company from a third party whose interests went against those of the client the firm was representing. Daniel learned that the firm had lost the case, despite mountains of documentation that should have guaranteed a favorable verdict. Daniel continued to investigate and started looking into similar cases: small cases where the firm had lost, despite having built a strong case with substantial evidence, most of which hadn't even been turned over during discovery as required. In each of these cases, Daniel plumbed the accounting files and found suspicious money transfers around the same time as the proceedings. Daniel decided to set a meeting with one of the partners to discuss the matter.

"Do you enjoy practicing law?" the authoritative, fiftysomething partner, Kenneth Whitmore, asked Daniel after he brought the details of the cases to light.

"Very much," Daniel said.

"I thought so," Whitmore said, pausing and considering his next words. He stood up, parting his suit jacket as he stuck his hands into his pockets. "If you want to keep practicing law, you have to learn boundaries. Your job is to handle the cases you're given. It's not your job to rifle through old documents and play detective."

"You knew about the third-party interests," Daniel said.

"Of course I knew. It's how we keep this firm powerful," Whitmore asserted, his tone unwavering in the face of judgment.

Daniel thought about this for a few seconds and said, "Then I have to quit."

"A noble man. Honorable. I like that about you," Whitmore said, sitting back in his chair with a sinister smirk. "You know, Williamson told me about you. Said you're 'indispensable.' He used that word. Said you're a genius with financials. Seeing patterns in numbers. I should have seen this coming now that I think about it."

"I'm glad to hear my reputation precedes me. But I do care about integrity. And with all due respect, I can get a job somewhere else."

"Are you so sure?" Whitmore asked, his cragged wrinkles stoically staying put.

"Are you threatening me?" Daniel asked, rising from his seat.

"I'm just asking the questions you should be asking yourself," Whitmore responded, even-toned as he reclined in his chair. "If I were you, I would wonder who those third parties were and what lengths they might go to ensure their interests are protected. You think you know those

187

companies, but you don't. Besides, I can give you opportunities here. I need whiz kids like you who know financial systems as well as they know legal code. Can you imagine? A person with your skill set, who knows how the firm operates...you could be *incredibly valuable* to this company. So, sit down. Let's talk."

"No offer is worth it," Daniel protested, but he took a seat as his resolve weakened.

"You haven't heard it yet. Besides. What's nobler than providing for your family?" Whitmore asked, getting a perverse joy from mocking Daniel's values. "Another thing I make sure I know: which attorneys in the firm have children."

"You don't know anything about my family."

"And you don't know anything about the companies we represent. This situation could be bad for you. Really bad. But I'm offering you an opportunity. A great one," Whitmore said, sliding a scribbled note to Daniel. "Here. Your new salary."

Daniel was astounded by the offer. This money would mean complete financial security. It would mean Rachel could quit her part-time work as a nurse if she wanted. It would mean Jake could go to school wherever he liked. Daniel nodded his head.

"I'll have Ted draw up the paperwork," Whitmore said, extending a hand. Daniel reluctantly shook it, knowing he'd made a deal with the devil. He left the office, shaken.

"Do you still need that sewing kit?" the receptionist asked Daniel as he made his way down the hall. She smiled her sweet, young smile.

"I don't think so," Daniel responded, defeated. "It's just a tear in the lining."

"I see."

"It's nothing," he said, walking toward his office in resignation.

Instead of taking up a needle and thread, Daniel kept wearing the suit on Mondays. He was careful when reaching for anything since the small tear might rip through the rest of the suit. He continued living like this, gingerly working around the constraints of the rip, until one day he decided he couldn't do it anymore. He was sick of worrying that the suit was going to fall apart any time he needed to grab a file, so he threw the suit into the garbage. The following day, Daniel bought an expensive, tailored suit to replace his father's old one. He wore the well-cut suit to work the next Monday, trying to keep his head up high as he broke a decade-long tradition of following in his father's footsteps.

Part II. The Emotional Triangles Cutting Through Sebastian Barnabas' World:

$\leftarrow$ $\leftarrow$ $\leftarrow$ 10

Sebastian's life was also about to grow more complicated as a result of his father's past. When Barrie Stevenson, disabled but alive, returned to Los Angeles from Vietnam in 1970, his father was dressed in full military attire to greet him. The khaki was ironed to a crisp, the medals pinned straight. After Barry stepped off the plane, the old man saluted him and embraced him, taking care to avoid knocking Barrie's maimed foot or his cane.

"Hell of a job you did, boy," Barrie's father told him in the car on the way home to Palos Verdes. "You see a lot in war. But I don't have to tell you. You're initiated now. I'm sure you've got plenty on your mind. You'll find a way to sort it. We all do. I just want to say I'm proud of you, son."

After Barrie's father pulled the car into the driveway of the family home, Barrie limped out to the nearby cliffs. The sun shone gently, the way it did during so many late afternoons in Southern California. The sea salt air cast a breeze in Barrie's direction. He closed his eyes and drank in the environment. He remembered Jacqueline and the dalliances they'd shared here before his deployment. He remembered her coy smile, her sweetness. He remembered the way her paisley dresses stood out among the dry grass. Jacqueline was still out there, not far away. Barrie sat and looked out on the edge of the world for twenty minutes before he squared himself with his obligation.

He drove toward Jacqueline's house. As he got within view of the place, he could see Jacqueline's parents, whom he'd only met a couple of times, playing with one-year-old twin boys on the front yard. These had to be Barrie's sons. Sons, plural. Jesus. Barrie didn't want her parents to see him, so he drove past their house and parked his car down the street. Barrie adjusted his rearview window so he could see the boys in the distance. One of the boys sat on a colorful blanket, amusing himself with the rattles, blocks, and stacking rings strewn about him. The other boy toddled around the periphery of the lawn, smelling flowers and touching bugs. Jacqueline's parents were smiling and attentive, each of them taking charge of one boy. The scene was idyllic, but Barrie felt like he didn't belong. He couldn't raise two kids. The thought of having one kid had been overwhelming enough. He might have felt more tied to his responsibilities if Jacqueline had been out there on the lawn, struggling to manage two wily kids alone. But she had better support than Barrie could offer anyway. So he left without looking back.

Barrie knew he couldn't stay in Palos Verdes Estates; it was a small enough town that his presence might force him into some degree of parenting. But Barrie saw an opportunity in his family's construction business, which serviced the greater Los Angeles area. So he packed up and moved to Hollywood to apprentice under his uncle, who was in charge of managing the operations there.

Barrie brought his guitar with him to his new apartment on Sunset, determined to pursue music during his time off.

He grew out his hair again, the way he'd worn it in high school. He hid his army ornaments in his closet, tucked away where he wouldn't have to explain them. He played his guitar into the night, inspiring the ire of his neighbors. Barrie didn't give a shit. After his rent and bills were covered, he spent every penny of his paycheck on LPs and marijuana and beers with whiskey chasers. Barrie wasn't a good enough singer or guitar player to make it. But whenever he crooked his fingers across the fretboard, plucked the strings, and sang out in union with his strumming hand, he expelled every toxin from his spirit. The terror of his memories, the loss of Jackie's companionship, the weight of his inaction—it was all suspended, captive to the music.

Barrie hit the Hollywood clubs as often as he could. He spent most of his time at the Whisky, which was a ten-minute walk from his apartment. Some weeks Barrie went there nightly, getting to know the bartenders and listening to the best music Los Angeles had to offer. Every so often, he'd meet a fellow vet there. They wouldn't talk about what they'd seen in Vietnam. They'd just drink together, bound in the fellowship of forgetting. Mostly, Barrie wanted to forget about Jacqueline, the children, and his obligation to them. For a few years, he successfully blotted them from his mind with substances and women. It wasn't until late 1973 that he couldn't ignore them anymore. His uncle had brought in another Palos Verdes guy to work as the bookkeeper at the office in Hollywood, someone whose father knew Barrie's father...that sort of thing.

"My uncle said you're from Palos Verdes," Barrie mentioned to the newbie, Ryan, during a break. "You know Jackie Barnabas?"

"I know *of* her. She's a mess," Ryan said in passing, grabbing a soda from the fridge.

"Jackie?" Barrie asked, trying to reconcile Ryan's description of her with the sweet teenage dream Barrie had impregnated.

"Yeah. Ever since her parents died, she's been hitting the bottle hard. It makes you wonder how her boy is going to fare," Ryan explained dispassionately, grabbing some chips.

"You mean her *boys*. She's got two, doesn't she?"

"You didn't hear? She gave one of the twins up for adoption. At least that's what everyone says. I see her sometimes with the boy. Cute kid."

"It's been a while. I didn't even know her parents died. Shit."

Barrie had rationalized his absence from his sons' life by convincing himself they were better off without him. But now that the situation stood as Ryan described it, Barrie couldn't solace himself with delusions anymore. It sounded like Barrie had already lost one son. He didn't want to lose another. The next day, he hopped into his car.

"Hey Jackie," Barrie said when she opened the front door to her parents' house.

"What the hell are you doing here?" she asked. She was upset but otherwise as beautiful as she'd been when Barrie first met her. Her long, black hair was still pin-straight, parted down the middle, and wading at her waist. She had bags under her eyes, but her green eyeshadow drew attention from the visible signs of fatigue on her face.

"Can I come in?"

"I don't know. Where the hell have you been?" she asked, on the verge of tears. "And don't even think about saying Vietnam because I know you've been back for years. Joey Blanick told me."

"Just let me in, and we can talk," he said, extending a hand toward her face. A four-year-old boy with a brown bowl cut approached from behind her and clung onto her leg.

"And who are you?" Barrie asked, getting on his knees to meet the boy eye-to-eye.

"Sebastian," the boy said meekly.

"Hi, Sebastian, I'm..." Barrie started, reaching out his hand.

"Don't," Jackie interrupted. "Just get inside."

Jacqueline stuck Sebastian in front of the television and led Barrie into the dining room. She cried for what seemed like half an hour, yelling at Barrie, who shouldered the abuse because he knew he had to.

"I want to be here now," Barrie said, heartfelt. "At least I want to try. I want to get to know my son. I want to get to know you again."

He wasn't just bullshitting her. As scary as the responsibility of parenting sounded, he wanted to be grounded to something, and a child bearing his genetic material seemed the surest anchor. And then there was Jacqueline, still alluring, still dynamic.

Jackie reluctantly let Barrie back into her life. She was a source of comfort for him. And he loved that kid. Barrie was amazed at how much this four-year-old boy sounded like a small adult, articulate and independent. They would play games together, running around the back yard that stretched for almost a quarter-mile. They would pull figs from the tree out back, sometimes eating them, sometimes smashing them against the stone steps gleefully. They would trek through the Palos Verdes wilderness, finding relics of civilization—a crushed beer can or an abandoned belt—and the two of them would play archeologist, refashioning the trash into artifacts of yore. Eventually, Barrie started sleeping over more often, playing the part of the father during the day and the boyfriend at night. At the beginning of his coupledom with Jackie, their nights were passionate. But the days grew tiresome, the parenting got harder, the boyfriending lost its allure, and Barrie itched to get out.

They fell into a pattern. Barrie would spend time at Jacqueline's place in Palos Verdes until they'd start fighting. He'd long for his bachelorhood in Los Angeles, so he'd leave for the city, sure he'd never come back. But after frittering away his money, he'd show up again at Jacqueline's door with apologies, excuses, and pleas. Some of these stretches together lasted longer than others, but they all ended in conflict.

"What's this?" Barrie asked Jacqueline at the end of one such stretch, picking up a package at the door that was addressed to Sebastian.

"Oh, that?" she said, opening the package and revealing a math book. "It's a New Year's tradition. Sebastian gets one every year."

"What the hell kind of a New Year's tradition is that? The kid is six. I don't even think *I* could understand half of this stuff," Barrie said, flipping through the book. "Who's sending these books to him?"

"You remember Dr. Fredrickson, that UCLA professor I babysat for when I was in high school?" Jackie said as she started cooking a box of macaroni and cheese.

"I guess," Barrie said, struggling to summon the memory.

"Anyway, he was grateful for everything I did for his boys. They loved me. After the twins were born, he started sending me these math books every year, saying the boys might appreciate them when they got older. Sort of a thank you."

"That's weird, Jackie."

"It's not weird. It's sweet," she pushed back, focusing more on the boiling water and the macaroni than the fight. "Besides, Sebastian likes looking at them. He likes numbers."

"Who is this guy, anyway?"

"I *told* you…" Jacqueline started, raising her voice and abandoning the pasta pot.

"Yeah, yeah, you told me. You babysat his kids. What, like seven years ago? This is fucking weird, Jackie, and I don't like it. Tell him to stop sending these books."

"Like hell I will," she said, throwing her wooden spoon onto the floor.

The conflict escalated until they engaged in an all-out screaming match. Barrie left the house for a while to cool off.

Later that night, while Sebastian and Jacqueline were passed out watching the New Year's Eve broadcast on the couch, Barrie quietly packed his things into his car. He scanned the rooms to make sure he wasn't overlooking anything when he came across his accounting calculator in the den. Barrie went to pick it up. The machine was heavy. He didn't want the burden of it. He had a thought. The calculator would make an excellent companion to Sebastian's ever-increasing math book collection. Barrie wasn't sure if Jacqueline would even notice his calculator or if she'd realize that he was leaving it behind in a passive-aggressive gesture. He wanted to leave it there regardless. So the calculator remained, but Barrie left for good, without considering the one-day man he was shaping in the process.

←　←　6　←

Question from the deposition of Sebastian Barnabas in the Specter v. Stanford wrongful termination case: Dr. Barnabas, how would you characterize your relationship with Mallory Specter over her years as a faculty member at Stanford?

Sebastian could tell whenever Mallory Specter was approaching in the hallways by the sound of her heeled pumps. She walked in quick, measured steps because her pencil skirts restricted the movement of her thighs. Every day, she pulled back her hair in a carefully parted, tight, low ponytail. She donned thick-rimmed glasses. Unlike the other female mathematicians on staff, she wore heavy makeup. She wanted to be taken seriously.

For years, Mallory and Sebastian were just impersonal colleagues. But then everything changed. It started when she bumped into him in the hallway, spilling her coffee down his shirt. Sebastian looked up, surprised to see her since she hadn't announced her arrival with her patented heels. She was wearing sweats, not a pencil skirt. Mallory apologized for the spill, following Sebastian into his office. She was a mess. She had mascara smudges underneath her eyes. Her hair was pulled into an untidy bun. Sebastian preferred the mess to the rigidity of her typical look. She was more human this way, and whether or not he felt fully human himself, Sebastian gravitated toward the flawed humanness in women he met.

"I know I'm a wreck. My husband just left me. Here, I can help," she said, wiping the coffee stain on his shirt with a napkin. "You know, I really admire your work."

She closed the blinds, unbuttoned his shirt, removed it entirely, and threw herself into him with the reckless abandon of someone who'd just lost everything.

Question: Why do you think Dr. Specter wasn't offered tenure?

There was always a bottle somewhere in her office, maybe a Hudson Baby Bourbon Whiskey or a six-year-old Templeton Rye. The liquor was always brown; it was always good, and it was sometimes exceptional.

One Friday, after about a month of sleeping together, Sebastian came into her office. She was hammered. With a clumsy smile, she walked toward him, spilling a glass of bourbon as she came. She pulled out a second crystal tumbler and insisted he drink with her. He refused. She was already too far gone, and he didn't want to use the fragile crystal, didn't want to be accountable for any breakage. He tried to reason with her, tried to ply her with a kiss in the right place. His efforts only enraged her. She took her crystal tumbler and threw it against the floor. The carpet absorbed the shock, keeping the crystal pristine. Unsatisfied, Mallory picked up the glass and chucked it against the wooden cabinetry. She smiled maniacally as the tumbler broke into shiny pieces that caught the light. She grabbed another crystal tumbler, then another and another, repeating the spectacle for Sebastian, forcing him to witness the destruction as punishment for not accepting the beautiful offering when it was intact. Mallory stumbled out of the office, which glittered with wreckage. Sebastian called out to her, unsure where she could be going. She explained: her T.A. was holding a study session for the final, and the students needed Mallory's expertise. He tried to stop her, knowing she was in no condition to teach, but she was already gone.

Question: Aside from her issues with alcohol, which she is in treatment for, in your opinion, are there any other legitimate reasons why she should not have received tenure?

During the first few years Mallory Specter worked at Stanford, her office drawer was filled with rejection letters. She'd shown them to Sebastian in one of her drunken rages. Given her failure to publish, it was a miracle Stanford had kept her on for so long.

Question: Dr. Specter contends the math department created a hostile work environment. Can you think of anything you might have done to contribute to a toxic work environment?

Once Mallory started the formal complaint process against Sebastian and Diana, some members of the math department circulated rumors that she'd gotten her job through sexual favors or the implied promise of them. Sebastian's colleagues approached him, asking if the stories were true. Sebastian responded, "Who knows?" He could have mounted a firmer defense of Mallory. He could have said, "That doesn't sound like her." Or "Mallory never mentioned any sexual relationships with anyone else at Stanford." Or "She wrote some brilliant articles before she got here." Or "She went through a devastating divorce that did a real number on her." But Sebastian stayed silent. Should he have felt compelled to do more when she was the one bent on destroying *his* reputation?

Question: Would you recount your experiences with Dr. Specter in San Diego last year?

Sebastian hadn't asked Mallory to go to the mathematics conference with him, but he also hadn't rejected her when she'd asked to come. During the car ride down, they had to overcome moments of friction. The first came when Mallory talked about how upset she was that her proposal to speak at the conference had been rejected. As someone who'd earned a spot on the list of invited speakers, Sebastian didn't know how to comfort her without calling attention to his successful submission. He tried to reassure Mallory that the organizers could only take a limited number of abstracts, and they rarely accepted multiple papers from the same university. That might have provided more solace if fellow Stanford professor Diana Hyland had not been elected to speak as well. A subsequent discussion proved thornier. As they passed through Los Angeles, Mallory suggested they meet one another's families on their way back home after the conference. Sebastian coldly rejected the idea. They barely spoke for the remaining two hours. Their first night at the hotel only heightened the tension. Mallory tried to create a romantic ambiance with candles and wine. Sebastian ignored her and fell asleep on the couch. The next morning, Mallory was frustrated. She told Sebastian she would spend the rest of the time in L.A. with her mother. She'd swing down to San Diego when the conference was over and pick him up so he'd still have a ride up North. He didn't plead with her to stay.

Question: And what happened after that? We know Diana Hyland was with you. Would you explain what happened between yourself, Dr. Hyland, and our client? ... Dr. Barnabas?

← 3 ← ←

198

Diana was still holding on to her piece of chalk when Sebastian kissed her in his hotel room. She should have dropped the chalk, as Sebastian had. Instead, she crushed it in her hand. Diana broke away from Sebastian's kiss to deal with the remnants in her grasp. She opened up her fist, turned to the side, and blew away the dust from her palm, imagining herself a fairy. She and Sebastian both smiled at the whimsy of the gesture. Diana took the larger fragments that remained in her palm and brought them to the waste bin near the desk. As she bent down to trash the chalk, Sebastian unzipped her skirt. He tugged the skirt against her thighs, past her hips, and threw it on the floor. Diana wasted no time sticking her hand down his boxer briefs. She aroused him with cultivated efficiency, backing off when titillation necessitated restraint and casting her hands elsewhere.

It was a night of good sex, the best she'd had in a long time. Sebastian was engaged and attentive. They talked for most of that evening, meeting each other's minds on a wide array of topics. But when she woke up in Sebastian's bed the next morning, she worried about what she'd gotten herself into.

She looked at the blackboard near the foot of the bed and eyed the dots they'd marked. She remembered the question Sebastian had asked her before he'd kissed her: how many times have you been in love? Diana found the marks she'd made in response to his question, a field of dots that formed a partition of the number five. How many times had most people fallen in love by this point in their lives? She wondered if she fell in love too easily or not easily enough.

Sebastian had never answered the question when she'd asked it in return. She imagined what his number was. Three? His reluctance to answer the question made her believe the number was low. But maybe she didn't know him well enough to tell. Still, she liked Sebastian. She rolled over and appraised his face, this time in the light of day. She liked his almond-shaped eyes, his stubble. She wanted to rub her hand against the coarse grain of his facial hair, but the better part of her wanted to let him keep sleeping. He really was...wait. Diana heard someone at the door.

"Sebastian," she said, nudging him awake as the door opened.

"Shit," Sebastian said, barely awake. "Mallory," he said, seeing her in the doorframe, key in hand.

"What the hell is going on? Diana?" Mallory asked in disbelief.

"I thought you were going to stay in L.A. for the next few days," Sebastian said as he sat up, composing himself. Diana started piecing together the situation.

"Surprise," Mallory said, her irritation and anger palpable.

"Mallory, I..." Diana started, working her way toward an apology she shouldn't have been responsible for in the first place.

"Get out," Mallory demanded, cutting her off.

"I don't want her to leave," Sebastian said.

"It's all right," Diana said, pulling a sheet over herself and grasping for underwear. "I'm going," she said, putting on her bra. Mallory picked up Diana's dress and jacket from the floor and threw them at her. Mallory's mousy face tightened as Diana readied herself.

"I guess we're over," Mallory said to Sebastian.

"I guess so."

"Then there's nothing stopping me from reporting you two," Mallory threatened. The prospect was enough to stop Diana in her tracks.

"Mallory, please," Diana begged, pulling her dress over her body.

"Go ahead," Sebastian replied assuredly. "We haven't done anything wrong."

"A department chair sleeping with a faculty member from her department? Sounds unethical to me," Mallory said, her forehead creased in self-satisfied judgment.

"Mallory, you don't have to do that," Diana pleaded. "Listen, I'm sorry this happened the way it did. I had no idea you were involved with Sebastian."

"And now that you know...?" Mallory asked.

"It's over," Diana said, catching a glimpse of Sebastian's troubled face.

"Just like that?" Mallory asked, taking a step in Diana's direction.

"Yeah, just like that. I never would've been with him if I'd known about you," Diana said, glad she could be honest in her defense.

"How's it feel to be cast aside so easily?" Mallory asked Sebastian tauntingly. He didn't respond but instead looked to Diana, questioning her with his expression.

"Whatever you two need to talk about, you should do it without me here," Diana said, slipping on her shoes and gathering her purse. "I'll see you both later."

Diana got out of there as fast as she could, running down the hallway toward her hotel room. Once she got inside, she went to her laptop and searched online for university policy. She read through 1.7.2 of the Stanford Administrative Guide. It didn't prohibit consensual sexual relationships between faculty members. Still, in cases where there was an imbalance of power, it did require the person in an authority position to notify the administration and recuse themselves from decisions that pertained to the more junior employee. Diana knew what she had to do.

It took her nearly thirty minutes to craft the email to the dean. It made her sick to write it. She had fought so hard to get her position as department chair, and she worried this would only confirm long-held suspicions about women's inherent weakness. She resented Sebastian for putting her in this position, even though she knew she couldn't absolve herself of blame. She did sleep with one of her subordinates. But the duties of department chair were not the same as those of other administrators. Diana considered herself a leader

201

among peers rather than someone with superior standing over her colleagues. When Sebastian's hand had grazed hers in the hotel bar, and their eyes had met with mutual interest, they'd seemed on equal footing, both mathematicians. Diana might have had a minor lapse in judgment, but it seemed just that: minor. Sebastian, on the other hand, had been far more guilty. He was the one who was carrying on with two women without informing either of them. He was the one whose entanglement with Mallory turned Diana's indiscretion from a passing mistake into a political nightmare.

Once she sent the email, Diana readied herself for the day and packed her bags. Even though the conference wasn't over yet, Diana wanted to get out of there. After she finished packing, Diana opened her door to see her old blackboard pressed against the doorframe with a note Sebastian had written on it. There were apologies, but there were also confessions. Sebastian admitted to a long track record of disappointing women. He recognized and mourned the corrupt part of him that had governed his behavior for the better part of his adult life. He expressed strong feelings for Diana, bandying the word "love," albeit in oblique ways. He still wanted her, and he talked about the way she tasted and the way she felt. He resurrected enough details that she couldn't avoid replaying them. She blushed. She wanted him too, but not at the cost of her integrity, position, or self-worth. She erased his words with her sleeve, making sure not to miss anything. She wheeled the blackboard into her room and left it there—someone else's problem.

Diana went home and processed all the paperwork. Life at Stanford resumed. She wrote Mallory a long apology letter. Days went by, but Diana got no reply. Whenever Diana saw Mallory on campus, Mallory turned and went in the other direction. Sebastian was different. About a week after the conference, he stopped by Diana's office with a gift.

"I thought you could use a new set," he explained, handing over a box of chalk with a bow stuck on it. "Just don't crush these," he smiled.

"Thanks," Diana said, placing the box on her desk. She considered rejecting the gift outright, but she didn't want to make a scene. If anything, she hoped to downplay the significance of his romantic gesture rather than give it importance by spurning it.

"I know I've said it before, but I want to say it again. I'm sorry about what happened in San Diego. I should've told you about Mallory," Sebastian said, taking a seat.

"Yeah, you should've."

"I know. It's just that Mallory and I never put labels on what we were. We never said we were exclusive."

"She probably just figured you were because you were sleeping together," Diana argued, less for Mallory's sake than for her own.

"Fair enough," Sebastian said without pain or defensiveness. "But the truth is, Mallory and I never had a real connection. I know you and I haven't spent much time together, but I want to change that. I want to see you again."

"Sebastian, I don't think you understand how serious this whole saga has been. I'm the department chair. I care about my position. My reputation. This mess has taken a toll on me. We can't get involved again. Not now. Not ever. We'll still have a working relationship. And we can be friends. But that's as far as it can go. You need to know that."

Sebastian tensed his face but nodded in acceptance of the situation. He stood up. "I get it. If you ever change your mind, you know where to find me," he said as he left.

Once he was gone, Diana closed her door, accidentally shutting it so hard the diplomas on her wall shook. She walked to her bachelor's degree and straightened it out with care. She moved on to her doctoral degree, adjusting it just as meticulously. She caught her reflection in the glass casing but didn't want to linger on it. Diana returned to her desk, but it was hard for her to refocus on work. She felt foolish, more like a teenager than the fifty-one-year-old woman she was. Why had she flippantly climbed into bed with Sebastian in the first place? She wasn't usually so forward or impetuous. This whole experience proved that she was not the type to plunge into affairs of the heart frivolously.

Diana hoped the worst was over. But in the weeks and months that followed, Mallory filed complaints to the Provost about Diana. Even though Diana had handled everything appropriately and the Provost had decided not to take action against her, Diana couldn't stop the political fallout. She noticed a change in her colleagues' tone, especially in emails. They abandoned the norms of professional discourse. They spelled out their grievances in all caps. They used personal insults to denigrate her when they were unsatisfied with the way she was handling an administrative decision. They blamed minor squabbles between faculty members on her poor leadership.

The contentiousness only got worse when Mallory filed her lawsuit against the university. The next day, Diana got to her office to find a note posted onto her door that read "RESIGN." She threw it in the trash. But once she opened her email that day, she found that this wasn't the sentiment of a lone rogue. One colleague after another had emailed her, expressing their lack of confidence in her as chair. The collective weight of their disapproval mounted until she had to concede and step down. But there was one saving grace: at least her professional undoing came at a time of personal triumph. Diana had been seeing a man for a couple of months, a dentist who lived in the same condominium complex as she did. He offered comfort during the siege against her and reminded her of who she was beyond her titles and reputation. When the settlement negotiations in the lawsuit broke down, and Diana learned the suit would go to trial, she felt daunted, but at least she had an ally.

Sebastian woke up alone on the morning of his scheduled court appearance for the Mallory Specter case. He treated the day like any other, drinking his coffee and smoking a cigarette with the rising sun. But once Sebastian entered the courtroom, he felt burdened by the seriousness of the situation. The high-vaulted ceilings, the cold marble walls, and the judge's elevated platform established a feeling of solemnity. The gallery was filled with secretarial women with lipstick on their teeth, stodgy older men who seemed like permanent fixtures in the courtroom, and twentysomethings with the scent of law school on them. Sebastian looked around until he caught sight of Diana. She was sitting next to a man in medical scrubs who had his arm around her. This man, balding but good-looking enough, turned to kiss her on the forehead as they waited for the proceedings to begin.

Sebastian took a seat a couple of rows behind them. His leg bounced. He couldn't stop staring. Diana kept fidgeting and adjusting her bobby pins, which secured her rambunctious curls into a knot on the top of her head. Why hadn't she left her hair down as she usually did? Why did she have on a necklace? And why so much makeup? None of this was typical. She wore a form-fitting but professional-looking dress he'd never seen before. Not the black dress pants she wore into the ground. Or the solid-colored, silky blouses. Or the floral-print ones. Those floral patterns were his favorite, in part because she'd been wearing a dress with pink roses on it when they'd been at the conference together. He remembered the way her dress had caught her curves, then remembered the feel of her full figure between his fingers. She squirmed in her seat. Sebastian hoped it was because she was uncomfortable with "Scrubs" keeping his arm around her.

Sebastian wondered: was it necessary for the guy to wear his scrubs to the trial? Couldn't he have changed into them afterward? Was he trying to broadcast his professional status? Sebastian clenched his fist and imagined punching Scrubs in the face. He could almost feel the man's bristled mustache against his fist. Sebastian wondered how Scrubs could care about Diana but not help her adjust the bobby pins she kept fiddling with.

The judge called the court to order, and the proceedings began. When Sebastian was called to the stand to testify, he answered the questions as directly as he could.

"Did you have a sexual relationship with Dr. Hyland while you were still engaged in a sexual relationship with Dr. Specter?" the lawyer asked Sebastian.

"Yes," Sebastian admitted. He looked over at Diana, whose face was tense.

"And at that point, you had been having a sexual relationship with Dr. Specter for a month or so. Is that right?" the lawyer asked.

"That sounds right."

"Did you ever stop to think about how your actions would affect Dr. Specter?"

"I mean, I didn't want to hurt her. But she wasn't my girlfriend. We weren't in a relationship. I guess I didn't realize how attached Mallory had gotten to me," Sebastian admitted. He could feel eyes on him as he spoke. Mallory was glaring at him from the plaintiff's table. He caught sight of another woman in the crowd, a younger woman who looked familiar. She had a cold but distant stare. He had to avert his eyes.

"Were you concerned about the fact that your relationship with Dr. Hyland, the department chair, might hurt Dr. Specter's career prospects?" the lawyer pressed.

"Not really. Relationships between colleagues happen. And Diana has always been professional. I never thought she would abuse her position, and she never did," Sebastian said, looking to Diana for a reaction. She smiled slightly, but she wasn't looking at Sebastian; she was looking at Scrubs, who rubbed her shoulder in reassurance.

Sebastian wanted to get off the stand as soon as possible. More questions followed, and Sebastian answered them. After his testimony concluded, the judge ordered everyone to break for lunch. When Sebastian made his way through the crowd, he saw Scrubs head for the restroom. Sebastian took the opportunity to corner Diana.

"Diana," he called out. "Hey."

"I can't believe this is happening," she replied. "Why didn't they just settle? You'd think Stanford would've wanted to handle this behind closed doors. Avoid bad PR."

"They tried to settle. Mallory was intransigent."

"I can't get over her. How can she argue gender discrimination? I'm a woman for Christ's sake, and I was the department chair," Diana said, fiddling with her jewelry. Poetically, she took out a tube of lipstick and reapplied it, using a compact in her purse as a guide. "It's ironic," she continued. "I'm the poster child of women's empowerment."

"I know," Sebastian said.

"No, I don't think you do. I'm literally on poster after poster, representing female achievement. Any time there's a new brochure or a marketing piece meant to stir up interest in the math department, I'm the face of gender-based diversity."

"Trust me, Diana. I know. I've seen them. I know every spot on campus where I can catch a glimpse of your face."

"Come on, Sebastian. Don't," she said, avoiding his gaze. He knew he would never get her back if he ever had her in the first place.

"Who's the guy in the scrubs?" Sebastian asked.

"Henry. He's a good guy. In fact, I should go wait for him."

"Sure," Sebastian said, watching her turn her back on him.

As Sebastian walked to his car, he saw a woman whom he thought he recognized: the same woman he'd locked eyes with when he'd been on the witness stand. She was in her twenties, redheaded with a bright face. She didn't seem to notice him. Sebastian had a strong suspicion he'd slept with her not long ago. Was she a bartender? He pursued her from a distance, trying to ascertain her identity.

She dropped her keys from her purse and bent down to pick them up. Sebastian noticed a familiar bird tattoo on her ankle. He must have slept with her. Sebastian grew paranoid. Suddenly, every woman he encountered looked like someone he might have been with. The middle-aged woman in the purple dress who adjusted her heel. The college-aged intern with an ID badge around her neck. The elderly woman being wheeled to the restroom. It was out of control. Sebastian knew his imagination was concocting liaisons that hadn't happened, but mentally placing these women into his bed was too easy.

After lunch, Sebastian returned so he could watch Diana's testimony. When he entered the courtroom, she was already seated. Henry wasn't with her. Sebastian thought to approach her but figured it would be best to give her space. He sat toward the back of the gallery, feeling vindicated by the other man's absence. Sebastian was the one who would be there for Diana during her moment of vulnerability.

Once the trial resumed, Diana took the witness stand. Sebastian fidgeted.

"When you started your sexual relationship with Dr. Barnabas, were you concerned about a conflict of interest since you were his department chair?" the lawyer asked.

"In hindsight, I should have been more concerned. At the time, I didn't think about it. I treated him like a colleague," Diana said, squirming in apprehension.

"But he wasn't just a colleague. You had the authority to affect all sorts of decisions related to his career. Decisions like the teaching assignments he received. Isn't that right?"

"I did initially, but once I disclosed everything to the administration, I recused myself from any decisions related to him."

"Dr. Hyland, before that night with Dr. Barnabas, how long had you been a department chair?" the lawyer asked with the confidence of someone winding up a blow.

"Three years or so."

"Do you believe that those three years gave you enough experience to understand the roles, responsibilities, and norms of being a department chair?"

"Yes, I think so," she admitted, her eyes already defensive of his mounting strategy.

"Then why did you break an important norm and sleep with someone you knew was a subordinate?"

Sebastian leaned onto his knees as Diana paused to think.

"Attraction. Recklessness. I made a mistake," she said, speaking slowly and deliberately, pained by the acknowledgment of her faults.

A mistake. Sebastian stared at Diana, but she kept her eyes on the lawyer who was questioning her. Sebastian left the gallery as discreetly as he could, knowing it had been foolish to think that Diana needed him there.

He was walking toward the elevator when he heard the click of heels running toward him. He turned around to see the signature red hair, and the compactly arranged facial features of the woman with the bird tattoo.

"You dropped this in there," she said as she neared him, handing him his wallet.

"Thanks," Sebastian said. "Wait, aren't you..." he started, squinting his eyes as if to search his mind.

"I'm Alice," she said. Her sensuality made Sebastian think she should come with appropriate labels: eat me, drink me. "Mallory was my advisor when I was working on my dissertation. I think I ran into you once or twice in her office."

"That's right. Sorry I couldn't place you."

"It's all right. Take care," she said before heading back into the courtroom.

Sebastian was relieved to learn he hadn't slept with this woman. But now he remembered wanting to sleep with her. He'd spotted the bird tattoo and thought there was something sexy about it: the rarity of seeing that sort of thing on an academic. He'd wanted to grip her leg and hike that ankle into the air so the bird could fly high, even if it were upside down. He'd slept with Mallory minutes after the young woman left her office. He'd positioned Mallory's leg over his shoulder and grabbed her naked ankle, imagining there was a bird inked on it.

Sebastian left the courthouse behind him, thinking he deserved to be on trial.

The Third Diagonals
Pyramidal Numbers: Life Gets Even More Complicated

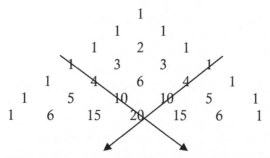

In Pascal's triangle, the numbers in the third set of diagonals (1, 4, 10, 20...) are also known as triangular pyramidal (or tetrahedral) numbers. These figures represent the number of dots needed to create a pyramid with an equilateral triangle base. The equation for determining triangular pyramidal numbers (where n = the number of dots and T_n = the total number of dots) is:

$$T_n = \frac{n(n+1)(n+2)}{6}$$

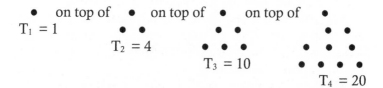

The triangles from the second diagonal enter the next dimension: building and building and building upon one another.

To minimize confusion, when Jake and Sebastian first started meeting up, it was typically in neutral territory—in a café, in a bar, at a park, or somewhere else in San Francisco proper—never in Berkeley or Palo Alto. There were practical reasons for this. Neither of them was keen on explaining their new relationship to people, especially since they were still trying to figure out what it meant to be friends, much less brothers. But with time, their similarities brought them closer to one another. They were both academics. They suffered at the hands of manipulative colleagues who had no qualms about tearing others down to serve their interests. They were both coming to grips with their families' lies. They understood one another in ways no one else could. So, they met up more and more.

Their increasingly frequent visits allowed them to explore San Francisco. Jake liked relaxing at Dolores Park in the Mission District. He liked browsing through the vendors' wares at the Ferry building and strolling along the Embarcadero. But there were times when meeting in the city wasn't ideal. Sometimes, it was more convenient for Sebastian to travel to Berkeley or for Jake to travel to Palo Alto. They decided to risk the potential consequences and meet on campus. Jake agreed to go to Stanford first.

"Are you sure that's such a good idea?" Lilith asked before Jake left. She seemed nervous, scratching her manicured fingernails against her thumbs.

"It'll be fine," Jake said.

"What if someone on campus mistakes you for Sebastian?" she asked, following him from the bedroom to the foyer as he grabbed his coat to head out.

"Lilith, Sebastian and I have gone over this. It's not that hard to explain now. It's not a big deal," Jake said, putting on his gray peacoat. He glanced at the mirror. Lilith approached him and directed his gaze to hers by touching his face.

"Jake, don't go to Stanford," she said, desperation in her voice. "I'm serious. I have a bad feeling about this."

Jake couldn't believe how shaken she was. She'd never been superstitious, but she was treating this "bad feeling" as a matter of importance.

"What's going on? Why are you so worked up?"

"It's probably nothing," Lilith said, straightening the collar on his coat. She paused in contemplation before asking, "Why doesn't Sebastian come to Berkeley?"

"He will," Jake said, rubbing her shoulders. "Eventually. Listen, the last thing I want to do is upset you. But nothing will happen. It's all going to be fine. You'll see."

Jake couldn't understand why she was so insistent, but he kissed her on the cheek, put it out of mind, and left.

When Jake arrived at Sebastian's office in Sloan Hall, the first thing he noticed was the disarray. It was so removed from the meticulous order of his own office that Jake felt like an intruder, stumbling into the mind rather than the physical space of his brother. Jake didn't understand how Sebastian could tolerate the books and academic journals and notebooks and binders shoved into bookshelves with such artlessness. Everything appeared on the verge of collapse, teetering with an instability that set Jake on edge. Aside from the anchor of a central computer, the desk was cluttered too. It was covered with papers and books and miscellaneous personal effects—ashtrays that housed a few cigarette butts in defiance of the university tobacco policy, salt and pepper shakers, generic coffee mugs, geometric paperweights, and a brown packing box brimming with items.

There was one decoration Jake appreciated: a set of large, intricately designed pyramids that dangled from the ceiling.

"Sierpinski's tetrahedrons," Sebastian said, noticing how Jake stared at them.

213

"Fractals," Jake said, recognizing the self-similar patterns of the smaller triangles embedded into the larger triangles on the faces of the pyramids.

"Right. They're beautiful, aren't they?"

Jake looked at the Sierpinski pyramids and agreed. They were like snowflakes, elaborate and delicate—triangles inside triangles inside triangles. But unlike snowflakes, all the pyramids had the same pattern. Jake looked closely for manufacturing flaws that might distinguish one from another, perhaps an uncut edge of plastic that didn't align with the rest of the pyramid or a color defect in the material. Jake considered how fragile they seemed. The centers of the Sierpinski pyramids were large, and he wondered how the shapes maintained their structural integrity with so much space carved into their middle.

"I'm ready to grab some coffee," Jake said, eager to leave the cramped office.

Jake and Sebastian made their way to a coffeehouse just off-campus. After Jake ordered his double ristretto, he headed to the restroom. When Jake returned, he saw the back of a dark-haired woman talking to Sebastian before she darted out of the coffeehouse.

"What was that about?" Jake asked.

"You don't know her?" Sebastian responded.

"I didn't get a good look at her. Why?"

"I figured she had the two of us mixed up. I've never seen her before in my life, but she came up to me talking about some email. She was upset. I don't know, said something about feeling embarrassed and surprised. I tried to explain to her I didn't know what she was talking about, but she just laid into me and left. You know anyone at Stanford?"

"I mean, I know some scientists from conferences, but no one I've talked to recently. What did she look like?"

"Pretty. Thirties. Wavy brown hair. Brown eyes. Tan complexion. Freckles across her nose."

"Selene," Jake muttered, mulling over the description. "But I haven't talked to her in years. She doesn't even live out here. At least, I don't think she does."

"The Selene you had an affair with?"

"Yeah," Jake said, racking his brain for any other possible women Sebastian could have met. But no else fit the description. *What if it was her?* he had to consider.

"Have you emailed her lately?"

"No," Jake said. He pulled out his phone and checked his inbox to see if he had any messages from her that he might have missed. He searched for her name. Nothing came up except some old emails from five years ago.

"Maybe I should reach out to her. Drop her a line. See if that was her," Jake said.

"Won't your wife get upset if she finds out you're talking to her?"

"'Upset' is an understatement. Yeah, it's a bad idea. Besides, maybe it was just some random person. Mistaken identity. I should let it go. Right?"

Sebastian thought for a moment before he spoke. "I don't know, Jake. If you had asked me a week or two ago, I might have told you to email her. But this trial with Mallory and Diana has shaken something loose in me. I think you have to protect your marriage. You've got something I don't have. Something I've never had."

"There's a lot you should be happy to have missed out on," Jake said in a knee-jerk reaction to the fights and tensions he'd experienced over the last five years.

"You might be right. But still..." Sebastian replied, then paused. His lips were open as he considered his next words. "Can I ask you something personal?"

"Sure," Jake said, drinking his coffee.

"How often do you have sexual thoughts about someone other than your wife?"

"That *is* personal," Jake responded, sighing and craning his neck, unaccustomed to such open conversations about sex.

"Sorry. Forget it," Sebastian said, reading Jake's discomfort.

"No, no, it's fine," Jake said, gripping his composure and remembering that this was his brother he was talking to, his double. He wanted to be open. "Are you talking about looking at a beautiful girl on the street or really thinking about being with someone else?"

"Anything. Could be in passing."

"I couldn't give you an exact number. A fair amount."

"Every day?" Sebastian pressed, one eye narrowed in curiosity.

"Why do you want to know?" Jake asked. His defensiveness around sex was programmed into him, and though he wanted to continue, his impulses tapped the brakes.

"I'm just trying to figure out how much of my damage is fixable and how much is hard-wired."

"Everyone thinks about sex," Jake assured him. Jake relaxed into sympathy, more encouraging once he realized this wasn't about his own sex life, not really.

"I know. It's just...being on the witness stand and talking about these women I've been with...I don't know. I just want it to be over. I can't believe Mallory didn't just settle."

"If there's anything I've learned, it's that when someone wants to destroy you, they're not content with taking a small piece of you."

"You talking about Radenport now?" Sebastian asked.

"Could be. I found out he's having an affair with a girl whose dissertation I'm advising. She's passing along information about my research to him."

"You're sure?"

"Yeah. I planted some false information about the meteorite when I was talking to her, and it got back to him."

216

"So...what? You think she's a spy?" Sebastian asked, only half-serious.

"Maybe. It's not the craziest idea in the world."

Sebastian didn't say anything, but he looked at Jake with more commiseration than skepticism. Sebastian's silence allowed Jake to believe that his suspicions about Jessica weren't entirely unfounded. Now, Jake simply had to figure out what to do about her.

 →   4   →   →

When Jessica Fleming was growing up, she was a latchkey kid, which is to say she was never a kid at all. On a typical day, she kept the spare house key wedged into the back edge of her sneaker. But when it got hot, and she wanted to wear sandals, she would secure the key to a metal chain she wore under her shirt, keeping it close to her heart like her Christian friends who tucked their crosses away from public eyes, held tight in private devotion. One time, to maintain the illusion that she was like her friends, Jessica gripped the form of the key through the fabric of her shirt and said an invented prayer over it, which seemed no less pretend than the way other kids treated the rosaries in their palms. But some part of Jessica knew the prayer wasn't pretend; the words were just different than the ones she would have said if no one had been around. In her fake piety, she articulated a real hope for salvation.

She went to a public school that was less than a half-mile from her house, and only a four-minute walk from a public library. Most of the time, she would go to the library in the afternoon and go home when it was time to cook herself dinner—some boxed macaroni and cheese or easy meals like tacos. The library was a sanctuary for her. When she was there, she'd pretend to be as scholarly as her parents, both Ph.D.s. She had a knack for academics from an early age, perhaps because her parents used words like "meritorious" and "anomalous" in casual conversation—at least when they were around. She developed a track record as an ever-precocious kid. In the second grade, she started a marine life conservationist society and recruited her friends to join in letter-writing campaigns to members of Congress. In the fourth grade, she spearheaded a fundraiser to furnish the school with more lab equipment. In middle school, she always had her hand raised in class.

Despite her perpetual hand-raising, the boys in Jessica's grade liked her. She was pretty and unafraid. Even though she knew her looks were the reason why she managed to have a string of boyfriends in middle school, why she lost her virginity when she was just fourteen, and why she distrusted her talkative middle-aged neighbor who stood too close to her, she still never believed she was attractive. Jessica had supreme confidence in her intellect but little confidence in her appearance.

When Jessica Fleming decided to double-down on the promise of her intellect and pursue her Ph.D. at Berkeley, she didn't think her looks would play any role in her academic experience. Her affair with William Radenport was not born of a compulsive desire to get ahead or an attempt to get a better grade on a paper. Instead, it was the product of more excusable personal weaknesses: her low regard for her physical appearance, her confidence in her mental prowess, and her attraction to people whose intelligence matched or exceeded her own. Like all professors, William Radenport was impressively smart. Jessica appreciated his intelligence, but she never saw him as a love interest until one day when they were alone in the elevator on their way to his class.

Jessica was ready to make small talk when he started fawning over an insightful paper she'd recently submitted. His compliments weren't measured—they were effusive, and because of the excesses of his praise and the intensity of his eye contact, his words felt sexually charged. She relished the intimacy of student-teacher relationships and felt the tug of attraction toward most professors she esteemed. He began asking her to visit during office hours to deepen their conversations from class. He asked her for extra copies of her work so he could use them as examples for future students. She was so flattered by his overtures that when he first kissed her, she believed she was worthy of his attention.

But when she'd first arrived on campus, Jessica hadn't hoped to earn the affections of William Radenport. She'd been more attracted to Jake Washington, even though Jake never gave her any sign of romantic interest. She knew Jake was married, like William. But Jake didn't seem willing to stray. He was always professional with her. And ultimately, Jessica didn't *aspire* to lure and entrap married men into her bed. She felt guilty enough about Radenport. She harbored sexual fantasies about her professors, sure, but except for William, she generally sublimated those desires into her academic work.

Jessica was daydreaming about Jake Washington when she came across him smoking a cigarette near the entrance to McCone Hall. It was almost as if he knew he was the object of her fantasies and had materialized to give form to the unspoken longing inside her. But something was off. Jake looked different. For one, Jessica had never seen him smoke before. Beyond that, Jake had also managed to grow a beard in a couple of days. Was it possible that she hadn't noticed his facial hair coming in during their last meeting?

"Jake," Jessica called out. "Is that you?" she asked as she neared him.

"Do I look different?" he asked, even his tone more relaxed than usual.

"I've never seen you with so much facial hair before," she said. She tried to conceal her smile. His facial hair contributed to his sexual appeal, lending an air of masculinity to his otherwise soft features. The interplay between his rugged and sensitive traits heightened the romantic image of a brilliant professor. Jessica had always noticed the scattered gray hairs on his head, but the grays in his beard were more pronounced. They made him look distinguished.

"Since when have you smoked?" she asked, eyeing his cigarette.

"Since college," he said, continuing to inhale his Lucky Strike.

"I didn't think any modern scientists smoked."

"Does it bother you?" he asked, gesturing a willingness to extinguish the cigarette.

"No," she said defensively. She'd been a smoker for a stint in high school when she'd turned eighteen, already adult enough to make bad decisions. She'd quit as an undergrad. But now the secondhand smoke awoke the teenager inside her in ways she didn't want to suppress. The scent summoned a flurry of hormonal jitters that made her feel electric. She ended up bumming a cigarette from him, eager to indulge in a shared ritual. She watched him handle his cigarette and focused on his lips as he projected smoke from his lungs. She appraised the fullness of his lips— perfectly average. She took inventory of the men and boys she'd kissed in her relatively short lifetime, trying to find an analogous set of lips from her catalog so she could better approximate the likely feel of his lips against hers. Meeting eyes with him, she worried her thoughts were showing. She took another drag of her cigarette and focused her eyes on the concrete.

"I know we're not meeting until tomorrow, but I've gone through the articles that you suggested at our last meeting. Could we talk about them now for a minute?" Jessica asked, trying to establish a more academic tone, even though every part of her wanted to keep behaving intimately, especially out in the open air.

"Listen, I have to come clean. I'm not Jake," he said. He extended his hand toward her in greeting: "Sebastian Barnabas. I'm a mathematics professor at Stanford."

It took her a second to process everything. "Jessica Fleming," she said, accepting his hand. "God, I thought I was going crazy. You look so much like him, but there was something...I don't know." She let out a sigh. "So what are you...his twin?" she asked, immediately realizing what a stupid question it was. He didn't seem to mind.

"Yeah," he replied. "You want to grab some coffee?"

She couldn't believe it. This man, this not-Jake-Washington who looked like Jake Washington, was asking to spend time with her. She gazed at him with lost intensity, as if she were looking at an optical illusion puzzle, trying to blur her focus while searching for traces of a different image beneath the surface of what she was seeing. She needed to unsee Jake Washington if only so she could finally see Sebastian Barnabas. She found that all she had to do was fixate on the differences between the two men: the added facial hair, the trimmer physique, the archly cool confidence.

"All right," she agreed. "We can go to the Free Speech Movement Café."

Once they entered the café and Jessica saw the familiar back wall covered in black-and-white photographs of protesters from the 1960s Free Speech Movement, she wondered if this was a good place for them to talk. She didn't want Sebastian to think about dissent when he was with her. The weather was beautiful anyway.

"Let's get it to-go," she said before she ordered her coffee. "I feel like walking."

Drinks in hand, they made their way toward Sproul Plaza, where Jessica led them to a six-foot diameter granite circle in the ground.

"You know about the Free Speech circle?" she asked, motioning toward the granite circle inlaid into the concrete beneath their feet.

"Nope," Sebastian said, then looked down. "THIS SOIL AND THE AIR SPACE EXTENDING ABOVE IT SHALL NOT BE A PART OF ANY NATION AND SHALL NOT BE SUBJECT TO ANY ENTITY'S JURISDICTION," he read from the inscription.

"It's a monument to the Free Speech Movement," Jessica said, placing herself inside one end of the circle. "You can say anything you want here. Step inside."

Sebastian obeyed, standing across from her inside the circle.

"How long have you been interested in my brother?" Sebastian asked flirtatiously. Jessica's heart raced as she processed his question.

"Excuse me?" she replied, trying to brush off the accusation.

"Listen, I'm not going to tell him," Sebastian assured her, "but I'm also not going to pretend that the way you were acting when you approached me was because of who *I* am."

"How was I acting?" Jessica asked, a sly smile building as she let down her guard.

"You know what I mean."

"I don't," she said, worried that she was blushing...*knowing* she was.

"Fine. Go ahead and be evasive while you're in the *free speech circle*. I guess it's your right. After all, lies are protected speech too," Sebastian said, playfully taunting her.

"Okay. Maybe I am attracted to him. But he's my dissertation advisor, and he's married. He could never think of me as anything other than a student anyway."

"I doubt that," Sebastian said, stepping toward her and entering the center of the circle. He looked her square in the eyes as he told her, "You're beautiful, after all."

His compliment felt surreal. Jessica had mentally constructed moments like this with Jake in mind. Those dreams had been so unconvincing that she'd written them off as fiction. But now, here was Jake's double, transporting her to an alternate universe where the object of her desire was not only single but attracted to her. Only instead of feeling pure elation, Jessica felt a mix of anxiety, excitement, and vulnerability.

"You think so?" she asked, taking a step in his direction.

"You don't?" he responded, getting closer.

"I don't know," she said. Jessica thought she might kiss Sebastian then, but she felt too self-conscious about what she'd just confessed. "Please don't say anything to Jake. I wouldn't want to make things awkward between us. He's going to be my dissertation advisor for a while. Besides, I'm seeing someone else."

Sebastian paused for a moment. "And it's serious between you and this someone else?"

"Define serious."

"Are you in love with him?"

"No. I wouldn't say love," she replied. Over the past couple of months, she and William had become closer, but she still kept him at a distance. The sex was fine, but the aftermath was messy.

"What would you say?"

"I don't know, I mean, he's married. So it'll never be love."

"You don't deserve to be anyone's second choice," Sebastian said.

"That sounds like a line," Jessica said, chuckling, taken aback by the stock remark. "Like, a *corny* line."

"Maybe it is."

"But I just told you I'm involved with someone."

"You said it wasn't serious," he replied, tilting his head with a knavish smirk.

"You know, you're nothing like your brother."

"I agree. Refreshing, isn't it?"

She laughed slightly, smiling at his audacity.

"Listen, I want you to forget about this other guy," he said, leaning toward her and grabbing her hand, "and come to dinner with me tonight."

"You don't think Jake would mind?" Jessica asked, guilt and excitement building.

"He doesn't have to know."

"What kind of a brother are you?" Jessica asked, half in jest. But she did worry that Sebastian's willingness to keep something like this from his twin spoke to his capacity for disloyalty. Sebastian and Jessica left the Free Speech circle as he explained his history with Jake. Jessica could barely believe the complicated path that had brought the two men back to one another after a life lived apart. Even if she couldn't fully understand the dynamic between Jake and Sebastian, she could understand how loyalty might look different between the two of them. Sebastian reached out for her hand once more. She looked up into his eyes. They were richly brown and expectant, and she knew she was in trouble.

→   →   10   →

The black-and-white newspaper print didn't capture Sebastian Barnabas' face well, but the small picture still caused Daniel Washington to do a double-take when he saw it. If you gave the man in the newspaper a good shave, he could be Daniel's son. Daniel started reading the accompanying article, which described a wrongful termination lawsuit against Stanford. He came across Sebastian's name and realized why the man in the picture looked so strikingly like his own son. The long-lost twin. Seeing Jake's near image in the newspaper was jarring enough, but as Daniel kept reading, he came across something that struck him just as intensely: the name of the law firm that was representing the plaintiff. Daniel stuffed the newspaper into his briefcase, grabbed some take-out, and headed home.

Once Daniel arrived, he put the take-out on the kitchen counter. He undid his tie and loosened his collar, stripping off his lawyerly persona. He moved more slowly than he used to. Back in the day, he could take his suit off in a flash and quickly acclimate to his native role at home where paperwork didn't exist. But after so many years in his field, the suit had a habit of sticking to him. Even the act of retracting one arm from an armhole took too long. When Rachel saw him struggling with his right arm, she came up behind him and slipped a hand under the jacket to help.

Daniel knew her assistance wasn't selfless. The first time she'd helped remove his jacket after a long day at work, she'd said, "You're getting too old for this." Whenever she eased the transition from lawyer to husband, she was trying to prove a point: the jacket belonged on a hanger rather than his body. This time, Daniel placed his hand over hers when she made contact. He felt the warmth of her hand and let it linger. He let go, and she hung up his jacket.

"You won't believe what I saw in the paper," he said, tossing the folded article onto the counter. Rachel picked it up and surveyed it.

"It's like looking at a ghost," she said, her eyes glued to Sebastian's picture.

"I know. Sebastian is part of a wrongful termination lawsuit against Stanford. Some sex scandal he was involved in. And get this. The plaintiff is Brian Whitmore's daughter. Kensington Whitmore is representing her in the trial."

"Did you know about this?"

"No," Daniel said. "But I'm going to ask Brian about it tomorrow. Maybe I can find out something about the case."

"What good will that do?"

"Probably nothing," Daniel admitted. "But I'm curious. I know Sebastian isn't part of our family, but he's Jake's family."

Rachel looked like she was about to cry.

"What's wrong?" Daniel asked, approaching her as she stood by the kitchen sink.

"I talked to Jake today," Rachel said, her wet eyes meeting Daniel's.

"And?" he asked gently, fearful of impending bad news. Rachel had always been the communication link between Daniel and his son. Though he loved Jake as much as a father could, his high-demand profession had estranged them from each other, making Rachel the conduit of affection and information between them.

"He's coming home for Thanksgiving," she said.

"Well, that's good," Daniel assured her, relieved that their son might return to the fold, no matter how slowly. "I know you were worried," he continued, rubbing Rachel's shoulders in consolation. Daniel wanted his son back too, but he didn't experience the sting of Jake's rejection as strongly as Rachel. He hadn't been the one talking to Jake on the phone weekly. He hadn't raised him day in and day out for decades. Instead, Daniel had clocked long work hours to keep the family prosperous; that had been his primary role.

"Yeah, you're right. It's good," Rachel managed, but tears halted her words.

"Then what's the matter?" Daniel asked, looking at her downcast head and raising it with a gentle finger under the chin.

"It was just the phone conversation we had. We hammered out the details, but that was it. I tried to ask him how he was doing, but he kept giving me these one-word answers. He handled it like a business transaction." Her full lips buckled against each other in pained frustration. Tears still muddled her teal-blue eyes.

"He'll come around. If he agreed to come home for Thanksgiving, that's a good first step. This situation isn't going to heal itself all at once," Daniel said, embracing her.

"I know. I just didn't realize it would take this long."

"Thanksgiving will be the perfect time to reconnect," Daniel said, disengaging from their hug and fixing himself a scotch on the rocks. "You'll see."

"He's going to see her while he's down here."

"Who?"

"Jacqueline Barnabas. Not on Thursday though. He agreed to that much," she said, arms braced against the kitchen counter as though she needed the granite to steady her.

"Don't worry about her. We're still Jake's parents. We're the ones who raised him. No one can take that away from us," Daniel said, approaching her with his drink in hand. "You want me to fix you something?" he asked her, waving his scotch.

"No, thanks," she said, smiling weakly. Her gaze drifted for a moment. "Maybe I should cook something special for Thanksgiving. What do you think? I have years-worth of food magazines I could go through."

"Make what you always make. There's a reason why everyone loves it."

"I'll still make all the staples. But I think I'll add a new dessert. Something sweet we can end on," Rachel said, opening a cupboard and pulling out a stack of magazines.

"Are you going to figure this out *now*?" Daniel asked, worrying that compulsion would overtake her as it sometimes did. "I don't want dinner to get cold."

"I think it'll make me feel better. I don't care if it's neurotic."

She looked through the spines of the magazines and separated the November issues from the rest. She began her search, rifling through the pages fanatically.

"Just put the magazines away. There's no recipe for what you want," Daniel said, eager to share dinner with his wife. After the tumult of the day, he wanted to unwind, which was at odds with her mania.

"You don't know that," she protested, continuing to leaf through the magazines.

"You should make your own dish," he suggested, hoping to end her quest.

"Without a recipe? Daniel, I'm not a pastry chef."

"You can handle it," he assured her, sidling up to her, casting a hand around her waist. "You don't need this," he said, lifting the edge of a magazine. "Just keep it simple."

"I guess I could come up with something basic," she relented, smiling as he detached from her and waved the plastic bags filled with Chinese food in her face. Daniel was glad to see her acquiesce. It was hard for him to watch her get into one of her frenzies. She put away the magazines, and they ate their dinner together.

Later that night, Daniel couldn't sleep. At ten o'clock, when Rachel was already asleep, he went to the kitchen and fixed himself another scotch. Sitting at the dining room table, he re-examined the newspaper he'd brought home. He couldn't stop staring at Sebastian's picture. He brought the paper into his study, where he took out a pencil and tried to erase Sebastian's beard. The ink was obstinate. Daniel pulled out a bottle of white-out and painted over the beard with the white-out brush, but the dead space looked unnatural. He grabbed a pair of scissors and cut the picture out of the article. He carefully carved around the whited-out beard and pasted the remainder of Sebastian's cutout face on a blank scrap of newsprint. Daniel used his pencil to recreate the bottom half of Sebastian's face, or rather, Jake's face, beardless, to forge a closer reconstruction of his son.

When Daniel surveyed his work, he was frustrated by the failure of his efforts. He had not created a portrait of Jake or Sebastian, but some twisted hybrid of the two of them. Daniel drank his scotch. He wondered what might have become of Sebastian if Daniel had been able to raise him alongside Jake. Would Sebastian be a better person? Would Jake? Would Daniel? More than anything, Daniel wished he could do more to remedy the identity crisis Jake was facing, but he knew he was powerless. He casually drank his scotch until he drifted off, falling asleep with his face on the newsprint.

The next day, with thoughts of Sebastian in his head, Daniel went to Brian Whitmore's office. Now that Brian was older, he was starting to look just like his father, Kenneth, had looked: chiseled wrinkles in his forehead, receding hairline, an extra thirty pounds in the gut, sleeplessness under his eyes. When Kenneth had passed away decades ago, Brian had taken over. The most Brian had done to change his father's office was to update items that fingered his old man by name: the diploma, the nameplate, the plaques. Daniel felt the same uneasiness around Brian as he had around Kenneth.

"Brian," Daniel said as he entered. "I heard about the Stanford case."

"The San Francisco office is working it," Brian told him, distracted by paperwork.

"Sure. But I was wondering if you could send me the case files anyway," Daniel said, taking a seat opposite Brian's desk.

"Why?" Brian asked pointedly, looking up with an accusatory glance.

"I might be able to help."

"Not on this one," Brian said, brushing him off and continuing with his work.

"Why not?"

"I told you, the San Francisco offices have it covered," Brian looked up, agitated.

"My son lives in the Bay Area," Daniel added in explanation, knowing better than to expose his real interest: Sebastian. "I could go up and help. I could see my son while I'm there. I just figured since Mallory is the plaintiff, you'd want as many eyes on this as possible. From what I've read and heard, the trial isn't going her way."

"Jesus, Daniel," Brian exclaimed, red-faced and jostled from his seat. "Could you keep your nose out of it?"

"There's money on the line," Daniel realized.

"Yeah. Important research coming out of Stanford that Carver-Jackson funds. Stanford has to come out on top."

"But Mallory's on the other side of that case. She's your daughter."

"You think I don't know that?"

"Does she know…"

"Of course not," Brian said, losing the energy for argument.

"This is a new low."

"I'm doing what's best for the firm, which is what's best for her too," Brian explained. Daniel judged Brian. But Daniel also knew that what he'd done all these years hadn't been much different: compromising his values to give his family financial security.

"I can't do this anymore," Daniel said, disgusted with Brian, disgusted with himself.

"You want out? Fine. But everything you know stays here," Brian said, pointing downward onto his desk for effect.

"That's what you're worried about? You think I'm going to sell you out?"

"If you did, you'd be making a huge mistake. You're implicated too."

"And now the threats? What if I did turn you in? What would you do?"

"Daniel," Brian explained, teeth gritted. "It's not about what *I* would do."

"What you would do, what *they* would do. I'm too old for this. You can threaten me all you want, but I'm done. Consider this notice of my retirement," Daniel said as he headed out the door.

When Daniel got home, it was still afternoon. Instead of opening the door with his key, he rang the doorbell and waited for his wife to answer. When she did, he smiled and walked over the threshold.

"What are you doing home in the middle of the day?" Rachel asked.

Daniel turned his back to her, lowered his chin to signal what he wanted her to do. He waited for her to slide her hand between his jacket and his shirt. He craned his neck and kissed her hand before she gingerly removed the jacket.

"You can put it in storage," he told her.

She smiled and retreated to a closet in the back where she threw the jacket into a box. Meanwhile, Daniel undid his tie, unbuttoned his collar, and took off every vestige of his former identity. Stripped down to his underwear, Daniel lay down on the couch, stared at the ceiling, and envisioned a new self.

→   →   →   20

Thanksgiving offered the twins a chance to piece together their family history. Trying to keep disorder at bay, they decided to keep the actual Thanksgiving Day simple: Jake would spend the day with his adoptive parents, and Sebastian would spend the holiday with his mother.

When Jake arrived at his parents' home in Glendale on Wednesday evening, he found the place decked out with traditional trimmings that harkened back to his childhood. Just as she did every year, Rachel Washington lined the front door with autumn foliage. There was a distressed wheelbarrow filled with decorative gourds and a fall wreath of twigs and gold ribbons. The door was unlocked, so Jake and Lilith let themselves in, and Jake called out to his parents. The autumn arrangements were just as elaborate inside the house as they had been out front. The dining room table was already set with silk runners, straw pumpkins, gold-leaf chargers, and china. The scene was perfect, and every other year, it had reflected the near-perfection of their family unit. But this year, it felt disingenuous.

"Give your mother a hug," Rachel said when she emerged and greeted Jake. The choice of words felt deliberate. He wrapped his arms around her tentatively, and she responded with a tight squeeze. "It means a lot to me that you've decided to come down and spend the holiday with us."

"You are my family," he said automatically.

"I was beginning to think you'd forgotten," she replied with a weak smile.

His father approached and greeted him, giving him a quick hug and saying, "I've missed you, son."

Aside from that admission of affection, his father acted as if nothing had changed since the last time they'd met. He chattered about the upcoming football game. Jake played along. This was his father's way: moving past conflict by ignoring it. If his mother wanted to talk about everything, his father wanted to talk about nothing.

Jake started unloading the car. After he put down the suitcases in the guest room, he noticed that his mother was standing in the doorframe, her arms burdened with thick books.

"Here," Rachel said, walking steadily toward Jake. "I made these for you."

"What are they?"

"Scrapbooks," she said. Jake held out his arms and accepted the stack. He dropped the scrapbooks on the bed where they toppled over.

"One more thing," Rachel said. She gave him a white, cushioned box and waited for him to lift the lid. She looked on expectantly, but when he opened it, he looked perplexed.

"What are these?" he asked.

"Those are your baby teeth."

"That's disgusting," Jake said, examining the teeth more closely in his revulsion.

"It's not disgusting. They were part of you," Rachel said, taking a seat on the bed.

"Exactly. Part of my *mouth*," Jake replied, looking at the yellowed matter that didn't resemble anything human anymore. "Why'd you think I'd want these?"

"It's a memory," Rachel said, her voice wistful, her face gentle. When Jake looked at her, he could see the woman she'd been decades ago. Even though she was nearing seventy, her hair was the same blonde color it'd been when he was growing up, still touched up by her local colorist. The wrinkles on her face were everywhere, but they were soft, and Jake found it easy to edit them out and restore his mother to the past.

"I get it," Jake said, looking at the box in his hand. "You know me best and have the dental records to prove it."

"I wasn't trying to…"

"I know you weren't," he interrupted, softening. "It's just weird. These teeth. I don't know what to do with them." He looked down at the decayed kernels. "They're broken, anyway," he observed. Some of them had even been ground into dust.

"That's what happens over time. But look, a couple are still intact," Rachel pointed. Even the ones that were whole were small and malformed.

"I barely remember losing my teeth," Jake said. "A couple of them, sure. I remember eating corn on the cob and feeling the tooth give way or pulling one out when it got shaky. But you're the one who remembers all of them. If anything, you should keep these, not me," Jake reasoned, giving the white box back to her.

"But you'll keep the scrapbooks? I made them for you."

"Yeah, Mom. I'll keep the scrapbooks."

"That's the first time I've heard you call me 'Mom' in a while," she smiled.

"Well, I guess that's who you are."

She gave him a long hug, then left the room to prepare food in the kitchen. Jake opened the first scrapbook, which captured his childhood as his mother remembered it, not as he understood it. There were floral backgrounds underneath the photographs, setting everything in a garden that bloomed artificially. It was thoughtful, beyond thoughtful, but when Jake looked at his ten-year-old self on the elementary school playground, he could tell from his expression that he'd never been as carefree as his mother wanted to believe he'd been. He'd been too serious; he was not convinced he'd ever been a child. Jake had been a tangle of nerves, even when there weren't any real responsibilities to deal with. In his youth, there had been too much that he hadn't known about the world, and knowledge was one of the few things he'd always wanted.

He opened a second scrapbook, one that contained the prizes he'd earned growing up. Unlike the photographs, the collection of accolades felt real to him. Nearly all the awards were for second- or third-place finishes, a slight that he remembered feeling acutely when he was a boy. But at least they were honorific, a sign that his name was worth something on paper. Now he had his meteorite, and he smiled at the prospect of exceeding the modest successes of his childhood. That night, he slept soundly.

On Thanksgiving Day, the men watched football in the family room while the women prepared food in the kitchen. Preserving these traditions and keeping the genders separate helped Jake adjust to the newness of his reborn family. He sank into the couch with a beer in hand and sports on the television. He and his father talked stats in their familiar way until a commercial came on.

"I'm glad you came home. How are you holding up?" Daniel asked casually.

His father was an expert at this sort of non-invasive probing, but Jake decided not to respond with the pleasantries that were typical of their relationship.

234

"Not great, if I'm honest. A bit better now, I suppose. But not great," Jake said, looking at his father, who dodged his gaze. Daniel's age disguised the man he'd once been. His hair was white and thinning in the back. His now-white eyebrows changed the contours of his face. His wrinkles were deep. Since retiring, Daniel always looked defeated.

"I'm sorry to hear that," Daniel said, sipping his beer.

"You know, you could have said something. This isn't all Mom's fault."

"I know. You're right," Daniel said, turning to Jake. "I owed you more."

Jake was surprised by this admission. Though his father was honorable, he'd never been forthright. Jake thought about pressing his father, but he resisted. He'd gotten enough from him. Besides, Jake was his father's son. He had grown used to the silence. He appreciated the way it allowed him to get around the emotional points that his mother would have mined for relentlessly had she been in the room. The commercial break ended, and their sports talk resumed. Now and again, Jake would enter into the world of women, grabbing another couple of beers from the fridge before getting shooed away.

Once four o'clock rolled around, the walls between the sexes lowered as they all gathered in the dining room and filled their plates. The dinner was traditional, a full spread: roasted turkey, mashed potatoes, green bean casserole, baked yams, spinach salad. The joy of eating masked any discomfort at the table. With a piece of fork-skewered turkey in one hand and another bite of the bird halfway down the gullet, everything *was* normal for once. But then they'd look up from their plates and recognize that something wasn't right.

"You cooked this perfectly," Lilith noted, trying to break the ice.

"Thank you," Rachel said. "I couldn't have done it without your help."

"Could you pass the salt?" Jake asked, spotting the shaker near his father.

"What needs more salt?" Rachel asked.

"Nothing *needs* it," Jake said, grabbing the shaker from his father, who kept his head down as he passed it off.

"Then why ask for it?"

"I like my mashed potatoes extra salty."

"This is the same way I've always made the potatoes. You've never once put more salt on them. I thought you liked how I prepared things," she said, clearly upset.

"Rachel," Daniel interceded, putting a hand on hers. "Don't take it so personally."

"It *is* personal," she said, getting up from her seat.

"Mom…" Jake started, but it was too late. She had already retreated to the kitchen in tears. Jake excused himself from the table and went after her. He approached her in the kitchen and hugged her. She wrapped her arms around him in return, dampening his shoulder with her tears. Eventually, she pulled away to speak.

"I know what I did was wrong," she said, her bluish eyes purpled by the surrounding redness. "I should've known better, but I didn't. I just loved you so much. I still do."

Though she'd made similar overtures on the phone, it was harder for Jake to remain toughened against her now, in her physical presence.

"I know, mom," Jake said, hugging her again. "I know."

"Come look at this," she said, pulling away from the embrace. She led Jake to the refrigerator and pulled out a chocolate mousse pie she'd made. "You want to try it?"

"Dinner's not done. Dad and Lilith are at the table. Shouldn't we wait for them?"

"I could use something sweet right now," she said, her voice still muddled by intermittent snuffles, her face imploring him with a smile.

"Make my slice big," he said, grinned in collusion.

"No slices," she said, handing him a fork. "We're not dividing up this pie. We're sharing it."

The two of them thrust their silverware into the middle of the pie and ate slowly. Eventually, Daniel and Lilith entered the kitchen, utensils in hand. They demolished the pie and licked their forks clean, making sure nothing was dirty by the end of the night.

* * * * * * * * * *

No one lovingly shared dessert at the Barnabas household during their holiday celebration. On Wednesday night before Thanksgiving, Sebastian took a slight detour before arriving at his mother's house. He stopped on Paseo Del Mar, a street that wound along the coastline. He parked his car on the side of the road and walked into a field of undeveloped land where dry stalks of yellowed grass grew among the cattails and weeds. This was one of the few places in the town where he felt at home, nestled among its wild edges.

When surrounded by the sprawling homes and the market squares and the suburban families, he was an outsider in his hometown. Palos Verdes Estates was a place where people defined themselves based on social titles, wealth, and traditional mores, and neither he nor his family had ever measured up to its expectations, at least not since the death of his grandparents. It was a town with a long memory, a place where everyone knew everyone, and no one forgot a salacious rumor. As a result, Sebastian had always been the child of that tragic Jackie Barnabas girl. He'd hated the local gossip and stares, but at least people knew how to keep their voices down when they judged you.

Removed from his neighbors, Sebastian looked out at the ocean and surrendered to the cliffs. It was almost as if the shore was cradling him, telling him everything would be okay. He knew that for all its hidden ugliness, Palos Verdes was one of the most beautiful places on Earth. Sebastian

237

breathed in, left the coast behind him, and made his way to his mother's home on Espinoza Circle.

"Sebastian," she said, greeting him at the front door. "I have a surprise for you."

Sebastian walked into the living room and saw Barrie standing there. Now that Barrie was sixty-one years old, he was worn around the edges and barely recognizable to Sebastian, who'd last seen him in his childhood. His hair wasn't long and shaggy but combed backward in a small puff, gray hair streaking the brown. He was relatively thin, but his face was bloated, his chin occupying too much territory. He wore jeans and an old, faded Credence Clearwater Revival T-shirt.

"What are you doing here?" Sebastian asked.

"Aren't you glad to see me?" Barrie responded. Sebastian didn't say anything. "I get it. You need time to adjust. I'll run to the corner store and pick up some beer. Let you two talk it out for a minute."

Barrie headed toward his car, and Sebastian looked at his mother in disbelief.

"Barrie's here?" he asked after the beat-up nineties-era Chevrolet Malibu peeled off.

"He needed a place to go. He asked me if he could come over. He's changed a lot. We've been talking again. I thought this might be a good chance for you two to reconnect."

"Reconnect? After all these years?"

"I told you, he's different now. And he's only going to stay for Thanksgiving. He's not going to be here the whole weekend. I haven't told him about Jake yet. I almost did. That was why I reached out to him last month. But now that I've been spending time with him again, I think it'd be easier if he didn't know."

"You say 'easier' like it means 'better.'"

"You'd rather make things hard?" Jacqueline said, her brown eyes narrowed in questioning. She was sixty, but she looked older. Her skin was not just wrinkled, but worn, sagging from the years of substance abuse. Her hair was died black, a shade darker than her natural color, but her roots were white.

"It's going to be hard either way," Sebastian said. Jacqueline disengaged and walked away. Knowing he wouldn't get through to her, he brought in his bags from the car.

Barrie eventually returned from the store with beer. "How about we watch some TV?" he said, walking into the family room with a cold one.

"You go ahead," Sebastian said. "I'm going to my room to lie down."

"While you're in there," Jacqueline called out, "would you go through the math books piled on the dresser? They've been kicking around the house since you were a kid. I'm sick of keeping them. Take any you want. I'll trash the rest."

"Sure," Sebastian said and retreated to his room.

Sebastian looked through the books on the dresser. Some were old textbooks on basic subjects: pre-algebra, algebra, geometry, calculus. But others were more academic books on topics like stochastic process or Cantorian set theory. Sebastian spent hours going through them. He opened up a book on chaos theory and leafed through the pages. He enjoyed scanning the beautiful swirls of Poincaré maps and the patterns of recurrence plots. But as he flipped through, he felt something acting like a bookmark, limiting the movement of the lower quarter of the book. He opened up to the anchored place and found an old photograph stuck there. The picture was dated in pencil on the back: 1968. There was also a handwritten note: *Never forget.* Sebastian recognized a teenage version of his mother in the picture, beautiful and pixie-like, flanked by two young boys around six and eight years old. A middle-aged man stood behind her with one hand on her shoulder and another on the older boy's shoulder. Sebastian went to the family room to talk to her, but she and Barrie were passed out on the couch already, empty beer bottles and a half-finished handle of Jack Daniel's strewn around them.

"Mom," Sebastian pushed her. "Jacqueline, get up."

"Not now," she said lazily, retreating to sleep.

It was no use. Sebastian decided to go to sleep. He woke up early the next day and stood guard in the family room. Once he saw her stirring on the couch, he assailed her.

"Who's this man?" Sebastian asked her, holding out the photograph. She groggily adjusted her eyes to the picture in front of her.

"Not so loud," she said once she processed the picture. She saw Barrie was still passed out. "Come here," she said, walking to the study in the back. Jacqueline closed the door. She and Sebastian sat opposite one another.

"Where'd you get that?" she asked.

"Does it matter?" Sebastian asked. "Who is he?"

"He was a professor at UCLA. A mathematician. I babysat for his kids when I was in high school."

"That's where I got the math books."

"Yeah. He wanted you to have them," she said, briefly glancing up at Sebastian. "He thought you'd get the math gene too. Hoped you would," she said, looking down at the floor, evading Sebastian's stares as she dropped her inferences.

"The math gene?" Sebastian repeated. "What are you saying? Is he my father?"

Jacqueline nodded, crying.

"How'd this even happen?" Sebastian asked.

"I was young. He was a smart man. Kind. My birth control failed. I didn't know what to do. My parents didn't even know about him. He already had a family. I couldn't tell anyone about us."

"Does Barrie know?"

Jacqueline's face crumpled in tension; her withered lips were pulled tight before they started trembling. "No," she admitted between tears.

"Mom, the man thinks he's my father!" Sebastian yelled, standing and pacing.

"Keep your voice down," she said, a worried head swiveling around. "You're right. And look how much he did for you when he thought you were his flesh and blood."

"He wasn't perfect, but that's because the war changed him," Sebastian said. It helped to think this way, even now. His mother had originated this narrative. Sebastian remembered being six years old and asking Barrie to take him to the local public pool or some other place. Sebastian remembered Barrie sitting in his recliner stoically instead of responding before Jacqueline would tell Sebastian that Barrie couldn't be around all the people, all the noise, all the children running around. It was because of the war, she'd say. These were the moments when Jacqueline stepped up most, taking Sebastian to the pool or the birthday party or the park.

"He was a coward," Jacqueline snapped back.

"He was a soldier," Sebastian said, recalling the khaki-green, standard-issue fatigues he'd found tucked away in a large trunk when he'd been a child.

"He was a deserter. His injury was self-inflicted. A way to get out. He was the worst kind of coward. The kind that pretends to be honorable."

Sebastian stopped pacing. He sat down to consider what his mother said and rested his head against his hands. He thought about the bullet wound. The barely noticeable limp. The time when Barrie had gifted him G.I. Joe action figures but refused to play with them. The way Barrie would admonish Sebastian whenever he'd cast a sheen of nobility over the imagined exploits of his toys. Sebastian had asked for the action figures, pleaded for them. But when Barrie left for good, he'd taken the toy men with him, an act that had felt cruel to Sebastian. Now Sebastian wondered if Barrie had taken the toys because he hadn't wanted Sebastian to valorize him, even in his play. Had Barrie been driven by guilt? By cowardice? By resentment over the war? By an urge to rebuke his role as a father? Sebastian didn't know him well enough to make an argument for one interpretation over another. He conceded that he never knew this man at all. Sebastian sighed, then lifted his head.

"Maybe you're right. Maybe Barrie was a coward. A deserter. But what about this professor? Where is he now?" Sebastian asked, hoping to reclaim something in the process of losing everything else.

"He died. Ten years ago. A stroke. Remember, he was much older than me."

Sebastian was crestfallen, sinking his head into his lap. He mourned the tragedy of another lost father. He tried to tell himself that nothing changed: he'd never had much of a father growing up; he didn't have one now. But there was a deep feeling of pain inside him, the dull ache of potential love that had been stripped from him, the deprivation of never seeing himself in anyone but his flawed mother until recently.

"Jesus, mom, why didn't you tell me any of this sooner! First, Jake, now this? All these years, I could've had a brother *and* a father. A father like me," he exploded.

"He wasn't like you," she shot back, angry in the face of Sebastian's resistance. "And he wouldn't have been a father. He wanted nothing to do with you. You think he would've cared about you? You think he sent those math books because he was a good man? I was seventeen when he got me pregnant. He was forty-four. I was a child. He was an adult. Sure, he was a mathematician. But he wasn't like you. At least I hope not," she said, scanning Sebastian in judgment, her face twitching before giving way to tears.

Sebastian knew he should comfort her, hug her, but he couldn't. He let her cry for a few minutes, softly sobbing in the chair next to him.

"So what do we do now?" he asked once her crying died down.

"We get ready for Thanksgiving," Jacqueline said, lifting her red-eyed face.

"You can't be serious. With Barrie? You're not going to get rid of him? He's not even my father," Sebastian said, anger rising in his voice.

"We can talk more tomorrow when Jake's here. I'll tell you anything you want to know. But not now. It's Thanksgiving. Let's give that to Barrie. To ourselves."

Sebastian relented. He showered and got ready. He spent the rest of the day on his own, walking the cliffs of Palos Verdes and working on the Twin Prime Conjecture in his bedroom. He surfaced for dinner as promised. Thanksgiving dinner came together as he expected. Jacqueline brought out paper plates, plastic utensils, a store-bought rotisserie turkey, instant potatoes, and canned cranberry sauce. Sebastian didn't want to talk. He tried to eat his food and be done with everything. But Barrie wanted to engage with him.

"You remember when we went to Disneyland? I got you that Mickey Mouse watch?" Barrie asked.

"No," Sebastian lied. "I was too young."

"Well, I remember," Barrie said, his face wrenched into an exaggerated smile.

"Why wouldn't you? You were an adult."

"Memories fade. You'd be surprised how many things you forget by the time you're my age. But not Disneyland. You know, my parents never took me when I was a kid. When I went with you, it was the first time I'd ever been there. Frontierland, Fantasyland, Tomorrowland," Barrie rattled off in advertisement.

Barrie glowed as he spoke about the theme park. Sebastian resented Barrie's easy reconstruction of uncomplicated moments rather than complicated ones. Barrie was no hero. He was just a man, an ordinary and pathetic man with a beer belly and a dream who wanted the simpler things in life. Sebastian finished his food, excused himself from the table, and waited for his once-father to leave. Barrie always did eventually.

←　←　10　←

When Jacqueline awoke to her alarm the morning after Thanksgiving, her bedsheets were still mangled from Barrie's legs, even though his body wasn't there. She'd gotten stuck with an early shift at the Ralph's grocery store in Rancho Palos Verdes because so many of her co-workers had taken the day off to camp out for Black Friday sales. As she rose from her bed, her head buzzed, foggy and pounding from too much wine. She put on her clothes without turning on the lights, helped only by the moonlight that shone through her bedroom window. She hopped in her car and rolled the windows down. The breath of the Pacific Ocean revived her as she lazily drove along the coastline curves of Palos Verdes Drive West, then turned onto Hawthorne Boulevard and reached the store.

"Remind me to stop taking six-o'clock shifts," she said to Clarence, the chipper middle-aged manager who greeted her when she arrived.

"You know what they say about the early bird," he remarked, guiding Jacqueline to a register with a hand on her shoulder, steadying her as though he had no confidence she could stand.

The benefit of the early shift was that there weren't many customers at the start. Jacqueline stood at the register for the first hour or two with her eyes shut, only roused into responsibility by a customer grabbing a bakery item or some necessities. Black Friday was especially dead. Even as the day picked up, the work was light. She scanned, bagged, scanned, bagged. Sometimes a finicky barcode harassed her, bunched plastic resisting identification. Whenever it happened, she'd manipulate the outer wrappings and hammer the item against the scanner, frustrated that the cost

244

of an object could hide so expertly. Sometimes she'd try to guess the value as she knocked the code against the laser, testing how well she could judge the price of everyday goods. She always failed. Good thing she'd be able to collect Social Security in a couple of years and leave this all behind her.

Toward the end of her shift, a thirtysomething woman approached the register a cart full of baby items: diapers, wipes, jarred food, bubble bath, teething rings, gas drops, infant acetaminophen, oatmeal, rash cream, and lotion. The woman looked sleepless but otherwise put-together with her hair pulled back into a tight topknot and her face lightly made-up. Jacqueline had rung up diapers countless times before, but today, she paused as she scanned them, realizing she'd never bought any herself. Her parents had done the shopping and gotten necessities for the boys when they'd been babies. She tried to remember how many diapers she'd even changed. Hardly any. Again, her parents had taken care of that.

She looked at the customer piling her goods on the conveyor belt. Her clothes were professional, black pants and a nice collared shirt. The woman probably had a career. Judging by the ring on her finger, she had a husband. Jacqueline wondered how her own life might have been different if she'd gotten pregnant at thirty instead of seventeen. It was too painful to consider.

Jacqueline eventually closed her register, removed her apron, and headed home. When she returned, she sighed as she crossed the threshold. After the door shut, Sebastian called out to her, "Don't forget, Jake should be here in half an hour."

Jacqueline felt an initial rush excitement at the prospect of seeing her long-lost son. She remembered how sweet he had been as a baby and a toddler, such a cautious and careful child. She summoned visions of him at his best, babbling semi-coherently with adorably dulled enunciations. But then she considered: what if Jake blamed her for giving him up? What if he judged her?

Her chest started to tighten. She struggled to breathe. She ran to the medicine cabinet in her bathroom and popped a couple of Xanax. She knew she'd feel better once the pills took effect, but for now, she felt the familiar, crushing weight of anxiety. She lay on the floor, curled up as she tried to will her way through her feeling of internal collapse. The medication took effect after about twenty minutes, but it wasn't working as well as it used to. Jacqueline retreated to the liquor cabinet and downed shots of vodka. Ten minutes later, the doorbell rang. Sebastian answered it and led Jake to the living room where Jacqueline was waiting.

"I can't believe it's really you," she said, hugging Jake awkwardly. He looked so much like Sebastian that he didn't feel new to her. But she was overwhelmed by the sight of the twins next to one another, double-teamed against her. She felt dizzy.

"It's really me. And it's really you."

"I guess it is," she said. Jacqueline lost her balance as she tried to sit and nearly tumbled onto the ground, but she braced the armrest tightly and composed herself. They all sat. Sebastian looked at her with suspicion, but she tried to ignore him.

"So do I just start asking questions?" Jake asked.

Questions? Was this going to be an interrogation? Jacqueline felt nervousness creep in, but the drugs blunted the worst of it. "If that's what you came here to do," she said.

"I just want to know why you gave me up. I mean, Sebastian told me the basics. You were a teen mom. Your parents died. But what I don't understand is, if you were so hard up, why'd you only give *me* up? Why'd you decide to keep Sebastian?" Jake asked.

Sebastian looked at his mother intensely.

"I couldn't let go," Jacqueline replied, shaken. She remembered the agony of those days, the hardship, the

246

loneliness. "I was grieving and alone. I needed someone with me."

"But you could let go of me?" Jake asked, his voice steady but probing.

"I didn't want to give up either of you. I knew I couldn't keep you both. It was too much. I couldn't handle it," Jacqueline confessed earnestly. Jake didn't seem satisfied with her response, and it triggered her defenses. Her voice grew louder, pointed, as she said, "I was young. I was so young. You can't imagine what it was like, neither of you can."

"It's fine, mom. We know," Sebastian said. "Calm down."

Jacqueline breathed in and out, closing her eyes and trying to center herself. She hated it when her son acted as if he knew better. Unfortunately, closing her eyes made her feel disoriented and woozy. She opened her eyes and saw Jake lean in toward her.

"But why'd you pick *him*? Why Sebastian?" Jake pressed.

Jacqueline looked over at Sebastian, who anxiously awaited her response. Her eyes started drooping, and she thought she might fall asleep right then and there. She fought her drowsiness. "It was chance," she explained. "Luck was all."

"Luck? I'd hardly call it luck," Sebastian scoffed. He took a moment to size her up. Jacqueline could feel his eyes on her. "Jesus, are you fucking high right now?"

"I'm fine," she said, trying to perk up and prove herself, though she could tell by how difficult it was to keep her shoulders steady that she wasn't doing a good job.

"I need to know why I wasn't good enough," Jake said, drawing still closer.

"I'm sorry, Jake," she said, letting her body flop against the curved back of her seat. "You were always...you were good. Good enough," she continued, her speech growing as lazy as the rest of her. "You were too good for me. Too good...I'm sorry for all of it, every *stupid* thing I ever...done. Did..." she muttered, her eyes fluttering in fits.

"And what about me, Mom?" Sebastian interjected, his voice rising as he leaned in.

"I'm sorriest for you, Sebastian," she said, trying to sound sincere. She wasn't sure if it was coming across right because Sebastian looked dubious.

"What about my father? Our birth father. You said you'd tell us about him," Sebastian said.

"I told you already. He's dead," Jacqueline spat out.

"You said he was a mathematician. Do you know what his focus was?"

"What do you think I am? An...an encyclopedia? You think I know anything about that math junk?" she asked, frustrated. "Look him up yourself. Arthur Fredrickson."

"Did he like science?" Jake asked.

"How should I know?" Jacqueline said, upset that her boys brought up Arthur at all. She'd hoped today would be about getting another son. Another chance. But as the tension escalated, she realized there were no more chances for her. It felt unfair. Did Jake or Sebastian care about what she'd been through? Did they have any empathy for her? Their faces were too grave. Too judgmental.

"You think I knew this man?" Jacqueline said. "I didn't know him at all. I thought he was...sweet. Genuine. A good man. But no. He wasn't. He sent some money at first. Some useless math books. That was it. And I was underage. Predatory. That's the word."

Jacqueline felt light-headed. Pressure mounted inside her, so she stuck her head between her knees. "Is the room spinning?" she asked. Her dizziness escalated. She could hear the boys asking her if she was all right, but she didn't feel like answering them. Not now. She lifted her head and looked at Sebastian, but she saw Barrie in his place. She looked over to where Jake should have been; only she saw Arthur Fredrickson instead.

"How are you doing that?" she asked, amazed.

"Doing what, Mom?" her son's voice asked, even as the alien face stayed the same.

"You. You're Barrie," she pointed. She turned, pointed again: "You're Arthur."

"What are you talking about?" her son's voice asked, from under the mask of Arthur.

"Are you all right? Mom? What'd you take? Tell me what you took," her other son's voice called out. Her eyes started closing. Both faces faded to black. She fell to the ground, losing her grasp on consciousness. In the darkness, she heard Sebastian's cell phone ring. She heard him answer and mutter incoherently into the phone. She tried to decipher what he was talking about. She heard the name Mallory, and then she drifted off.

← 4 ← ←

From the time Mallory Whitmore Specter was an infant, her father groomed her to be a tiger. As far as he was concerned, Princeton was the only acceptable college for her. She didn't have the grades to warrant admission, but sizeable donations from the family secured her a place. Once she got to Princeton, Mallory blended in as best she could, but she struggled with feelings of fraudulence, especially when she underperformed academically.

The night before her first Dean's Date—the date at the end of the semester when all written work was due—Mallory was up late finishing papers for her classes. She was trying to focus when her roommate, Olivia, whisked her away to Holder Courtyard. Throngs of preppy coeds were packed together, all waiting to take part in the Holder Howl, a midnight tradition where students howled to let out their end-of-the-semester stress. The din of conversation was everywhere.

"This is stupid," Mallory told Olivia. "I have work I should be doing."

"Stupid or not, you're howling," Olivia demanded. "Besides, it'll only take a minute. And if there's anyone who needs this, it's you. You need to come up for air."

"I'm breathing just fine, thank you very much," Mallory said.

"How can you say that when you *literally* hyperventilated an hour ago?"

"I wasn't *quite* hyperventilating. Besides, you think *screaming* will help?"

"You'd be surprised what good old-fashioned catharsis can do for you. Aristotle knew his shit," Olivia argued. "Besides, we are motherfucking tigers, aren't we?"

Mallory didn't respond. She wasn't so sure. In the next few seconds, the countdown started. At the four-second mark, Olivia realized Mallory wasn't counting down and nudged her with an elbow until she joined in. At the end of the countdown, Mallory closed her eyes and inhaled deeply. She took her beat and waited for the spirit to move her while the collective roar rang out.

With a ferocity she didn't know she had, Mallory howled as she was supposed to, animalistically from the most primal part of her. Her ululations joined the chorus, and she could feel the intoxicating pulse of inclusion race through her. In the middle of the night, mouth open, she finally belonged among the other feral elite. She could feel her teeth sharpening and her claws surfacing, transforming into a beast. When the other tigers ceased their howling, Mallory continued, unleashing a semester's worth of anxiety and self-doubt and torment into the space left by less hungry, less ferocious tigers. It felt appropriate to be alone in the final throes of her wail. She was divorced from the collective that had always been alienating for her, even in moments of acceptance.

"I told you. You needed this," Olivia said. She put her hand on Mallory's arm while the transfiguration undid itself.

"Fine. You were right," Mallory conceded, but she worried the transformation wouldn't last. And it didn't. The next afternoon, Dean's Date, Mallory was the last person to submit work to McCosh Hall. She couldn't help but feel like it was a sad metaphor for her life at Princeton. She carried that experience with her; but fortunately, it reigned alongside her memory of the Holder Howl. No matter how often Mallory felt down on herself, she tried to remember that she could be an animal. This reminder was the only thing that saved her from herself when she was at her lowest points.

"I'm Mallory," she said after one such low point, "and I'm an alcoholic." It took her a while before she ever stood up at one of the meetings to speak, but when she did, she often talked about her time at Princeton. In her mind, those were the formative years of her disease when it grew roots inside her: the binge drinking, the escapism, the feelings of inadequacy.

At the beginning of her litigation against Stanford, she started attending meetings regularly. She reached out to one of the meeting organizers to see if he could help her find a suitable sponsor. The problem was that Mallory struggled to connect with the veteran alcoholics she met at the meetings. She told the organizer she needed someone more like her, someone with a Ph.D. It took a while to track someone down, but eventually, he found one. It wasn't perfect. He hadn't been able to find a female academic to sponsor her, but he could find a male one, not too close, but over in Berkeley, which was a reasonable distance away for such a specific request. William Radenport.

As it turned out, Mallory and William were an ideal match. He understood the pressures of publication as much as the next professor. Like Mallory, William had been jaded by the pitfalls of growing up with too much money and not enough guidance. He opened up to her about the years

251

between his Oxford degree and his journey to the States, when he had drunk his way through all the pubs in London, squandering his potential until he was sure he had ruined his chances of being the scientist he thought he could be. William told her about the ethically questionable means he'd used in his desperation to get published before he'd applied to schools in the States. She opened up to him about her suspicion that she wouldn't have gotten her position at Stanford if not for her father's impressive tenure at their law school. The two of them understood one another.

Eventually, Mallory opened up to William about the trial with Sebastian. She hadn't been prepared for Radenport to know who Sebastian was, but William had learned about him from Jessica Fleming. Once William explained the connections that bound him to Jake as inimically as she was bound to Sebastian, Mallory felt that Radenport had been matched as her sponsor through an act of fate. They hadn't known one another for long, but Mallory valued his support. They both stayed in town for Thanksgiving and met up the day after. They talked through their issues, bridging the emptiness inside them that longed for alcohol. There were depths to Mallory's depression that no one could breach, but William helped. At least their animosity toward two men with the same face united them.

1

Jake and Sebastian watched as the paramedics lugged Jacqueline's passed out body into an ambulance on the Friday after Thanksgiving. Before the crew got there, Sebastian had already done what he could to piece together how Jacqueline had fallen apart this time. When he'd approached the wet bar, he'd seen an open vodka bottle. When he'd gone to the master bathroom, he'd found the Xanax bottle on the countertop. His mother could never be a master criminal. Sebastian told the paramedics his suspicions about what she'd taken. He told them about the symptoms she'd been exhibiting before she passed out. Jake looked distressed but not Sebastian. He was too accustomed to this sort of scene. Jake offered to come with Sebastian to the hospital, but Sebastian let him off the hook. Jake left, but before he did, he and Sebastian agreed to caravan on their way up north come Sunday.

After a few hastily smoked cigarettes and a couple of freshly brewed cups of coffee, Sebastian got into his car to go to the hospital. When he started the engine, he saw that a peacock was blocking his exit. Sebastian rolled down the window and shouted at it. He honked his horn. The bird was unfazed. The peacock approached his car and began pecking away at it, assaulting the car with flapping wings. The bird opened its mouth and let out the classic honks that Sebastian remembered from his childhood. Sebastian got out of the car to chase it away, but as he did, he stopped to pick up one of the feathers that had fallen to the ground. Sebastian used to collect them as a kid.

When he was young, Sebastian liked the peacocks in the neighborhood. They were the exotic locals who didn't seem to belong but were entirely at home. Many of the town's residents regarded them as pests, but there was no denying their beauty: the bright blue chests, the blue-and-green trains that trailed behind them. His mother had discouraged his feather-collecting hobby. She'd told him it was dirty. Feather in hand, Sebastian got back in his car. He remembered his mother telling him that peacocks were some of the stupidest animals on the planet. She'd told him that they pushed their babies off roofs to see if they could fly. Sebastian wondered if that was true.

When Sebastian got to the hospital and tracked down his mother's room, he spoke to the doctor about her condition. The staff had already pumped her stomach, and they were giving her fluids. She was stable. The doctor spoke about the extreme danger of mixing Xanax and alcohol as if Sebastian were the one who needed the lecture. Sebastian listened patiently, nodding his head as appropriate. Once the doctor left, Sebastian spent some time sitting in a chair, watching his mother sleep in her medical bed with IVs attached to her arms. After an hour of waiting, he decided that he shouldn't have to be there anymore. Not in another hospital room. Not talking to another emergency responder or doctor. Sebastian wrote his mother a note. He let her know that he hoped she'd recover soon and that he'd be spending the next couple of nights in a hotel before heading up to Palo Alto. On top of the note, he left a peacock feather. The blue eye of the feather seemed to watch him leave.

On Sunday, Sebastian and Jake met up to begin their northward caravan home. They decided to take the 101. They could have shaved off an hour or more by taking the 5 through farmland, but they wanted a nicer view. Besides, neither of them was interested in passing by the cow pastures that blasted the stench of manure through the air conditioning. So they hopped into their cars that morning, braved Los Angeles traffic, made it past Ventura and Santa Barbara, and stopped in Solvang for lunch.

"This place is crazy," Jake said when he met up with Sebastian in a local parking lot. Sebastian watched Jake look around admiringly. The Danish architecture was something to behold. Windmills. Brown slats of wood in geometric patterns on the buildings. Old fonts on wooden signs. "It takes you to another place and time."

"It's pure Denmark," Sebastian replied, breathing in the scent of æbleskivers baking nearby. "I thought you'd like to see it. I can't believe you've never been."

"It reminds me of the illustrations in the fairy tales my mother used to read to me," Jake said, his face full of reverie.

"I bet," Sebastian said, remembering how he'd thumbed through the pictures in his own childhood books, making up stories when no one was willing to read them to him.

"Speaking of fairy tales, there's a bust of Hans Christian Andersen close by."

Sebastian and Jake visited the statue. After the brief stop, they found a Danish restaurant and grabbed a table inside.

"So, how's your mom doing?" Jake asked once he and Sebastian had sat down and ordered their food—plates of sausage, sauerkraut, and potatoes.

"Fine as far as I know," Sebastian said. "She was recovering when I left her at the hospital. Plenty of able physicians to care for her."

"You haven't called her since?"

"No. I know the drill. She's fine. She always is."

"You weren't kidding about her. She's a piece of work."

"Classic Jackie Barnabas. But it's for the best that she was such a disaster when you saw her. Hopefully it crushed any fantasies you might've had about her."

"I'm sure you're right," Jake said, fidgeting with his napkin. He was slow to talk, considering his words as he continued. "But it's hard for me to see it that way. When I watched her stagger around and get confused and pass out, I kept thinking, this is where I'm from. This is *who* I come from."

"Welcome to my life. At least you didn't have to meet Barrie. You didn't have to think he was your biological father for too long. I can't believe my mom brought him over for Thanksgiving. The guy's a child. He hasn't seen me since I was six years old, but he had the audacity to bring up memories of Disneyland at dinner as if he'd just come back from a work trip or something."

"Is it a relief to know he's not your father?"

"It's complicated," Sebastian said, hoping Jake would let it go. Sebastian didn't want to spend another minute thinking about Barrie, the deserter.

"Are you holding on to fantasies about our biological father?" Jake asked, curious.

255

"No. Maybe. I don't think so," Sebastian faltered. "After my mom gave us his name, I did a little research on him. I was able to track down some articles he published. They were compelling. Well-articulated. He wasn't a pure mathematician, like me. He did applied mathematics. Computer sciences. Cryptology. But he's still a mystery to me."

"Well, we do know one thing about him. The man didn't have the strongest moral character if he could treat your mom like he did."

"I guess not," Sebastian said. "But we do have his genes. And it's not like either of us is a paragon of morality. I mean, you cheated on your wife, and I…"

"Once. I cheated on my wife once," Jake interrupted forcefully. "And I didn't do it with a teenager. And I didn't impregnate anyone or leave behind a couple of kids."

"You're right," Sebastian said. "False equivalence. Sorry."

Sebastian knew that Jake was entitled to be upset. Still, Sebastian couldn't excuse himself so readily. He had to reckon with his sins. But he wanted to be a different type of man now. Sebastian got up to use the restroom, in part to ease the tension that was building. When he returned, he noticed that Jake looked even more upset than he had earlier, his face drawn in rigidity. Jake ignored the steaming hot food that had arrived.

"You got a text when you were in the bathroom," Jake said, nodding his head in the direction of the cell phone that Sebastian had left on the table. "When were you going to tell me that you were seeing my dissertation advisee?"

"Soon," Sebastian replied. "I'm still getting to know her. Besides, I didn't realize it would upset you."

"I told you she's been having an affair with Radenport."

"Right. You did. I forgot about that. When you told me, I didn't even know who she was yet. When I first met her, she told me she was seeing someone else, some married guy, but I didn't put two and two together."

"I don't trust her."

"She's harmless."

"What's her angle? First Radenport, now you?" Jake said, eyes narrowed in suspicion.

"You seriously think she's doing something sinister by dating me? You think this is part of some elaborate plot? Give me some credit here."

"Maybe you're right. Maybe she's interested in you. But don't tell her anything about my research," Jake said before shoveling sausage into his mouth.

"I hadn't planned to. It's not like we spend all our time talking about you," Sebastian said in frustration.

"Just be careful," Jake replied, nodding his head as he cut his food.

Sebastian was annoyed that Jake saw him as an unwitting dupe being manipulated by a young woman. The implicit judgment against Sebastian was as frustrating as the implicit judgment against Jessica. She was not some scheming Jezebel. Sebastian had already been on a date with her, and it had gone well. She'd been charming. Intelligent. They'd ended the night with a kiss rather than a lay, but it'd been one hell of a kiss. Sebastian was still thinking about her when he and Jake left the restaurant. On the way to their cars, they passed the famed Little Mermaid fountain that featured a half-scale replica of the original statue from Copenhagen. Sebastian stopped to marvel at the copper girl, poised on a mountain of rocks. Her face was the lightest part of the sculpture, a mask of white that looked like marble. The rest of her was mottled: oxidized and corroded in patchwork patterns. She didn't look tarnished, just neglected. To Sebastian's surprise, her legs were human, a depiction of her after her transformation. A young woman, not a Siren, she wore a serious expression that stuck in Sebastian's mind for the rest of the car ride home.

Shallow Diagonals

Fibonacci's Sequence: Golden, (Almost) Perfect

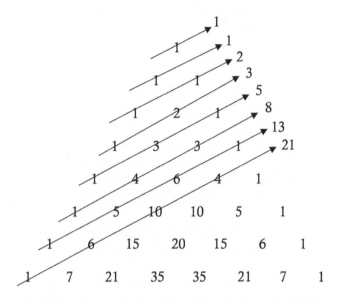

If you draw shallow diagonals through the rows of Pascal's triangle and add up the numbers, the sums will recreate Fibonacci's sequence. Fibonacci's sequence follows the recurrence relation:

$$F_n = F_{n-1} + F_{n-2} \text{ where } F_n > 1 \text{ and } F_0 = 0 \text{ and } F_1 = 1$$

Fibonacci's sequence is related to the Golden Ratio ($\approx$1.618034), which is represented by either the tau symbol (τ) or the phi symbol (φ). Here is a related limit:

$$\lim_{n \to \infty} \frac{F(n+1)}{F(n)} = \varphi$$

A limit describes the number that a function infinitely approaches but never reaches. In the limit above, F represents the function of Fibonacci's sequence, and "n" represents the position of the number within the sequence. As n reaches infinity, the ratio between two successive numbers in Fibonacci's sequence gets closer and closer to the golden ratio.

Mathematicians, philosophers, biologists, and artists have long investigated the golden ratio. When applied to architecture and the arts, the golden ratio provides a harmonious sense of balance. Some scientists have contended that the golden ratio occurs organically in nature and that the spiraled designs of certain plants and vines are beautiful because they conform to the golden ratio.

In short, the golden ratio represents an ideal. Given this function, the previously mentioned limit using Fibonacci numbers takes on additional weight. Essentially, the ratio between successive terms in Fibonacci's sequence endeavors to reach the golden ratio, that paragon of perfection. As the terms ascend in value, their ratio gets closer and closer to being "golden" but will never reach perfection.

---

1 ...

It was hard for Jake to believe what he saw. He had dreamt it before, almost exactly like this. Selene Thessalonia was maybe a hundred feet away from him, wearing a slinky, golden gown with a neckline that plunged toward the empire waist of the dress. Her hair was pulled back with a braid laced across the top. Jake thought it suited her perfectly. It was youthful but complex, elegant but whimsical, structured but organically messy. Her look was Grecian, harkening back not only to her nationality but to the more ancient sources of her beauty, which from Jake's estimation must have sprung from Olympus.

Jake had always hoped that one day he would run into her again, by chance or design; now, as if by magic, she was here. It made Jake wonder: *had* Selene been the girl who'd approached Sebastian at the coffeehouse in Palo Alto? Ever since then, Jake had thought about Selene nearly every night before going to sleep, tossing and turning with the restless fantasies of love or obsession. He couldn't tell which took hold of him; he only knew for sure that it was one of the two because nothing else had ever felt so needful. Every night, she gave Jake hope that he could reclaim a different existence, one unmarred by the mundane disappointments of everyday life. He never suspected that he would see her again, not after he'd put his wedding ring back on and acquiesced to a life of modest expectations. But now, she was not a phantom of his pre-sleep consciousness. She was here, and he felt the pounding sensation of living a realized dream.

He was suited for the occasion, dressed in one of the nicely tailored tuxedos that Lilith made sure he wore whenever he attended one of these functions. He put his hand on the knot of his black tie, tightening and adjusting it like a dapper Hollywood film star. But the longer he looked at Selene with his fingers on the knot, the more strangled he felt. The sensation of breathlessness was not new. He remembered the other time Selene had made him feel this way, back when he'd been in his spacesuit, ignoring his oxygen tubes. This time around, Selene locked eyes with him, but her gaze didn't inspire comfort because she didn't smile. She had an icy assurance he didn't recognize, and he worried that the tie around his neck was more a noose than an accessory. Jake approached her anyway.

"Selene," he said, interrupting her conversation with a few other guests.

261

"I'm in the middle of something," she explained, brushing Jake away like he was a child who needed coddling. "You were saying?" she said, redirecting her attention to the man at her right.

"Pardon me," Jake managed as politely as he could, taking Selene by the wrist and pulling her toward him. From a distance, Jake could see Lilith watching the scene. He retreated farther away with Selene to avoid the withering stares of his wife.

"What?" Selene asked once they reached a private alcove.

"That's all I get?" Jake asked, genuinely hurt. He didn't know how to read her curt responses, her round dismissals of him. Her cold reception shook him.

"What were you expecting?"

"I don't know. Something more. The last time we saw each other..." Jake started, gently grabbing her wrist and grazing her forearm with his fingertips.

"I need to get back," Selene interrupted, pulling away.

He clutched her wrist again, forcefully this time. "You came here because you wanted to see me," he said, channeling confidence he rarely had.

"What makes you think that?" Selene said, her brown eyes wide with spite. She was still beautiful in her anger, fiery and dynamic. Her prominent cheekbones had a sheen of pearlescent makeup smeared on them that caught the light and made her glow.

"My wife's wine company is one of the main sponsors of this charity ball. The event is in Berkeley. You must have known I'd be here," Jake reasoned, grasping at any hope.

"A date brought me here," she said. His heart sank. "And if you remember, you hardly told me anything about your wife. Not her job. Not her company. Not even her name. So don't flatter yourself. I had no idea you'd be here."

She turned to leave, only this time, Jake didn't grab her. He didn't want to have her by force. Watching her hips sway in high-heeled steps killed him with desire.

"You know I loved you back then," he called out, hoping this might bring her to him. Even as he said it, he wondered if it were true, but his attraction to her overrode his doubts. She stopped and glanced back at him.

"That's not enough."

She walked away, and Jake had the displeasure of looking at her exposed back with her sparse freckles reminding him of when he'd once been close enough to touch them. He didn't understand what could have changed so much. The passing of years was never kind, the reality of marriage even less so, but he still found it inexplicable that Selene could look at him with disdain, recoiling from him as if he were more monstrous than flawed.

He tried to console himself, thinking he must have been right earlier. She had to have come here expecting to see him. At the very least, she must have hoped it was a possibility. But then he considered: she was in the Bay Area and hadn't contacted him. The most she had done was *maybe* yell at a man who looked like him at a coffeehouse. Even that was dubious. His spirits sank. When Jake walked back into the main ballroom, he saw Lilith staring at him. She would have looked lovely, elegantly robed in a glittery, silver gown, if not for the scowl on her face. After experiencing Selene's disdain, he didn't want to have to deal with Lilith. He could tell she was going to make him pay for speaking a few words to this other woman.

"Did you know Selene was going to be here?" Lilith asked in hushed anger, leading Jake by the elbow to an empty corner of the room.

"I didn't even know she was in the area."

"Well, why *is* she here?"

"Apparently, a date brought her," Jake said. "Besides that, I don't know."

"That's it?"

"We didn't talk long," Jake said, stoic in his defense.

"What else did she say?" Lilith asked after a beat, her hands on her hips.

"Nothing, Lilith. She didn't say anything."

"I find that hard to believe."

"She doesn't want anything to do with me. You have nothing to worry about. I'm getting a drink," Jake said firmly and walked away. As he approached the bar, Jake looked at Selene, who'd rejoined her earlier conversation. She was masterful at acting oblivious to his stares. She was the picture of effortless socializing, happy and carefree. Jake circled Selene from a distance and stole his glances to avoid arousing the suspicion of his wife. Like a camera panning, he captured Selene at every angle, committing her to memory. By the time Selene left, Jake had stocked his brain with a catalog of material on her: facial expressions, quirks, laughs, stances, movements.

Once she was gone, Jake had no more interest in staying. He hoped to get home as quickly as possible so he could savor his recollections before they became too murky with the stains of time. Lilith seemed to sense his urgency. She insisted they stay longer. She had people to speak to, and this was business, after all.

"Okay, fine, we can go," she said two hours later. Jake called a taxi.

"You know I hate these things," Jake said, undoing his tie as they headed outside to wait for the cab. In front of the hotel, they stood next to one another distantly.

"Usually you do. But maybe tonight was different," Lilith said, side-eyeing him.

"You can't mean that. Tonight's gala was more agonizing than the others."

"That's not exactly a consolation. It might even be worse."

Lilith held her head high. Her chin pointed away from him toward the darkness. Jake knew he'd been unthinking, perhaps even cruel. He hadn't wanted to be. He reached out for Lilith's shoulder, touching it briefly before she brushed his fingers off with a shrug. Jake didn't like seeing her hurt. He noticed her jaw quivering. Her hand brushed at her cheek, a response to tears that Jake couldn't see. He felt pity for her, but the animal part of him also felt aggrieved. He spent the taxi ride stewing in frustration.

When they got home, Jake went straight to bed. Lilith took her time undressing and getting ready for sleep. She left on the lights, bumped around in her closet, opened too many drawers, and even took a shower before joining him in bed.

"I know you're tired," she said as she climbed in. "But I wanted to say something. I think it was a good thing, seeing her tonight. Now we can put everything in the past."

"I'm glad," Jake muttered from his pillow, wishing they didn't have to get into it.

"Before I saw her in real life, she was so much more threatening. Like a ghost. But once I saw her...I don't know. She was just human. I felt better. You know what I mean?"

Jake didn't respond. He was frustrated that she was centering this experience on herself, but he knew he didn't have the moral high ground to complain about his hurt. He closed his eyes. She leaned toward him and kissed him full on the mouth, her thin lips a stark reminder to Jake of the woman who was lying beside him: his wife. An intelligent and strong wife, but one who wanted to claim ownership over him. One he didn't like at that moment. His lips accepted hers half-heartedly, and he released a deep breath.

"I guess you don't want to talk about this," she said, pulling away from him.

He didn't want to talk about it. Even now, as Jake rested his head on his pillow, he was reinventing the details of Selene Thessalonia that he'd carefully memorized earlier that night. In the past, his re-creations had never been vivid enough, too divorced from her basic shape since they were crafted from the few pictures he retained from their time in Utah. Reliant on those old images, he could only imagine her static, posed as she was in the photographs, unable to move an inch or show any emotion other than the one she inhabited when the flash went off.

But now, she was fresh in his mind. She could move the way she moved that night, using a hand to wipe away the tendrils that escaped her braid. More importantly, she could smile. She hadn't smiled at him at the charity ball, but she had smiled at other people. Fortunately, in his bed, Jake could change his position relative to her and transform that smile into one reserved for him. She was perfect, never so perfect as in that dress, made up for the ripest fantasies. He continued his quest as a historical revisionist, imagining conversations that never happened, fabricating kisses, touches, and other acts of reciprocation that reminded him what infatuation felt like, every sticky part of it. But no matter how he tried to cling to the fiction, he couldn't dispel the knowledge that none of it was real or would ever be real. Now and then, Lilith would breathe too loudly or turn over in her sleep, and Jake would be thrust back into the bed they shared, feeling alone.

1 ... 1 ...

Sebastian didn't bring Jessica with him to hear the verdict in the Specter v. Stanford trial, but he smiled as he drove toward the courthouse, knowing he was going to meet up with her later that night. They had already seen one another twice since he'd gotten back from Palos Verdes. He was taken with her. She was the stuff of fairy tales, sprite-like in her purity and vivacity. She could be puckish, and whenever she was, she would lift an eyebrow like a cartoon character. He'd asked her about the eyebrow maneuver on their first date. She knew she was capable of the trick and had pulled it out at parties to draw a laugh, but its regular use was an involuntary tic. After Sebastian brought it up, she grew self-conscious. The second time they met up, her eyebrows took on a new shape: a nervous quiver that straddled the line between relaxed and arched, as if she were fighting away the gesture. She told Sebastian that she didn't like being read so easily, but he assured her it was endearing.

He thought about her eyebrow as he pulled into the courthouse parking lot. He had a good feeling about the day. After parking his car, Sebastian spotted Diana getting out of a nearby vehicle with the same man from before…Scrubs. What was his name again?

"Good morning," Sebastian said, approaching them as Diana locked her car.

"Hey, Sebastian. This is Henry, by the way," Diana said, introducing them. They shook hands. Henry nervously met Sebastian's eyes, but Sebastian did his best to signal a truce. Sebastian no longer wished this man any harm, even in his imagination.

"How're you feeling about our odds today?" Sebastian asked Diana as the three of them walked toward the courthouse.

"Great," Diana said. "Stanford's lawyers were excellent. The evidence was persuasive. I wonder if Mallory considered how much the lawsuit could backfire."

"She probably didn't mind going down as long as she could take the rest of us with her," Sebastian said as they closed in on the imposing building.

When the three of them entered the courtroom gallery, Henry and Diana led the way toward seats near the front. This time, instead of hanging back, Sebastian followed and sat next to them. At first, Diana seemed nervous. But Henry grabbed her hand and started massaging it. Diana and Henry talked in low whispers. None of this upset Sebastian. It relieved him. He didn't particularly want to make small talk with them, but he also didn't want to be rude and sit somewhere else among strangers. Sebastian was glad that Diana had this man in her life. Sebastian didn't want to be the one massaging her hand. He didn't want to be the one responsible for an outsized portion of her happiness. With the promise of Jessica on the horizon, Diana was just a colleague again. Sebastian scooted over to give Diana and Henry some space when a woman approached Sebastian on his other side.

"Mind if I sit next to you?" she asked Sebastian. He looked up to see that it was the red-haired girl he'd met last time at the courthouse, the one with the bird tattoo on her ankle. She was dressed professionally in gray pants and a white blouse. Her hair was in a French twist, and her small nose wrinkled as she spoke.

"Not at all," he responded, smiling warmly.

"Alice," she said, placing her hand on her chest. "Remember?"

He did remember. He remembered it all: the fantasies that he'd had about her, the suggestiveness that her name and tattoo had evoked in him, his initial concern that he'd slept with her and forgotten her name.

"You were Mallory's advisee, right?" he asked.

"That's right."

"Are you sure you want to sit next to me? It seems we're on opposite sides of this case," Sebastian said.

"What makes you say that?"

"You mean you're not here to support Mallory?"

"I'm here to watch her break," Alice said meekly, evading his gaze as she confessed her motives. "She was a worthless advisor. Beyond worthless. Sometimes I think she was deliberately trying to sabotage my work."

"I hadn't realized she was that bad. Not with her advisees, at least."

"You know, I picked her as my advisor because she was a woman. One of the few in the department. I thought she'd understand me better than a man would. More empathetic, maybe. But it was always a competition with her."

268

"She's a difficult person," Sebastian said, happy to have an ally next to him. "I'm sure you're better off without her. What are you working on now?"

Sebastian and Alice spent the rest of the wait talking through problems they were working on. She ended up being helpful. When Sebastian brought up his work on the Twin Prime Conjecture, she helped him consider how certain sieves might prove fruitful. They were in the middle of a solid intellectual conversation when the court convened. Sebastian took a breath before the verdict was read. He was sure that Stanford's lawyers had outperformed Mallory's, but there was the possibility the jury wouldn't see it that way. He braced himself for a potential defeat, even as he hoped for victory.

The verdict was delivered, ruling in favor of Stanford. Sebastian and Alice uttered exclamations of relief. Diana hugged Henry before turning toward Sebastian. She quickly embraced him in solidarity. Ordinarily, this small gesture would have been enough to send Sebastian into a protracted reverie about taking her somewhere and gripping her body against his. But this time, he felt nothing more than camaraderie. She smiled at him weakly. Sebastian felt like a changed man. Light was pouring in from the windows on the left side of the courtroom. He could feel the warmth on his face, and he closed his eyes. This was his moment in the sun, dismissive of the past. He basked in the present, golden and still. He opened his eyes, sure that nothing could dampen his spirits. He was wrong.

There was one issue that prevented Sebastian from being entirely happy: Mallory. Sebastian saw the look on Mallory Specter's face. There was a quiver in her forehead as she tried to will away her tears. She locked eyes with Sebastian across the room and lifted her chin a bit higher, trying to seem unfazed while letting some of the hurt show through. She turned her face away and cracked, taking off her glasses and collapsing into her palms.

269

When she did reemerge, her black eyeliner was smudged up to her eyebrows; her lipstick was smeared up her cheekbones. She was one of those women who looked better wiped clean. When she'd arrived at the courthouse earlier that day, fully made-up, it had been easier for him to dismiss her. But now that the seams were showing, Sebastian wished he could remove the makeup and restore her to her natural condition. He couldn't fully rejoice in his victory, not in the face of her collapse.

1 ... 1 ... **2** ...

The night after the trial concluded, Sebastian picked up Jessica Fleming, and they drove to the California Academy of Sciences at her suggestion. The Academy was hosting an event with a live band, cocktails, and access to all of its exhibits. When Sebastian and Jessica got there, they stood in line at the bar and people-watched as they waited to get their drinks. Jessica was the expert, able to pick out details to support her hypotheses about who these strangers might be. She fabricated all sorts of backstories for passersby. She spotted an environmental activist doing recon for a protest, a taxidermist waiting on an animal to die so he could stuff it, a douchebag trying to impress a girl he met on the internet, and an old man who insisted that people refer to him as "the Captain."

Sebastian couldn't get enough of her inventions. Jessica pointed to a couple kissing in the corner. "They're having an affair," she said. "See? One's wearing a wedding ring. The other isn't."

"Why would a man wear his wedding ring while he's with his mistress? Wouldn't he take it off?"

"Sometimes that's part of the game," she said, smirking.

"Maybe they're married, and the wife misplaced her ring."

"Maybe. But they're all over one another. In public. That doesn't say years of solid companionship to me. That has illicit affair written all over it. I would know," Jessica said. Almost immediately, she seemed to regret her last sentence. She changed the topic before they made it to the front of the line and got their drinks.

After they drank their cocktails, Jessica dragged Sebastian to the aquarium.

"Aurelia aurita. Moon jellyfish," she said, approaching the creatures floating in a cylindrical tube.

"You know the species by name," Sebastian said.

"They're my favorite. I come here a lot."

The lights in the artificial habitat changed at intervals. Purple. Pink. Blue. Green. Orange. Red. The natural glow of the circular jellyfishes took on the color of the lights around them, transforming from hue to hue every ten seconds or so. The saturation of the colors was so intense that the transparent bodies looked like they were on fire.

"They're beautiful," Sebastian said.

"Bioluminescence. It's lovely. A natural defense against predators."

"You'd think the light would make them a target. Lure in all sorts of animals."

"It can startle enemies. Confound them," she said, arching her eyebrow. Sebastian smiled at the gesture but didn't call attention to it. She put her hand against the glass, drawing her fingers along the path of a jellyfish as it ascended in the water.

"They don't change direction too often," Sebastian noted.

"They can't. The currents mostly determine where they go."

"That sounds terrible."

"I don't know. They're in touch with their surroundings. You ever go to the beach and just exist? Sit on the sand, dig in your feet, and let the breeze guide your thoughts?"

"Not the beach usually. Cliffs," Sebastian said. "Is that the same thing?"

"Sure," she said, combing his hair away from his forehead with her fingers. "Any cliffs in particular?"

"Palos Verdes. South of Los Angeles," he said, looking into her blue eyes.

"So you get it," she said, smiling. She pulled away and circled the jellyfish tank.

"Get what?" he asked, chasing her as though they were playing a game.

"The Pacific. I'd let it take me wherever it wanted," Jessica said, twirling around with her head tilted toward the ceiling.

"I thought you were a control freak," Sebastian said, taunting her with a finger prod at her side.

"When did I say that?" she laughed, defensively slapping his hand away.

"You didn't say it exactly," Sebastian said as they kept walking. "It's small things. Like the way that you rearrange your cash in your wallet after you pay for something. The bills facing the same direction. The denominations numerically ordered. Or the way you eat every last bite of your vegetables before touching your steak."

"Those are just quirks. Compulsions."

"Listen, it's not a bad thing. I wish I had more order in my life," he said, catching up to her brisk walk and placing an arm around her waist.

"I've always needed order. It's how I cope with everything."

"Cope with what?"

Jessica launched into an explanation, starting with her childhood. Like Sebastian, Jessica had all but raised herself. But unlike Sebastian, who delighted in discarding the responsibilities that he hadn't been able to abandon in childhood, Jessica took on more duties every year, growing more stable with each new task she undertook. Sebastian admired her reliability. She was an anchor tethering him to the person he should have been, even in the face of the person he was.

After she revealed so much about herself, Sebastian felt compelled to do the same. For once, he opened up to a woman about the complicated and burdensome details of his life. He talked to her about his past, which he'd thought was best left in the past until she convinced him it would be an unremitting part of his present unless he confronted it. She knew about that sort of thing. She'd been reluctant to go into therapy until she almost gave up on her life at twenty-one. He felt better when he talked to her.

That night, he took Jessica to his place and slept with her for the first time. There was passion, but beyond that, there was comfort. When Sebastian woke up, Jessica was lying next to him, her back bare. He cast his hand across it. He looked at the birthmark on her shoulder. It wasn't dark. He could only faintly distinguish it from her surrounding skin. He hadn't even noticed it before. But now that he was aware of its existence, Sebastian tried to discern a form within its shape, an animal or flower or fruit, something organic that connected her body to life outside of it. He traced the outline, trying to think up an image that could stick, but ultimately, the design was too amorphous. He decided it was better this way. If he had been able to trace a pear, she would have been defined by that pear. If he had been able to locate a star, he might have read too much into the magic and otherworldliness of it. She was born as she was, attached to nothing, bearing a mark that destined her for scrutiny. She had to be decoded, not using archetypes that already existed, but by accepting that she was a new archetype, one that others would doubtless imitate.

Sebastian liked that she made him think, even when she was doing nothing. She got his mind turning so much that he decided to pull out a notebook from his bedside table and work on the Twin Prime Conjecture. Sebastian combined a

273

sieving tool with a function that tweaked the definition of the level of distribution. He ran through the numbers while Jessica rested next to him. The moment couldn't get any better. He hoped this would last.

It did. Jessica started spending more time at his place, especially on the weekends. She and Sebastian did activities reserved for couples: going to brunch together, meeting for dinner with her friends, and driving to San Francisco to picnic in Alamo Square. Some mornings, she made him instant pancakes, and he oozed with warmth and nostalgia.

Eventually, Sebastian surprised her at her office at Berkeley. Once she'd wrapped up her work, he led her to the Free Speech Monument in Sproul Plaza, the same place she'd taken him the first time they'd met. Once they got to the granite circle in the ground, Sebastian positioned Jessica's toes right against the six-inch hole in the center of the monument. He placed his toes against the opposite edge of the hole.

"Are you ready to tell me why we're here?" Jessica asked.

"I brought you here to tell you I love you."

She looked at him for a moment. She raised her eyebrow.

"You couldn't have told me this in my office, huh?"

"I wanted to chart new territory in a new territory. Another jurisdiction."

"You know this isn't actually another jurisdiction, right?" Jessica responded, her face mischievous and light-hearted. "I know the inscription makes it seem like it is, but the artist never went through the bureaucratic red tape to make the space sovereign or independent or whatever. It's an unfinished work."

"Would you stop trying to kill my romantic gesture?"

"I'm sorry," she said, wrapping her arms around him. "I love you too," she said. She kissed him above the hole in the ground, smack in the middle of the 60,000-foot invisible column of freedom. "Now can we grab dinner? I'm starving," she said.

274

Sebastian reached for her hand, and they left the granite monument behind them. He radiated with happiness until he realized something.

"This is crazy to even ask, but you're not still seeing Radenport, are you?"

"No. I mean, I still see him around campus but only professionally. Did I just tell you that I love you, or did I only imagine that?"

"Sorry," Sebastian said. "You did. Don't mind me." He knew he should forget about Radenport. But suddenly, the moment that had seemed so perfect was no longer as flawless as he'd hoped.

1 ... 1 ... 2 ... 3 ...

After so many years spent alone, there was a glow about Jacqueline Barnabas now. She felt flushed whenever she looked at Barrie. There had always been something transgressive about being with him. When they were teenagers, it had been his long hair, his bell-bottoms, and the way he wore his fringed vests to school without a shirt on underneath, flaunting the body that construction work with his father's company had given him. He had rock and roll inside of him, and he was a pro at letting it sing through his guitar; he strummed with a violence that had felt like passion to seventeen-year-old Jacqueline. Her parents, Palos Verdes conservatives who'd mourned the passing of the fifties with audible groans, had hated him, even before Jacqueline had gotten pregnant, and he'd made himself scarce. There was still that danger inside of him. He might leave her any minute; he might damage her; he might betray her. But for now, he was doing nothing of the sort. Living on the edge was preferable to being on a road to nowhere. They lied together on the living room couch.

"Remind me what happened again," Jacqueline instructed him, stroking his elbow where the joint failed to bend properly.

"Old football injury. Flares up here and there," Barrie explained.

"You played long enough to do that kind of damage? I thought you only played for one season in high school," she said, staring up at the ceiling and caressing his arm.

"It's not about how *long* you play. It's about *how* you play. And I was reckless."

"You don't say…" Jacqueline teased, her face craning toward his as she lay on his chest. "What about your leg? The one with the bullet scar. Does it still hurt?"

"Sometimes. But I don't want to talk about it."

Of course he didn't want to talk about it. Barrie had only discussed the injury once before: on a night when they'd both been high out of their minds, and he'd confessed to shooting his own leg so he could get out of Vietnam.

"The insurance is still covering everything, right?" Jacqueline asked.

"Yeah. And as long as I keep this job, the insurance will *keep* on covering me."

"There's no way you're going to lose your job, is there?" she asked, her fingers playing with the joints in his hand.

"No chance. They love me there," Barrie said, referring to a new construction firm.

"You're sure?"

"I wouldn't have come back to you if I thought I couldn't provide for you."

"So…now you're going to tell me that's why you left in the first place?"

"Well, it was. You deserved better."

She said nothing in response but snuggled further into the valley between his arms, knowing that this time around, he was the one who deserved better.

"Do you think the rehab is going to fix your joints?" she asked innocently.

"You worried?"

"I want you to feel better."

"That's not what you're worried about."

Jacqueline thought about playing coy, but she decided not to pretend. They were too old for games, and they both knew what was at stake. The past couple of weeks together had been perfect. They'd been able to retreat into a life with Oxycodone, the antidote to every sadness they used to fall victim to. Barrie received the pills for chronic pain from his joint problems and recent hip surgery. Jacqueline loved the warm sensations that flooded her body every time she crushed up one of the pills and snorted it. While on the opiate, she could lie on her bed doing nothing, floating away in pure bliss. She craved the drug more and more, even as the intensity of the rush diminished with each hit. She enjoyed the ritual of preparing the powder, which reminded her of those years in her twenties and thirties when coke was all the rage and she never went to a P.V. party without doing some amount of blow—the South Bay was brimming with the stuff, rich kids with too much money and too much time, and she was never one to refuse an offer.

Now that she was older, she didn't have to worry about the responsibilities of motherhood. And since Barrie was gainfully employed, she reduced her hours at the grocery store and didn't worry about much. Occasionally, the oxy would make her nauseated or itchy, but she knew how to deal with the side effects when she had to. They were worth riding out. Sometimes, Barrie would roll a joint of his medical marijuana, and the euphoria of the oxy would be all the more idly pleasurable when coupled with the taste of pot. The cannabis also bridged the gaps between oxy highs since they had to ration their pills—the doctors had been generous in their supply but not generous enough to cover the type of habit they'd developed. Whenever they were coming down, they amused themselves with one another to forget the pain of life without oxy, retreating into sex like the teenagers they'd been when they'd first met. Everything was as ideal as it would ever be, but it wasn't sustainable. Jacqueline dreaded the day when Barrie's prescription would run dry, but she never assumed there might be other obstacles destroying her Shangri-La.

"What the hell is this?" Barrie asked, finding some old letters and photographs from Jackie's affair with Arthur. "Who the hell is this guy?"

"You've been looking through my things?" Jacqueline asked.

"Answer the question, Jack."

Jacqueline thought about lying, but she could see it wouldn't do her any good. "I babysat for him back in high school. I think you might've even met him a couple of times."

"Come on, Jackie. I'm not dumb. You did more than babysit for his kids. These letters. They're fucking love letters," he shouted, face red and pained.

"All right. Fine," Jacqueline erupted. "You're right. I had an affair with him."

"These pictures, they're all from 1968. That's when *we* were together."

"I know. But back then, you spent your time with other people too. I was never your only girl. You slept around. I knew all about it. The girls, they talked."

"Jackie...Am I Sebastian's father?"

She held her tongue.

"Jackie," Barrie yelled, jolting her with the force of her name. "Am I his father?"

"Don't, Barrie. Just don't."

"Answer me," he said, pulling her by her shirt.

"No," she confessed. Barrie let go of her shirt and shoved her to the ground.

278

"I knew it. I knew this was a mistake. You were always a mistake. Do you know what I did for you? I went to fucking *war* for you!"

"I never wanted you to fight. I pleaded with you to stay."

"I went to war to get away from you. From the kid. You're poison, Jackie. Poison," Barrie spewed, pointing emphatically at her with his insults. "I took a fucking bullet! And for what? For a kid that's not mine?"

"Listen to yourself!" Jackie shouted, rising from the floor and following Barrie as he walked around the house, grabbing his things. "You went to *war* to avoid taking responsibility for yourself. To avoid being a dad? Which of us is poison?"

Barrie raised his hand as though he might hit her, but instead, he started for the door.

"Barrie! Barrie!" Jacqueline called out, insistent and shrill.

"What?" he responded, turning around for an instant.

"Could you at least leave me some pills? I don't need many. Three? Two? Even one would be something," she pleaded, softening her voice.

"You're unbelievable," he said. He took one of the pills from his prescription bottle, threw it across the house as far as he could, and left.

Jacqueline ran to the sliding glass door where the pill had fallen into the crevice of the railing. She dusted it off and washed it down with some liquor before eventually falling asleep. When she woke up the next morning, the paradise she'd made for herself was in shambles. All the drugs were gone, and so was her lover. She ran around the house, upturning everything in her path, hoping that an errant pill had fallen underneath a piece of furniture. She spent the rest of the day in a cold sweat, wishing for the warmth and love of the oxy. Instead, she found the blunt pangs of withdrawal and a painful reminder that trying to cultivate the perfect life decimated every chance of having a decent one.

There is a perfect place in this world for everyone. For Rachel Washington, that perfect place was the coastal Californian city of Carpinteria outside of Santa Barbara. For decades, she'd dreamed of selling the family home in Glendale and moving there. She longed for a future without perpetually gridlocked traffic on congested freeways. She imagined a place with less smog where it didn't hurt to breathe. She envisioned life in a smaller community, divorced from the bustle of the greater Los Angeles area but not too far from a city. Part of the dream wasn't where she'd spent the rest of her life but with whom. She'd spent years dreaming she could reclaim her husband again and wrench him from the grips of his job. Since she'd retired from nursing in middle age, she'd spent too many years alone in her home, waiting for Daniel to come home from work, only to see him continue working after dinner. The only fights they'd had in the past fifteen years had been about when he would retire or cut back his hours. He'd kept promising it would happen. He'd even agreed to move to Carpinteria when he left the firm. But each year he kept working was another year that Rachel had to put off her dreams and accept the reality that her husband might work himself into the ground and she might die in Glendale.

Rachel had been watching the real estate market in Carpinteria closely, dreaming about one house or another before it eventually sold. She lived vicariously through pictures on the internet, mentally transporting herself to local events. She admired online photos of the flower nurseries and the sea glass festival and the outdoor movies in the park. She built an entire existence in Carpinteria in her head before claiming a residence on its streets.

The day after Daniel told her he was retiring, she'd hopped into her car, driven up the coast, and looked at the houses on her radar. She fell in love with a five-million-dollar estate right on the shore. The price tag was high, but if she'd sacrificed so much on the altar of her husband's high-paying job, shouldn't she reap some of its benefits? Besides, their Glendale home had appreciated tremendously in the decades since they'd bought and remodeled it. She took Daniel to the Carpinteria house on the weekend of his retirement and practically coerced him into making an offer. They entered escrow, and thirty days later, it was theirs.

"I can't believe we're here," Rachel said, unpacking boxes in the kitchen in the early evening on their first day in the new place. "And the move went so smoothly."

"I'm glad you kept your eye on the market for so long. This place was a real find. Even though the last owners were a nightmare..." Daniel said, stretching out on the nearby living room couch. He lay there in contemplation as Rachel unloaded the plates and silverware. "You don't think it's too quiet?" he eventually asked.

Rachel got up and opened the windows, letting in the sound of the waves crashing on the shore. She abandoned her unpacking and joined Daniel on the couch.

"Listen to that," she said, curling up against her husband.

"It's nice, obviously," Daniel said. "But still a bit quiet."

"You know what's quiet?" Rachel asked, rising from the crook of his arm and looking in his direction. "An empty house in the suburbs."

"Fair enough."

"You'll find things to do here," Rachel said. "It won't seem so quiet."

Daniel smiled weakly. That half-smile summoned Rachel's fear that Daniel wouldn't know who he was without his career. It was something she'd considered a lot in the past days and months and years, but it struck her with new force when he seemed unable to relax in one of the most relaxing places on the planet. But beyond thinking about him, Rachel started to worry that she wouldn't know who *she* was without his career either. He was entirely hers now, ready to give her the sort of constant companionship she thought you were supposed to get when you signed your marital contract. In many ways, it already felt nice. When he laughed or smiled, Rachel saw the twentysomething boy she'd fallen for all those years ago. But she also knew that they would have to redefine their relationship as the barriers of work routines fell away. She didn't want the walls of her own identity to collapse in the process.

"Get up, grab your coat, and take off your shoes," Rachel said, rising from the couch.

"Why?"

"Just do it."

Daniel obliged. Rachel grabbed his hand, leading him down to the beach. They walked along the shore, and the sand got into the crevices between their toes. The sea-salt breeze swept their hair across their faces. The tide was mellow, a hum at their side. The sun was setting, and orange lit up the sky. Rachel found a piece of sea glass in the sand and bent to pick it up. She spotted another not too far away and grabbed it. She looked at Daniel and held out the polished blue and green stones for him to see.

"The simple things in life," she said.

"Or the not so simple things," he said, nodding his head in the direction of their impressive house behind them.

"We've certainly built something for ourselves, haven't we?"

"Is it everything you wanted?"

"More," she said, sending an arm around his waist and leaning her head against his shoulder as they continued walking. "Can you believe this was part of someone's beer bottle?" she asked, admiring the sea glass.

"It doesn't matter what it was. It matters what it is."

"I love how smooth the edges get," she said, manipulating the stones between her fingers. "But it's strange the way the colors get murky. Like the glass develops cataracts or something."

"You still say the funniest things."

"Listen, husband. I'll have you know I am a profoundly unfunny person. I thought you knew that by now."

"There you go again."

She took the sea glass and sent it back into the ocean, throwing the stones with the full strength of her good arm.

"What'd you do that for?" Daniel asked.

"I want to make sure there are still some for me to pick up tomorrow."

"You don't want this place to get old."

"How could it possibly get old?" she asked. "It's perfect." She paused for a moment. "You think Jake'll like it?"

"How could he not?" Daniel replied. "After all, it *is* perfect."

And to Rachel Washington, it was. The house, the town, the neighborhood.

But the following week, something happened that shook her. Rachel noticed a black sedan cruise by their house every so often, stopping and idling nearby. At first, she didn't think much of it. She assumed the car belonged to a neighbor or the friend of a neighbor. But the more often it surfaced, the more suspicious she became. One morning, Rachel could have sworn someone was taking pictures of the house. After that, she couldn't calm her mind all day. Daniel noticed something was off with her. That night as they drank wine on their deck and looked out at the ocean, Daniel reached out to her.

"It seems like something's bothering you," Daniel said. "Want to talk about it?"

"You'll think I'm crazy."

"I already know you're crazy," Daniel said jokingly, "so what's the harm in talking about it?"

"Haha," she said in mock humor. "I'm serious. I think someone's spying on us. Maybe they're casing our house? I don't know. I could be paranoid."

Daniel was silent. He drank his wine and looked out at the ocean. His face was blank. The waves crashed against the shore and filled the wordless expanse. Rachel wished she'd kept her sea glass so she'd have something to fiddle with right now.

"Daniel?" she asked, searching for a response. "What is it? You think I'm crazy?"

"I don't think you're crazy," he said, looking at her stoically.

"Then what're you thinking?"

"I don't even know where to start."

"Now you're making me nervous," she said. Daniel looked over at her, mired in the darkness. The moonlight reflected off his eyes, serious eyes. It took him a while to speak, and Rachel grew more distressed with each passing second.

"I'm not the man you think I am," Daniel said, turning to her and hunching over, his elbows propped on his knees.

"What do you mean?"

"The work I did for Kensington Whitmore. It was crooked. Maybe not *all* of my work exactly. But the company was crooked, and I knew it. I helped them. And I promised I'd never say anything about it to anyone."

"I don't understand," Rachel said, struggling to reconcile this new information with her husband, whose virtue had never been beyond reproach in their decades-long marriage.

"I know you don't. I don't expect you to."

"You think the car that's been hanging around here is related to your work?"

"Yes."

"Are we in danger?"

"I don't think so. It's not like I'm going to become a whistleblower or anything. I'm going to keep my head down, live my life here, and forget everything about that place."

"I just…" she said, rising from her chair and pacing in disbelief as she gathered her words. "I thought you cared about honor. Ethics."

"I do…I *did*," Daniel clarified, his voice dropping in shame. "The money they offered me…that was what gave us the freedom to live our life. The freedom to buy this house. Pay for Jake's private education. I did it for the family. And most of the time, the wrongdoing, it affected big companies. Profitable companies who could afford it."

"My god, Daniel. This is a lot take in," Rachel said, continuing to pace. She didn't know how to process what her husband had told her. She couldn't believe he could have kept something so serious from her for so long. At first, it felt like a betrayal, but she considered why he hadn't told her anything. It must have been shame that had kept him silent all those years. After all, he was a good man. Rachel was sure of that. She looked out at the ocean and thought about the cost of their property, financially and otherwise. She worried she was complicit. She'd never questioned their bank statements. She'd never asked him about business colleagues who'd seemed unsavory. And whenever Daniel had seemed distraught over work, she'd written it off as typical lawyerly stress. She'd wanted a good life for her family: emotionally but materially too.

"I'm going to take a walk," Rachel told Daniel, getting up from her chair.

Rachel took off her shoes and walked along the edge of the shore, letting the frigid water lap at her feet. She looked down as she walked, hoping to find some sea glass along the way. But it was too dark for her to see anything, so she planted herself in one spot to search for treasure, bending down and digging her hands into the sand. Her fingers froze up in the wintered earth, but she continued groping for something buried, anything buried. Eventually, Rachel withdrew her hand in pain, dropping a sharp piece of broken glass onto the sand in the process. It wasn't a bad cut, but it startled her. She carefully picked up the glass from the ground and held it up to the moonlight. It was clear, unmarred by the stains of time. She kept it with her so no one else would fall victim to it. She made her way home to her mansion on the waterfront. She wondered at her home's beauty. But as she listened to the wild waves encroaching on the land of men, she was no longer blind to the turbulent world that had helped create that beauty.

1 ... 1 ... 2 ... 3 ... 5 ... 8 ...

To Jake Washington, there were few things on Earth as beautiful as natural formations born from land, sky, and water. Rocks. Meteorites. Crystals. Geodes. Canyons. His mother used to tell him his obsession with rocks was practically as old as he was. According to her, whenever she'd take Jake on a walk in their Glendale neighborhood in his youth, there were certain houses she'd have to avoid because she knew if Jake passed by a gravel area, he would plop down, play with the stones, and refuse to leave.

The love affair with rocks kept going. When he was eight, Jake got a rock tumbler for Christmas, and he collapsed onto his knees at his parents' feet in gratitude. Sometimes when he'd use his rock tumbler, he'd spend the night in the garage so he could fall asleep to the sound of the rocks clanging around and the motor whirring. The transformation was like magic. When he'd open up the tumbler after days of rumbling, he'd see the beauty emerge from the rocks' dirty exteriors. His favorite rock had been an amethyst he'd found near the schoolyard that polished up nicely, pale purple with strands of white woven throughout.

But now, Jake was older, he had his Martian meteorite, and no other rock could compare to it. Martian meteorites were rare enough, but Jake thought there was something extra special about his specimen. It was just a feeling. Or maybe an illusion. Either way, Jake's expectations were high. When Jake had led Jessica Fleming to believe that he'd stumbled upon a revolutionary discovery, he'd implied that his meteorite demonstrated evidence of life on Mars. After all, that had been the dream. The more he analyzed the meteorite, the less likely it became that he had such proof on his hands. But Jake found something else in the meteorite: remarkable crystals. Since crystallography wasn't his specialization, Jake teamed up with eight other scientists around the world who were more versed in the field. He sent them samples of the crystals so they could analyze them using a variety of methods and high-tech equipment. The findings floored Jake.

"Sebastian," Jake said when his brother stopped by his Berkeley office. "You have to see this," he continued, pulling up an image on his computer.

"What am I looking at?" Sebastian asked.

"A scientist in Tokyo captured the image in a transmission electron microscope. It's an electron diffraction pattern from the crystals in the meteorites. Turns out, they're not even crystals at all. They're quasicrystals. Take a look at this symmetry: ten-fold," Jake said. He admired the image as if for the first time. It was a pattern of bright white orbs arranged in concentric circles against a black background. The glowing white circles spread out like an intricate constellation, with larger orbs and smaller orbs arranged in an ordered design. The pattern looked like a firework when it first explodes in the air before gravity causes the shape to melt and deform in the night sky.

"It's lovely," Sebastian said. "But what are quasicrystals?"

"They're aperiodic crystalline structures that don't have traditional crystalline symmetries. Until the eighties, people disregarded them or thought they couldn't exist. Scientists thought all crystals had to have two- or three- or four- or six-fold rotational symmetries. Look at this one," Jake said, pulling up an image that looked like wallpaper with patterns of white dots in small, almost circular structures. "This one was taken using high-resolution transmission electron microscopy."

"They're Penrose tilings," Sebastian said, recognizing the self-similar, non-periodic designs. Jake was glad he could share his research with Sebastian. He was thankful that Sebastian could use his mathematical brain to see the world as Jake did.

"That's right," Jake said. "Quasicrystal patterns are related to the golden ratio."

"So how rare are these quasicrystals? If people started researching them in the eighties, is there any chance of breaking new ground in your work?"

"Scientists have analyzed hundreds of quasicrystals, but they were almost all created in labs. Until now, there was only one known naturally occurring quasicrystal. This meteorite contains the second. It's a relatively new field, so there's a lot of potential."

"That's great news," Sebastian smiled, hand on his shoulder. "Honestly. But I should take off. I just stopped by to say hi. I promised Jessica I'd take her out tonight."

At the mention of Jessica's name, Jake tensed up. He knew it was irrational, but he couldn't fight the feeling that she might exploit Sebastian's trust and team up with William.

"Don't tell her about the quasicrystals," Jake cautioned. "I don't want Radenport to know about them."

"She's not even seeing him anymore. She broke it off with him."

"As far as you know."

"Yes, as far as I know. I don't think she's lying to me. Calm down. Radenport isn't going to ruin this for you," Sebastian said with an earnest look. The next minute, he left.

Jake couldn't stop thinking about Jessica and her potential mutiny against him. It could all be paranoia. After all, Sebastian trusted her. He loved her. He'd told Jake as much. Whenever Jake saw Sebastian and Jessica together, her interest in Sebastian seemed genuine—so genuine that it made Jake's meetings with her a bit awkward, pulled taut by the knowledge that she was dating someone who looked like him. But Jessica's interest in Jake's work also seemed genuine. She'd already used many of his articles as foundational sources for her research. There shouldn't be any reason to distrust her. And yet, Jake couldn't get it out of his head that she was in league with Radenport. Feminine wiles were powerful; Jake knew as much. Jessica knew how to smile and make people around her feel important. She could ruin everything for him.

To distract himself from these concerns, Jake brought out a collection of rocks and gemstones from his cabinet. Pyrite. Alabaster. Sandstone. Obsidian. Petrified wood. Serpentine. Limestone. Sulfur. Some sparkled, some shone. The colors ran the spectrum. Most of the rocks weren't ones he'd found, but ones he'd purchased, true beauties that were too rare to find along the suburban paths of Glendale. He held some in his hand and massaged their smooth edges in his palm. They felt nice. As he touched the smaller stones, he looked over at a large geode displayed on his desk. Its crystals were beautiful: cragged and lustrous. Jake thought about the quasicrystals in the meteorite, and they buoyed his spirits with their promise. They were an incredible find, maybe even the key to his future, but he couldn't stop worrying that Radenport would find a way to take this away from him too, the way he always did.

1 ... 1 ... 2 ... 3 ... 5 ... 8 ... **13 ...**

Jake Washington had every reason to be paranoid, though he should have directed his suspicions elsewhere. William

Radenport was not a threat to him. The real danger came from a company that Jake didn't even know he should worry about: Carver-Jackson. Carver-Jackson was not just a conglomeration but an empire. Decades of mergers and acquisitions had fattened its britches such that its shadow stretched across oceans. Few people knew it by name, which made it all the more powerful, especially since its anonymity as a parent company contrasted its easily recognizable subsidiary companies. Most of the population assumed that the "big names" of these television companies and cosmetic giants and internet providers and the rest were large enough to function without an overseer.

People bought all sorts of products without ever knowing that Carver-Jackson owned the companies that made them: electronic toothbrushes, top-of-the-line kitchen stoves, stainless-steel cookware, curling irons, anti-aging skin cream, color-match foundation, digital video recorders, LED screens, internet bundles, cable channels, telescope eyepieces, surveillance equipment, and the very microscopes stocked in Jake's lab.

Carver-Jackson had thrown capital behind Stanford years ago, bankrolling research that could revolutionize the conglomeration's technology. Protecting their investment, Carver-Jackson had paid their long-time ally, the law firm of Kensington Whitmore, to sink the wrongful termination lawsuit against the university. So when Daniel Washington learned about Carver-Jackson's arrangement, quit Kensington Whitmore, and made threats as he left, the conglomeration decided to surveil the Washington family. Their investigation proved that Daniel was a typical retiree, uninterested in divulging secrets about the Stanford case or any others. The Carver-Jackson team was about to stop the surveillance entirely when a telephone call piqued their attention.

"I have news," Jake told his mother when he called her on the landline. "And I wanted to share it with you."

"What is it?"

"Well, you may not understand the significance of this, hell, I don't know that *I* do, but my team and I found naturally formed quasicrystals in the meteorite. It could lead to some groundbreaking research. It might have cosmological implications," Jake explained.

Though "cosmological implications" were hardly interesting to Carver-Jackson, a tech on the surveillance team flagged the conversation just in case. He forwarded the recorded conversation to Carolina Thackeray, the head of research and development at Carver-Jackson. The executive smiled. She'd already seen the applications of quasicrystals in everyday technology. It was promising. Several qualities made quasicrystals desirable for developing products, including their corrosion and abrasion resistance, low conductivity, high hardness, and low friction coefficients. One of the first applications that scientists discovered for quasicrystals was kitchenware, specifically non-stick pans. Companies used small quasicrystalline particles in their manufacture of stainless-steel instruments and products, which resulted in more durable, corrosion-resistant metal. Other applications of quasicrystals allowed LED companies to improve the photon extraction efficiency of their products. For obvious reasons, these scientific innovations were important to Carver-Jackson, a corporation whose subsidiaries sold kitchenware and electronics and other devices.

Having a natural sample of the quasicrystals' structures could mean big business. The first natural sample discovered had a high crystalline structure, as good, if not better than any produced in labs. Who knew how durable this new crystalline structure would prove? Carolina Thackeray saw the potential. There was still work to be done, but that was no matter. Something almost perfect had landed right in her lap. The only catch was that the meteorite wasn't hers...yet.

1 ... 1 ... 2 ... 3 ... 5 ... 8 ... 13 ... **21 ...**

Lilith Washington couldn't believe her luck when she landed a lunch meeting with an executive from Carver-Jackson. The executive had business at Stanford, so Lilith agreed to drive to Palo Alto. After Lilith parked and started toward the restaurant for the meeting, she came across a farmer's market. She'd arrived early, so she perused the market.

She walked by flower stands and spotted some lovely alstroemeria. She was about to lean down to inspect them when she saw her: Selene Thessalonia. Selene was admiring an apple at a nearby fruit stand. Lilith followed her. Selene browsed other stands, glancing up intermittently as if to catch a wandering eye. But Selene's roving looks were not aimless. A man approached Selene, and when he reached her, he kissed her. The man was good-looking. He wore thick-framed glasses and a flannel shirt, just the sort of hipster that belonged with a girl like Selene. The two of them held hands as they strolled down the lane of the farmers' market, occasionally sampling the wares that vendors offered. They smiled and laughed, nuzzling one another with the affection of new romance. Nothing could have made Lilith happier. Now she could stop compulsively checking Jake's email in case Selene responded to the email Lilith had written in his name. Lilith breathed out and headed to the restaurant for her meeting.

When she got there, she saw Carolina Thackeray dressed in a clean, black suit with minimal makeup and a tight bun at the base of her neck. Carolina smiled as Lilith approached, but there was a sharpness to her, too many edges. Lilith shook hands with Carolina, introduced herself. They took a seat and got down to business.

"I'm very interested in your husband's research," Carolina said. "There isn't much public information about it, so I was hoping you could give me more insight into how his work is coming along. Obviously, I can talk to your husband directly if I need to know any particulars. But I'm not a scientist. I'm a businessperson. So I thought I'd talk to you because of your position on the Board at the Berkeley Foundation. I'm trying to figure out the best course of action here. Carver-Jackson does a lot of philanthropic giving, but we also offer grants in the sciences and technology. I'm not sure if we should donate money to the foundation directly or if we should encourage your husband to apply for a grant instead."

"Jake is always writing grant proposals for one thing or another so it wouldn't be a bother, but I'm not sure he needs any funding for his meteorite research right now. It might be best for you to donate to the foundation, and I'll find a way to make sure that your contribution can help sustain his research if his current funding runs out. I'm happy to handle the donation for you," Lilith said.

"Thank you. That would be helpful."

Lilith couldn't believe how well this was going. Usually, when she'd meet with potential donors, she'd have to do a hard sell. There'd be plenty of legwork before ever broaching the subject of donations. But this was different. Carolina Thackeray had been the one to reach out to Lilith.

"Great," Lilith said, deciding to press her luck. "I also had another idea that I wanted to run by you. I don't know if anyone told you this, but aside from my work with the foundation, I'm also the senior vice president of marketing for Silversun Wines. I'd love to get in touch with someone from one of your production companies about cross-promotional opportunities, maybe on a cooking show or something like that."

"I can send you some contacts. But I'd like to get back to Jake and his research. I know you said you don't understand much of the science behind what he does. But I'm more interested in the man behind the meteorite. What he's like. What his process is. Where he works. Who he works with.

More of the broad strokes. Personal backstory type of information. That sort of thing helps me pitch for him."

Lilith was happy to oblige. She gave as many details as she could summon about Jake and his working process. Carolina Thackeray listened eagerly. Lilith left the meeting feeling great. She was all but sure that Carver-Jackson would give the foundation and Jake a hefty amount of funding.

Lilith felt like the day couldn't get any better. When she got home, she had the place to herself. She went down to the wine cellar to find something to celebrate the promises of the day. She held a bottle of 2002 Louis Roederer Cristal in her hands, mulling over whether or not to open it. Lilith had drunk her first bottle of Cristal on her twenty-first birthday; it had been a present from her father, who'd said exceptional champagne was the only way to celebrate a milestone. Lilith agreed. The 2002 bottle had earned nearly perfect ratings, but it hadn't fully matured yet. There were other bottles of champagne in the cellar, but she kept going back to the Cristal. If she opened it now, she could give it time to breathe; that would help some.

Resisting the internal voices telling her to wait, Lilith uncorked the bottle and poured herself a glass. She put on some music and drew herself a bath while the champagne opened up. Eventually, she took up her glass and brought it with her into the bathtub. The nose of the champagne lured her. She could feel the effervescence of the carbonation tickling her as she breathed in. The first sip was perfection: loud, mineral-heavy, and full of citrus that lent a crisp but measured acidity. Her muscles relaxed in the warm water. She let herself go limp and let her head fall back against the rim of the tub.

Lilith closed her eyes to better enjoy the taste of the champagne and the stillness of her limbs. She thought about Selene Thessalonia. Selene had rejected Jake at the gala, but Lilith had kept worrying about her. But now that Lilith had seen Selene clutching that other man at the farmer's market,

294

Lilith was sure she had nothing to worry about. Even Jessica Fleming was no longer a threat because she was dating Sebastian. Jake could be Lilith's again. The thought of it made her itchy for sex. She decided that after her bath, she would put on her sexiest black lingerie and seduce her husband when he came home. She knew she could still excite him when she wanted to. In the middle of her reverie, the phone rang. She got out of the tub and wrapped a towel around her, picking up a nearby receiver.

"Jake's out," Lilith said to Rachel Washington, whose number showed up on caller ID. "He should be home soon if you want him to call you back."

"No, that's all right," Rachel said. "It's nothing urgent. Something's come up, and I thought you two should know about it. It's probably nothing. I'm just calling you as a precaution anyway. I'm sure it's not even worth the phone call."

"A precaution?"

"Daniel's retirement has been a bit…messy. I guess his firm had some shady business interests. I just want you and Jake to be on alert."

"Be on alert? What's going on, Rachel? What kind of business interests are we talking about here?"

"Again, it's probably nothing, but I'm worried someone's watching us. Daniel doesn't think anything is going to happen, but I still thought you and Jake should know. Daniel thinks it might be tied to that huge conglomeration, Carver-Jackson."

"Carver-Jackson?" Lilith asked, nearly dropping the phone.

"Yeah, they own a bunch of tech companies and media platforms, I think," Rachel said. Rachel gave Lilith a full explanation of everything she knew. Lilith could barely keep her composure as she silently took it all in.

"Well, thanks for letting us know, Rachel. I'll tell Jake. We'll keep our guards up. Have a good night," Lilith said before hanging up the phone.

Lilith stood in the bathroom, dripping water onto the carpet until she could compel herself to move. She towel-dried her hair, drained the bathtub, and threw on comfortable underwear and an oversized shirt, leaving the lacy lingerie in the drawer. Lilith refilled her champagne flute and drank it in silence on the living room couch. Not long after, Jake came home, put down his things, and poured a glass of champagne.

"The 2002 Cristal," he said, sitting down next to her and kicking up his feet, glass in hand. "The meeting today must have gone well."

"I thought so," Lilith said, trying not to seem too somber.

"What's wrong?"

"Nothing," she said. "Nothing's wrong. I just want another glass."

The Seventh Row
The Power of Prime Numbers

```
                    1
                1       1
            1       2       1
        1       3       3       1
    1       4       6       4       1
1       5      10      10       5       1
1   6      15      20      15       6       1
1   7      21      35      35      21       7       1
```

Whenever the first number after the initial 1 in a row is a prime number, then the subsequent numbers in the series will be divisible by that prime number.

Examine the seventh row. The first number beyond the 1 is a prime: 7. The other numbers in the row are 21 and 35, both of which are divisible by 7.

Like all prime numbers, seven is beautiful because of its indivisibility; no number other than one or itself can evenly divide seven without leaving a remainder.

The fact that prime numbered rows exclusively produce their multiples is a testament to their legacy. For as odd, strange, and (relatively) uncommon as primes are, they are undoubtedly powerful.

There is now a consensus that the number 1 should be excluded from sets of primes. But in the past, some mathematicians treated it as a prime number.

1 : : : : : : :

Prime Numbers Generally Stand Alone

On Sunday, Jake woke up with a hangover from the
champagne and whiskey he'd downed with Lilith the night
before. But worse than the hangover was his lingering
suspicion that he hadn't locked up his meteorite in his
cabinet. The misgiving was strong enough that Jake decided
to push past his headache, hop into his car, and make a quick
trip to his office. When he arrived, he noticed that the
meteorite wasn't on his desk. He unlocked the cabinet and
opened the drawer. Nothing. He kept searching. Nothing.
Jake started to sweat. He thought he might throw up. His
headache worsened, and he had to sit down and breathe. In
his mind, there was only one explanation: William
Radenport. Jake tried calling Radenport's cell phone. No
response. Jake's next call was to the police, who came to
investigate the scene. They offered little hope.

His next call was to Sebastian. Jake needed to see him.
He arranged to meet him at the Golden Gate Bridge one
more time.

"Interesting choice," Sebastian said, greeting him.

"It felt significant. This is where I felt like we connected
for the first time."

"And look at us now," Sebastian said, patting Jake on the
shoulder.

"Yeah," Jake responded sullenly.

"Is everything all right?"

"No. Not at all. That's why I could use a walk."

Jake left the visitor center and headed toward the bridge.
He tried to walk off his demons, keeping a brisk pace that
Sebastian barely matched. The day was clear, which made
the size and scope of the bridge feel imposing as they neared
it. The last time they were here, they had met in the fog,
when it had been easier to pretend that the bridge was

298

smaller, more adequately scaled to the size of human affairs. Walking along the pedestrian bridge in the sun, Jake felt insignificant. Jake steadily increased his speed until he was running. Sebastian trailed behind. Jake didn't know why he felt the urge to take off, but it was the only thing that made sense to him at the moment. In his fury to move forward, he grazed against other pedestrians, stumbling as he went.

"Slow down, would you?" Sebastian called out. "What's going on?"

Jake cleared past the pedestrians and broke into a sprint until his body lost steam.

"It's gone," Jake yelled back at Sebastian when he finally stopped and rested, huffing in exhaustion and looking out onto the bay. "The meteorite. It's gone."

Sebastian caught up to Jake. "What do you mean, 'it's gone'?" he asked.

"It was stolen. I went into the office today, and the meteorite was gone."

"Jesus. Did you file a police report? Maybe they can get it back."

"I did. But I doubt they'll find it. It's gone. I know it's gone."

Suddenly, Jake heard faint traces of music. He tilted his head toward the bay. Drumbeats thumped and thumped. Other instruments were playing too, softer and barely detectable: flutes or piccolos, something higher pitched that carried the melody.

"Do you hear that?" Jake asked.

Jake and Sebastian leaned against the railing and looked down. Fort Point was visible below them, and there were small figures assembled inside.

"It's a Civil War re-enactment or a historical celebration or something," Sebastian explained. "I read about it in the local paper, but I'd forgotten about it."

Jake watched the participants below move in military formation. The drum rolls recommenced, this time in the pattern of a march.

"I only see blue uniforms," Jake noticed as he leaned against the railing.

"Makes sense. California wasn't exactly a Confederate stronghold. It's not like there was any actual fighting out here. At least I don't think there was."

"What a weird goddamn thing to do in this city," Jake said, intrigued by the patterns below and confused by the event. It was a distraction, but it felt unwelcome. "I thought they only did re-enactments in the South. It's like nothing makes sense anymore."

"I'm sure it feels that way," Sebastian said, turning toward Jake and cocking his head closer to him. "But listen, Jake. It's going to be all right." Even though Jake could tell Sebastian's words were sincere, Jake remembered why he was here in the first place.

"No thanks to you," Jake said, turning toward Sebastian and meeting his eyes.

"What's that supposed to mean?"

"Jessica."

"What are you talking about?" Sebastian spat out, losing his patience.

"The quasicrystals. You told her about them, didn't you?" Jake pressed, serious.

Sebastian was about to speak when there was a round of artillery fire. The men inside the open-aired plaza of the fort raised their arms and shot their rifles. The gunfire continued, and Jake imagined the bullets careening into the sea where they would sink to the bottom, useless. As the shooting trailed off, Jake considered the more likely reality that the men were shooting blanks that wouldn't go anywhere.

"Jake, I swear, I didn't tell her," Sebastian said. Jake looked over Sebastian's facial expression, trying to detect any signature tells. His affect was flat, his lips parted by his lazy jaw. His almond eyes held still. Sebastian's eyes were similar to Jake's but were slightly farther apart, reminding Jake that this person was not him. Sebastian didn't seem like he was lying, but Jake couldn't shake his suspicion.

"What about Radenport? He must have known. I ran into him on Friday, and he acted like he knew. I hadn't told anyone at Berkeley about the quasicrystals. But you knew. You, who's gotten so close to Jessica, even though I warned you about her. I *told* you about her connection to Radenport. And now he has the meteorite."

Another echo of artillery fire rang out, only this time, it was a cannonball sounding.

"You don't know that Radenport took it," Sebastian said once the cannon fire relented. "I doubt he did. It wouldn't make sense. He couldn't publish any findings on the meteorite without implicating himself in a theft."

"Maybe he doesn't want to publish his own findings. Maybe he wants to sabotage mine. The man is spiteful and vindictive," Jake shot out, upset that Sebastian defended Radenport on any level.

"I think you're overestimating his malice."

"I think you're underestimating it."

"Whatever's the case, you'll get through this. It's not as if that meteorite defines you," Sebastian said. His voice was kind, but his kindness showed how ignorant he was about the whole situation. About Jake.

"Jesus, you don't understand anything, do you?" Jake exploded, gripping his fingers in anger, his forearms tensed in front of him. "This was my chance. I could have made a name for myself. A *real* name for myself. Without the meteorite, I don't have anything."

"You can't be so defeatist."

"Defeatist? I had everything taken from me. My undergraduate research. My sense of my parents. Who they were. Who they *are*. My whole fucking identity. And now, my career. The most important fucking thing there is."

"You have a family who loves you," Sebastian yelled back, his bulging neck veins responding in kind to Jake's tense arms. "You have everything, and you don't even see it."

"Maybe I have my parents," Jake relented. "You're right about that. But even they aren't the same parents they were before. They can't be. Not entirely. Everything is so fucked. My life was fine before I met you."

"As if this is my fault?" Sebastian asked, head shaking in disbelief. "I'm your brother," he continued, somber and forceful, gripping Jake's forearm.

"Biologically," Jake responded, hoping the slight would sting. Sebastian pulled away, his head nodding slowly. Jake had a flash of regret and wondered if he needed Sebastian. But he pushed away the thought. "You know, you're nothing like me. I would never betray people like you have," Jake said.

"Who have I betrayed? You? By dating Jessica? Is that my sin?"

"I told you she was working with Radenport. She passed information to him before, and she's done it again. I *know* they're behind this."

"Jessica had nothing to do with this! I had nothing to do with this!" Sebastian yelled. "Hell, I'm not even sure Radenport did. You've fucking lost it, man."

"I need you out of my life," Jake said, stoic in the face of Sebastian's anger.

"But Jake, I..."

"No. Don't. Just leave."

"Fine," Sebastian said, throwing his hands up in surrender. "If that's what you want. But for the record, I'm not sure you and I are as different as you think."

Sebastian walked away, but Jake stayed on the bridge. Maybe they weren't so different, but Jake wanted to believe otherwise. He continued to watch the make-believe soldiers below him. They were no longer in formation. Instead, the men were consorting with the public, shaking hands with spectators. There were no enemies on the fort. There was no war. No blood had been shed, and despite the sounds of warfare, the fort remained unshakeable, firm in the defenses it had mounted. The music continued, and the soldiers became dancers, approaching women dressed in hoop skirts and petticoats. The men ushered them to the center of the plaza for a waltz. The twosomes moved artfully, and from Jake's aerial perspective, they seemed to function more like collective units than discrete individuals. As he watched, Jake thought about the relationship he'd been a part of minutes earlier. He mourned the loss of his brother, cried at their failure to connect. But Jake was convinced that he didn't need Sebastian. He didn't need anyone. Not anymore.

:   7   :   :   :   :   :

Prime Numbers Don't Handle Internal Division Well

By the time she was seven, Mallory Specter (then Mallory Whitmore) had amassed an impressive collection of tokens from Chuck E. Cheese's Pizza Time Theatre. There was a location near her father's office, so it was the ideal place to drop her off when he needed to do work, and she was on his watch. For the most part, she kept the gold coins in her jewelry box for safekeeping, but many got scattered around her room. She could have spent the tokens. Ostensibly, that's what they were for. That was why her father handed her real money in the first place. He figured she might use the coins to play Skee-Ball or a video game or shoot baskets. That was what he imagined she did. He never noticed that she didn't come home with the chintzy prizes other kids got: the bouncy balls, the paper fans, the candy. Instead of playing games or winning tickets, Mallory had another routine. She'd convert her father's money into coins, stick the tokens in her pockets, then wait for an animatronic show to start.

She loved watching the robotic animals jerk around in imitation of life, their big eyes opening and closing so deliberately. It made her feel less alone.

As an adult, Mallory rarely thought about her time spent in Chuck E. Cheese's Pizza Time Theatre, but now and again, one of the tokens would turn up unexpectedly, and the memories would be fresh. The other day, she grabbed a handful of coins from the coin jar in her living room, not knowing there was an old token in her fistful. She shoved the coins in the cubby of her dashboard so she would have change for the meters. The next day, Mallory parked in a meter and reached for the money. Once she realized that she had something other than currency in her hand, she stopped to separate the real from the counterfeit. She pulled out the Chuck E. Cheese's token and read the inscription on it: "IN PIZZA WE TRUST." That was an easy enough maxim to stand behind, Mallory thought.

She didn't throw away the token. Instead, she put it in her cup holder, which housed other important tokens: the measures of her sobriety. The saying on those tokens was far harder for Mallory to live by: "TO THINE OWN SELF BE TRUE." There was something hollow about the phrase to her. She got the sense that it didn't mean anything at all. She preferred the image of Chuck E. Cheese and his long rat nose to the triangle of unity, service, and recovery on her AA token. She left all the tokens behind and got out of her car.

She entered a downtown San Francisco restaurant. It felt too formal with its white tablecloths, overly serious tableaux, and vaulted ceilings. Her father waited in the entryway, decked out in a navy Brooks Brothers suit, black loafers, and an impatient expression.

"*Now* you're here," Mallory said, approaching him. "But when I needed you, you were nowhere to be seen," she continued, giving him a quick hug to keep up appearances before the host guided them to a table.

"You know I couldn't litigate your case from Los Angeles," he explained as they took their seats.

"You could have worked up here during the trial. There is an office here."

"I have other clients who need me," her father said, glancing over the menu with half of his attention as he spoke. Mallory resented his indifference, his misplaced priorities. As he focused on the menu, her frustration built.

"If you had been the lead attorney, do you think you could have saved me?" she finally asked, feeling more of a child than ever. Her father looked up, his brow furrowed by his deep wrinkles. He closed his menu.

"No one could have saved you. It was a tough case."

"Are there any other legal remedies you can help me with?"

"No," he said, readjusting his tie, his chin lifted.

"So why did you come here?"

"I wanted to see how you were," he said, but there was no concern in his voice.

"It's a bit late for that. My life is shit, thank you very much."

"I wish we could've gotten you what you wanted."

"Do you?" she asked, frustrated that her father hadn't come up for the trial, hadn't been there when the verdict was read, hadn't called after the case had concluded. "Because this is the first time in a long time that I've seen you express an interest in me or my case."

"That's unfair," he responded, still calm. "Our firm took the case, didn't we? Some of the best attorneys in the nation and you didn't have to pay a cent for them."

"Yeah, and look what good those attorneys did me," she shot back, resentful that he always defended himself by listing the money or services he'd provided as if she owed him.

"Sometimes these things don't work out."

"I lost my job," Mallory emphasized.

"You can get another one."

"My dignity was stripped from me in public."

"You knew that was the risk when you went to trial. Your counsel urged you to settle," he reasoned. "Frankly, I don't know why you didn't take the payout."

"This was never about the money," she said, her low-pitched voice rising an octave as she raised her volume.

"Then what was it about?" he asked.

Mallory knew he'd never understand. "Nothing," she managed. He turned his attention to his cell phone, thumb scrolling on his Blackberry.

"Listen, Mallory, something important has come up with a case. I can't waste time traveling back to L.A. before I handle it. I'm going to have to stay up here for a day or so and take care of everything from the San Francisco office. Is there any way I can stay the night at your place in the guest room? I know you weren't expecting me, but maybe that will give us a chance to talk through all of this. I can bring home some dinner for us."

"Fine," she relented, not in the mood for a fight.

"I knew you'd understand," he said, rising and kissing her on the forehead. "I've got to go. I just got new information about the case, and there are some time-sensitive matters."

"But you haven't even had lunch," she said as if that might make him stay.

Mallory watched him go, took the napkin from her lap, and tossed it against her empty plate. She got up, apologized to the hostess, and drove home in tears.

Though she was frustrated by her interaction with her father, she still hoped to mend things with him that night, as promised. But throughout the evening, Mallory's cell phone calls and text messages to him went unanswered. Eventually, she got takeout for herself and went to bed, accepting the cold reality that her father had never had any intentions of bringing home dinner and reconnecting with her. She woke up intermittently throughout the night, wondering when her father would show up. At two in the morning, she noticed that the door to the guest room was shut. She went into the living room and saw his jacket thrown over one of the chairs.

Unable to sleep, she went to her computer to browse the internet. She clicked the Gmail link bookmarked on her browser, but once the page loaded, the background was different than hers. The messages in the inbox were from people she didn't even know, which confused her until she saw that her father's email account was logged in. He must have checked his email when he'd gotten in and forgotten to log out. Out of curiosity, she searched for and read through the emails that pertained to her case. She stayed up nearly the whole night, sifting through the evidence of his betrayal before falling asleep on the keyboard. When she woke up, he had already gone.

"Daddy!" she yelled as she stormed into his law office that morning. Secretaries and other employees were trying to appease her.

"He's in a meeting," one woman told Mallory as she wove through the offices.

"I don't give a shit," Mallory said. "Daddy!" she called out again, eventually locating him in a conference room with glass walls. She opened the door forcefully and launched into him. "You threw my case for some extra corporate dollars?"

"Mallory, calm down. I'm in a meeting. I'll come see you in a minute," Whitmore tried to assure her, looking nervously at the fourteen other men in suits that were passing dubious glances at one another.

"You whored me out for money from Carver-Jackson!"

"You don't know what you're saying," he said, approaching her and wrestling her violently before she crumpled in tears on the floor.

"I'm your daughter. Doesn't that mean anything?" she cried.

"You're making a scene," he said quietly, putting both hands on her shoulders.

"I can make an even bigger one," she said cuttingly, looking him squarely in the eyes like a savage animal tracking its prey. He placed his hands underneath her armpits and pulled her up to a standing position. He led her out the door while all of the suited men looked on and murmured.

"I'm sorry, Mallory," he said once they were alone. "I never wanted you to find out. But these cases. These dealings. These companies. They're how I get the money to support you. You want to live on unemployment until you land another job? Or are you still happy to take my money every month? You have to understand. I did this for you."

"You did this for yourself."

"Let me take you out to dinner tonight. We can talk. Right now, I have to smooth everything over with those men in the conference room. I'm utterly fucked because of what you said. Not that I'm blaming you," he backpedaled, "but we'll talk tonight."

"No, we won't. I'm going to report your firm and expose the scummy shit you do. Then I'm never talking to you again unless it's through a glass pane," she said, leaving.

When Mallory got back into her car, she stuck her hand into her cup holder and pulled out two tokens: the Chuck E. Cheese coin and the seven-month sobriety coin. She fiddled with them in her hand, using her thumb and her middle finger to shift between holding one, then the other, then one, then the other. Fatalistically, Mallory shook up the two coins and separated them, blindly placing one in her right hand and the other in her left. She submitted to the whims of chance in the way that only lost people ever did. She inverted her palm toward the sky, opened her left hand, and saw the face of Chuck E. Cheese winking at her, goading her to accept a life of fantasy and pleasure. She repeated the process, thinking she needed another sign to be sure that a fickle guide wasn't misleading her. Mallory opened her hand. This time, in the center of her palm, she read, "IN

PIZZA WE TRUST." She called a place on Divisadero Street and ordered a whole pizza for herself, not content to limit herself to a slice or two. As she drove toward the restaurant, she took her sobriety token and threw it out the window where it fell into a gutter.

After picking up her pizza, Mallory walked down Divisadero. She came across a liquor store. It seemed like a humble enough establishment, but when she looked through the specialty spirits locked away in a glass case, she saw a bottle of Pappy Van Winkle's Family Reserve, a bourbon so rare she couldn't imagine how this small liquor store had gotten it. The price tag reflected the rarity of the whiskey, but Mallory didn't care about the cost. She bought it and left. When she got home, she called William Radenport.

"You have to talk me down," she said into the phone, eyeing the bottle of bourbon in her condo. "I need a drink like you wouldn't believe."

"You don't need a drink," William said. "You're having a hard time, but drinking will only make everything worse. You called me because you don't want to do this."

"You don't know what it's been like," she said, crying on the floor of her dining room, back against the wall, the pizza box open between her splayed legs.

"You're right. I don't know what it's been like. But I do know alcohol isn't going to make it better. Mallory, why'd you get sober in the first place?"

"I was fucking up my life," she said, digging into a piece of her prosciutto and basil pizza. It was nothing like the pizza she'd eaten at Chuck E. Cheese's as a child; this pizza was thin, authentic. For whatever reason, call it nostalgia, she wished she could have the bready, greasy pizza of her childhood rather than the fancier adult variety.

"Right," William said. "Now remember what it was like before when you were at your lowest point. Try to remember everything about it, every last bloody detail. Do you want to go back to that?"

"I don't know," Mallory said. She held the crust of a pizza slice in her hand while the cheesy center oozed downward. She considered the past. She invoked the blackouts, the sickness, the hangovers, the drama. But she also invoked the feeling of relief she got when she downed a tumbler of whiskey.

"You don't know," William said slowly, deliberately.

"I don't care," she eventually settled on, realizing she needed a remedy, some balm, a fast-acting soothing agent. "To be honest, this feels like a new low."

"It sounds like you should go to a meeting. Have you gone to one today?"

"No," she admitted, taking a bite of pizza, knowing what William would say next.

"Go to a meeting."

"You don't understand. I can't even stand up much less go out," Mallory said, feeling powerless on the floor. The only thing motivating her was the food in her hand and the bottle by her side.

"Mallory, you'll get through this," he said, waiting for a response. She didn't say anything but breathed shallowly into the phone and returned her half-eaten pizza slice to the box. After an extended pause, William resumed talking: "I must go. You should go to a meeting. Or at the very least, get out of the house, go to a movie, do something."

"That's it?"

"I'm sorry I can't do more. I am," William said flustered.

"I'm still on an emotional fucking precipice, and if you hang up now, I'm going to have a drink, and it'll be on your conscience."

"I want to be here for you, but I'm a wreck myself. I can't have another hour-long conversation right now. I know I'm a bloody awful sponsor, but the last thing you need is someone unstable trying to guide you. Take my advice. Go to a meeting. I know you'll feel better if you do," he said, hanging up the phone.

"Asshole," Mallory said when she heard the dial tone. She tried calling a couple more times, but he didn't pick up.

She tossed her phone aside and ate her pizza. After she finished her seventh slice, leaving only one to spare, she examined the bottle of Pappy Van Winkle. There was an image of an older man on the label, smoking a cigar. Mallory thought he looked like Freud. She didn't even remember when she'd seen a picture of Freud, but she was sure that these two men, balding and bespectacled, were cut from the same cloth, both experts at dealing with people's pain. She thought about Rip Van Winkle, the story she'd read in high school where the old man slept for twenty years and woke up to a new world, one where his weapon was rusty and loved ones had died. Most of the people in her class had felt sorry for Rip, but Mallory hadn't. He got to sleep through war, through the struggles of everyday life. She envied him. Without her usual appreciation for the quality of the bourbon, she downed tumbler after tumbler of Pappy Van Winkle in rapid succession until she drifted off into an alcohol-induced sleep. But unlike Rip Van Winkle, Mallory never did wake up.

: : 21 : : : : :

Prime Numbers Are (Almost) Always Odd

Sebastian Barnabas showed up to teach his morning lecture on Monday the way he usually did: coffee in hand, some papers shoved under an armpit, feet crossing the threshold a few minutes late. He unfurled his things onto the professor's desk before turning his attention to the sparsely populated auditorium. Sebastian surveyed the students in attendance. Most students looked no different than they did any other day, but there was a small group clustered in the center of the lecture hall who looked morose.

"Where is everyone?" Sebastian asked the class, picking up his coffee. "Is today some unofficial holiday no one told us about?"

"Probably people grieving," one of the somber students said.

"Grieving? Who died?"

"Mallory Specter," the same student responded. "A lot of us had her as a professor."

Sebastian shrank inside himself at the sound of Mallory's name. He looked out at the students who seemed to be appraising his reaction. He didn't know what to say other than to ask the obvious question: "How'd she die?"

"No official word yet, but there are rumblings about suicide. Pills and alcohol, I think," the student said, looking at Sebastian with a hardened affect.

"My God," Sebastian said, swallowing hard. He thought for a second then spoke again. "In light of all this, let's cancel today's lecture."

There were no complaints. The students quietly packed up their bags.

"Thanks, Professor Barnabas," one of the female students said as everyone filed out. She approached him and whispered, "You know, no one blames you." She smiled weakly and left. When every last kid was gone, Sebastian took a seat at his desk and pressed his head against its hard surface.

No one blames you. It's the type of thing someone says when people are definitely blaming you. Sebastian wondered what share of guilt he deserved. Taking in as deep a breath as he could manage, he lifted his head from his desk and got up. He headed to Diana's office down the hall and knocked on her door.

"I'm guessing you heard about Mallory," Diana said as Sebastian entered.

"My class was practically empty this morning. Students were talking about it," Sebastian said, taking a seat opposite her.

"Yeah, I was about to send an email to the department," Diana said, clicking her mouse on her computer before redirecting her attention to Sebastian. This was the Diana he was used to now: the relatively distant yet consummate professional, still acting like a department chair, even though she'd relinquished her seat long ago.

"Chiang isn't going to handle the messaging?" Sebastian asked, immediately regretting that he brought up her successor's name.

"He hasn't yet," she said tersely. "And people should know."

"What are you planning on telling everyone?"

"Whatever I *can* tell them, which isn't much. Not a lot of official details."

"Suicide?"

"That's the prevailing theory," Diana said, nodding her head gravely.

"Do you think Mallory would've killed herself if she'd won the lawsuit?" he asked.

Diana's expression became even more severe, the edges of her full lips tensed in wrinkles. She paused, then said, "We can't possibly know the answer to that."

"No, not for sure. But what do you *think*?"

"There's no value in thinking about that. Sure, the lawsuit might have been a factor in her decision to hurt herself. Let's say that it was. What good does that do us? There's no way we could've known this would happen."

"We ruined her," Sebastian said, guilt prodding him.

"Mallory was already ruined. That woman was a mess. Don't give it another thought. You can't think like that."

"You're right," Sebastian muttered, not so sure. "I know you're right."

313

"Take the day off," Diana suggested. "Get your head screwed back on."

Sebastian took her advice. He left work behind him and got into his car, only instead of heading home, he made his way to 2100 De Soto Drive. Mallory's house. He parked nearby and looked at her property. There was crime scene tape fluttering over the front gate like the sash on a pageant contestant. Sebastian idled in his car, recalling his experiences inside the place. He knew the home intimately. After all, she'd led him on a deliberate quest to "fuck away her husband." But Mallory had kept an awful lot of relics for someone trying to forget. Sebastian remembered the framed wedding photograph in the living room. He remembered the stack of worn-in T-shirts, frayed polos, and collared shirts she'd offered Sebastian when he'd been over.

Reflecting on everything, Sebastian knew Diana was right: Mallory was a mess even before he or Diana had appeared in her life. Regardless, Sebastian couldn't fight the feeling that he'd played too significant a role in her downfall to absolve himself of blame. He'd been the one screwing her. Never tenderly. She'd never wanted that. She'd demanded brute force, as though she'd wanted him to stake her to the ground. Toward the end, as she'd gotten softer, he should have recognized her growing attachment and cut things off. He knew that now.

A few days later, new information surfaced about Mallory's death. It was no longer being treated as a suicide but as a murder, probably induced by a hard-to-detect poison. While this revelation minimized Sebastian's guilt, the thought of someone killing Mallory disturbed him. Sebastian wanted to talk about it with someone. His first instinct should have been to call Jessica, but he didn't want her to misconstrue his feelings about Mallory in the wake of her death. He decided he'd talk to Jake. Even though their last encounter had seemed final, Sebastian couldn't help but hope there was something left to salvage.

Sebastian arrived at McCone Hall on Berkeley's campus in the early evening on a Friday. When Sebastian exited the elevator, he saw Jake down the hallway, entering an office that wasn't his own with the help of a janitor who unlocked the door. Sebastian discovered that the office belonged to William Radenport. He stood outside, waiting for Jake to come out.

"Jesus, you scared me," Jake said, jumping at the sight of Sebastian. Sebastian noticed a pair of used nitrile gloves in Jake's grip.

"What were you doing in there?"

"It's not important," Jake said, dismissing Sebastian as he walked briskly toward his own office and settled in there. Sebastian took a seat as Jake flitted around.

"I don't understand why you're here," Jake said.

"Mallory Specter died."

Jake stopped frantically moving around papers and books and looked Sebastian in the eye. "I know," Jake said. "William Radenport was the one who found her body. He's been out of the office since the news broke."

"Radenport? I didn't even know he knew Mallory."

"Apparently, he was her AA sponsor. Small world," Jake said. Sebastian was already on edge, and all of this strange new information, not to mention the peculiar behavior of his brother, only increased his unease.

"So...are you going to tell me why you were in his office?" Sebastian asked.

"I forgot something in there. That's all."

"What'd you forget?"

Jake hesitated. It was clear Sebastian had caught him in a lie.

"You were wearing gloves," Sebastian noted as Jake struggled for words. "Why were you wearing gloves?"

Jake's face went slack, abandoning his pretenses. "You don't understand. That man is evil. Pure evil."

"Jake, what did you do?"

"I just helped things along."

"What's that supposed to mean?"

"Listen, Sebastian. Radenport's worse than you imagine. He stole my research. He stole my meteorite. He's unscrupulous. I told you he was the one who found Mallory's body. They're saying it's a murder. It had to have been him. I know it."

"And you did *what* exactly?" Sebastian asked.

"I made sure his office was well stocked. Thallium. Potassium chloride. A few other potentially toxic compounds and substances."

"Jesus, Jake!" Sebastian exclaimed. "You're trying to frame him? How the hell can you be so sure that he even did this?"

"I'm sure."

"How can you possibly…"

"I'm sure, goddamn it," Jake interrupted. "And if he's not, I have to trust that the criminal justice system will exonerate him. He is an educated white man, after all. Besides, even if he's innocent of murder, that doesn't mean he's innocent."

"This is crazy. You've got to see that. You've got to undo this."

"Just leave, Sebastian. Go."

"Fine. If you want me gone, I'm gone. But I'm telling you, you should go back into that office and get those compounds back. You're going to regret this. This isn't who you are. You're a good man."

Jake said nothing. Sebastian left, shocked by his brother's madness. When he got back to his car, his hands shook. There were so many feelings rushing through him: pain that he'd lost his brother for good, concern for Jake's mental well-being, disgust that this person who was so much like him was capable of something so wrong. He broke down into tears, immobilized by the way their relationship ended.

Prime Numbers Are the Building Blocks of Bigger Multiples

Elizabeth Bentley, a veteran fixer for Carver-Jackson, flipped on the television and turned to the news coverage of Mallory Specter's death. There were rumblings about William Radenport, who had found her body. The police were not naming him as a suspect yet. Through her surveillance efforts, Elizabeth knew that Jake had planted potassium chloride and other substances in Radenport's office. He'd also just called in an anonymous tip to the police. But that alone might not lead to an arrest. Elizabeth knew a good idea when she saw one, and Jake had given her a lead.

"We need to plant the IV syringe," Elizabeth said, talking into the phone while the news played in the background. "It has her DNA on it. Without it, the evidence is too circumstantial. William Radenport might not be arrested, let alone tried."

The man on the other end of the phone voiced his concerns.

"I understand that," she said. "But no matter how clean the scene was, it wasn't clean enough. Otherwise, no one would have challenged the initial suicide ruling."

He spoke again, trying to dissuade her.

"It's not a risk," she explained. "Doing nothing is the risk. It won't be long before the search warrant gets approved, and the potassium chloride won't be enough. The syringe needs to be in Radenport's office by then. It's the safest route we have. We need a legitimate suspect to divert the cops and take the heat off the spectacle she made at Whitmore's office." She was growing impatient with her associate's obstinacy. "Get it done."

It wasn't long before the police stumbled across the syringe in William Radenport's office, analyzed them, and found traces of Mallory Specter's blood on the tips and residual potassium chloride in the empty vial. The media firestorm heated up. All sorts of stories about Mallory came to the surface: stories about how she had been cutthroat and underhanded while at Princeton, stories about how she'd been naïve and duped by a philanderer at Stanford, stories about how she'd threatened her father when the lawsuit hadn't gone her way, stories about how she'd recognized her addiction problems and sought out help. The media outlets would decide which of these stories would become central to her narrative. Elizabeth rifled through her wallet and found the business card of Britney Tates-Ryan, a thirty-five-year-old producer for a Carver-Jackson-owned news network.

"We need the right commentators for the coverage of the Mallory Specter story," Elizabeth advised Britney over the phone. "We need the right spin."

"I know how to do my job. I'll get the right people," Britney assured her.

"Well, so far, you haven't gotten the angle you need."

"And I bet you're going to tell me which angle I should take?"

"Listen, our company has interests to protect. The way you handle this story will affect your ratings and your bottom line, which in turn determines our bottom line."

"We may be a subsidiary of Carver-Jackson," Britney recognized, "but that doesn't mean we're beholden to your content decisions."

"That's exactly what it means."

"I'm going to go further up the ladder on this. I'll get it straightened out."

"I'm the top of the ladder," Elizabeth said, her gravelly voice stony with assurance.

It took Britney a second to respond. "I give up. What do you want?"

"I want Miranda Jones," Elizabeth said.

The next night, Elizabeth turned on the television, hoping she had succeeded.

"The case of Mallory Specter shows us just how misogynistic the world still is," commentator Miranda Jones noted. "The woman was discriminated against based on her sex, she was ridiculed for shedding light on that discrimination, and when she was suffering as a result of these societal failures, she was manipulated by a man who used her depression to cover up his heinous crime. And now, some organizations, major organizations, are coming to the defense of this man and trying to call Mallory's character into question. This is one of the grossest examples of blaming the victim I've ever witnessed."

"Your characterization of the facts doesn't seem fair," Eugene Bonaventure, a reporter for the *Times* argued. "The point these organizations are making is that, for one, William Radenport hasn't been convicted yet, and may be innocent, as he claims. Secondly, Mallory was not the paragon of virtue you're making her out to be. She didn't lose her lawsuit because the system was misogynistic. She lost the case because there was no evidence of wrongdoing on the part of the university. We need to see Mallory Specter for who she was: a troubled woman who was severely depressed. She probably ingested the alcohol voluntarily. There's surveillance tape showing her purchasing the bottle that evening. No gun to her back. No one with her. And as far as the other substances are concerned, we don't even know if she was injected unwillingly. Far from being a murder case, this might've been an assisted suicide. Until we know all of the facts, it doesn't seem right to give this man a public flogging."

"To anyone who has been following the case, it's obvious that William Radenport is guilty," Miranda Jones responded, "and any claims to the contrary are rooted in your prejudices. If this man were a woman and the situations were reversed, you wouldn't be so quick to excuse the culprit and attack the victim's character. I think even you would be assured of the murderer's guilt."

319

Elizabeth had to give her credit: Miranda Jones knew how to gender bait. The man who calmly and rationally challenged her contentions was nowhere near as magnetic as Miranda was. Elizabeth knew that would be the case. Miranda Jones had a power to her, even if some people found it disgusting.

Elizabeth drank a scotch neat and let the television play. She tuned out, focusing on the image of Miranda Jones: teased hair, bright lips, power suit, heavy eye makeup, shiny veneers, and a fiery expression of righteous indignation. Elizabeth believed that this was what she owed Mallory Specter: martyrdom shouted from the mouths of the faithful. It was the best compensation Elizabeth could provide. After all, it was better to make Mallory appear like a misunderstood woman, wronged at the hands of men, rather than what she truly was: a misunderstood woman, wronged at the hands of both women and men. Elizabeth was sorry that Mallory had to die, but what Elizabeth offered in exchange was longer-lasting than life. Besides, with Mallory's death, Carver-Jackson would remain powerful, and Elizabeth's career would continue to burgeon, immaculate and promising.

:　:　:　:　35　:　:　:

There are Infinitely Many Prime Numbers

The Berkeley campus was twittering with speculation when Jake went into the office the day after William Radenport's arrest. Everyone was grappling with the shock of seeing police officers launch a search of William's office the previous morning. The police hadn't found the meteorite in Radenport's office, but Jake held out hope that the police might find the rock elsewhere, perhaps in Radenport's home. Jake sat at his desk. Even though he was no longer in possession of his meteorite, he still had the data he'd already

320

extracted from the specimen. He knew he should continue with his data analysis, but he found it hard to focus. His mind was too distracted by what awaited him after work: DVR'd recordings of the news. Lots of recordings.

After an epically unproductive day, Jake rushed home to watch the footage. He sank into his couch. He turned on the television and navigated to the DVR. With the "live" news coverage in the past, Jake fashioned himself into a god, manipulating the course of time with his remote. He zoomed past the coverage of the Republican primary. Jake continued scanning. The three forward-facing triangles moved the world ahead, and he watched California burn at high speed. There were arson fires in Los Angeles, torching the county that had been his home growing up. Jake saw aerial footage of the destruction, the gyrating blocks of yellow and orange surrounded by billows of black smoke. It was a blur of devastation, but the impersonal distance compelled him to continue fast-forwarding.

Finally, he got to the coverage of Mallory Specter's death. This was what Jake had been waiting for. When William Radenport's mugshot came on the screen, Jake reveled in the dour expression on Radenport's face. The man still looked like an academic, but he was an academic with a darkness to him, and now the whole world could see that darkness on display. Jake stared into the screen for hours, cobbling together footage from a variety of television programs and constructing a patchwork quilt of schadenfreude. Friends of Radenport's wife talked about their long-held suspicions that William had been having an affair. Forensic psychologists postulated about the mindset of Mallory Specter's killer, noting the ways that Radenport aligned with or differed from the profile. The whole thing made Jake nauseated, but he couldn't stop watching.

"Could you shut that off already?" Lilith asked when she walked into the room.

"Radenport spoke with Mallory on the phone the day before she died," Jake reported. "And she called him three times the night of her death," he added, craning his neck away from the television.

"Don't look so happy," Lilith said from the distance of the kitchen.

"Why shouldn't I be happy?"

"This is a man's life we're talking about."

"Yeah, but let's not forget which man," Jake said, his eyes focused on the television.

"I don't care who he is, delighting in his downfall is a sickness," she contended, moving from the kitchen and joining Jake on the couch in the living room. She nervously scratched the edge of her manicured nails against the flesh of her thumbs.

"Why are you so defensive of Radenport?" Jake asked, turning to her.

"I think you're being too harsh," she said, her green eyes raised upward in a show of sympathy for William. She continued fidgeting with her nails.

"You got a manicure," he noticed.

"Yeah," she said, evading his look and focusing on the television.

"What's going on?" Jake asked, processing her nervous movements, her rigid posture. "You always get your nails done when there's something on your mind. And now you're acting weird about Radenport."

"I told you, I don't think you should be so hard on him."

"The man stole my meteorite!" Jake yelled in frustration.

Lilith kept quiet but pursed her lips in contemplation. "William didn't steal your meteorite. At least I don't think he did," she eventually said.

"What are you talking about? Of course he did," Jake responded. Lilith picked up the remote and turned off the television. Jake thought about turning it back on in defiance, but her face was too serious, so he stayed put. Lilith told Jake about everything: the corruption in Daniel's job, the potential surveillance, the probing questions Elizabeth Bentley had asked when she'd met with Lilith to talk about Jake's research. Lilith laid out her case for why she thought Carver-Jackson was behind the theft.

"You think *a corporation* stole the meteorite? What would Carver-Jackson want with it?" he asked, hoping Lilith was wrong.

"You tell me. They have their hands in almost every industry you could think of."

Jake thought everything through. The more he considered what Lilith said, the more convinced he became that she was right. He started remembering small details that had only seemed strange for a second: the clicking sound at the end of the phone line, the sensation of being followed one night, the stares of a woman from across a café.

"What are you going to do?" Lilith asked, gently putting a hand on his arm.

"What *can* I do?"

"I don't know," Lilith murmured, her face looking away in resignation.

"They have an empire. Even if I wanted to get the meteorite back, my resources are nothing compared to theirs. I'm outmanned, outnumbered, and out of luck," Jake recognized, gazing off blankly while the implications of this sank in. "You really don't think that Radenport..."

"No, I don't think that he did."

"And I..."

"You what?" Lilith asked.

"Nothing."

"God, Jake, I'm sorry. I'm so sorry."

"I know. This isn't your fault. But I need to clear my head. I think I'll take a drive and do some stargazing. Get my mind off things," Jake told Lilith. He packed up the car and drove into the hills where he could be alone with his equipment and the sky. The drive passed in a blur. He arrived at his usual sky-gazing spot, got out of the car, took out his telescope, attached a 35mm eyepiece, and shivered in the cold.

Once the machinery was set up, Jake retreated to a wilderness inside himself that he hadn't known existed. He approached the telescope feverishly. Radenport was ruined, thanks to the evidence Jake had planted. And for what? Revenge? For something Radenport might not have done? Jake breathed out. Stargazing would calm him. It had to. He angled the telescope. But in his haste to see the stars, Jake forgot to remove the lens caps. His eye stared into the nothingness, paralyzed centimeters away from the eyepiece. The blackness shook Jake. There was a simple solution to the issue he faced: he could unscrew the dust cap. Unfortunately, when he did, his world was still upturned. Before that moment, he'd been intrigued by the infinite scope of space, shrouding it in a childish mysticism that allowed him to feel like part of a larger, benevolent order. But suddenly, the immensity of the universe was no longer comforting but isolating.

Jake stepped away from the telescope. He sat on the hillside and reflected on what he'd done in his madness. How much he'd destroyed. Sebastian probably hadn't told anything to Jessica or colluded with William. But Jake had pushed his brother away in distrust. And there was William. Jake knew he could take a moral stance. He could confess to what he'd done, exonerate Radenport. But he'd be ruined personally and professionally for it. No, Jake decided. He wouldn't. Not for William. Jake coldly accepted his devolution with a twinge of regret. Nothing could stop the momentum. He was growing further away from the person he once was, doomed to continue on that trajectory indefinitely. He knew the darkness would grow asymptotically toward the limits of his body, where it would possess his innermost thoughts if it hadn't already.

*Prime Numbers Leave Remainders in the Wake of their
Destruction*

Jacqueline Barnabas awoke with the same sting of
withdrawal, anxiety, and depression she'd been grappling
with ever since Barrie left. Since there was no more
Oxycontin left in the house, she'd resorted to drinking to
alleviate her insomnia, agitation, and pain. The alcohol
didn't help. She knew it wouldn't, at least not in the long run.
But there were still stretches of time when she'd be the right
amount of drunk.

When the alcohol's magic wore off, Jacqueline thought
about going into town and trying to find a hookup, someone
who could score her something, anything. But she
remembered where she was. She remembered *who* she was.
Jacqueline was a washed-up, sixty-year-old Palos Verdes
resident. There were no roving drug dealers she'd be able to
find. Drug dealers existed. Palos Verdes thrived on drugs.
But you didn't get them on the street like a common junkie,
and you didn't get them without plenty of cash to handle the
suburban mark-up. Barrie wouldn't take her back. She'd
tried that already. She thought about other men she knew,
suckers who knew how to score. But her skin was worn. Her
beauty, deteriorating. Now her feminine charms only
worked on familiar burnouts like Barrie, and most of the
guys who fit that description had gotten married or been
priced out of the neighborhood long ago.

So Jackie got out of bed and resigned herself to another
day of struggle.

She stumbled to the kitchen to take some ibuprofen. As
she swallowed the pills, a loud noise pierced her ears and
magnified her headache. The familiar shrill notes kept
sounding over and over again. Jackie followed the noise,
opened the front door, and stepped onto her driveway in her

robe and slippers. She saw the culprits: seven peafowls digging into the overgrown garden that she'd neglected. There were more on her neighbors' lawns. The suckers were everywhere. She counted twenty-one within eyesight—an infestation.

"Get away," she screamed, matching their strident cries with her own.

Some of the peacocks made their way onto her roof. Jacqueline threw one of her slippers at them. A couple of peahens continued eating away at her garden, oblivious to her theatrics. One of the peacocks on the ground fanned out its feathers in upright spectacle, circling her and the nearby peahens like a courtier. The rows of dark blue eyes on the feathers mesmerized her with their undulating movements. The overwhelming number of focal points destabilized Jacqueline until she got dizzy and fainted on the lawn.

When she came to, there was a fallen peacock feather tickling her nose. She brushed it off in repulsion. She remembered the peacock feather Sebastian had left on the bedside table in her hospital room over Thanksgiving weekend. She felt renewed puzzlement over the gesture. He'd left her a letter, but the note had been so brisk that it hadn't explained much. Jacqueline stormed inside and phoned Sebastian.

"Why did you leave that peacock feather in my hospital room?" she shouted the minute Sebastian answered his phone.

"What's this about? Are you on something?"

"Do we have to do this every time we talk? I'm not on anything. I just want to know about the feather," she insisted, her guttural voice creaky with frustration.

"You never let me collect them," Sebastian said as if that explained everything.

"That's it?" she asked, stunned that the answer could be so simple. So meaningless. "You're hanging on to some childish grudge?"

"You know, Mom, I'm glad you called. Because this is exactly what I don't need in my life anymore. I started therapy. Jessica encouraged me to go."

"Who the hell is Jessica?"

"The girl I'm dating. Anyway, I'm glad she pushed me to see someone. The psychologist says I've got a lot of damage to work through. But for the first time in a long time, I feel like I can unpack some of what you've dealt me."

"What I've dealt you?" Jacqueline yelled. Now she was furious. "Do you ever stop to think about my life? You think I wanted to get pregnant when I was seventeen?"

"Mom, I love you. I do. Somehow. Despite all this. And I know your life has been hard. But a lot of that is of your own making. I can't be dragged into this anymore. If you want to get clean, I'll help you. I'll pay for rehab. But until you get clean, I can't keep pretending our relationship is healthy. I need a new path for myself."

"I can't believe you're making all of this about you. I'm in pain here, and all you seem to care about is yourself..." she said, angrily gritting her teeth as she seethed.

"I'm going to stop you there. Call me when you want to get clean," Sebastian said and hung up.

Jacqueline couldn't believe his gall. He wasn't experiencing withdrawal. He wasn't drifting toward oblivion. Okay, he wanted her to get clean. But it wasn't so easy. If she were clean, how could she stem the tide of dissatisfaction that haunted her?

Jacqueline hadn't been clean since she was a teenager, since before Barrie. It was hard to remember those days now. The days of mini-skirts and mod dresses and colorful headscarves. The days of having nowhere to be and nothing to do and no one to parent and no one to sleep with because all you needed was a deep kiss every so often from the right boy, and that was fantasy enough to occupy your dreams for months on end. She missed those adolescent days, back when a minute was a long time and pleasure came in staggering but brief waves that swelled and swelled until they seemed like they might knock you over. She knew that her reliance on substances was a way of chasing that same hyper-concentrated pleasure. The only options she had now were synthetic, and she still needed them. Her son didn't understand. Couldn't understand. He had the luxury of hanging up the phone on his mother and cutting her out of his life. Jacqueline would give anything to be able to get angry at her mom, yell at her, or slam the phone in the receiver. But she didn't have the chance to hate her mother because her mother was dead and all Jacqueline could do was love her mother's ghost for the rest of her natural life. She resented Sebastian for not understanding how lucky he was to have her alive.

Jacqueline wanted Barrie to come and fix everything because weeks before, he *had* fixed everything with his pills and his affection. She closed her eyes and thought about the way his sagging skin puckered around his scars. She remembered how comforting it had been to run her hand over the bullet wound, how soft it had been. She imagined him in the jungles of Vietnam, evading enemy gunfire. Then she recalled how he'd gotten his injury.

Jacqueline opened her eyes. She grabbed her cell phone, stuck it in the back pocket of her jeans, and went out to the front yard with a plan. The peacocks were still there. She walked to the side of the house to get the ladder, brought it around the front, and positioned it against the lowest eaves of the roof. She climbed up. Once she was on the roof, she stood up and stared at three peacocks that accompanied her. She thought about lunging toward them, but she didn't want to accidentally fall from the wrong part of the roof. She needed to remind herself that the peacocks were only important as a pretext anyway. The birds don't matter, she told herself. Their screams and squawks don't matter. Their brightness and beauty and strangeness don't matter. They aren't special, she thought. They're nothing but pesky locals, walking around and sticking close to the neighborhood as if no one told them they had wings that could take them elsewhere.

Jacqueline looked over the edge of the roof and walked toward the overhang above her large flowerbeds. The soil looked soft. There weren't any objects nearby that could cause a severe head injury. She closed her eyes and leaned forward. She shifted her weight from the back to the front as slowly as she could, trying to protract the moment before she fell, but the whole process only took a matter of seconds. Before she knew it, she was on the ground. She tried to push herself up, but her right arm gave in and flopped limply. She rolled onto her back, pulled out her cell phone using her left hand, and called the ambulance with a grimace that became a smile.

:   :   :   :   :   :   **7**   :

Prime Numbers Can Come in Twins

Jessica Fleming was on the couch in Sebastian's condo, taking notes on an article for her dissertation, when the hospital called his cell phone. She tried to focus on her work, but she kept getting distracted by his conversation.

"Everything all right?" she asked when he hung up the phone.

"Fine. That was Torrance Memorial Hospital. My mom fell off her roof. She broke her arm and bruised some ribs, but she'll be okay."

"Shit. Are you going to go see her?" Jessica asked, putting down her work and sitting up at attention.

"No. I can't keep doing this. I told her she needed to get clean just hours ago. She was probably hammered. She never changes, so I guess I'll have to."

"That sounds healthy," Jessica said, but she could see that Sebastian was uneasy. He grabbed a tangerine and picked away at the rind. "Did I ever tell you about the day trips my parents and I would take?" Jessica asked, hoping to distract Sebastian.

"I don't think so," Sebastian said, continuing to pick away at the tangerine. He didn't eat the fruit once he'd peeled it but kept tearing up the rind into even smaller parts.

"I told you that my parents never wanted kids. They weren't cruel or anything. Just indifferent to me. But they knew they acted that way, and sometimes, they'd feel guilty about ignoring me. They'd make a big deal about these day trips to different parts of California. Nothing too far from Santa Cruz, but far enough that it felt exciting. My favorite trip was to Point Reyes. My dad busted out his marine biology expertise when we were at the tide pools, and I sort of fell in love with science out there. I say tomorrow we take the day, head out there, and forget about this bullshit with your mom."

"Yeah," Sebastian said, biting into his first slice of citrus with a wince. "That sounds great." He walked over to her and kissed her on the forehead before retreating upstairs.

Jessica went to her computer and looked up the tide charts for Duxbury Reef. She found that low tide would be at 7:01 AM. Early. Couldn't be helped. When Jessica and Sebastian hit the road the next morning, it was still dark outside. By the time they got to the tide pools, the sky was checkered with streaks of light, but the sun hadn't fully emerged. Jessica and Sebastian used their flashlights to illuminate the marine life at their feet. The low tide exposed brilliant purple sea urchins, green sea anemones, and pink coral: a garden of living flowers. The tide pools were beautiful, but they weren't as Jessica remembered them. She didn't remember so many of the animals squeezed between the rocks. She didn't remember thinking about what it might feel like for the starfish to desiccate outside of the water. The ambiance was also different. Since it was early on a winter morning, there was no one around. No children were jumping from rock to rock the way she recalled so many compatriots doing when her parents had brought her here. But this trip with Sebastian was supposed to be about forgetting, not remembering, so she tried to explore the life around her with fresh eyes.

Jessica squatted onto the balls of her feet. She closed in on a sea urchin that was submerged in the shallows and thought about sticking her finger between its spines, letting the organism pucker around her touch. She used to do that as a kid. Instead, she just rippled the water's surface with her pinky and left the urchin alone.

"They're pretty," Sebastian said, crouching next to Jessica.

"Yeah. Pretty thorny bastards."

"That's the way I like them. Pretty, thorny bastards," he said, brushing her hair over her shoulder at the word "pretty" and narrowing an eye jokingly at the rest of the sentence.

The glow of the new morning brightened his smile. Jessica liked being his pretty thorny bastard, and she was glad he was hers.

"Better than the barnacles on the rocks," Sebastian added, walking toward another section of the tide pools.

"You don't like barnacles? I think they give a place character. Make any location seem ancient and sea-worn," Jessica said, following him and hopping from rock to rock. She made a game out of it, balancing on one foot and switching feet between bounces, playing hopscotch as she neared an invisible winners' semicircle by Sebastian.

"They're practically parasites. Attaching themselves wherever they please and sealing themselves off in their shells. Besides, looking at the patterns of their holes triggers something inside me. Total disgust."

"Trypophobia," she said. "That's what you have. My friend posted about it on Facebook the other week."

"Facebook...the source of all knowledge," Sebastian joked, prodding her as she got close. "Call it what you want.

I don't need to stare at anything that looks like the plague," he said, admiring a starfish that was basking on a nearby rock. He neared his face to the creature. Jessica liked the way he wrinkled his nose to inspect its beauty.

"Barnacles are so cool, though. They're heartless hermaphrodites," Jessica said.

"Heartless hermaphrodites are your definition of cool?"

"Obviously," Jessica said sarcastically. "Listen, you're not young and hip like me, so trust me on this one." She sidled next to him and ribbed him with her elbow.

"Even though you just called me old and unhip, I'm going to give you a pass and tell you I *always* trust you," Sebastian said, turning his attention to Jessica. He pulled her close to him. "The sun's finally out," he said, nodding toward the horizon.

Sebastian and Jessica spent a minute or so in an embrace, taking in the vibrant colors of the skyscape. She kissed him for being everything she needed him to be. The tide came in. Water lapped at their rubber boots. It wouldn't take long for the water to submerge the plants and shells and creatures into an entirely different environment. Even though the incoming water meant that Jessica would need to leave, she relished the thought of the high tide, when the currents would pull the anemones' tentacles to and fro in a hypnotic dance.

"What next?" Sebastian asked, kicking away the moisture from his boots.

The two of them made their way to the car, and Jessica drove toward the Cypress Tree Tunnel. She parked near the Historic KPH Station at the end of the tree tunnel and told Sebastian to get out. Jessica wrapped her arms around him and took her first steps toward the towering trees. The colossal cypress trees lined a quarter-mile path. The bent boughs and branches wove a latticed roof over their heads that made the tunnel feel like a portal into another dimension. Jessica remembered how unbelievably large the trees had seemed to her as a child. She was surprised that her considerable growth since then had barely shrunk her perception of the trees' size. It was nice to feel small again and to have Sebastian feel small alongside her, the two of them comfortably compact while the world impressed her with its bigness. She loved that the tree tunnel was equal parts fairy tale and nightmare, gorgeous in its gnarled hideousness. She and Sebastian couldn't help but look upward at regular intervals, focused on the nest of twigs and leaves that kept them from seeing the heavens but invited them to see the earth. After one such upward glance, Sebastian pivoted his eye downward.

"I wonder how big the roots are. The roots we can't see, I mean," he said.

"I'm sure there's a massive maze under our feet."

"There used to be these ficus trees in the backyard of my childhood home. They formed a natural barrier on the property line. But my mom eventually had to call someone to uproot them. The roots were invasive. Pried loose some of the foundation. The trees weren't even that tall. You wouldn't know they were capable of so much damage. The rest of the neighborhood had a bunch of them too, and they cracked the sidewalks everywhere. I didn't mind, though. I was fine jumping over the gaps in the concrete. I liked the look of the trees. They made this green wall out back. I convinced my mom to keep some of them. The ones farthest from the foundation. She yelled at me about it a few years ago when the roots overtook the plumbing line again."

"At least there's no foundation nearby for these cypress trees to damage. The maritime radio station back there seems comfortably far away."

"That's what the art deco building is? A radio station?" Sebastian asked.

"Yeah. They have a museum inside, but it's hardly ever open. You can see the old radio equipment and ship-to-shore communication systems from the past. Relics from the days of Morse code."

"Dots and dashes," he said. He grabbed Jessica's wrist, inverted it, and began pounding out short and long beats. He used two fingers like people do when they take your pulse. She concentrated on the rhythm, trying to decode the message of the pulsations.

"What's it mean?"

"You think I know?" he responded, smiling and kissing Jessica as she jokingly hit him and pulled away.

Once they reached the end of the Cypress Tree Tunnel, Jessica yelled, "Race ya!" and bolted in the direction they'd come. She ran clumsily in her rubber boots, but she was fast. Sebastian lagged behind her, but he ran at a decent clip. She hoped he would speed up and catch her, grab her, slow her down. When he finally did, he swept her up and carried her to the car like a baby.

They made their way to the last tourist stop of their day trip: Point Reyes Lighthouse. As they walked down the long route of stairs toward the lighthouse, the fog rolled in. Jessica and Sebastian held hands. They could see one another, but the rest of the world receded in blurred detail. The wind surged and created so much noise that they could barely hear the foghorn blaring in the distance. It was cold, but at least Sebastian's hand was warm. They descended deeper into the whiteness until they arrived at the lighthouse. It was rusted and defunct, reduced to a historical artifact. But there was a nearby, automated light now that the lighthouse was retired.

"I love it," Sebastian said, wrapping up Jessica to keep her warm.

"Too bad it doesn't work anymore."

"Sure it does," Sebastian said, pointing to the rotating light on top of the visitors' center.

"You know what I mean," Jessica said. "I wish we could see the old lighthouse with its huge windows all caught on fire with light. It would be so much more romantic."

"That's not what I call 'romantic.' That small light over there," Sebastian said, pointing to the automated light once more, "that's romantic as hell. Steady. Reliable."

"But you don't need anyone to manage that light. Tending to this old lighthouse was a twenty-four-hour-a-day commitment. People needed to put in the work. Keep it up."

"You still have to replace the bulb now and then on the automated light," Sebastian said. "You can't neglect it. You just don't have to work as hard for it. But if it means that much to you, I'll change my tune and admit you're right. I'll concede that the old rusted pillar over here is more romantic."

"No, it's okay," Jessica said, pulling his arms around her. "I like it when you disagree with me. Keeps things interesting. If I dated someone just like me, I'd go insane."

The two of them stood at the edge of the lookout. The fog blinded them, but they were content to exist together in the emptiness.

"I meant to tell you," Sebastian said, still holding her in the mist. "I'm pretty sure I finished my proof of the twin prime conjecture."

"That's huge!" she said, breaking away from him in a moment of exultation and shock. She jumped up and down and kissed him fast. "Why didn't you tell me earlier?"

"I still need to check my work. Make sure I got it right."

"I'm sure you got it right," Jessica assured him, peppering him with quick kisses.

"I think I did," Sebastian said once she gave him some space.

"We'll have to celebrate tonight," Jessica said, hugging Sebastian. He accepted her embrace before pulling away to look her in the eyes.

"This has been a perfect day," Sebastian said, earnest. "I don't know how it could get any better. Thanks for taking me out here. You're my family now."

Jessica liked the idea of supplanting her family and replacing them with Sebastian. She was already doing it. Years down the road, when she thought about Point Reyes, would she think about her father rattling off facts about marine life, or would she think about Sebastian squinting at a starfish? She knew the answer. She loved this man and wanted him in the rest of her memories, even if they pushed out old ones.

"Jessica," Sebastian said seriously. "I have an idea."

: : : : : : : 1

One was Once Contested as a Prime Number

There was one memory from their childhood that both Jake and Sebastian retained when they grew older, though they dealt with the memory in different ways. Because the memory captured the earliest event that either of them could recall with any detail, it felt significant and potent, but it was also easy to discount. Sebastian's memory of the event had been starker and more crystallized since he'd grown up knowing about Jake's existence. Jake, on the other hand, had written off the hazy, residual recollection as a childhood fantasy. It wasn't until the two men discussed the event as adults that Jake realized it had happened.

The memory centered on their third birthday party, not long before they were separated from one another. There were animals everywhere: stuffed animals, animal-print paper plates, banners with animals on them, the works. Only this party was not a jungle-themed party or a petting zoo party. This was a Noah's Ark party.

In keeping with the concept, the parents that attended were given matching animal props when they came through the door: the Smiths secured pig snouts over their noses, the Pasternaks placed headbands with cat ears on their heads, and the Laramies put lion-mane-covered elastic bands around their faces. The few singles who came—a divorced parent and a wife whose husband was working—refrained from wearing animal accessories to keep the image of paired animals pure. Jake and Sebastian wore the same lion costume—a footed onesie that covered every part of them but their faces, which peeked out from open lion mouths. Other kids also wore animal costumes, and those that hadn't brought costumes wore scaled-down animal accessories like their parents.

For a good deal of time, the kids ran around the backyard, pretending to be the animals they looked like. Everyone snorted and growled and kicked up dust, often crawling around on four legs. The girls in the bunch were usually the kittens or the bunnies, cutely socializing and staying on the outskirts of the yard. Jake and Sebastian, along with the rest of the boys, were the wild animals, parodying blood lust, aggression, and volatility with empty threats of violence and ferocious snarling. But what Sebastian remembered the most about this party was not being feral but being tamed. He remembered retreating into the house for juice when a middle-aged man picked him up and thrust him into the air before pulling him to his chest. He remembered smiling and laughing when a middle-aged woman came over to kiss him on the cheek. Sebastian knew that his mother had been there too, but he didn't remember her in the same way that he remembered those two doting people: his grandparents who'd raised him until their fatal car accident. This birthday party was the sole memory that Sebastian had of them. The only way he could be sure that these two people were his grandparents was because he'd seen pictures of them.

Sebastian remembered his grandparents bringing in birthday cakes, lit up with candles. He remembered the singing, the joy. Sebastian also remembered the party favors: bubbles. Once their friends left the party, Jake and Sebastian played with the extra sets of bubbles. They unleashed a torrent of small bubbles in the living room before their grandparents herded them outside. Out on the front lawn, Jake learned to breathe more slowly and deliberately, creating bigger bubbles. Sebastian tried to do the same, but he couldn't moderate between blowing too strongly and too weakly. So he watched Jake. Sebastian thought about bursting a huge bubble that his brother formed, but he liked the iridescent colors in the film. Jake waged a competition against himself, trying to outdo himself with each new blow. Finally, he created a massive orb that exploded all over him while Sebastian looked on unscathed, warm inside the un-wetted comfort of his animal onesie.

The Last Realm
Infinity

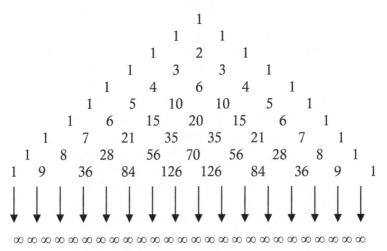

As with the numbers in a number line, there is no end to Pascal's triangle. The series continues infinitely. The number ones in the first row start so close together. But as they journey down the triangle, they grow further apart, even as the complications inside of the triangle tie them together. The distance continues with forever in its sights.

∞

I have to close my eyes, or else the brilliance of the sun will flood every inch of me, and I'll have no sense of darkness. The truth is, I don't own any sunglasses, even though I'm a native Californian. For as long as I can remember, I've always liked looking into the sun, squinting to regulate the entrance of light. When I was growing up, the sunshine was the only consolation I had. Now that I've wrenched myself from that life, I hold on to a sliver of darkness—the shadows left by a too-luminous sun—just so I never lose sight of the person I once was. I can already feel the sunlight seeping into my pores. The warmth enlivens me as the passing breezes temper its strength.

There is nowhere else in the world I'd rather be, but I'm stunned that I'm here. The Pacific hums in the background, but it is not the same stretch of ocean that I'm used to. There is no one on this part of the beach other than Jessica and me. She's sleeping on a towel next to me, letting her back brown while she dreams of something that I hope is as perfect as this moment. Her bikini is undone. The strings languish beside her, fit to be tied but idle while she is equally so. I like watching her nostrils move as she breathes in, breathes out. It reminds me that she is alive, and I am alive, and little else matters.

The sun catches the new golden band on her finger and stings my eye with its sharpness, so I divert my face and look at my ring. No one from my past would recognize me now if they even remembered who I was in the first place. There is no need to think about any of that now. The sun is shining, and the water is still. There is a new life ahead of me, and the promise of it is enough to make every event of the past few months fade into oblivion. Eventually, the sun begins setting on the last day of 2011. I think about waking Jessica, but she seems too calm to stir. We have a lifetime of sunsets ahead of us; there is no need to disrupt her when we have forever to waken one another with surprises more significant than this. It's also a moment I would like to spend alone since I still believe that I own the sun. The tropical sky is striped with fuchsia, but the exotic vista melds with the familiar woman beside me, and I feel at home, even though I am hundreds of miles away from the place where I live and work. I am not saddened by the descent of the sun or the passing of the year. Now that I live with so much light, I know I can handle the darkest of the dark.

Acknowledgments

This book wouldn't exist without the support of many people. I will always owe a debt of gratitude to my incredible parents, Karen and Gabor Jilly. I cannot begin to enumerate everything they've given me—materially, emotionally, and intellectually. Their generosity, love, and encouragement are foundational to my identity and to anything I produce. Likewise, my husband, Michael Wachell, sustained me through the odyssey of completing this book. His patience, input, and support enabled me to write and keep writing. This book has seen many, many drafts, but there is no way it would be in its current form without the help of my Cabal—Shawn Chen, Jonathan Westerberg, and Matt Wheeler. I will always think fondly of our writing circle sessions, and I'm so thankful that you three invested so much time in giving me feedback on my work. Your perceptive notes, insightful comments, and enduring friendship made this book infinitely better. To my sister, Christie Jilly-Rehak, scientist extraordinaire: thank you for helping me refine the details of Jake's scientific research to make it more realistic. That being said, I would like to mention for the record that none of the scientific inaccuracies included in this novel in the name of fiction are your fault. To Margaret Diehl, whose professional line edits and developmental edits made this book much tighter and stronger: I truly appreciate your work. To my dear friends, Quincy Howerton and Diana Sieker: thank you for being important sources of emotional support for me over the years. To my children, my hearts: thank you for helping me understand motherhood and the deep love that comes with it. Lastly, to anyone who has read portions of this book at any stage, including Dan Frey and David Piorek: thank you, thank you, thank you.